THE CRIMSON SCAR

BY HANNAH PENFOLD

THE HOUSES

HOUSE OF RAVEN:
Ravens consist of vampire and royal blood. They have the power of heightened senses, considerable strength & sharp fangs. Unlike vampires, Ravens can sustain their bodies with both normal food and blood. They are able to walk in sunlight without being burnt and are known for their ruthlessness.

HOUSE OF BANE:
Nightshades consist of unicorn and royal blood. They are well known for their intelligence and thirst for knowledge. Nightshades can come into contact or ingest poison with no repercussions making them extremely useful allies and terrifying enemies.

HOUSE OF SUN:
Ceslestials consist of angel and royal blood. They have the power to create sunlight and heat. They are known for their divine beauty and incomparable fighting abilities. They are close companions with dragons whom they have ridden for hundreds of years.

HOUSE OF VELVET:
Silkens consist of siren and royal blood. Best known for their sly and cunning nature, they are able to control a person with their voice alone. Amongst their abilities of manipulation they have a reputation for being deceitful and self-serving.

HOUSE OF CREATION:
Briars consist of fae and royal blood. Deemed the most magically powerful house of the six, Briars are a dangerous kind to challenge. Slow to trust but extremely loyal, Briars' faithfulness will know no bounds.

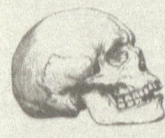

HOUSE OF GLASS:
The Severed consist of demon and royal blood. Closely related to the fallen angels, the Severed have the ability to sense death - even going as far as seeing the dead. Having demon blood, they do not have shadows thus making them extremely artful in the conduct of spying.

*The Hex consists of one representative from each House and will consist of three females and three males. If death occurs to a member of the Hex, they will be replaced at the first opportunity.

This book is dedicated to the three most special women in my life:
My Nan, my Mum and my Sister in Law.
Without your support and belief in me, this would never have
been possible.

GLOSSARY

ANNIE (An-ee) - A royal healer, dameer

ARASIDE (Ah-rah-side) - Magical medicine that helps those with vampire blood to give birth to more than one child at a time

ASH - Eldest brother of Scarlet, breeder Raven

BADGER'S SETT - A fighting establishment situated in Rubien

BLAZE - Older brother of Scarlet and twin of Ember, fighter Raven

BLOOD BENDER - Someone with the power to manipulate blood

BRANDE (Brand) - Current Raven of the Hex, younger sister of Ruby Seraphine

BREEDER RAVEN - A Raven whose duty is to reproduce and maintain the Raven population

CARMINE (Car-mine) - Competitor in the Hex Trials, fighter Raven

CHAMPION - A Raven who has support from a member of the royal family during the Hex Trials

DAMEER (Dah-mear) - A human born with magic

DIMITRI (Da-me-tree) - Scarlet's best friend, vampire

ELDER RAVEN - Leader and figurehead of the House of Raven

EMBER - Older sister of Scarlet, fighter Raven, competitor in the Hex Trials

FIGHTER RAVEN - A Raven whose duty is to train and fight for their kingdom

GUARDIAN - A dameer member to the Hex

HALF-BLOOD - Someone whose parents are different species

HANRAH - A kingdom found in the North known for its hot desert climate

HELLFIRE - Fire that originates from the Underworld

HEX - A group of magical beings who protect and serve all people regardless of race, culture or influence

HEX TRIALS - A deadly competition to find the next representative of the Hex

HOLY HANRAH! - A common phrase used when cursing in Kingdom Hanrah

HOUSE OF RAVEN - An army of Ravens created to serve Hanrah and its sovereigns

HUMAN - Someone born without magic

JACK WILDE - Competing guardian of the Hex Trials

KING ERYC (Eh-rick) - King of Hanrah

LIQUID GOLD - An alcoholic drink that tastes vile for anyone underage and delicious to those of age

MARIE WILDE - Current guardian of the Hex, Jack's mother

MASTER JEPP - Teacher in the House of Raven, fighter Raven
MASTER LENNOX - Teacher in the House of Raven, fighter Raven
MATILDA - Works at Rubien Tea Shop, human
MEELA (Me-lah) - Nurse at Rubien hospital, dameer
MERCY - Merlot's guardian in the Hex Trials
MERLOT KINSMAN (Mer-low) - Competitor of the Hex Trials, worker Raven
PRINCE JULIEN - Heir of Hanrah
PRINCE CHRISTIAN - Prince of Hanrah, eldest triplet
PRINCESS VICTORIA - Princess of Hanrah, triplet
PRINCESS OLYMPIA (Oh-lim-pee-ah)- Princess of Hanrah, youngest triplet
PRINCESS LEONORE (Lee-o-noor) - Youngest princess of Hanrah
QUEEN ADELA (Ah-dell-ah) - Queen of Hanrah
RAVEN - Half vampire, half dameer (royal blood specifically)
RAVEN'S NEST - The main square within the House of Raven where Ravens gather for announcements
RED RAVEN - The moniker for Brande Seraphine
ROUX (Roo) - Eldest sister of Scarlet, breeder Raven
RUBIEN (Roo-bee-en) - Underground city in Hanrah where the humans and dameer reside
RUBY - Mother of Scarlet, worker Raven
SENNASTONE (Sen-nah-stone) - A continent, the large mass of land that holds the six kingdoms
SERAPHINE (Seh-rah-feen) - Scarlet's surname
SILVA- Fortune teller, dameer
SILVER SNAKE TAVERN - A tavern situated in Rubien
SONGBIRD CASTLE - Royal residence in Rubien
SKINSEAL - A white jelly-like substance that protects the skin from getting burnt in fires
TAYLOR - Ember's guardian in the Hex Trials, dameer
TEALWATERS- A kingdom found in the West known for its tropical climate
THE PHOENIX - Scarlet's fighting name at the Badger's Sett
THE PIRATE - Fighter at the Badger's Sett
THE TEACHER - Fighter at the Badger's Sett
VERMILION FANG (Vuh-mi-lee-uhn) - The moniker of Ruby Seraphine
WINELLA (Win-elle-ah) - Competitor in the Hex Trials, fighter Raven
WORKER RAVEN - A Raven whose duty is to work and keep the economy running

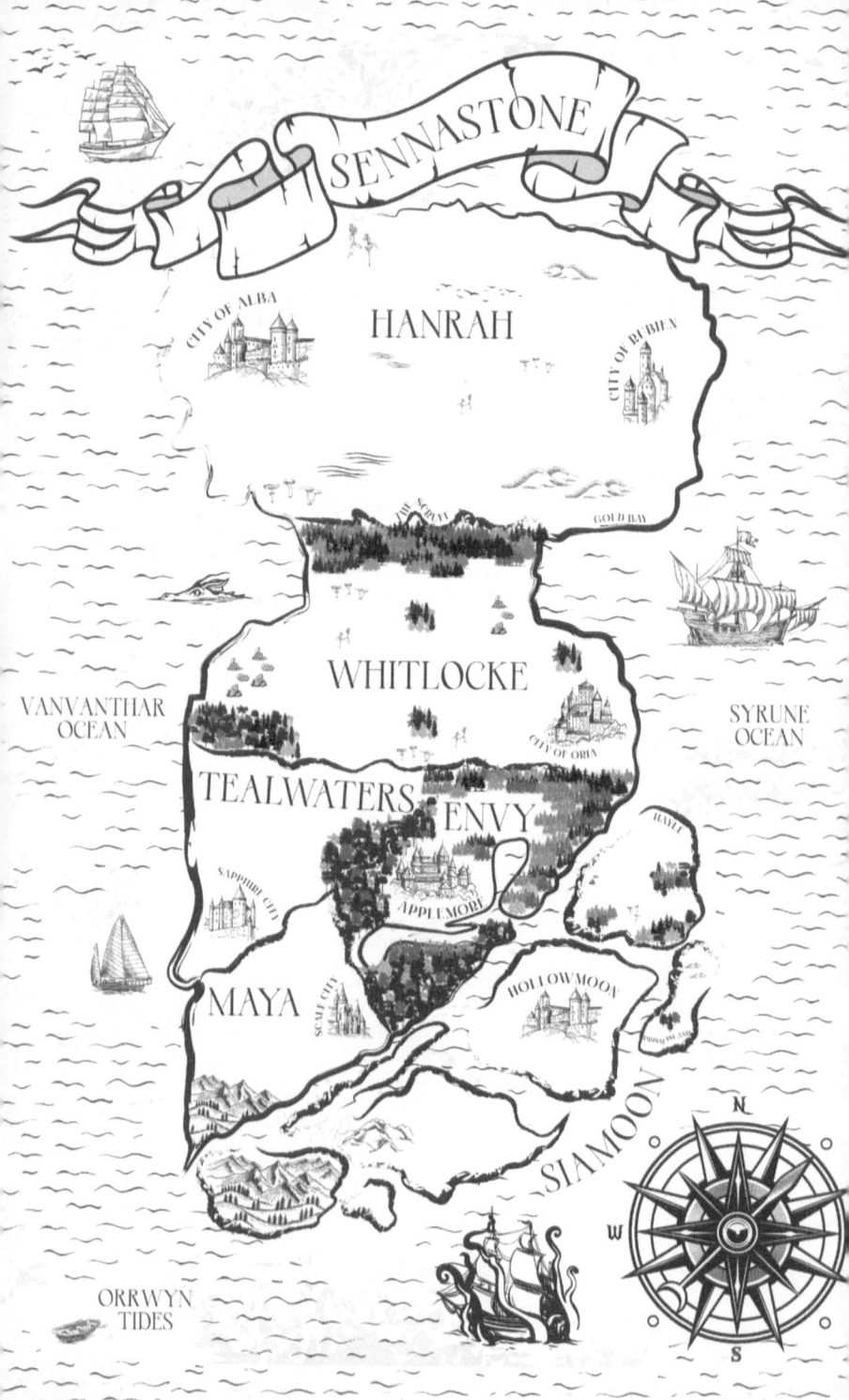

PART ONE
The Hex Trials

SCARLET SERAPHINE

I

I breathe in the smell of sweat as spectators roar at me, their shouts loud and invasive from outside the fighting ring. All I need to focus on, though, is the man in front of me. He's perhaps a few years older — early twenties. He has a mop of dark, messy hair upon his head, and from the way he smells, I can tell he is dameer — a human born with magic.

Spit flies from his mouth as he attempts to dodge my attacks. Occasionally I let his fists collide with my bare skin to keep the fight interesting, to let him think he has a chance. I glance quickly at the manager of the joint. Storm, a burly man with pure white eyes, gives me a nod of permission.

You can finish the fight now, he conveys silently, and I grin wickedly.

My first fight, I was told off for ending it in less than thirty seconds, Storm scolding me for not performing to his liking. 'Make them beg for a victory,' he'd said.

If I triumphed within seconds, it wouldn't be as enter-taining for his customers, and the more they are enter-tained, the more money they throw his way.

My opponent swings for my gut. I'm quick to elude the attack. My own fist flies towards his jaw in answer, the crack loud in my ears. *Bingo.* In one smooth movement, my opponent's body falls to the floor, his eyes rolling back into his head.

'And the winner is the Phoenix!' Storm cries out, sending the crowd of spectators into a roar of equal amounts of delight that I've won and horror that I've lost them money.

One voice I hear above the others is the vampire who is a regular here and who just so happens to be my best friend. Dimitri Thunders' cheers of happiness are loud compared to everyone else's. I turn towards Dimitri, who grins widely, and I mirror him in high spirits.

'Nicely done,' he says with a nod as I approach the small wall that divides the fighters from the spectators. We clap hands as we usually do after every win, my fingerless gloves damp with sweat and blood.

'Thank you,' I whisper with a grin.

I reach under my hood and wipe at my eyes. The mask makes it difficult, but I'm used to it. A rule here at the Badger's Sett is no fighter is allowed to show their identity, and thus, fighters are made to wear hooded costumes and masks to cover the face – eyes not included.

Workers drag my opponent away for the next fight to commence. Storm announces who the next fighters will be and urges everyone to get their bet and beer ready for the next round.

I jump over the small wall and follow Dimitri to the bar. Some men slap me on the shoulder in congratulations, while others scowl at me.

At the bar, a young man called Andre is serving. When he sees me in my fighting gear, he starts moving. Two glasses of Liquid Gold are ready on the counter when I reach him.

'There you go, love.'

I nod my head in silent thanks. I smile under my mask, knowing he won't be able to see it, but I still see a twinkle in his eyes, a common reaction for humans to have in the presence of the Phoenix.

The next match is about to begin, so Dimitri and I head upstairs. We walk past private rooms all designated for the fighters to unwind and safely unravel their hidden identities. Dimitri heads for the end chamber, my preferred space, called the Green Room.

The walls and furniture are all shades of forest green, and it has a minibar within that Dimitri and I take full advantage of. It's also a safe place for me to take off my hood and sweaty mask.

'That was fun,' I state happily, adrenaline still coursing through me as I untie my long dark red hair, the tension instantly soothed the moment my locks spring free of their plait.

'You kept your guard up well, Scarlet. He didn't have a chance,' Dimitri says loyally as his glamour drops.

While in my fighting form, known as the Phoenix, Dimitri holds the glamour of an older gentleman, a father figure watching his child win fights. The first time I saw his disguise, I thought it was hilarious, his belly slightly rotund and his beard long and highlighted with grey.

But when I am simply Scarlet, he is the complete opposite of a simple human man. Dimitri without magic is a tall, dark-haired vampire with fangs longer than mine and a smile just as deadly.

I take a long swig of Liquid Gold from my glass, letting the alcohol soothe me. As the name suggests, the drink is pure gold in colour and stains a person's mouth metallic, but I don't care – I've earned it.

Gold liquor dribbles from the side of my mouth as I drain my glass, and my tongue pokes out to catch it before it trickles down my chin.

'Good?' Dimitri asks, taking a swig of his own.

Liquid Gold is a special beverage that tastes like the individual's preferred flavour. A drop of magic makes it delicious to anyone over eighteen and vile to anyone underage.

'Like chocolate and mint,' I tell him, rubbing my belly to show how tasty it is.

'Like strawberries and cream,' he counters, rubbing his own stomach.

A warm sensation courses through me as I relish the alcohol before shouts from the balcony echo through the room. We both head to the terrace, a pane of one-way glass protecting us from eyes below, and see two men. One is new, from the looks of him, while also young and toned. The other is a crowd favourite. They call him the Pirate, as he has a wooden leg and massive arms that can easily crush a man's skull. I've yet to fight him, but I'm not eager to.

'Put your bets in,' Storm shouts from the ring, hands up in the air to get the audience's attention. 'We have the Pirate and the Teacher.'

I share a look with my friend. 'The Teacher? What type of name is that?' I scoff.

There aren't many names that sound good here in the Badger's Sett. I chose the Phoenix because I thought it sounded distinctive and intimidating, but the Teacher? It doesn't even *sound* menacing.

'Maybe he wants to be a professor when he's older,' Dimitri ponders.

I shrug, not bothering to watch the fight – I know the

Teacher will probably be beaten within minutes. I head back to the Green Room to change into my normal clothes, my belongings waiting in a trunk.

I'm stuffing my sweaty clothes into my sack when I hear Dimitri shouting. Rushing out to the balcony, I find a look of astonishment upon his pale face.

'What happened?' I ask.

'The Teacher.' He points to the fight below. The Pirate, on his backside, looks up into the eyes of the young masked man. 'He trounced the Pirate. Flipped him like a pancake!'

The Teacher's body language shows he isn't threatened. He seems to know he has won, and the crowd screams around him as he puts his boot upon the Pirate's stomach in warning.

As if knowing he is being watched, the man looks up at us. I don't baulk but rather tilt my head questioningly. I can't help but be intrigued by the stranger.

Who is this new fighter?

The Teacher stares in our direction for a moment more, light blue eyes stony. Then he salutes as if sensing us still observing him.

'Cocky bastard.' Dimitri laughs, clapping his hands for the fighter as he returns to his opponent and helps him up onto his feet. 'What a show. You missed a good one there, Scarlet.'

'Yeah, shame I missed it,' I answer half-heartedly, curious as to how someone of the Teacher's size could defeat a half giant like the Pirate.

Dimitri and I stay most of the night at the Badger's Sett, watching fights and downing Liquid Gold. Unfortunately, being part vampire, I can't get drunk on alcohol, and neither can Dimitri, but we still enjoy swindling newcomers with drinking games.

The evening is quiet when we leave, most households in bed, already sleeping as we stroll leisurely through the streets. The cavern above us is pitch black and menacing, the cave much colder now than it is during the day.

The homes here are painted bright colours, their front porches decorated with potted plants and creative welcome mats. Here in the city of Rubien, the humans and dameer live happily together.

'Sometimes I wish I were human,' I murmur.

Dimitri nods in understanding. His human life was taken from him too soon, and for hundreds of years, he's been living the life of a blood drinker. He would never complain to me about it, but I know he hates his food choices.

'It's hard,' he agrees, his hands finding his pockets. 'But I can't complain to *you*, of all people. I'm accepted for who I am here.' He waves to the city around us.

It's true – the people of Rubien accept Dimitri, sympathising with his past. It isn't uncommon for humans and dameer to be caught in the wrong place at the wrong time. Vampires can be dangerous and scary creatures – at least the foul ones – and when caught, it is near impossible to run away from them.

'They are coming to accept me. It's slow, but I've noticed a change over the years,' I reply, knowing deep down the people of Rubien would have embraced me sooner if it weren't for my Raven heritage.

We approach the wall that divides the city of Rubien and the House of Raven. It's an intimidatingly tall stack of jagged rocks that was created as a barrier to keep the humans out. Or as the humans claim, to keep us Ravens out.

We walk along the barricade, sharp stone edges poking out, before we reach a tunnel. The temperature here increases a few degrees. As the only entrance to my home, it's the only way I can travel to see Dimitri.

He stops suddenly, his hand shooting out to grasp my shoulder. I'm suddenly on high alert, my hands out in case he faints, in case he stumbles. It wouldn't be the first time that's happened.

'Dimitri?' My senses sharpen at the seriousness of his expression as he comes back from wherever he just went.

'I had a strange feeling.' Dimitri's gaze wanders to the tunnel, the same tunnel I've been travelling through for years now, as if it's dangerous. His bright red eyes dart around the opening, surveying the space.

Peering down the entrance myself, I find nothing out of the ordinary. 'My hand isn't bleeding,' I say, checking my palm for any blood.

My right hand, scarred with a jagged silver line, peers up at me. From birth I've had it, and from birth it has been able to sense when danger is coming. When I came across a stray dog once, my scar opened up, pouring out crimson – the dog nearly bit my hand clean off right after. But currently, the scar is silver in colour and sealed shut. I know I'm safe. For now.

Dimitri grimaces, his brow creasing with thought. It's not uncommon for him to have these strange feelings. When he was a dameer, a human born with magic, he could see the future. However, now, as a vampire, the only inkling of his ability comes in the form of various strong feelings and blurry visions.

'I think it's safe for you to get home,' he declares.

I wait a beat to see if he will explain himself, but he doesn't. He simply waves me down the tunnel instead. The hole in the wall is the furthest he will go. The reason for him never stepping foot in Raven territory is one I've never had the courage to ask.

I slowly make my way through, and when I get to the end, I take a cautious look around. Again nothing seems out of the norm.

'I'll be fine,' I tell Dimitri, meeting his watchful gaze across the way, waving my scarred hand at him. 'Nothing happening here.'

He doesn't look convinced, but he nods. 'Okay. Go straight home. No shortcuts.'

'Yes, sir.' I salute, making his lips twitch with amusement.

2

It's quiet in the House of Raven, much like the city of Rubien, but that's where the similarities stop. Here, the houses aren't colourfully painted like those of the humans over the wall. Instead, they are cold and neutral in colour and blend in with the dull cave interior. None of the Ravens have bothered to decorate their homes – no plants or personal belongings to set each place apart from the others.

I follow one of the lava rivers that flow through the depths of the cavern. It bubbles beside me, reminding me how painful it will be if I topple into it. I take a few steps away to be safe.

The stream leads me to the end of my street, where homes are packed together in close proximity. In this part of the cave, the stalactites dangle intimidatingly above me, the cavern ceiling we all live under a dark, gaping hole where bats and other nocturnal creatures sleep.

After passing a number of small stone homes, I come to my own household. I can see from the gap underneath the front door that a light is on.

Who is still awake at this time of night?

Stepping through the entrance, I'm welcomed by my older sister Roux at the dinner table, her face cautious until she registers it's me. A single lantern illuminates her striking features, sharp and clever crimson eyes and a smile that can turn from kind to cunning in seconds.

'Hi.' She smiles, in the middle of cutting off the skin of an apple.

'Hi there. Cravings?' I ask, watching her eat the juicy red skin of her fruit. She nods, and my eyes fall to her swelling belly. 'How are they faring?'

Roux's hand automatically goes to her pregnant stomach, rubbing it affectionately before answering. 'I had another check-up today.'

I sit at the table alongside her. I don't particularly like to talk about her check-ups – the House of Raven is well known for its clinical way of reproducing.

Roux is classed as a breeder; her duty is to procreate. She's to keep breeding as many Ravens as possible so that our House will thrive for generations to come. Being female, she is allowed to stay home, but my older brother Ash isn't so lucky. He is forced to lodge with other males in a shared residence near the breeding clinic, forbidden to have visitors.

'And? How did it go?' I probe, noting Roux's downcast gaze, the apple in her hand temporarily forgotten. Suddenly her eyes become teary, and I'm reaching for her, not sure why she is upset. 'Roux, what happened? Is something wrong with the babies?'

Roux stares up at the ceiling, trying her best not to blink. I know this is a way of preventing herself from crying, as I do the same when I'm trying to hold myself together.

'The healers don't think they'll make it through the birth,' Roux admits in a whisper.

My shoulders sag at the news. 'What? *Why?* Why do they say that?'

'Purely because they're twins.'

I shake my head in frustration. 'Yes, but Ember and Blaze are proof twins can be birthed without complications,' I argue, mentioning our other siblings. 'What makes *your* babies any different?'

'Me,' Roux states coldly, her voice turning hard like she truly believes she's the problem. 'I can't birth them without some sort of help. They don't think *I'll* make it through the birth, let alone stay alive long enough for the babies to survive.'

Fear instantly wells up inside my chest. Heartbreaking images of Roux and the babies fog my mind. Desperation claws at me. I can't lose my sister. I can't lose my future family. Not like this.

'What type of help are we talking about? What can aid you, Roux?' I demand, my voice loud enough that she hushes me and looks with worry at the staircase that leads upstairs to where our mother sleeps.

'It's taken Ruby hours to get to sleep,' Roux explains, pressing a finger to her lips.

When I nod in confirmation that I won't start shouting again she continues.

'They mentioned a certain medicine I can take leading up to the birth, but it's very hard to come by, and as you can imagine, it's in high demand due to its magical ingredients.'

My mouth twists in frustration. I remember Ruby mentioning taking special medicine when she was in labour with my brother and sister. What did she take, and how did she acquire it?

'Well, that's utter horse shit,' I mutter before silence envelops us both. I meet her gaze, and we both watch each other as tears fall from our eyes. A tear each for a future we can't prevent.

'Other than that, the babies are happy and healthy.' Roux wipes at her face, already looking guilty for revealing the reason for her sombre mood. She takes my hand and squeezes it, as if *I'm* the one who needs the comfort right now.

'Roux,' I say, but I have no idea what to say. Roux is in danger. Her children are at risk. Surely there is something I can do – a solution I can unearth before the birth. 'I'll find the medicine for you. We have time.'

'That's sweet of you, Scar, but if the healers can't obtain it for me, I doubt you'll be able to.'

I think of the money I've won from my fights, the velvet bags I've accumulated over the years, which I keep stored at Dimitri's place. 'It doesn't matter how much it costs. I will get the medicine for you. I don't care what I have to do. You and the babies will pull through.'

'You don't—' Roux begins, but I cut her off, my feelings tumultuous at this point.

'No, Roux. I don't care how I acquire it. I'm going to save you all. Raven's promise.'

Always the intelligent sister out of us, she doesn't bother arguing. She knows once I set my mind on something, I'll work hard to prove I can do it, and with this, I promise myself I won't give up until I find a way for Roux to watch her children grow up.

3

'Y ou're looking for Araside, love. Very powerful stuff,' the woman tells me. 'A simple but life saving tonic to help your kind successfully birth more than one child at a time.'

I'm up early the next day, walking the markets of Rubien and asking anyone and everyone I can about this mysterious medicine that can help pregnant women deliver babies. It seems very few people know what I'm talking about but only because the tonic is not used for humans – only those with vampire ancestry.

The woman beholds my confusion, seeming to enjoy my lack of knowledge on the matter. 'Vampires are unable to breed unless a male finds a human woman. Ravens though, you can breed one child fine enough. But to give birth to twins or triplets ...' She laughs to herself as if the thought of it is preposterous. 'Your vampire blood is your disadvantage. You need the aid of Araside or else the mother and children will die.'

Die.

The word rings inside my head.

Die. Die. Die.

I can't think of Roux ... *dying*.

'Araside is also very expensive and extremely rare,' the woman goes on, oblivious to my growing panic. 'I wish you luck on finding it.'

'So I won't be able to obtain Araside without leaving this cave?' I ask, doing my best to conceal my emotions.

The woman shakes her head with a sympathetic grimace. 'No, love. The last I heard of it, it was found near the forests of the kingdom of Envy, which without a portal would be at least a few months travel on horse,' she answers, looking at the metal bracelet around my wrist, the one all Ravens wear – a bracelet that prevents us from leaving this cave.

I grimace, wanting nothing more than to scream and shout with frustration. 'Thank you for your time.'

After hours of zero luck, I decide to head back to the House of Raven, defeated and angry. Somehow I have to find a way to retrieve a substance that comes from a kingdom I can't get to. What has my life become?

'Hello, Gem,' I say as I walk into work, entering the large double doors of a stone-walled barn full of horses. In a cave, wood is a hard material to come by, so everything is mainly made of rock or metal. The whole place lacks a homely feel, and I despise it.

I pet Gem on her soft nose and give her neck a scratch. 'What am I going to do?' I whisper to her, my mind reeling with questions. Gem softly grazes my clothes, looking for a treat I don't have. 'Okay, okay. I'll get you something to eat.' I chuckle half-heartedly while turning for the tack room.

I stop in my tracks, sensing something not quite right. The horses don't seem to feel threatened, their heads poking out of their stalls like usual when I arrive. I sniff the air – no smell other than the animals, but that means nothing. All of us that possess vampire blood are born without a scent.

Silently I peer over Gem's stall, taking a look inside to see if there is someone there. There isn't. I move to the next stall, where a mare called Torment lives, but again no one is there. I repeat this for all the horses until only the tack room is left.

I reach for a broom that leans against a nearby wall before I twist the handle on the door. The moment I open it, I can't help but smile.

Sitting on a bucket, wearing his fighting leathers, is my older brother Blaze. He is cleaning his boots with some oil when he looks up at me, his curly red hair bouncing when he moves.

'What are you doing here?' I say in greeting, watching him finish off his boots. They look pretty good after a polish.

'I thought I'd stop by and say hello, but you weren't here. So I thought I'd spend my time doing something useful while I waited.' He shrugs, crimson eyes gleaming with amusement.

He starts to put the polish and brush away, stashing them in the wrong places. I roll my eyes and move them to their correct spots, earning a fanged grin from my brother, his teeth inhumanly white. He takes the broom off me and twirls it around, expertly spinning it around his body with ease.

'You've been out a lot lately. Is everything okay?' he asks, walking through a routine of strikes and defence movements.

I shrug because I don't know how to answer. Lately I've been fighting a lot at the Badger's Sett, which Blaze and the rest of my family don't know about.

I watch with mild interest as he continues his fight with

an imaginary opponent, his body supple as it attacks and counter-attacks his invisible foe.

'Yeah, I'm fine. Just doing ... stuff.' I shrug again when he looks my way.

'Doing *stuff*?' he echoes, pausing for a brief moment.

'Yes. I've been working hard to get some extra money.'

He seems to defeat his unseeable opponent and decides to call it a day, placing the broom against the wall. 'Why do you want extra money? Is there something you're saving up for?'

My freedom, I think sourly. If I had enough money, I could pay a trustworthy blacksmith to take this awful bracelet off my wrist, and I could run to another city – preferably with my family in tow.

Instead, I say, 'New boots.'

Blaze surveys my tatty old brown boots and scowls. 'Your masters don't give you new ones every year?'

I give him an irritated look. Like Roux, my brother has a duty, but it's to fight. As a fighter, he trains for the occasion when we may go to war, or for when the royal family needs him for a more specific mission.

'If they do, they've forgotten to swing by for the last three years,' I counter.

I'm not classed as a fighter; I'm classed as a worker. Someone who's given one job to do for the rest of their life. In my case, I tend to the horses and get paid very little money for it.

A sudden sensation in my right hand makes me look down in surprise. Blaze surveys my scarred palm with a scowl, the usual silver jagged mark now seeps crimson blood as if it's a fresh wound. Right now my blood is a red flag warning me something is coming.

I hurry to the entrance of the stables, where I find Master Jepp pouring buckets of water from each of the stalls onto the floor. I refrain from shouting rude remarks at him.

'What is the meaning of this?' the older male asks, his black uniform with red detailing sleek and intimidating as he prowls closer. 'You give these wretched animals dirty water?'

He runs a hand through his bright red hair, the same colour as Blaze's, the same shade as every Raven's – except mine.

'I fill their buckets up with fresh water every morning,' I answer matter-of-factly, willing my face into neutrality. I keep my hands behind my back to hide the bleeding and to stop myself from wrapping them around his stupid neck.

'What are we paying you for around here?' Master Jepp snaps.

You barely pay me at all, I want to answer, but I don't, knowing if I play along with his little game, I'll be sent to the leader of our House for punishment, and that's the last thing I want.

Master Jepp slowly approaches me, looking me up and down with distaste. 'You never did have a backbone, half-blood,' he mutters, circling me like an animal would its prey.

I stand very still, willing myself to breathe as slowly as possible, to focus on that instead of his words.

'If I were Ruby, I would have given you away to the humans and never looked back.'

An aching pain in my mouth informs me of my rising anger. My fangs grow slowly as frustration begins to swell inside my chest. As a child, I would have slapped him by now, but I slowly learned that people like him thrive on power, and if I played the victim, he would indulge in my squirming.

Master Jepp's smile falls further the longer I stay quiet,

ignoring his jibes. 'Do your job properly *half-blood*,' he spits, sensing my need to bite back slowly fade away. 'Or else *she'll* hear about this.'

Finally breaking eye contact, the master notices Blaze behind me. His features quickly morph into a rare smile as he forgets me instantly. 'Good to see you, Blaze. How is your twin?'

'Ember is very well,' Blaze says politely.

'How is Ember's combat training coming along? Still top of the class?'

Blaze's mouth twitches at the dig, but he stays composed. 'Excelling as usual, Master.'

'Marvellous. I look forward to her joining my classes. I've heard she is a remarkable student.' Master Jepp nods pleasantly before turning on his heel and leaving us without another word.

I turn to Blaze with a scowl, hatred still simmering in my bones. 'Holy Hanrah! How does anyone cope with him? He is the bane of my existence.'

Blaze shakes his head. 'He's not that bad, really. He's actually a really good teacher to have. It's only you he's a bastard to.'

'Good to know,' I utter, looking at the buckets of water that need refilling. 'I swear he only visits me to make my life harder.'

Blaze leans against a stall, the horse closest to him curious enough to sniff him. Blaze eyes the stallion up before meeting my gaze. 'Ruby would never give you away,' he blurts, making me blink with surprise. 'She's never regretted having you, Scar.'

Discomfort weaves its way through me. It's strange to have Blaze feel sympathy for me, or for him to feel sorry enough for me to think I need reassurance that our mother loves me.

'I know that.' I shrug.

Ruby, our mother, was once as loved and adored in the House of Raven as our sister Ember is now. She grew up as one of the youngest breeders and had four children. Then, having surpassed her duty at an early age, she was invited to become a fighter and join the Raven army, but that all changed when she had me.

She would never admit it, but I know Ruby misses her old life, training like Blaze and Ember do every day. Now she serves as a barkeeper at the local tavern and works long hours to keep us fed and watered. Not once, though, have I heard her complain about her job, and she has never made me feel any less than my siblings for being a worker too — even though it's seen as lower class in our House.

'Master Jepp only says things like that to aggravate me. He'll find any excuse to send me off for punishment,' I clarify, finding a rag and wiping the blood from my hand. Now that Master Jepp has left, the once-crimson scar appears as a silver stripe upon my palm again.

Blaze nods, crossing his arms. Silence envelops us for a moment before I approach him.

'So what's the real reason for your visit? Gossip on any new trainees? Or have you been missing me?'

My brother's face widens into an amused smile, bright red eyes looking down at me. 'The last one, I think, is stretching it a bit.'

'You would be surprised how many visits I get in a day from people needing to see this beautiful face,' I counter with a wide smile.

He grins, but it doesn't reach his eyes. I know then that his visit has something to do with what I've been thinking about since last night.

'I'm worried about Roux,' he admits, lowering his voice. 'She's pretending everything is fine, but I heard her cry today when she thought she was home alone. It can't be good for the children.'

I grimace, feeling the pressure rise inside me. Time – I just need time to think of a solution.

'I've been asking around the city,' I say, gaining Blaze's attention. Unlike me, he never visits the city of Rubien, having been brought up to think humans are not worth his time.

'And?' he prompts, leaning forward slightly, anticipating my next words.

'I'm told the medicine Roux needs is called Araside, but it's found in the kingdom of Envy.'

'Envy!' Blaze blurts with horror. 'How are we supposed to get there?'

I shrug. 'We need a portal. We need a witch or a wizard to take us there.'

Blaze lifts up his arm, putting the metal bracelet on his wrist up to my face. 'And how are we supposed to deal with these?'

My eyes roam over the band. It's said that once a Raven leaves the cave, the bracelet will begin to burn them, a precaution for Ravens who feel the need to leave their House and desert their loyalties. Personally, I think it says more about the leadership than us.

'It will hurt immensely,' I state without hesitation, and Blaze reluctantly nods.

Our conversation is interrupted by a sound I've not heard in years. A bell.

It chimes, echoing through the stables. The horses go crazy in answer. I mirror Blaze's frown when I meet his gaze.

'The Elder Raven? What does she want?' Blaze wonders.

'This better be good,' I huff, hurrying to lock up the barn before making my way to the Raven's Nest.

T he thunderous ringing noise reverberates along the cave walls, making me cover my ears in discomfort.

What is happening?

Opposite the stables, huge crowds begin to flow out of the gigantic training arena. Hordes of Ravens march over the grey stone bridges that pass over rivers of hot lava and into the busy streets.

Passing fountains of gurgling molten lava and ducking down dark alleys between dwellings, Blaze and I walk alongside the crowd that parades towards the Raven's Nest, Blaze greeting a few of his friends.

With similar uniforms of black leather, identical bright red hair and matching crimson eyes, the fighter Ravens are the image of formidable. Soldiers born and bred with vampire and magical dameer blood to create an army – the House of Raven.

The lanterns that float in mid-air burn brighter than usual, illuminating the stalactites that hang precariously above. A thick darkness coats the cave ceiling.

As a child, I used to wonder what the world outside the

cave would look like. I wondered how the ocean would feel if I ever stepped in it, how the trees would sound when the wind caught their leaves. All things I would likely never experience.

'In formation!' a female shouts, her fangs long and intimidating as she shoves the crowd into orderly lines. Her uniform, detailed with red piping, indicates her position of master, much like Master Jepp's. The Ravens obey her, taking her orders as law, because they know the consequences if they step out of line.

Blaze and I travel down cold streets made of rough rock and past buildings built of sharp grey stone. We pass an array of shops, the local tavern, the small, haughty library and the breeding centre, where even pregnant Ravens stagger out into the streets for what is to come.

Nearing the main square, we travel through the quieter back streets in hopes of finding a familiar ladder. It clings precariously to the side of a jagged stone building well known as the tailor shop, a place where Ravens get their uniforms made, altered and fixed.

I race up to the rooftop, Blaze following closely behind, and reach the top of the building. I lie on my stomach and crawl to the edge of the roof – my secret spot that has the best view of the entirety of the Raven's Nest.

My eyes roam over the sea of red below, the absence of any humans normal for our part of the cave. Unlike me on my visits to the city, humans would never dare step inside the Ravens' domain, fearing their lives would be at stake.

Standing intimidatingly to one side of the crowded square is a tall stone structure that holds the chiming bell. Finally it stops, and the crowd goes silent. The only sound remaining is the lava rivers that flow endlessly around the circumference of the piazza.

I feel my heart pound with anticipation. Never in my

life have I seen so many Ravens in one place at the same time. Whatever is happening must be *really* important.

A small figure appears on the front steps of the bell tower, and I exhale a shaky breath.

'The Elder Raven,' Blaze whispers, anticipation lining his words.

Her face is hostile, the image of a cruel and dangerous creature. Her short red hair is tied away from her face, showing harsh cheekbones and a mouth with fangs so long they make mine look insignificant in comparison.

'Ravens,' she says in acknowledgement of the crowd, her voice loud as magic helps project her words. Her presence is fierce and frightening even at a distance. 'You may wonder why I have gathered you all here today. As the ruler of our monumental House, I have the pleasure of announcing some exciting news. We are soon commencing the Hex Trials.'

A gasp of excitement runs through the audience. I frown, not understanding what the Hex Trials are.

Blaze shuffles closer and whispers, 'It's a competition where Ravens fight each other to the death for a grand prize – to be in the Hex.'

'For generations,' the Elder Raven continues, 'our House has been known for being mighty in more than strength. We are known for our skill, our unfailing judgement and ability to outmatch any opponent that comes our way. Today, we will begin our search for our next champion and Raven of the Hex.'

I know only a little about the Hex. It consists of one champion from each of the six kingdoms, and their job is to protect and serve all people regardless of race, culture or influence. They serve all kingdoms, serve all beings and have immense authority everywhere they go. No one in the whole land is ignorant of who they are – my family especially. For as long as I can remember, my aunt Brande has been the Raven of the Hex. She's been able to travel the six kingdoms, visit famous landmarks and monuments, all while helping people from all over the lands as her job. I just didn't realise that to gain that position, she had to compete in a deadly competition.

'The Raven of the Hex cannot be just *anyone*,' the Elder Raven continues. 'As tradition states, all female Ravens from the ages of thirteen to thirty can participate in the Hex Trials. They will be tested on their strength, honour and skill, to distinguish the weak from the elite. The winner will be awarded the privilege of representing our House.'

'Ember is going to be pleased.' Blaze scowls.

'Don't tell me you're disappointed.' I gape at him. I can't begin to think why he would want the opportunity to compete in such a dangerous game.

'I could prove myself.'

My brother is described best as the shadow of Ember, her reputation surpassing all her peers, and being her twin, I can see why Blaze would feel like she's always one step ahead of him.

'You could die,' I counter, making him glare at me.

'That's what I was born to do, Scar. I'm a fighter. One day we may go to war, and I'll be on the front line, as I've trained to be my whole life. How is this any different?'

I shrug, trying not to display my unease at his remark, but he does make a good point. I glance back at the Elder Raven, who walks along the front of the bell tower with long strides.

'In previous years, competitors have dwindled in number. This will not do.' Our leader shakes her head unhappily. 'So in these Hex Trials, I am willing to be generous. Every family here needs something. Something *important*. If you compete, you will be rewarded handsomely, and if you *win* ...' The word hangs in the air for a short moment, the audience seeming to hold its breath for what's to come. 'You will receive the possessions your family is most in need of.'

Slight chatter echoes through the cavern. The Elder Raven allows it for a moment before raising her hand. Everyone becomes silent once more.

'A letter has been sent to every household in hopes our females will sign up for this momentous opportunity. Remember, this is history in the making. The Hex Trials are an enjoyable event where we come together and support our peers. I'll see you in the arena.'

The Elder Raven walks back into the bell tower, and echoes of excitement and questioning resonate through the cave the moment she is gone, hundreds of voices speaking over each other.

Observing the mass below me slowly disperse, I can't help but try to find my family in the crowd and wonder what they think of all this.

'So, are you going to compete?' Blaze asks me, making me blink in surprise.

'Me? Definitely not. I'm a worker, not a fighter.'

He shrugs, his red eyes on the crowd below us. 'Worker or not, it could be fun.'

'I wouldn't compete in the Hex Trials unless I had the chance of becoming the next Elder Raven. Only then might I consider it.'

'Why would you want to be the next Elder?' Blaze frowns.

'Because then I could ban foolish competitions like this.'

5

Blaze and I pass homes made of uneven rock and scorching hot rivers of flowing lava before setting foot on our own street. As we approach our family home, I can identify a faint burning smell and loud yelling coming from within. My mother's voice is loud and thunderous.

Opening the door, I find Ruby pointing a pale finger across the dining table, a small flame flickering across her skin as magic fills the air. Sitting on a rickety chair is my older sister Ember, who is the spitting image of Blaze. She stares back at Ruby, her crimson eyes gleaming with defiance.

'Ember Seraphine, when are you going to stop being a pain in my arse?' Ruby hisses.

Hearing the door open, Ruby turns around to acknowledge us, her beautiful pale face set in a deep scowl, her fangs on display. She's a small woman, but her presence is the opposite – strong and captivating, especially when wearing her current expression.

'Are we interrupting?' I ask, taking a seat at the dining table. I notice two new handprints burnt into the light wood, as well as a small piece of timber discarded in the middle of the table. Looking down towards the floor by Ember's feet, I realise the timber is the other half of a table leg that's been ripped off. So *that's* what the argument is about.

I turn to Ember with a sly smile. 'You need to control that *hot* temper of yours better. This is the second table you've burnt this month.'

Ember stands up abruptly. Fire lights up along her arms, making me feel uncomfortably sweaty. I hate it when she uses her fire magic – the thought of it touching me makes me want to recoil.

The flames crackle loudly as I watch her face turn irritated. 'I'll show you hot,' she threatens.

'You don't have to. I can look at my reflection for that,' I joke, making her scowl.

'Did you end up seeing the Elder Raven's announcement?' Blaze asks. I turn to him questioningly, and he gives me a warning look.

Don't rile her up, he seems to say.

Ember's eyes still burn with annoyance. I simply shrug and ignore her.

'Yes, I did,' Ruby states, taking a seat at the table. 'I've received the official letter already.' She holds up a crimson envelope, then places it on the table in front of her before getting up again.

I stare at the envelope like it's about to burst into flame.

Moments later Roux waddles in and takes a seat beside me. She smiles timidly, and I mirror her in greeting.

'How are you feeling?' I ask.

She nods, seeming to be in a better mood than she was last night. 'Fine now I've had a nap.'

'We all feel better after a good nap,' Blaze agrees before

pushing the envelope closer to Ruby. 'I'd also feel better hearing what the Elder Raven has written.'

Ruby's fingers unfold the piece of paper inside the envelope, and her crimson eyes dart across the crisp white paper in silence. I notice her body stiffening slightly before she lays it out for the twins to read first.

They mirror one another, body language the same as they scan the words. It fascinates me how they move, as if flowing and ebbing with one another without realising it.

'Well, I'm going to sign up,' Ember announces, looking at Ruby. 'If you and Brande competed, I want to continue the legacy.'

'I'll support you no matter what you decide.' Ruby nods as if unsurprised by this.

I'm also not surprised by this decision.

Ember leans back in her chair, crossing her arms over her chest. 'Plus I could do with an upgraded uniform and a new sword. Mine are old and need updating.' She looks down at her almost pristine uniform of black. It hugs her body like a second skin, the material fireproof to accommodate her fire abilities.

I scowl, looking at my own attire – my trousers, which are smeared in horse shit; my shirt, which is ripped at the bottom from when Gem nibbled it; and my boots, which have a hole in the bottom where my big toe is.

Blaze notices my self-inspection and smirks. 'I think Scarlet could do with new clothes over you.'

Ember surveys me and wrinkles her nose. 'Yeah, and perhaps something to cover the smell. You stink like an animal.'

'Are you done?' Roux asks, snatching the letter out of Ember's hand. 'We aren't here to listen about your superiority. Scarlet smells fine.'

Ember's eyes narrow, but she doesn't snap back like she

would with me. Ember is indebted to Roux for being a breeder for the family. Without Roux, Ember would have to step down from her life as a fighter and reproduce, and that's something we all know she'd never like to do.

Roux places the letter between us, and I read the cursive writing eagerly.

> To the Seraphine family,
> Tomorrow we commence the Hex Trials, an important day for the House of Raven. We implore you to compete in the trials not only to gain honour for you and your family but to take part and test your skills against your peers.
> By signing your name below, you consent to partaking in four trials, one every month, all of a dangerous nature.
> As promised, you will be rewarded with not only a higher allowance for competing but a choice of two items in the list below if you win:

My eyes scan the list slowly as I absorb what items Ravens are desperate enough to sign up for. I stop on item number twelve. My heart stutters, and my hands become sweaty.

> 12. Araside (birthing medicine)

Shit.

I feel my heart sink inside my chest. Araside. The medicine that can help my sister. It seems the Elder Raven has been watching us closely and knows our family, or more specifically Roux, needs medicine.

I feel someone watching me, and no longer can I ignore them. I look up to see Roux, and she is shaking her head vigorously at me. She has spotted item number twelve and has realised what it is.

'What?' I ask, showing feigned ignorance.

'No,' she blurts. The temperature rises between us, her fire magic radiating from her body.

'But—'

She doesn't let me finish. She stands up and slams a fist on the table, making me jump, another burnt fist print left on the wood. Her eyes are scrutinising, and her voice is low in warning. 'No, Scarlet. Don't you *dare*.'

Ember knocks on the table to get our attention. She regards the spot Roux has burnt and glances at Ruby, seeming to wonder why our mother won't tell our sister off for vandalising the furniture. 'What's the problem, Roux? What's got your big belly in a twist?'

Roux doesn't answer. She only has her sights on me. I break eye contact, and I find Ruby watching us too. She must know from past experience that Roux needs the Araside, but she doesn't interrupt, doesn't intercept. She is letting us work it out between ourselves.

Ruby nods encouragingly. *Go on*, she seems to say.

I take a deep breath.

'Roux,' I say carefully. I point to the list, my finger circling item number twelve. 'This is the medicine you need, and I can try to get it for you. This is a sign.'

'I don't care. You are not competing in these trials. You could *die*!' she shouts, the words sharp as they dig into my heart.

'If I *don't* compete, *you* will die!' I snap, regretting the words the moment they are out of my mouth.

She freezes, every inch of her on high alert, hands covering her stomach protectively. 'Please, Scar,' she whimpers, curling in on herself. Her head tips downwards as if to rest on her chest. 'I won't forgive myself if something happens to you.'

'Roux, Araside is the only treatment that can help you birth your children. Don't you want to take this chance? This is not a coincidence. They know we need this.'

Slowly, I take her arm gently. It's hot to the touch, but I don't let go, silently willing her to sit back down. She refuses me at first, but after a few light tugs, she obeys and takes her seat again. Ruby is behind her immediately, rubbing her shoulders to ease the tension.

'If you want Araside,' Ember says from across the table. 'I'll get it for you. It's not a big deal.'

I glare at my sister. '*Not a big deal?*' I repeat, fangs slowly growing.

She shrugs and waves her hands towards Roux. 'If she's so desperate for some medicine, I can arrange that. The winner will receive two prizes. I don't mind sharing one.'

I jump to my feet, infuriated by how unconcerned she is about it all, but Ruby's hand is around my wrist in seconds, her nails digging into my skin. I can hardly feel them.

'You are so self-absorbed—' I begin, but Ruby interrupts me before I can say much more.

'Ember, that's very nice of you. With both you and Scarlet competing, we have double the chance of saving Roux and her children.'

'You can't be serious!' Roux cries, staring up at our mother. 'You can't let Scar compete. *You*, of all people, should know what the consequences of that are.'

Ruby glances at me briefly but doesn't snap back. Before my aunt Brande became Raven of the Hex, both she and Ruby must have competed in the trials. Ruby has never mentioned what horrors she endured, but I sense from the expression on her face that whatever it was mustn't have been good.

Ruby leans towards me, her lips twisting in thought. 'Scarlet.'

I dip my chin to let her know she has my full attention.

'Will you sign up for the Hex Trials regardless of whether you have our blessing to compete or not?'

I swallow, and it feels difficult to do so when I can feel everyone in the room watching me, but I've decided. I know I have to do this, as Ember could retract her offer. If I step down and give in to Roux's wishes, to have Ember later change her mind ... I will never forgive myself. When it comes to Roux I won't risk Ember fucking it up for her. My eyes flicker to my pregnant sister, 'Yes, I will.'

Ruby nods once and gives Roux a knowing look. 'I have five children. I know when it's a losing battle.' She caresses a strand of my sister's hair before she removes herself from the room, slowly walking up the stairs. 'I need a moment alone. Sign your names, and I'll post it later,' she says towards Ember and me before silence envelops us all. A scribbling ink pen is the only sound as my older sister writes her life away.

Ember sighs loudly and slaps Blaze's knee once she's done. 'Well, that's our cue to leave. We have training. See you both around.' She waves lazily before exiting, leaving the front door open for her twin.

Blaze gives Roux's shoulder a gentle squeeze. 'Don't be too hard on her,' he whispers, before peering sidelong to give me a thin lipped smile. The door closes with a soft click with my brother's exit and the sudden quiet seems to cage me in.

Roux sits quietly as I take my turn to sign my name upon the white paper. I watch the wheels rotate inside my sister's head as she digests what's happening, the decision

I've made. I don't regret it, not even when I've folded the paper back in its blood-red envelope.

'I won't ever agree to this,' Roux mutters quietly.

'You don't have to.'

She leans back in her chair before sliding down to lie across the seat, her eyes staring up at the ceiling. 'If I'd known I would have to choose between my little sister and my future children, I would never have agreed to this breeding bullshit.'

'Why do you see it that way? Why can't we have it *all*?'

Roux shakes her head slowly, a tear sliding down her cheek. 'The Hex Trials aren't for children, even if the Elder Raven does allow thirteen-year-olds to participate. It's a test of physical and mental strength against the toughest of fighters. You haven't trained for this like Ember has. You will be left in the dust, and no one will come to your aid. You will be *alone*.'

She meets my gaze finally, conveying her feelings through her stare. I can't pretend I'm not scared. I am. But when I survey her, all I can think about is what will happen if I *don't* do something? I can't sit around and hope for some miracle to happen. These trials are my one opportunity to help my sister, to win the medicine and watch my future nieces or nephews grow up. This is our *one* chance.

'I would do anything for you, Roux,' I whisper.

She reaches blindly for my hand, returning her gaze to the ceiling, but I catch her fingers and hold on tightly. Tears begin to stream down the sides of her face, the flickering lanterns making it shine across her pale cheeks.

We stay like this for a long time before she says, 'I know, Scar. That's what scares me most.'

6

Dimitri walks beside me, listening while I vent. As we stroll through the streets of Rubien, city dwellers wave at him with warm smiles, and he greets each of them back. He has respect in the city, and I'm given the chance to walk peacefully beside him – the humans' distrust of Ravens is understandable.

A beam of light showers down on me from the cave ceiling. It temporarily warms me up. It feels amazing on my skin until I step out of the pocket of sunshine. Dimitri noticeably avoids the light and keeps his distance until I step back into the shade.

Unlike in the House of Raven, there is no lava here. No giant arenas for anyone to train in, no one who walks with weapons on their person. Instead, the civilians are more carefree and enjoy the soft wind that flows from the ocean side of the city.

My favourite thing about Rubien, though, is the dameer. They're humans born with magical abilities, and they are scattered throughout the swarms of people. Within minutes, I notice a window cleaner who controls water as it splashes against the glass of a jewellery shop, a young messenger boy delivering envelopes and newspapers at superspeed and an artist selling his paintings in the street, his paintbrushes moving of their own accord as he charms passers-by.

'So now I've signed up to compete in the Hex Trials,' I say after telling Dimitri about the Elder Raven and her announcement. I sigh heavily. Dimitri knows without me explaining that I will never back out of my decision, but I assume he can still sense my nerves, my fingers fiddling with the cursed bracelet around my wrist.

He's silent, and that makes me worry. Looking up, I find Dimitri's bright red eyes averted, but I can see they are full of concern. In moments like this, it's hard to find Dimitri scary, as vampires are described to be, but he's different. After all this time, he *remembers* being human.

'Say it,' I urge.

'I've lived for many years ...' He trails off, making me feel on edge.

Normally, I would take the opportunity to jest about my best friend's old age, but looking at his pale face, I know now is not the right time.

'The Hex Trials are incredibly dangerous and are not for the faint-hearted.'

'What are you saying?'

Finally he meets my gaze, his strides slowing until he finally stops. He rubs the back of his neck, his long fangs gleaming as he tries to find the right words. 'The Elder Raven has put you and many others in a position you can't back out of. Once you sign up, it's a contract for your life.'

I purse my lips. When I signed my name beside Ember's on the piece of paper, I felt like I could do anything, but now, thinking it over, I wonder if my recklessness will affect my family in more ways than one. What if I don't make it through the first trial? What would I achieve for Roux then?

'I saw no other way of saving my sister,' I say, needing to defend myself.

Dimitri's inhumanly handsome face shows no sign of his typical humour as he stares down at me. 'I know, but this isn't your average fight at the Badger's Sett. For one, you won't be fighting the people of Rubien; you'll be pitted against your own kind.'

I grimace, hating his words. He's right, of course. Humans and dameer are not as strong as Ravens, including half-blood Ravens.

Ravens are hybrids of vampires and royal blood – the most powerful dameer blood in the kingdom. Throughout the years, Ravens have bred with other Ravens to create a powerful House. But me, I'm not the same. I have a Raven mother and a human father. I have a mix of the strong and the weak.

How can I possibly compete against them?

'You're overthinking the wrong things.' Dimitri clasps my shoulder, forcing me to look at him again. 'These trials will be testing the very depths of you and your peers. All you have to do is be *smart*. Work out the best way to win. Don't simmer on the what-ifs, because your opponents certainly won't.'

He begins to walk again, making me follow like a loyal puppy. It's only when I realise we are in part of the city I don't recognise that I ask where we are going.

'I think you should see this,' Dimitri answers.

He leads me to a cavern wall that from a distance looks completely normal. As we close the distance I see depictions all up the wall, and I realise what I'm looking at.

'The Hex Trials have taken place for many years to find a Raven skilled enough to represent your House,' Dimitri explains, waving his hand over hundreds of scenes carved into the rock wall. 'For a long time, Ravens used to mingle with the humans here in the city, until they became predatory, more savage, and deemed humans and dameer too weak to associate themselves with.'

'But we were originally made to protect humans,' I argue, not understanding.

'Yes. Originally you were made as an army to protect Hanrah from any form of invasion, but your House became more its own entity.' Dimitri walks along and points to various pictures. 'These are what the Ravens left behind. These are what some of the trials consisted of many years ago.'

I gape at fanged beings being hung by their fingers and Ravens fighting giants and creatures with wings or sharp talons. I examine trials of water and ones of the earth swallowing up competitors. I gulp at the horrendous scenes before me and wonder what I've got myself into.

'I am going to die,' I murmur, shaking my head. 'Why did you show me these? This does not help!'

Dimitri grabs my shoulders, staring deep into my eyes. 'You are *not* going to die, Scarlet.'

His deep confidence in me is not surprising but it *is* comforting. My heart however still races furiously. My best friend's gaze lowers to my throat, most likely hearing the thrum of my pulse.

Dimitri smiles softly, letting me go to motion towards the depictions. 'These are all moments in history we can *learn* from. These are potential trials you'll have to face.'

I find my hands running through my hair. 'You and your learning,' I grumble, unconvinced.

'We will train every day so you'll feel ready. We will read of prior trials and research solutions for them all,' Dimitri says calmly, his demeanour the opposite of mine. 'And besides, you have an advantage that no other competitor has.'

Dimitri tugs me away from the carvings, towards another set of drawings. These are victorious scenes, Ravens smiling with a severed head in their uplifted arms, winners on a stage with their competitors lying dead on the floor. It looks like carnage and doesn't help settle my panic.

'And what is that?' I ask.

'You have been trained by the very best.' Dimitri grins.

I roll my eyes, trying my best not to smile back. '*You* train me.'

'Exactly. I have more experience, more *knowledge* than all those Ravens put together,' he answers with a slither of pride. 'They have been trained by the same masters for generations and they will know each other's tricks – each other's strengths and weaknesses. *You* however are seen as the outcast, a worker Raven who supposedly cannot fight.'

'I am a mystery,' I agree, starting to understand.

'A secret weapon.' He nods, crimson eyes shining.

7

The next morning, the house is quiet with anticipation. I sit at the dining table with my sisters, Blaze sitting on a step on the stairway. As soon as a knock sounds at the door, Ruby rushes into the room and swings the door open wide. She takes a crimson envelope from a young Raven boy.

My mother rips it open with swift fingers. 'It's from the Elder Raven, an invitation to join her in the training arena in half an hour.'

'And so it begins,' Blaze murmurs.

'Right. This is it,' Ruby says sternly. She puts the letter down on the table and sips from her cup, the smell of lemon wafting through the room. 'Now, all of you go and sort yourselves out. We leave in ten minutes.'

Moments later, I'm already dressed in a dark tunic I usually wear working at the stables – the oldest one I own, in case it gets ruined – as well as some generic black trousers and my pair of brown boots, which smell like horses.

I stand with Ruby, Roux and Blaze as we wait for

Ember. They all wear their usual black leather attire, which makes their toned bodies look exceptionally sleek and strong, the raven emblem on their chests showing they all belong.

I look down at myself. Compared to my family, I look nearly homeless, and what makes it more frustrating is that with the money I win from my fighting, I *could* look exceptional. However, I recently bought a new grooming brush for the horses, and if I were caught wearing new clothing without explanation for how I earned the money to afford it, it would lead to questions and potential punishment. I don't want punishment; it isn't worth it.

The sound of Ember coming down the stairs distracts me from my thoughts as I lay my eyes upon her. My sister's attire, kept for special occasions such as this, is completely red instead of black. An emblem showing a raven's head stands out in black on the right side of her chest. Printed on her back is a bold outline of a raven, its wings spread out to either side of its body, ready for flight. To top it all off, the suit is fireproof, so my sister can use her fire magic and not burn her uniform to ashes.

Ember comes to my side, smirking at my clothing. 'Nice gear.'

'Thanks. This is all my allowance gets me,' I answer, hoping to get some sympathy out of her. From the expression she gives me, I know she is far from caring.

'It's a shame, really. I think this uniform could make anyone look impressive, even you. But don't worry. The suits won't help the weaklings in the trials. They are just leather, after all.' Ember walks to the full-length looking glass by the door to check herself out. She grins at her reflection. 'At least I'll look good when I beat them.'

'Okay, that's enough. We need to go,' Roux announces,

heading for the door while pushing anyone in her path out of the way.

We file out into the stone streets, and I follow my family towards the largest building in the House of Raven. The training arena is menacing with its size and its walls made of dark grey stone. A soft orange glow from the lava river lights up the dull rock.

Throughout the years, I've heard much about the amphitheatre. Having sat at many family dinners while my siblings all spoke about their training, I grew up curious to see what it was like. A couple of times, I even tried sneaking in, but I was caught and punished each time.

Walking under a set of twin arches, we enter the grand stone structure. Ember and I receive numbers to pin to our attire. My feet stop. I did not expect *this*.

As my heart races, my eyes roam over the whole scene. I find myself in the middle, among stone seats that tier upwards towards the very top of the arena and downwards from my family until the seats stop abruptly. A tall wall borders a large fighting pit that is sunken into the ground and covered in dark red sand. Lava lamps beam down on us all, making my hands sweat slightly.

'Impressive isn't it?' Blaze gives me a friendly nudge.

I notice flags and banners decorate the premises, bright red against the dark architecture, the black raven emblem taking pride of place everywhere I look.

Ruby steps closer, her hand lifting to point towards the wall that separates the audience and the sandpit. 'Can you see the shimmering?'

Concentrating on what my mother is referring to, I nod slowly. Around the fighting ring, a magical glamour has been formed. It gives off a faint smell I can't quite place, and it acts as a curtain of illusion.

'So the fighting pit isn't usually full of sand?' I wonder.

'This is an exact replica of what it looks like most days,' Ruby answers, ushering Roux and Blaze towards the seats lower down. 'But I assume for today, something interesting is waiting behind it, but they can't reveal it yet.'

As we take our seats, which are conveniently close to the action, my siblings converse with other Ravens dressed in their crimson garb. Ruby acknowledges a few of her friends who sit close by, chatting about what they expect from today's invitation.

I, however, am being stared at. Unknown gazes watch my every move, most likely pondering my presence. A worker in the arena is a bizarre sight, but a half-blood? Even more so.

I'm not one to feel intimidated easily – I fight rivals twice my size daily at the Badger's Sett – but here I feel isolated and caged in. My family is oblivious to my internal worry, of course. Most of them have been fighters in their lifetimes, and they are very comfortable being in this environment.

The echo of excitement dies down as Ravens begin to turn towards the top of the amphitheatre. Spinning around, I spot what is grabbing everyone's attention. On the highest step, the Elder Raven stands patiently, pale hands clasped together, as she waits for her subjects to calm themselves. Once silence ensues, she begins to walk down the steps, taking her time as the audience watches her every move.

'Today we begin to trial our females until we have only *one* remaining,' the Elder Raven begins, her eyes cold even from this distance. Magic no doubt makes her voice louder so everyone in the establishment can hear her. 'We will find our warrior, our huntress, our protector, and the next Raven of the Hex.'

Whispers echo across the seats, enthusiasm spreading for what's to come. I fidget in my seat, my curiosity and unease growing stronger the nearer the Elder Raven edges toward my family.

'We want a female with strength, with power, and most of all, we want a loyal female to represent our House. The Hex is a true honour, and we will choose our winner within the next few months.' The Elder Raven raises her hands to quiet down the loud enthusiasm around us, and the audience obeys within seconds. 'The Hex Trials will consist of challenges that will test the agility, intelligence, loyalty, strength and magical abilities of our challengers. We will have no less than the best to represent us. As a Hex member, you will need to learn to expect the unexpected. Today you will experience this first-hand. Your first challenge will start momentarily.'

The Elder Raven's gaze lands on me, crimson eyes showing silent questioning before she notes my competitor number. Her smile is sly, and it does nothing to calm my hammering heart.

'We are going to have a trial *now*?' I say, mostly to myself.

'Not one to waste time, is she?' Roux murmurs uneasily. She glances at me and grimaces at my expression. 'You can back out. You don't have to do this.'

I ease my features into neutrality and squeeze my sister's leg in reassurance. I've signed my life away but regardless, I won't back down from this. My eyes meet hers and I smile softly. 'I've got this. We're *both* going to be fine.' I stroke her stomach, hoping it won't be the last time.

Her hand covers mine, her warmth seeping through me. 'Please be careful.'

I nod before standing up. Blaze gives me an encouraging smile. Ember is already making her way down the stairs to join a group of older females who look intimidatingly ready to battle for their desired prizes.

An arm wraps around my shoulders and pulls me along. 'I can't imagine what you must be feeling right now, Scarlet,' my mother murmurs, leading me down the arena steps. 'But know this – you are strong, and no matter how far you go, I will always be proud of you and what you stand for.' Ruby's smile is faint, but her eyes convey enough for me to feel slightly better. She's done this before, years ago. She knows how I'm feeling. 'Stay focused and look for weaknesses. Everything and *everyone* has them. Once you find the fragile link in their armour, you can succeed in anything.' Ruby nods, squeezing my shoulder to give me comfort.

'Thanks, Ruby,' I murmur.

'It's okay to be afraid. The best warriors always are.'

Taking a deep breath, I follow the competitors down into the dark tunnels below. Ember leans against the stone wall, leg propped up casually as she waits for me to reach her.

I try not to think about failing, that soon I could be hurt or worse. Instead, I try to keep Roux in my thoughts, the happiness of her birthing the twins, of her delight in watching them grow up and become their own people.

'Don't look so glum,' Ember states, walking beside me as we travel further away from the heat and into the cool air of the underpass.

'I'm not glum. I'm just thinking.'

Ember grabs my shoulder and stops me before we head into a room full of Ravens, their scarlet uniforms making me feel self-conscious and out of place.

'Listen. Stay in one piece, all right?'

'Is that your attempt at encouragement?' I ask with an

amused smile. Ember has never been one for affection, but watching her try is comical.

'Ruby wants you safe, and Roux wants you alive. Just make sure you're one hundred per cent sure you want to compete, because right *now* is your only chance to slip away.'

I examine the waiting room. Ravens sit on metal benches as they await their next orders. They look happy – excited, even – about what is to come. Right now the females look harmless, their wide smiles animated and full of enthusiasm, but I know from years of listening to my siblings talk about the arena that it is no place for fun and games. The Hex is going to be hard. It's going to test the very depths of my skill set.

It's only when I turn back to Ember that I notice her peculiar look.

She expects me to bail, I realise, *perhaps even hopes for it.*

She most likely wants to do this alone and gain glory from it. I don't trust her enough to help Roux, though. Ember's mind is always on herself, and relying on her is not a risk I'm willing to take when it comes to our sister.

'No. I'm ready.'

She is good at hiding her disappointment, but she nods. 'You can't expect me to protect you out there. I don't know what they have in store for us.'

I narrow my eyes at her. Classic Ember, thinking I'll be dead weight for her.

'And remember I won't be there to save *your* back either,' I counter.

She grins, but it doesn't reach her eyes. 'Funny.'

A male Raven enters the waiting room as we appear in the entrance. He looks across the room of pale faces. 'Ravens, prepare yourselves. The first group will follow me.'

Competitors who wear red numbers on their backs instead of black are chosen first.

Ember claps me on the back. 'Looks like you're in the first group.'

I gulp down a flutter of fear.

'Let the best Raven win,' I hear Ember say as I'm pulled away to the first trial.

8

The metal gate lifts with a screeching sound that makes me grimace. Following my group, I take in my surroundings and see the glamour is now gone.

We stand on an island of sand that overlooks a pit of bubbling lava, the heat rising into my face like a boiling kiss. Looking out onto the scorching pool, I see a small piece of land in the middle of sharp, jagged rocks, a tower of stone in the centre rising sky-high. Sitting on top is a bird-cage, and inside, waiting patiently, a midnight-black raven.

'Careful you don't fall in,' someone behind me says. I turn to find a girl with long, wavy hair, crimson in a way that reminds me of fresh blood.

'This is ridiculous,' I say in answer with a shake of my head.

'What's ridiculous is that they think we'll be able to reach those boxes.'

I didn't notice at first, but floating around in the lava are several boxes. Somehow they don't melt, and somehow they move in synchronisation. Above us are more of the same boxes, which rotate and float through the air of their own accord. The sight makes me feel unsteady.

A commotion on the other side of the fighting ring echoes through the arena. The other group, Ember included, march out from behind another metal gate and gather on the opposite island.

'This whole place is symmetrical,' I think out loud.

'I suppose it will be a race. Whoever gets to the middle wins, perhaps,' the girl ponders, making me nod slowly.

'I think you're right.'

The girl offers her hand to me, and I stare at it like it's a trick. 'I'm Merlot Kinsman.'

Hesitantly I grasp her hand. She shakes it eagerly.

'Scarlet Seraphine.'

'I know.' She smiles.

The male who's in charge of our group points up towards the ceiling, breaking my attention away from the female before me. 'Take note. The Elder Raven wishes to speak.'

Above, our leader stands on a floating piece of rock, her voice loud and clear for everyone to hear. 'Ravens, your first challenge is to travel from one side of the arena to the middle, climb up this rock formation and release the caged raven. You will be up against the team on the opposite side of the course. The first Raven in each pair to set free the bird will go to the next round. How you get across the lava is up to you, but beware – your opponent may be faster, may be smarter and may beat you. Choose your weapons carefully, as the only rule I will allow is there are *no* rules. In the outside world, enemies do not fight fairly, so the trials will be the same.'

A loud, excited roar from the spectating Ravens echoes through the arena, the cheering and whistling from the audience making my heart pound quicker.

A cabinet of weapons stands behind us. Inside lie swords, poison darts, maces, spears and all kinds of deadly devices. Merlot chooses one hunting knife.

I raise a brow at how simple she is going.

She smirks and shrugs. 'You'll see.'

As I reach for a weapon next, my hand is swatted away by the male, his eyes pinning me down. 'The Elder Raven has given me orders that you will pick last,' he claims.

Frowning, I peer up to see the Elder Raven glaring at me, her expression warning enough not to step out of line. I gulp and obediently wait my turn.

It's not worth it, I tell myself.

Once the last Raven has chosen her weapons, I pick the last bow and remaining four arrows, a handful of daggers and some rope that no one seems to want, hoping a plan of attack will arise sooner rather than later.

'Who will start us off?' the male Raven asks.

Beside me, Merlot puts her hand up. 'Wish me luck,' she says with a tense smile as she heads for the starting point, a large red cross on the ground.

The male claps her on the shoulder, clearly impressed by her confidence. 'Strength to you.'

'Ravens at the ready,' the Elder Raven shouts.

Merlot cuts her forearm with the large knife she carries. A long gash opens up, oozing dark crimson blood. I refrain from looking on in awe as the blood drops start to float into a straight line by her feet.

'Go!'

A bang goes off, and Merlot jumps into action.

Lifting her foot, she steps onto the line of hovering blood. The line stretches out like a tightrope, holding her weight as she tests its strength.

'What is she doing? That's incredible,' a Raven who looks too young to be competing says.

The male Raven peers around with an approving expression. 'She's a blood bender.'

Merlot quickens her pace, noticing her opponent is also gaining distance quickly. The other Raven's ability is controlling stone, and her hands are outstretched as she commands the floating boxes to transport her from the lava to the top of the rock tower.

Merlot sets into a sprint, keeping her free hand up towards the ceiling. The line of blood moves up, lifting her higher to prevent her from having to climb the rocky pillar.

She meets her opponent at the top of the rock tower. Her opponent swings a left hook, but Merlot dodges it with ease. The bird squawks as they duel, magic coming into play. I find myself holding my breath as I watch the females battle it out, both of them so near the edge that multiple times the audience gasps in anticipation.

It's minutes later when blood starts to run down Merlot's face, and her opponent doesn't look much better now that the fight begins to see its end.

A kick to the face sends Merlot's opponent wobbling. Her tired body stumbles and topples off the edge of the stone tower. The female form catches on the rocky edge of the tower before falling head first onto the stone bottom. The sound of crushing bone and skewered skin makes me want to be sick.

Standing still, having watched her opponent descend to her death, Merlot finally lets out a breath. Her shoulders sag, showing how tired she is. Slowly she approaches the birdcage, and the raven is released.

An eruption of cheers and clapping for the winner echoes throughout the arena, making me feel uneasy. I watch the bottom of the rocky tower, wondering if someone will come for the dead body. No one does.

The floating stage that carries the Elder Raven nears

Merlot, who stands waiting. With a respectful nod in greeting, she steps up onto the stage, and the pair talk briefly before the female ends up sitting on the edge of the floating stage, her legs dangling off the side as she finally relaxes, gaze wandering around the audience.

The black raven cries as it flies back into its cage, which closes itself for the next two opponents.

'Next round!' the Elder Raven shouts, and my group shuffles nervously with movement.

A finger points in my direction, and my heart freezes.

'You, you're next,' the male declares, yanking my arm and placing me on the starting platform. My feet move even though I don't want them to.

I stand looking at the scene before me, the heat of the lava at my feet, and I feel the large distance between where I stand and the floating boxes below. I feel fear setting in as I realise I can't make it across. I have to either attempt something seriously dangerous or stand and watch like a coward.

My family is watching, I remind myself, the sudden pressure overwhelming.

I grit my teeth in growing panic and frustration. I try to remember all my lessons with Dimitri, every piece of advice he's shared with me over years of training.

Everything seems to go quiet. My mind calms down as I begin to calculate my chances.

I can fight, regardless of what everyone thinks.

My lack of power means I have to use other skills; I have to *think* my way out of this.

'Ravens at the ready,' the Elder Raven shouts.

Frantically I explore my options. Ruby's words spring to mind: *Look for weaknesses.*

I cannot swim in the lava like Ember can, but I may be able to jump onto a floating box if it floats my way …

Too time-consuming. I rule it out immediately.

The floating platforms above are also not an option – the distance is too far for me to jump, and my height is too insufficient to successfully grasp the edge. So that leaves no choices.

Then again, no rules apply.

Who said anything about going *across* the lava? Maybe if I just went around ...

'Go!' the Elder Raven calls out.

9

I spring into action and push past the group of Ravens as I sprint towards the closest wall. My arms pump at a rapid speed as I count the seconds in my head. One hand reaches for my belt, letting loose one, two, three knives into a ladder of blades up the wall. Thanks to Dimitri, my aim is perfect, and I prove it when I jump from handle to handle, scaling the wall without hesitation.

This is the first time in my life I've had the chance to test my limits like this and for a brief moment it feels exhilarating. I can feel my muscles bulge under my clothes, my body mastering the large wall better than I expected. When I jump onto the last knife, I realise I'm going to be too short.

It's all or nothing.

With one last leap, my arms stretch up, fingertips skimming the rim of the wall. The audience looks down at me with mild interest as I grin with delight at my small triumph.

I hang for a second while adjusting my grip, then pull my weight up and over to straddle the wall, surprising the observers around me. I give them a giddy smile before getting to my feet.

I take off in a sprint and run around the thin edge of the pit, lava bubbling on one side of me and spectators on the other. I try to keep an eye on my opponent, who is succeeding in catching a floating box.

Stopping halfway around the stone wall, I analyse my next step, eyes darting in all directions to come up with a plan to somehow get to the tower.

I grab the rope wrapped around my waist, a plan becoming firmer the longer I ponder it. Thinking I must be mad to pull this off, I take the bow from my back and pull three arrows out. I quickly wrap the rope around each of the arrows and make sure they are securely attached with a double knot. I aim them all at the floating stage the Elder Raven and Merlot watch down from, creating a triangle on the platform's edge. Merlot's eyes widen with surprise when they hit their mark.

Putting the bow back over my shoulders, I tug at my now tightly strung rope. I take a deep breath, making sure not to think of the potential death I will endure if the rope doesn't hold.

I think of Roux before jumping off the wall and refrain from screaming as my body flies through the air. The rock tower rushes towards me, sharp edges closing in at an incredibly fast speed. Gritting my teeth with quiet terror, I let go and somersault through the air.

My body crashes into the birdcage, my legs coasting over the edge. I grapple for the enclosure – its metal bars are thankfully glued to the stone. I exhale a breath of relief that it holds my weight as I dangle over the side.

Fingers aching, I pull myself up to find my rival waiting patiently. She grins, sharp fangs on show.

'Why, hello, half-blood,' the female growls.

The stranger has her hair scraped back into multiple

buns on her head. Her facial features are sharp and chis-elled, much like the Elder Raven's.

'Hello there,' I utter back. I don't need to look at my hand to know it's bleeding – my palm is damp with blood.

Danger! Run away! It seems to tell me, but I stay put.

Cautiously I study my rival as she circles me, and I wait for the female to make the first move. Her pale fingers dance with anticipation, and I know she is eager to fight me, to prove herself. It's only when she narrows her eyes that I sense she is about to spring. She jumps at me, and I dodge with ease, readjusting the bow on my back.

My opponent has long, thin claws that slash out as she charges me. I do my best to duck out of their range, keeping a strong defence, but I have to keep moving precariously close to the edge to do so.

'You're fast. Faster than I thought,' she says, seeming genuinely surprised.

'I *am* a Raven,' I grunt in reply, trying not to take offence.

She strikes out once more, ambushing my right side as I stumble away. She's quick, and I'm beginning to tire. I need to end this soon, or I'll be thrown over the edge to a rocky death like the female before me.

'You are *not* a Raven. You have human blood. Human blood means *weakness*, and you know we Ravens are far from the frail and delicate creatures *they* are.'

I roll my eyes. This female has probably never met a human.

'Humans may be weaker in terms of magic, but they certainly don't talk as much shit as you,' I counter.

I tackle her around her middle. She falls onto her back, eyes dazed for a moment. I wrap my hand around her neck tightly enough that I have her full attention but not enough to truly hurt her.

'Listen to me.' Her eyes meet mine, and she lies there, my right boot pinning down one arm while my free hand holds the other, her claws unable to move. 'We can end this in a more civil manner. We don't have to go as far as killing one another,' I say.

She doesn't move. Doesn't react.

'No,' the female spits. 'I will gain honour from the Elder Raven if I kill you.'

She bucks her hips, and I fall head first into stone. Hands wrap around me and shove me back roughly, removing my advantage over her. She's on her feet, standing over me with a grin.

'You should have taken the opportunity to finish me off. No matter, though. I'll enjoy taking the victory instead.'

She smiles, her talons slashing for me. I raise an arm, and her claws cut through my shirt and skin as if they were paper. I hiss in pain as she readies for another strike, but I kick my feet out, twisting her legs from underneath her. In seconds, I watch the female fall over, roll along the platform and go careening off the tower, her feet the last thing I see.

Her scream sends shivers through me as I quickly crawl over to the edge. As if in slow motion, she plunges to her death. I don't hesitate to ready my bow and last arrow. I aim for her heart without thought. The shaft hits its mark, and before she hits the rocky bottom, silence envelops me. I prevented her from suffering serious pain, but that doesn't make this outcome any better.

Ashamed, I look away, unable to see the final product. The sound of her body is enough to make me gag. I curse to myself. 'I've killed someone,' I can't help muttering, realising my hands are now bloody in all senses of the word.

Numbly approaching the raven, I unlock its cage, but it

doesn't fly away like it did before. It simply sits and stares at me with its dark, beady eyes. I feel its judgement of me, and I try not to break down, not to cry.

A ripple of pain rushes up my arm, making me grit my teeth in agony.

'Holy Hanrah! What the—'

Looking down, I inspect where the female has left four large gashes across my skin, the wound bubbling with black and red liquid. My face creases into a grimace.

Poison, I think grimly.

I kneel as I extend my wrist out for inspection, searching for something to help. The poison courses further through my veins the longer I take to think of a solution. Finally I decide to rip at my flimsy sleeve, easily tearing off the material around my wound. The veins around my injury turn black as the poison spreads up my arm.

My eyes flicker with pain as my fangs begin to grow, gums aching. Using them to bite into my infected arm, I suck hard on the wound before spitting the vile black substance out. The taste makes me want to vomit. Again and again I suck, repeating the step until the black finally fades from my veins and my head becomes dizzy from blood loss.

Footsteps sound behind me. I lift my head groggily as Merlot kneels down beside me.

'I think you got the most of it.'

'Do you think so?' I murmur back.

She pulls me to my feet, and together we slowly approach the Elder Raven, stepping up onto the floating platform. My leader ignores me, giving me nothing more than she would any other half-blood Raven.

Letting the insult slide, I stand proudly on the winners' stage, slightly disorientated. When I find my family in the crowd, I give them a small wave. Roux and Ruby gesture back enthusiastically. Blaze, beside them, gives me a thumbs-up.

A half-blood on the winners' stage, I think with pride. *Who would have thought it?*

10

'Y ou did very well, Scarlet.' Dimitri smiles at me.
It's been two days since my first trial, and I'm still pondering over how I managed to stay alive. Now I'm somehow a different person. I actually *killed* someone. True, she had been on the way to imminent death, but I chose to pierce her through the heart with an arrow I wielded, and I've not been able to sleep properly since.

'I got poisoned. Wouldn't class that as anything spectacular,' I answer, taking a gulp of Liquid Gold and wishing for once the alcohol would affect me as it would a human – take away my memories and untangle the feelings inside me.

We sit at our usual table in the Badger's Sett. The music is loud and the fighting not so busy tonight, the newbies on show for a change. A small crowd shouts at two young boys who fling their limbs around like there is no tomorrow.

'I didn't use the word *spectacular*,' Dimitri quips.

I catch his stare, and he smirks at me. I punch his arm lightly.

'However, you held yourself well and made a clever

decision to go *around* the lava.' He hums cheerfully to himself, taking a large sip of his drink, which smells of lamb blood.

Somehow Dimitri knew what happened in my first trial before I saw him, surprising me beyond belief. 'Did you visit the House of Raven? Is that how you know what happened?'

'No, I will never step inside the Elder Raven's domain.' His fangs are on display as his mischievous smile grows. 'Don't ask me any more questions, Scarlet, you'll only frustrate yourself figuring it out but know this, I won *a lot* of money because of you.'

'Oh so you and your friends are making bets on the Hex Trials now? You should be a gentleman and give me half.'

My eyes trail down to my pale arm, the skin still showing spiderwebs of darkness where the toxins lingered. My stomach rolls, remembering the feeling of poison flowing through me.

'This is only the beginning, I'm afraid,' Dimitri murmurs, noticing my gaze, his voice low enough that only I'm able to hear it.

I glance up to find him watching me, his pale skin similar to mine, his youthful face, even after centuries of living, looking worried for me. He cracks his neck, his fangs gleaming in the light. They are larger than mine and permanently on display for the world to see, an obvious sign of his power.

'I shouldn't have let her get that close to me,' I murmur, swirling the gold liquid in my glass.

The fighting ring erupts with noise. They have found their winner, it seems.

'Always seeing the negative in yourself,' Dimitri says, tutting.

His red eyes are as bright as mine should be, if only I

didn't have a human father. Mine, as my best friend once described, look more like red wine. Dark and dangerous.

His hand gently rests on my knee and gives it a quick squeeze. 'You made me proud out there, Scarlet.' His gaze roams over my face, wanting me to believe his words. 'You should be proud of yourself too.'

'I'll be proud of myself if I make it out of these trials alive,' I counter with a grimace before emptying my glass.

'Then let us train.' Dimitri smiles while standing up, waving his hands towards the fighting ring. 'Let us make history by showing those Ravens that a half-blood can win against them all.'

I nod, wishing it were that easy. 'Okay.'

'But first I must do something. Stay here.' Dimitri winks and waltzes away.

I lean back in my chair, arms relaxed across my stomach. I let out a long breath. What have I got myself into? I've competed in *one* trial, and already I feel scared to death about what's to come.

'Rough day?' someone asks behind me.

I don't move, but my eyes automatically look to my right hand. The scar is silver and unopened. I relax and nod slowly, inhaling the scent of salt and fresh air. *Dameer*, I conclude, smelling a hint of magic on the stranger.

The voice walks around my table, and I'm surprised to see it's the hooded fighter from the other night, the one who beat the Pirate within minutes.

'The Teacher,' I recall, making the fighter nod.

'The one and only.'

I straighten as he takes Dimitri's empty seat. He watches me with light blue eyes, eyes that are shadowed by his hood. If I were human, I wouldn't be able to tell what colour they are, but as he surveys me, he seems to realise I'm perhaps not what he thought I was.

'You're a Raven,' he states.

'Indeed I am.' His gaze roams over me in the way a fighter would an opponent, finding weaknesses in case they need them in the future. 'Am I a threat to you?'

He leans back, surprise showing in his stare. A gloved hand rests on his armrest. His ankle rests on his knee. It's an attempt to show he feels at ease, but he's still tense. 'No. Why would you say that?'

'You're looking me up and down as if calculating how to overpower me.'

With his mask covering his face, I can only assume he's smiling, perhaps amused, from his temporary silence.

'You're safe from me. I won't fight anyone unless it's in that ring over there.' The stranger motions to the fighting. This time, two girls are wrestling each other, and they look horribly young – younger than me when I started wrestling random strangers for some coin.

'Phew,' I answer, wiping my forehead in jest. 'I don't know if I would have a chance against the *Teacher*.'

His head whips around to face me, narrowed eyes regarding me and my sarcasm. 'You don't like my fighting name?'

'No, not particularly,' I answer honestly.

'Why not?' He doesn't sound offended, but rather, intrigued.

'It has no significant meaning, has no ...' I try to find the word, my hands waving around in the air. 'Allure.'

I spot Dimitri talking to Storm, and the conversation looks animated. I predict he won't be back for a while, so I put my feet up on the stranger's chair. He stiffens slightly, but his eyes don't waver from me.

'You want me to be more *alluring*?'

I tilt my head, wondering what he would look like under his mask. 'You want people to gamble on you, to be in your corner when you fight. Why in the royal family's name would anyone pick a fighter with a name like the Teacher? Do they want to learn some history when they come here? Or learn how to read?' I quip.

He considers this for a moment, and I wait for him to answer.

'What name is your favourite out of all the names of the fighters?' he asks.

I pretend to ponder over his question, but of course, I choose my own. 'The Phoenix.'

'And why do you like that name better than the rest?'

'Because it symbolises immortality and resurrection. A phoenix will die and be reborn from its ashes. I think it's a captivating story for a fighter to portray, that no matter the outcome, they will come back again and again and keep fighting.'

'I suppose it *is* a good fighting name,' he says reluctantly, his sapphire stare intense.

'I watched the Phoenix's first-ever match. Storm usually likes to drone on about a fighter and things about them so we spectators can decide whether we want to bet on them. The name stuck with me, and I've never been able to forget it.'

We sit in silence for a moment, my words sinking in. I don't know what the stranger is thinking, but he watches the ring with new interest. I can't help but break the silence between us.

'Have I offended you?'

The Teacher shakes his head softly. 'No. I was just thinking.'

'About what?'

He doesn't answer. Instead, he stands abruptly enough to make me flinch back. He walks around the table and gives me a polite nod.

'I'm sorry, but I must go. I forgot I have plans, and I'm already late.'

He turns to leave, but I grasp his wrist, his glove giving way to cold skin. I grit my teeth but don't let go. His hand turns into a fist at the contact.

'Why did you choose the name Teacher?'

He slowly comes face to face with me, contemplating what to say, by the look he's giving me. Finally he sighs, so softly I wonder if I really heard it.

'I chose that name because I make sure to teach people a lesson.'

I blink as he gently removes himself, leaving my hand hovering in mid-air where he once was.

11

The Raven's Nest is full of those needing their weekly shopping, the main square full to the brim with red-headed vendors and customers. I stroll along with Ruby and Roux, a basket in the crook of my arm, and I watch them pick out some fruit scattered on a table, receiving a few glances from passers-by.

'Did you like the oranges I bought before?' Ruby asks me, pointing to a juicy stack.

I nod. 'Yes, they're nice, but they're also too expensive.'

The male working behind the table scowls at me.

'We don't need them. Just get the basics this week,' I urge Ruby, knowing most of her wages go on feeding all her children, and it's not cheap.

'We've run out of broccoli,' Roux says to no one in particular. 'Don't forget it, like we did last time.'

Taking in the rows of tables, I notice a stall of vegetables further down the market lane. I squeeze Roux's arm. 'I'll get it now. I'll be back in a moment.'

She nods and carries on filling Ruby's basket with red apples.

'Stay within sight,' Ruby warns.

As a half-blood, I'm an anomaly in our House. I'm not powerful enough to be deemed a full Raven, but I'm not human enough to be deemed useless either. Some Ravens accept my presence, simply ignoring me in hopes I pay them no attention, while some would rather make a scene and make me wish I had never been born. Ruby, more than anyone, knows of the abuse I've endured for the absurd things, some punishments handed out purely because of *what* I am, not because of what I've done.

Approaching the pile of green vegetables, I reach for two trees, but a hand slaps mine away.

'No. I'll get them. Let me bag them up for you.' Merlot Kinsman grins at me, the female from my first trial looking unnervingly happy to see me.

She puts my purchases into a sheet of brown paper, rolling them up like a present before tying the package with string and handing it over. I give her a few coins, and she accepts them with a cheerful incline of her head.

'You look better,' she says, motioning to my still healing arm.

I stare down at the four scars across my forearm. 'Yes. It was rough for a while, but I'm on the mend.'

Merlot nods like this is good news.

I hold up the package and turn to leave. 'Well, I'll see you around, I guess.'

'Scarlet, wait!' Merlot runs around her table, her arms out as if to keep me from leaving. Instantly I'm on edge, wondering why she is being nice to me. Usually, no one is this pleasant to converse with.

'Yes?'

Merlot glances around the market and lowers her voice. Not a chance would someone *not* hear her, Raven hearing being nearly as good as vampire hearing. 'I wanted to ask you something ...'

I wait because I'm not sure where this conversation is going. Is she going to make me polish her horse-riding boots? Does she need me to do something for her that will get me punished? Will I be able to say no to her in front of this many people?

'I wondered if you wanted to join forces and guard each other's back against the other contenders during the Hex Trials.'

This takes me by surprise. Her face grows more concerned the longer I'm silent. Flustered, I look around, not knowing what to say.

'You want to be allies? With *me*?' I clarify, wondering why, of all the competitors, she is asking me.

'Yes. You clearly have brains and a natural talent for fighting. I feel like we are similar in the way others treat us. Being workers, I mean.'

I nod because I know what it's like to be looked down on for not being a fighter or breeder.

'You're a worker?' I ask, having never seen her at the market before.

'Yeah. I'm usually based in the dressmaker's, but some family stuff has come up, so I'm here as well.' She shrugs nonchalantly, and I wonder what the circumstance is.

'I'll think over your offer,' I state, noting Ruby watching us like a hawk. 'I have to get back.'

'Scarlet.' Merlot stands so close I can feel her breath on my cheek. 'I know why you're competing. I want to let you know that if we partner up, I'll make sure to get the medicine for your sister if you somehow can't.'

I stare at her, dark crimson meeting fire red. 'I don't know what you're talking about.'

She gives me a pointed look. 'Your sister is big enough to be carrying twins, maybe triplets. No Raven can birth more than one child at once without medical help. I assume, with the allowances your family receives, you can't afford the treatment she needs once she's in labour.'

Averting my eyes, I stare at Roux as she explores a table, her hands covering her belly protectively around so many people. I grit my teeth. 'I don't know what you're playing at, but if you so much as go near my sister—'

She holds a hand up, stopping me mid-sentence. 'I am competing for the same reasons. My mother is sick, and we also need medicine. However, I don't have any siblings as backup in case I fail.'

I lean back in surprise. She's desperate, I assume, to tell me a weakness of hers within the short time of knowing each other. Ravens rarely get sick, as diseases don't affect us as they do humans, so Merlot's mother must be in deep trouble.

'Why not ally yourself with my sister or someone with more experience with fighting? Why would you ask me?' I whisper, giving Ruby a friendly wave. Her face has been hardening while Merlot has been standing close.

'Those that compete for glory will not go far. Their motivation to win isn't enough for me to count on. I need someone whose very *being* relies on winning these trials, and by the way you look at your sister ... I know you'd do anything for her – including competing in a set of deadly trials created by the Elder Raven.'

She smirks, and I can't help but roll my eyes. She's right, of course, but it doesn't make me feel any better.

'If I win the Hex Trials, I'll get the medicine your sister needs. If you win the Hex Trials, you'll get the medicine my mother needs,' Merlot offers, sticking her hand out.

It's another chance to help Roux, I reason with myself.

I glance at my sister once more before shaking Merlot's hand. 'Fine. We have a deal.'

ROUX SERAPHINE

12

It seems every four weeks, Ember and I can expect a new trial. In preparation for the second trial, all competitors have been sent a letter asking them to meet at the tunnel that separates the city of Rubien and the House of Raven.

Ember and I stand along with the rest of the Ravens. I can tell at a glance the group is not as big as it was before the first trial. Over half the participants either were unsuccessful or are dead.

'What is taking them so long?' Ember fusses, crossing her arms in frustration.

'Why? Are your nerves taking a toll on you?' I ask, feeling somewhat relaxed as I lean back against the rock wall. The tunnel is no new sight for me with my daily visits to the human side, but I don't think my sister has been through it. She probably has no idea what the other side looks like.

'I'm not nervous,' she snaps, her fiery red eyes glaring at me. 'I just hate wasting time.'

It's at this point that the Elder Raven comes into sight,

her entourage trailing behind her loyally. Everyone straightens and bows her head in polite greeting as the Elder Raven reaches the group. I find myself hiding behind bodies in hopes she doesn't notice me – her glare is extremely intimidating.

'Ravens. Today we are going to meet the royal family,' the Elder Raven says with a harsh smile.

Whispers surround me as my heart thumps loudly. *What?*

'The royal family members have been the judges of the Hex Trials since the beginning. Their opinions matter immensely, and you would do well to remember your fate is in their hands. Make sure to make a good first impression.'

From inside her sable uniform, the Elder brings out a penlike object. She uncaps the device and starts drawing a large circle in the air. The sound of sizzling piques my interest as a portal forms, its edge crackling like fireworks.

The Elder Raven lifts a leg and steps through the floating opening. 'Everyone follow me, and do not touch anything, or you will be sent back home without your hands attached.'

One by one we climb through.

The first thing I notice is the colours – emerald green, sapphire blue and lustrous gold adorning everything. The kingdom's colours are evident in all the decor of the place we now stand in. I look up, and the ceilings are frighteningly high. Chandeliers dangle proudly throughout the space, and light pours in from the ceiling windows, making me gape at the room's beauty.

'That chandelier probably costs more than our house and furniture combined,' I say to Ember, but she isn't listening. Instead, her stony gaze is surveying the new environment as if it were a battlefield.

'Welcome to Songbird Castle, the royal family's personal residence when visiting Rubien. It was first constructed over five hundred years ago and was one of the first structures to be built here underground.' The Elder Raven rambles on about some more history as she leads us through hallways as long and windy as a river. The walls are adorned with antique lanterns and bold, embellished wallpaper.

We finally come to a grand hall that's lavishly decorated and bigger than anything I've seen before. The windows here are stained glass and display depictions of the royal family. Several platforms perch high above us, with ropes and ladders hanging down. Wooden cabinets border the space, as well as racks of weapons filled with items I've never seen before, displayed for everyone to fawn over. The further I walk into the room, the more small details I note, such as the springy floors and glass cupboards of liquids that look alarmingly like poisons. I conclude it's a training room of some sort.

Three golden thrones sit on a dais at the far end of the room, one large and two smaller on either side. On the centre throne sits Queen Adela, a woman adorned in a silky gown of gold. Her dress shines under the lights, contrasting with her long midnight-blue hair, which is pinned up under her emerald-studded crown. It shows off her startling dark blue eyes and stunning face. She looks like a woman I wouldn't want to mess with, her face set in stone and her gaze intelligent and all-knowing.

On one side of her is her son Prince Julien, who wears a suit of sapphire blue that complements his dark blue eyes. With a demure smile, he watches us with keen interest.

The third throne, however, is empty. The sight is strange and disconcerting. Surely, if it weren't in use, they would remove it. My mind theorises all sorts of reasons for its presence.

'Welcome, Ravens. Please come in,' Queen Adela says in greeting, and we gather around at the bottom of the steps.

The Elder Raven bows, and everyone is quick to follow, including me. I peek up from under my eyelashes, and the queen finally shows a hint of a smile.

'I am overjoyed that today is here at last. Our family has spoken about this event for years, in preparation for the Hex Trials to finally commence,' Queen Adela says, motioning to her successor. 'As you know, my husband, King Eryk, is back in the capital, running the kingdom, while I stay here and watch the events unfold. With me I have brought your prince, who is extremely happy to come along and watch you all compete.'

I try to remember how many children the queen has. *Five*, I recall. Prince Julien, the heir to the Hanrah throne, the triplets – Prince Christian, Princess Victoria and Princess Olympia – and the youngest, whom no one seems to know much about. I wonder why none of the other children wanted to come.

'This is our private training hall,' the queen continues as she stands, her dress reminding me of Liquid Gold as it pools at her feet. 'You will come to know this chamber like your own home. It has everything you will need to become the next Raven of the Hex.'

A shiver runs down my spine. In the midst of trying to survive the first trial and thinking only of Roux, I forgot that some Ravens are here purely to join the Hex, the team of warriors who protect the lands. I peer at Ember, and her smile is enough for me to know she is imagining herself as a member of that team.

'Today we will start with introductions. I want to speak to you all individually and watch how you fare with our training courses. Some are particularly hard, but I know you Ravens are talented in solving difficult obstacles,' the Queen of Hanrah states, moving down the steps to greet the Elder Raven personally.

From the sly smile on the Elder Raven's face, I know today is going to be an interesting one.

It's been hours since we arrived. I'm hanging from a climbing wall when I realise I'm one of a handful still left to be spoken to by the queen. Merlot, whom I found not long after arriving, has been interviewed by the queen, as has my sister – both of them are on the opposite side of the room to keep tabs on who has been dealt with.

Climbing higher, I admire the view. From here I can see everything, including the intricate detailing of the ceiling. I reach up to touch it, and it's smooth, the swirl design recently dusted and possibly cleaned. I shake my head in amusement. I don't envy the person whose job is to keep the ceilings clear of cobwebs.

'And that must be everyone,' I hear from under me.

The queen stands from her throne, looking proud of herself. I, on the other hand, dangle off the wall, wondering whether I should mention they have forgotten me.

Merlot, who is looking around, seems to notice I'm missing. 'Excuse me, Your Majesty, but I think you have one more Raven to see.'

The Elder Raven's eyes roam up, narrow in displeasure at the sight of me. She frowns but says nothing. I quickly descend, my feet nimble as they find their marks.

I feel the moment all the competitors stare up at me, their eyes burning holes in my back.

Finally I land on the floor with both feet and turn to the Queen of Hanrah.

'Your Majesty.' I try to bow, but I feel awkward and out of place.

'Ah. I see,' she responds, making me feel even more self-conscious. 'Come, then. Everyone else can carry on.'

I follow her to the throne, a set of guards coming to my side. She motions for me to stand a step below her while she sits. Dark blue eyes survey me as I attempt to stay as still as possible, refraining from fidgeting.

'Please forgive my forwardness, but as you can probably imagine, I am tiring after the events of today.'

I nod, trying to look understanding.

'You do not look like the other Ravens. Your hair.' She squints at my face. 'Your eyes. They are both much darker than those of your peers.'

It's not a question, but she looks at me like she wants me to explain regardless.

'My mother is a Raven, and my father is human. I think my colouring is because—'

'Ah.' The queen nods and steeples her fingers. 'You are Scarlet Seraphine, the half-blood.'

I'm surprised she knows my name, but I nod numbly. 'Yes, Your Majesty.'

'I see. Well, that explains it.'

She writes on a piece of paper that perches precariously on the arm of her throne. I try not to watch, but the word *mongrel* catches my eye as she places it next to my name. Along with mine are written the other competitors' monikers, all with a tally next to them. Points, I assume. I lock my jaw to prevent myself from doing or saying something I'll regret.

'Why are you competing in the Hex Trials, Scarlet? Do you see yourself as the next Raven of the Hex?'

'No, Your Majesty. I am here to win the prize.'

Quickly her head rises. 'What prize do you want, exactly?'

'Medicine for my sister.' She narrows her eyes inquisitively, and I quickly add, 'Your Majesty.'

Since being in the presence of the Queen of Hanrah, I have sensed her feelings towards me shift drastically. I can hear her heart beat slightly quicker, her breath catch, and I wonder what I've said that would make the most powerful woman in the kingdom react in such a way.

'Are you well?' I ask, stepping closer, but a large hand catches my arm to stop me from moving any closer. Frowning, I turn to a guard, who shakes his head in warning.

I'm about to move back when I notice a faint line across my boot. I refrain from rubbing it away, wondering what comments the queen will write if she spots my less than pristine boots. I scowl but move my attention back to the queen whose gaze is on me.

I clear my throat, feeling silly for being worried about the state of my footwear when in comparison my whole outfit is probably worse. 'Apologies, Your—'

'What do you see?' she asks, standing up and pointing to my boot.

I hesitate, and a guard grabs my collar and shakes me firmly. 'Answer your queen.'

'I see a silver line. I'm sure it's simply dust or ...' I trail off, unable to say much more. I don't know what it is, but why does the queen worry about it?

'Can you see it now?' Queen Adela asks, her questions starting to feel like an interrogation.

Studying my feet, I find the line, faint silver in colour,

expanding. It circles up the steps as if encompassing the throne she sits on. I frown.

'Yes, it's there.' I try pointing it out, but no one seems to be looking where I'm signalling. 'No, right *there*.'

Queen Adela smiles and motions for me to ascend a step. I do as I'm told, but I feel a sudden resistance, like my body is being pushed back down. My eyes flicker to my queen, and she is smiling.

'How interesting. You can see my shields.'

Again she writes upon her piece of paper. I don't bother to watch this time, not wanting to know what other names she may be referring to me as, but my mind spins.

What does it mean to see Queen Adela's shielding magic? Does no other Raven have the ability to see it?

The Elder Raven comes to the queen's side and leans down to whisper in her ear. I quietly contemplate how long the pair have known each other as they converse.

'Scarlet, you are the last on my list. You therefore will not be spending as much time with me, unfortunately. So I wish you to fill out this test as swiftly as possible. Then we are all done for the day.'

I'm handed a crisp white booklet of paper, all of the twenty-five pages having written questions on both sides. A guard motions for me to sit on the step.

'I'll give you fifteen minutes to complete it. These marks will go towards my judgement of you and your capabilities. The higher the mark, the better,' Queen Adela instructs as she begins to descend the stairs. 'You may start.'

I look through all the questions first, determining which are easy and which I should leave to the end.

What is the capital city of the kingdom of Siamoon?
Moonhollow, I write automatically.

What is on the national emblem for the kingdom of Whitlocke?

A crown of vines.

What are the four types of elemental shifters?

Ocean, sky, ember and earth.

My pencil scribbles over the pages, reading questions not only in our language, Hanrae, but also in dialects from the other kingdoms. It makes an easy test slightly harder, but thanks to Dimitri's lessons throughout the years and his obsessions with languages in particular, I'm well prepared.

Time seems to pass too quickly. The point of my pencil is nearly blunt as the quarter of an hour runs out, and the side of my hand aches.

'Time,' a guard says, holding a hand out, into which I surrender my test.

'Did you struggle with the questions?' a voice asks. I turn to see the Elder Raven behind me, staring at me with her fiery red eyes. She glowers at me like a piece of dirt on her shoe, so I wonder why she is talking to me.

'No,' I lie, internally wondering if I've answered well enough, if I've answered with enough description.

The Elder Raven moves through the guards to my side. They move out of her way, and she escorts me down the steps, hand grasping my upper arm, nails digging in painfully.

'I assumed you wouldn't survive the agility trial.'

I blink in surprise at her candidness. Her grip doesn't waver, and my arm throbs slightly under her fingers.

'I created that trial to kill off the weaklings before the royal family got to meet any of you. I thought you would fail, but surprisingly, you were lucky and walked away with minor injuries. However, I warn you now, half-blood – the following trials will make the first look easy. I suggest you go back home and leave the Hex Trials to those who deserve to win, and those who *want* to win. You will not survive these challenges. I promise you that.'

My heart hammers in my chest. She lets go and leaves me with the group, as if the conversation never happened.

Merlot approaches and gives me a friendly nudge. 'Are you all right? You look like you've seen a ghost.'

The Elder Raven converses with other Ravens, asking how they did in their tests.

I swallow. 'I think I just got my first death threat.'

13

Arms tiring, I hit the fighting dummy once, then twice before giving it a kick to its straw-filled head. Sweat drips down my back, and I wipe my forehead with my forearm. My breathing is haggard, but I don't care – I feel good, and I need to let go of the tension building inside me.

Leave the Hex Trials to those who deserve to win, and those who want to win.

I swing again, imagining the dummy as the Elder Raven. Who is *she* to say I'm not deserving?

The Badger's Sett is my favourite place to unwind without judgement or fear of punishment. No masters or family members know of this establishment, and no Raven would ever consider walking through the tunnel to find me. It's my place of solace and my favourite place to *think*.

My knuckles are cracked from sparring, lines of blood threatening to spill if I keep up with the punches. Hands on my hips, I decide to call it a day.

'You are quite exceptional.' The Teacher walks up to me, pointing to the dummy, whose head looks nearly severed.

He wears his usual garb, his face mostly hidden by a dark mask and hood.

'You say that like you're surprised,' I counter, rubbing at my sore hands.

I grab my water canteen from the table and drink heavily. The Teacher's gaze follows my every movement.

Interesting.

'Do you want some?' I ask. Sky-blue eyes meet mine, and I wonder what he looks like under his disguise. 'Are you ever going to take that mask off?'

Amusement fills his voice as he replies, 'So many questions.'

'And not enough answers,' I quip, giving him a pointed look.

He walks to a nearby cabinet that lines the room, bringing out several supplies and placing them on a tray. 'I like being a mystery,' he admits, his back turned to me. I admire the broad shoulders beneath his cloak, his tall strong frame and unique smell of salt and fresh air.

'Mysteries are made to be solved,' I murmur softly, taking note of what he is grabbing as he approaches the table and sets the tray down upon it.

'Are they?' He takes the canteen from my grasp and gently places it back on the table. I don't object, merely because I'm curious about what he is doing.

The Teacher dips a small white cloth into the small bowl of water. Carefully, he reaches out a gloved hand and takes one of mine, running the cloth over my knuckles, cleaning the cracked skin. The act is strangely intimate, the way he bends his head to closely inspect my hand, the way he steps closer and seems to fill my senses with his scent alone. Once he is done, he takes my other hand and repeats the process.

My eyes lift, needing to find those sapphire eyes. To my

delight, I find him already staring. A tingle of something I've not felt before causes me to shiver.

Is he trying to unnerve me?

'In my opinion, I think mysteries *are* meant to be solved. Otherwise what is the fun in them?' I attempt a smile, looking up into his hood. It takes all my restraint not to look away, to cower in my sudden self-consciousness when he gazes into my eyes, but in the end my cheeks burn.

He considers this while putting away the cloth and begins to take off his gloves. My attention snags on his tanned hands – strong and calloused. They remove the lid of a small jar where yellowish oil resides. He dips his fingers in and reaches for me once more, smearing the healing oil across my knuckles.

'Are you blushing, Raven?'

I bristle but can't find the strength to pull away. 'I'm hot and sweaty,' I insist. 'If you didn't notice before I have been exercising.'

'Hmm, if you say so.' He massages the oil in, his touch making my chest tighten as his thumbs circle my stinging knuckles. It feels nice, comforting even.

'What power do you possess?' I ask suspiciously.

He pauses, meeting my gaze. 'Why do you ask?'

'No reason,' I lie. The silence grows thick between us, the need to fill in the gaps making me itch. 'I must say your lack of answers is rather frustrating.'

He releases my hands, now finished with his task and wipes his hands off of oil. Slowly he pulls on his leather gloves, hiding himself once more. My lips press into a thin line. Under his disguise he is grinning.

'Fine,' he relents. 'No, I don't want any of your water, but thank you for offering.'

I roll my eyes.

'And no, I won't take this mask off. It keeps me safe.'

'From what?'

'From *who*,' he corrects.

'Fine. From who, exactly?'

'From Ravens with too much curiosity.'

'Hilarious.'

'I really am.'

We stand close, and I can sense his body stiffen. The smell of him makes me smile. Magic, salt and fresh air – like the ocean breeze that wafts into the cave occasionally.

'And my last question ... What is the answer to that?' I prod, needing to know if his magic is the reason for my strange reactions to him.

He hums with amusement, and I wonder if he will take the bait. This stranger is a puzzle indeed, and one I seem to be failing to figure out.

'You can try picking and prodding at me all you like, Raven,' the Teacher drawls, leaning down. His face is so near that his mask is nearly touching me. 'But you'll be disappointed.' He leans back and ponders a moment before adding, 'Perhaps not disappointed in the way I look, though.' He gives me a wink, and I shake my head, unimpressed.

'Humble and mysterious. What a lethal combination.'

'The only lethal thing around here is that right hook of yours,' he declares, motioning to my right hand and noticing the silver scar upon it. 'Looks nasty.'

It's not a question but a statement. I wonder if he is always so careful with his words – words that will never risk him giving himself away.

'My right hook isn't the only lethal thing about me, *Teacher*.' I smile widely before pouncing. I grab his wrist, yanking it down. I twist his body, the element of surprise on my side as I pin his arm behind his back. He falls to one knee as I grab around his neck and pull his head back so he looks up at me, smiling demurely down at him.

My arm around his neck loosens, and my hand instead creeps up to his hood, which threatens to slide down. His blue eyes look slightly dazed. Standing over him makes me feel powerful, and I can tell he knows this.

'If I wanted to know who you are,' I murmur softly, leaning close. 'I would know by now. Your hood is not enough of a barrier for someone like me.'

Unexpectedly, his free arm wraps around my nearest leg, and his gloved hand grasps the back of my calf. He softly caresses it up and down. I frown down at the bold gesture, trying to ignore the pleasant feeling it brings me.

'I wouldn't dare dream of thinking you weren't capable of exposing my identity. However, I think you have a quality your *kind* doesn't seem to possess,' he murmurs.

His hand squeezes my leg, and I loosen my grip on him, thinking we are done playing around.

In seconds, his pinned arm is ripped out of my grasp. He spins on his knee, and my arms are wrapped behind my back. Standing with him before me, one of his hands forcing my hands back, the other trailing up my leg, I can't help but feel suddenly warm.

As he peers up at me with playfulness, his hand slides higher, cupping behind my thigh as he slowly brings himself to his feet, his body up against mine in an act of defiance.

'And what's that?' I ask, my body on high alert.

His hands come away, releasing me from their hold, and for a moment, I feel myself pouting before I remember myself.

He twirls a piece of my hair, and I watch it as if mesmerised.

'A consideration of those around you and what they feel.'

I lift a brow in question, not understanding his meaning.

'You wouldn't rip my hood off, because you know I don't want you to. It would be more satisfying to you if I *chose* to reveal myself.'

I twist my mouth, knowing he's right. 'You're not wrong,' I admit.

'Of course I'm not. I rarely am.'

And just like that, he steps away, making me feel like I've lost a game I didn't know we were playing.

'It's been lovely talking to you, but I must go.'

I refrain from huffing. 'Let me guess. You have somewhere to go, and you're already late?'

The delight in his gaze is instant, and I kick myself for remembering his parting words from the last time we met.

'It seems you are more interested in me than I first thought.' He circles me, his tall frame looming over me easily as I stand still. If I don't react, I can potentially save face. 'I quite enjoy the thought of you thinking of me, wondering what I'm doing when I'm not around.'

I pause, trying to calm my thundering heart. I turn my face upwards, and he's there already, staring down at me with those captivating eyes. The blue of the sky, the blue of the ocean.

'You look rather pretty with flushed cheeks.' I find his amused eyes once more and we both know I can't find an excuse for my body's reaction to him this time. *Bastard*. The Teacher strokes my warming cheeks so softly I restrain myself from leaning into his touch. 'So pretty, like I thought they would be.'

Turning away with embarrassment, I lock my jaw in frustration. Why is he getting under my skin?

'Aren't you supposed to be going somewhere?' I remind him, refusing to look his way.

His cloak grazes my back as he walks to my side. 'Yes, but I look forward to the next time we see each other. It seems I'm not the only one whose curiosity is piqued.'

I stop myself from meeting his gaze, despite wanting to read his expression to see if he is lying. Instead, I lift my head high and make my voice confident and no-nonsense. 'You put those words in my mouth. I said nothing of the sort.'

'You didn't need to, Raven. Your face told me enough.'

Whirling around to confront him, I'm ready to argue, but he's already gone.

14

Two days pass, and I'm sitting on a bench with Merlot, watching a pair of Ravens duel with long wooden sticks. The sound of cracking echoes through the courtyard, the ground beneath me cobbled like the streets of Rubien.

'This place is so extravagant,' Merlot murmurs, nudging my leg as she subtly surveys our surroundings.

The queen has insisted we train under her watchful eye three times a week. The remaining Ravens in the trials are assembled in the parade ground, which is situated outside. The castle wraps around us like a cage, the old building like a fortress.

'Imagine *this* as your home.'

I think of my small family home, my bedroom, more specifically, a tiny room with three beds, which I share with both my sisters. I can quite easily imagine a room to myself, where I don't have to suffer with a sister who burns everything when she is angry – which is a lot of the time – and a sister who gets up to pee at night every half an hour.

'It would be bliss,' I answer.

I quietly spin towards the queen, who sits upon a lavish

throne. Her son is absent today. Beside her stands the Elder Raven, reminding me of a guard dog and its owner. I visualise a collar around my leader's neck, the queen holding the leash in her firm grip.

The thought makes me smile until I notice a chalkboard with all the competitors' names on it by the Elder's feet. A list of names ranked best to worst, my name being very close to the bottom.

Suddenly cheering erupts, distracting me from my worries. Ember has been chosen to fight next. My sister's opponent looks uneasy, and I don't blame her. Ember has no regard for anyone's safety, especially when she can win something. The pair begin to spar, and my sister is quick, her jabs calm and calculated as she finds the weaknesses of her opponent.

'She's amazing,' Merlot says in awe before turning to me, her expression becoming serious. 'What do you think the next trial will be? Because if I have to fight your sister, I'm going to be shit scared.'

My brow rises. 'You're a *blood bender*, what do you have to be scared of? You could beat everyone here in seconds.'

She is silent for a brief moment and I know by the shift in her expression I've unwittingly hit a nerve.

Merlot leans towards me, lowering her voice. 'Blood bending I'll admit is useful at times but it comes with its downsides too. I only use it if I *absolutely* have to.'

This explains why she didn't use it on her opponent in the first trial.

My lips twist with indecision. I want to press her more for details but from her straight back and hard expression I don't think now is the right time.

'Perhaps we will be tested in weaponry in the next trial,' I say, noticing a wave of relief sweep through her. 'What do *you* reckon is next?'

'I'm not sure, but I don't have a good feeling about it,' she replies, her gaze falling behind me.

Spinning in my seat, I find two Ravens standing tall and demanding. One has a pixie cut, and I know her vaguely as Carmine, purely because she has come by the stables once or twice for horse-riding lessons. The other female wears a crown of plaits, and I think she is called Winella.

The pair stare at me menacingly, and my scar begins to dribble blood. They mean business.

'Yes?' I ask, looking between the pair. 'Can we help you?'

'You killed our friend,' Carmine states, crossing her arms. Her red uniform creaks slightly, making me assume she's recently been gifted it. Her leathers look new, unlike my own tatty outfit.

The picture of the girl falling from the tower projects itself inside my head, an arrow I held shooting straight through her heart. I keep my features neutral, hoping they can't detect the horror of that moment on my face. 'I'm glad your observation skills are intact,' I answer, heart racing at the confrontation.

Merlot gives me a concerned look, her gaze contemplating as I continue to watch Ember – trying but failing to ignore the pair still behind me. The surrounding Ravens give us curious looks as Carmine clears her throat.

'I'm not finished,' Carmine claims.

She grasps my shoulder, digging her nails into my thin tunic. It hurts, and on instinct I grab her wrist. Our gazes meet, and I hope mine conveys to Carmine that laying a hand on me will be a mistake she won't forget.

I pull with such force the Raven is hurled over my shoulder and lands loudly on the stone ground at my feet. The young female seems to register her disadvantage as Merlot and I look down at her.

Merlot elbows me, and I find Queen Adela and the Elder Raven glancing our way.

My fangs lengthen in an innocent smile. 'You touch me again, and you'll feel more than a sore back,' I whisper to Carmine, hoping the Elder Raven won't hear. 'Now take your friend and go away.'

Body on alert, I watch the female closely as she lifts herself from the ground, brushing herself off with an amused smile. Winella rushes to her side with a look of contempt on her pale face.

'You think you're so high and mighty, don't you? You disgusting half-blood,' Carmine spits, not caring that the queen is watching, not caring that the Elder Raven's attention is on us.

It's just another insult to add to the long list I'm used to receiving, but Merlot seems surprised by the female's affront. 'What did you just say?'

'Oh, sorry. I meant it in the *nicest* way possible.' Carmine smiles towards her, her face the picture of sarcasm. 'I didn't mean to hurt your *feelings*,' she adds, looking at me with a smirk, implying I have none to hurt.

'Your face will hurt if you don't leave us alone.' I notice out of the corner of my eye that Ember and her opponent have stopped fighting, and the next pair are beginning to duel. 'Now, run along. This isn't a playground.'

Winella, clearly offended, launches herself at me with her fangs out on full display, eyes narrowing with anticipation. I'm pushed back off the bench to land heavily on my back as the Raven scratches my face and punches at my stomach, her anger winning out.

As my fangs lengthen in response, I note mine are much larger than Winella's. Hers haven't fully grown yet. I bite the Raven's hand, resulting in Winella's glorious scream. I shove her away and stagger to my feet as swiftly as I can.

Merlot sits stunned, watching the fight unfold, but she, too, stands, probably to back me up, but Ember comes up behind her and lays a hand on her shoulder. 'Let her work this out.'

'What?' I blurt before I'm taken off guard.

Carmine attacks with a knife in hand, swiping for my chest. I barely dodge the blade before I drop to the ground and swing my leg around to clip her ankles, but the young Raven anticipates the move and jumps away, gaining space to recover.

Winella jumps me from behind. Her legs wrap around my middle while her hands roughly yank my long dark hair. The stinging sensation through my scalp makes me hiss in pain.

I grab Winella's hands, which are curled into my locks, and hold her so tight she can't jump off. Then I run for the nearest stone wall. Twisting at the last moment, I crush Winella against it with a loud crack. The female groans with the impact and tries to let go, but her hands are trapped within my firm grip, and I refuse to release her.

Realising her friend's dilemma, Carmine comes to her aid, but I land a swift kick straight into her face, catching her off guard, and she falls to the ground unconscious.

'Let go,' I hear faintly from my back, Winella whispering her words of surrender.

I finally rip Winella's hands from my now-messy hair and shove her away, making her stumble.

She is clearly not as used to fast-paced combat as I am, so I study her as she finds her breath. I tense my jaw to stop myself from shouting profanities at her in front of the large audience now watching us.

'How dare you!' Winella seethes. She takes a small knife out of her boot as she looks at her friend, still knocked out. 'You don't even *look* like a Raven. Why should you have the chance to be in the Hex? We deserve better. Your *kind* doesn't belong here!'

Hands on my hips, I scoff, finding blood staining my right side. 'Is that all you want? You want me to admit that your friend was more deserving than me for this chance to be the next Raven of the Hex?' I laugh coldly, giving Winella a harsh smile. 'Do you not think that if I stand here, then I am a threat regardless of diluted blood or darker colouring?' I motion to my hair, a significantly darker shade of red than everyone else's here.

Carmine, having regained consciousness, stares at me with quiet rage from the ground. I give the Ravens a pointed look, trying to quiet my anger. My fists open and close in response as I try to calm myself.

'When you kill me, *then* you can say I'm not worthy. Until *then*, let's see who climbs to the top,' I say, needing to hear the words as much as these two fools do.

Merlot's nod of encouragement makes me feel slightly stronger.

'I didn't realise you half-breeds were so full of shit,' Carmine spits, recovering from the high kick. Her nose is at a strange angle. The female picks up her discarded knife, touching her face tenderly as blood dribbles down her chin, and clambers to her feet. 'Your mother must have been pretty desperate to fuck a *human*.'

Rage like an inferno ignites within my chest. My head pounds painfully as the words wrap around my thoughts. The insult to my mother and the father I never knew, so harsh and cruel.

I don't realise what I'm doing until my hand snatches the knife from Carmine's, too quickly for the female to realise what I have planned, and I strike at the Raven's stomach with all my might. The female screams so loud it's like music to my ears. Carmine stumbles against the wall with blood flowing down her legs.

Winella growls, throwing her own knife at me. It sinks into my shoulder with a wet thud. Anger overtaking any other feeling, I pull the knife out without flinching – most likely looking insane. I throw the weapon back, and the hilt hits Winella's head with a loud thud and temporarily knocks her out, body and knife tumbling to the floor.

Standing numbly, I look down on one female with bite marks on her hands and a bruising forehead, then the other, with a bleeding stomach and a broken nose.

It's only when the anger slowly ebbs away and the tense silence around me becomes very loud that I feel fear start to kick in. The realisation hits me hard enough to make me feel unsteady.

I turn to find the queen looking surprised, clutching her chest, but even worse, the Elder Raven looks insanely furious, her flaring nostrils and wide crimson eyes pinned on me like I'm her next target.

'Fuck,' I murmur, catching Merlot's troubled expression.

15

I'm promptly escorted away by two male Ravens, their hands wrapping around my upper arms to drag me away. Out the corner of my eye, I note a messenger boy is sent to fetch the royal healers for Carmine and Winella.

A portal opens before me, and the males force me through. I peer around this new environment. It's unfamiliar and cold. I assume we are back in the House of Raven, but where exactly, I'm not sure.

'You shouldn't have done that, little bird,' one of the Ravens murmurs, the other smirking in response.

'What? Defend myself?' I can't help but bite back.

'You didn't, though, did you? You attacked those females.'

I gape at his accusation. Is that how this is going to play out? Everyone ignoring the beginning of the story to make *me* the villain?

The males stop at a set of double doors, large and made of metal that looks inconveniently heavy. The doors open, and I'm pulled inside and shoved into a plump crimson chair with the most uncomfortable back.

The room is spacious, clean and chilly. A stone desk sits centrally, and a pile of books lines one wall. Lanterns glow within the chamber, but they bring no warmth or hospitality to the place. If anything, it reminds me of the breeding centre – clinical and unfeeling.

I sit wondering what's going to happen, the males staring me down with excitement. The Elder Raven finally enters the room, and the Ravens stand taller, their features relaxing into neutrality. She takes a seat behind her large desk.

The moment the Elder Raven's eyes meet mine, my right hand begins to bleed. I don't look at my scar, but I curl my hand into a closed fist, hoping to contain the blood so the Elder Raven can't see it.

Run away! You're in danger! it screams at me as blood oozes out slowly, making my fingers damp.

'Come now' is all the Elder Raven says, confident in herself as she motions me to stand.

I obey, knowing that if I don't, I will be punished. If I comply, maybe she will sympathise with me.

'You can't go around hurting Ravens because you feel like it.' She stares at me as if I'm the troublemaker, as if I started the fight. Her face is set in stone, her fangs displayed in warning, and I can't help but gulp at the sight.

'It was self-defence. Those females attacked me first,' I murmur, my voice coming out strangled.

I've never been sent to the Elder Raven's office before, but the masters under her employment I have experience with. Those like Master Jepp take any opportunity to leave me beaten and bruised, to cut and torture me when they can, but the Elder Raven doesn't seem to be readying for a punishment like that. She merely sits back in her chair and steeples her fingers as if in thought. A small flicker of hope within me thinks she will see my side of the story.

'I don't believe you,' she says.

Well, there goes my sense of hope.

'You want me to believe that you, a half-blood, did not hurt those females because you are envious of them? That you didn't want to teach them a lesson or show everyone you are somehow capable?' She stands up and walks around her desk to stand face to face with me.

This close, I can smell her perfume, and it surprises me. Vampires and those with vampire blood, like Ravens, do not have a scent. It's part of the package deal of being a creature of death, but here before me, the Elder Raven wears something that humans – a species she supposedly hates – also wear. It's disorientating.

'I do not envy them, nor do I randomly start fights to show my *capabilities*,' I reply fiercely, my anger obscuring my fear. 'I didn't want to fight them, and I certainly didn't mean to hurt them.'

'But you did,' the Elder Raven drawls, sitting on the edge of her desk.

Her body language is casual, but I don't relax. I can feel this conversation building into something I'm going to regret getting myself into.

'They insulted my family. I reacted without thinking,' I admit, grimacing at the memory of Carmine's words.

Your mother must have been pretty desperate to fuck a human.

'It won't happen again,' I insist, hoping the Elder will accept my apology and call it a day.

A pale hand lifts into the air, and the Elder Raven's fingers slowly near my neck until long nails scrape lightly against my throat. She digs her fingers in.

For a moment, I think she looks afflicted, but not with sadness. It's as if she's silently deciding how to discipline me. Slowly the feeling of heat begins in my hands, setting off my heart in panicked fear and making my hand bleed faster, the blood now oozing through my fingers.

The Elder Raven watches my blood trickle to the floor. 'I will deal with you accordingly. My magic will douse your inflated ego, and I will set you back on the path you were meant to stay on.'

I shake my head, not understanding her words, but she clutches my throat now with strength a human would find unbearable, the heat of her touch growing torturously slowly.

From childhood, I've known what her power is – to create invisible fire that burns a person from the inside out without a trace on the body. Everyone calls it Unforgettable Fire, an inferno that whoever has endured it can never forget, the nightmares of its torment haunting them throughout their lifetimes. A nightmare I'd now have to endure.

Fire blazes through my spine suddenly, and my back spasms as the Elder Raven holds me upright by the neck, her nails cutting deeply into my skin. I gasp for air as her magic consumes me, my screams ignored as I claw at the Elder Raven's firm grip.

'You were my biggest regret,' she reveals, pushing me roughly to the floor, the stone cold against my now-scorching body.

Invisible fire roams over my arms and legs now, making my body wither with uncontrollable pain. My whimpers and cries go unheard by the males in the room, who watch with quiet delight.

The Elder Raven lets go of my neck and instead looms over me, her magic still working even without contact. 'I wish I had never told Queen Adela of Ruby's pregnancy. As usual, her typical human heart won over, ordering me to wait till you were born in case you came out a warrior like the rest of your siblings.'

Clutching my hands together, I try to stop myself from scratching away the heat, from trying to rip at my skin to get rid of the fire beneath it. I look up, and the Elder Raven's face twists into mild amusement.

'You came out weak instead, your dark hair giving you away as human, a sign of your inconsequential father.'

The Elder Raven bends down to touch my forehead, pressing hard, adding fire to my skull. I howl in agony.

'What really gave you away, though,' she continues, standing back up, 'is that scar – even the Gods marked you as an outcast in our House. Yet our noble queen wanted to keep an eye on you, to see how you grew up, and I was forbidden to kill you.'

The Elder turns abruptly and walks around her desk to sit in her chair. The invisible fire momentarily ceases. I'm unable to get up, my body still shaking, my breathing still unstable from the torture.

'Forbidden until now, that is.' The Elder Raven's cold eyes roam over me with excitement.

Inside my chest, my heart pumps rapidly. My breathing is erratic, and my hand is drenched in steaming blood that burns my palm.

All injuries from my earlier fight seem insignificant in the face of the hurt I feel now. My wounded shoulder is easy to cope with compared to the burning sensation that simmers through my muscles.

'You started a fight in the presence of royalty. I believe you will be forgiven for your actions by our dear sovereign. I, however, am not so generous. These trials will be my one chance to get rid of you, Scarlet Seraphine. You mark my words – you will *never* live through them, because our fates depend on it.'

My leader smiles coldly as the two males grab me and start hauling me away. They deliberately pull me across uneven stone floors and down hard stairs, knowing I have no fight left in me to retaliate.

We approach an exit that leads outside the bell tower and into the main square, where the Elder Raven made her big announcement over a week ago. After walking into the middle of the Raven's Nest, the males dump me like a pile of unwanted trash by a lava fountain. My body slumps to the ground, quivering and heaving still, as they leave me looking up into the darkness of the cave ceiling.

16

H alf an hour later, I find myself falling through Dimitri's door. My own home is the last place I want to be, and witnessing me in this state is the last thing Roux needs.

Dimitri is beside me in seconds thanks to his vampire speed. 'Holy Hanrah, Scarlet. What happened?' he asks, his cold palm covering my sweaty forehead. He flinches away as if I've burnt him. 'Fuck, you're scorching hot.'

He shuffles his arms under my body, attempting not to touch my skin, and he carries me through his home like I weigh nothing and sets me on his bathroom floor before filling his bath with cold water.

'S-sorry,' I stammer, my mouth opening and closing. I want to say more, but Dimitri shakes his head, red eyes wide with worry. He takes my clothes off and puts them neatly in the corner, along with my dirty boots, leaving me in just my underwear. In normal circumstances, I'd be embarrassed, but right now I couldn't care less what he sees.

'Don't talk,' he orders, getting a pile of towels ready, as well as a sponge.

I know I'm in safe hands, even though the pain is nowhere near over. A spasm of hotness overcomes me so abruptly I grit my teeth to prevent myself from biting my tongue off.

'Focus on me, Scarlet.'

His words are low and soothing as he turns the tap off. My chest heaves erratically, the heat making breathing difficult. I want to tell him what happened, but the amount of effort I need just to breathe is overwhelming.

My eyes land on his shaking hands as he goes to lift me again. He puts me into the cold water, taking care of my head. Guilt consumes me instantly.

'This is going to make you feel better,' he promises.

My body withers in the cold, steam rising from the bath. His hands keep my body under, his grip like steel as I thrash, reacting as hot and cold fight each other. The torture eases only slightly while I'm submerged in the ice-cold water.

'Th-thank y-you,' I whisper, watching as Dimitri searches my limbs and inspects each wound I've received today while cleaning me up.

He grimaces as he looks over my scarred hand, which is covered in dried blood and makes the water turn a diluted red colour. He looks saddened as he finds the nail marks on my neck, his fingers tracing them as he tries to hide his worry. Running a sponge over me, he comes across the nasty knife wound in my shoulder. His eyes harden as he meets my gaze.

'Who did this to you?'

'T-t-training,' I manage as he cleans my arms and legs.

Disturbed by the bruising skin around my forearms and sliced-up knees from where I was dragged, he brings out a small knife from the back pocket of his trousers. I watch as he slices his own hand open.

'Take as much as you want,' he says, presenting his bleeding palm. He edges it towards my mouth, and I gingerly open up.

On any other occasion, the thought of drinking blood would be revolting to me, but as I am part Raven, it can sustain my body like food and water can. Vampire blood, though, has healing qualities, which is the only reason I allow myself to drink it now.

The effects are nearly instant as I swallow my first mouthful of blood. My body stops shaking, my fingers uncurling as my muscles relax slightly.

Time goes by, and Dimitri regularly refills the bath with fresh cold water.

The heat still radiates off me hours later, the smell of burnt flesh still acrid in the air, but the pain slowly becomes more bearable.

I close my eyes, a wave of fatigue hitting me as the day catches up with me.

'Thank you, Dimitri. I owe you one,' I whisper, letting the darkness envelop me.

I end up staying overnight. My body temperature finally becomes somewhat normal, the feeling of burning alive having faded.

Not needing to sleep himself, Dimitri sits in an armchair beside me as I lie on his sofa, its decorative cushions piled under my head. His cold hand covers my forehead to keep my temperature down as we talk about what happened with the Elder Raven.

Dimitri's crimson eyes don't turn away from mine, his thoughts out in the open for me to see clear as day. He detests the Elder Raven, always has since I told him about our clinical ways of reproducing, but now more than ever, he has reason to loathe her, now that she's hurt me so brutally.

'She's power-hungry. And she's attempting to keep you quiet and compliant. I mean, she has the perfect magic to do so. It's just strange she would drag *you* away when those Ravens attacked you first.'

I sigh, knowing the reason. I'm a half-blood, and she never wanted me born. She clearly has a vendetta against me for some reason.

'I don't think it matters who started the fight. She seemed adamant that I'm some show-off wanting to display my skills.' I pause as I remember something. 'She did mention something odd, though.'

Dimitri hands me a glass of water, and the liquid soothes my sore throat. 'Is this before, during or after torturing you?' he drawls, mad I wasn't given the chance to stand up for myself.

No one can imagine fighting a power such as hers. It's something no one can understand until they experience it first-hand. But from what I know of Dimitri – which is a lot – I sense my best friend has had his fair share of pain, even if he wishes not to share such stories.

'She said, "I will set you back on the path you were meant to stay on,"' I recall, my brows creasing in thought. 'What path am I on that I wasn't on before? The trials? Does she think I'll ruin the challenges for her?'

He shrugs, unable to answer. We sit there for a while, contemplating her motives, what reasons she has to hate me.

'She mentioned my father, and it's clear she hates him,'

I say slowly, moving into a more comfortable position. Dimitri's hand falls from my forehead. I glance at my friend, trying to remember the conversation as I shuffle to the edge of the sofa. 'I mean, he's human. To the Elder Raven, he is dirt on her shoe, but the way she mentioned him, it sounded personal.' I scowl, questions piling up inside me.

'Maybe the fact he got Ruby pregnant is enough for the Elder Raven to hold a grudge against him. Maybe they had a relationship she didn't approve of,' he ponders, and I eye him sceptically.

I never knew my father, nor do I care much what happened to him. I've always assumed he died. But the thought of Ruby being affectionate with someone, being *in love* with someone, let alone a human man, makes me crinkle my nose at how bizarre it sounds.

Ravens in general have children through the breeding centre, a place where female Ravens are inseminated and kept under the strict and watchful eyes of our Elder and masters. There is no affection or passion involved.

'Ruby wouldn't have fallen for a human,' I state, trying to persuade myself it's not true.

'Are you sure about that? You're proof that Ravens have travelled to the other side of the wall. Perhaps your mother did the same and met your father.'

I stagger to my feet, wobbling slightly.

Dimitri's hand is out, holding my arm to steady me. 'What are you doing?'

'I need to find out. I need answers,' I say, walking for the door.

Dimitri is there in seconds, hand on the doorknob. 'You've never bothered thinking about your father, but now you want answers? Why?'

'All my life, I've been different. I'm more human than

anyone in the House of Raven, and they see me as weak. My father is human, a measly human in the eyes of the Ravens, but for some reason, the Elder Raven *remembers* him. Why would a random man with no magic or any powerful qualities make an impression on the Elder Raven? It doesn't make sense.'

'Unless he did something to her,' Dimitri guesses.

I nod. 'Precisely. So Ruby is the best person to talk to – plus she's probably worried sick wondering where I am.'

'You sure you don't want to stay and rest a while longer?'

My face makes him sigh in defeat.

He steps to the side, letting me pass. 'Fine. Let me know how you go, and be careful, all right? I don't want to see you battered and bruised again, unless it is during our training sessions.'

He opens the door for me and waves me out.

'I will. See you later,' I promise, stepping into the streets.

The tunnel is only a ten-minute walk from Dimitri's house. The wall separating our homes is tall and looming as I follow a small stream towards the tunnel entrance.

A small plopping sound echoes off the wall, making me pause. It sounds like a stone being dropped into the water. The street is empty when I turn around, but I feel the presence of something.

I don't move but instead close my eyes, and my senses confirm something is near. Glancing at my hand, I note it isn't bleeding. My body relaxes slightly with the knowledge that whatever is out there doesn't have bad intentions.

'Hello?'

Silence envelops me. The only sound present is my slowed breathing and the trickling stream.

'I won't hurt you.'

Turning in a slow circle, I try to pinpoint where the phantom is. With no luck after several minutes, I give up, the presence clearly not ready to show itself.

I head back to the tunnel, the feeling of being watched following me still, but I don't give it another thought.

17

Normally, I can ignore the stares, but today I can feel them like brands on my skin. Ravens pass me with looks of mild disdain, some with sneers on their pale faces. It seems the news about my punishment from the Elder Raven has been circulating. Unsurprisingly, the House of Raven is always full of gossip.

My sigh of relief is loud when I approach my house. Dimitri is right – I'm still weak and need more rest. I yearn for my bed and a long nap, my body still tired and achy.

It's quiet as I swing the door open, welcomed by stern looks from Roux and Ruby sitting at the dining table. Pausing, I realise my mistake. I've forgotten my wounds before entering. Roux's red eyes glare at the bruises along my arms.

'Where have you been?' Ruby demands, distress lining her words. 'Are you all right? What happened?' She inspects me, her gaze running up and down frantically. She comes to my side and strokes my neck, my cheek, and she scowls at the hole in my shirt where the knife skewered me. Thanks to Dimitri's blood, it is no longer a major concern to me, but it still looks fresh and sore.

'I've been with a friend.' My voice comes out tired, and I can't hide my exhaustion. My energy was zapped when I was burnt alive with invisible fire.

'Good. Sit down. Let me make you some tea.' Ruby ushers me to a seat, then dashes around the kitchen, heating a cup of lemony-smelling substance with her bare hands. Flames lick up the side of the mug. 'Oh, goodness. It's boiling now.' She's flustered, and I try not to look worried for her.

'It's fine, Ruby. It's perfect.' I'm given the hot tea, and I sip it, the liquid burning my tongue. I hide my grimace of pain behind the cup.

Looking between my sister and mother, I see the family resemblance. Their features are nearly identical, with catlike eyes that are bright and intelligent, and wavy red hair that is long and flows around their chiselled pale faces. Their expressions, however, couldn't be any more different. Ruby looks troubled, unsettled, seeing me like this, but Roux, she looks at me like I've ruined her day. Displeasure and rage flicker in her eyes. I swallow and avert my stare.

'I was told you were dragged to the Elder Raven's residence yesterday,' Ruby states, a crimson eyebrow rising in question. 'Ember said you were being punished.'

It takes me a moment to compose myself, to refrain from scowling upon hearing Ember has snitched on me. I take a deep breath and wrap my hands around the hot mug, focusing on the heat wafting from it.

'Yes. I hurt two Ravens during training,' I say before looking up, 'but I didn't mean to. I swear it.'

'I believe you, but why did you hurt them?' Ruby asks, her expression without judgement.

Sitting opposite Ruby, I watch carefully for her reaction. I've never mentioned my father before. It isn't a topic that comes up, but now I have the perfect opening.

'One of them spoke about you and my father. She was extremely rude, and I reacted badly, using her knife against her and her friend.'

Roux's eyes turn slowly towards our mother, and I can't help studying her as well.

'I lost control. The vile things they said were too much for me to handle,' I go on, carefully choosing my words. 'All I saw was red.'

Ruby, for a split second, seems shocked at the mention of my father, the man whom I know nothing about but who I have suffered for since birth. I don't look away as her crimson eyes find mine. If anything, I stare her down, willing her to say something, to tell me something about this mystery man.

Ruby blinks quickly, her gaze becoming misty, and she abruptly stands and makes for the stairs.

She's running away, I think with confusion.

'Was it really such a terrible time in your life? Was I such a mistake?' I ask, chasing her up the steps. My legs are wobbly as I follow her, and my recovering lungs struggle with the sudden exertion.

Ruby stops and spins so quickly I nearly collide with her. 'You weren't a mistake, Scarlet, but you don't need to know about him.'

'But *why*?'

I'm cut off as Ruby raises her hand. For a moment, I think she is going to hit me, and I flinch, expecting punishment, but Ruby's hand caresses my cheek instead, hurt welling in her eyes as she tries to soothe me.

'I would never lay a hand on you. You are a *gift*, just like all your brothers and sisters are. You, however, need not know about the man who helped create you. He is in the past, and we must focus on the present and future.'

To say I'm startled would be an understatement. Ruby

runs the rest of the way up the stairs and goes to her bedroom, closing the door with a definitive thud. I find my heart thundering with a mixture of emotions.

It takes me several minutes to calm down, to descend the stairs and sit back down with Roux. My sister shifts in her seat as she watches me return to the table.

'I won't bother scolding you or telling you how dangerous this path is that you're running down without care.'

My head hangs, weariness taking over me suddenly. 'Leave me be,' I croak.

'I worry about you, Scar. We all do. How can we sleep at night when we see you like *this*?' She grasps my wrist, and my head jerks up. 'How can I not be concerned for your well-being when you have a bruised face and two black eyes?'

I press my fingers gently to my eye sockets. They are indeed tender to the touch, but I don't let my tumultuous feelings show. 'Perhaps by not looking at my face.' I'm unable to keep the bite out of my words, the need for sleep growing more urgent the longer I stay in her presence.

'You're tired,' she states, to which I nod. 'Go to bed, and when you wake up, we'll have a chat.'

'Can't wait,' I mutter, heading for my bedroom, my sweet bed calling my name.

As I reach the third step, Roux calls out for me once more. 'You passed, by the way.'

'What?' I frown.

'You passed the queen's test.'

I've forgotten all about the first meeting with Queen Adela. The booklet I had to fill out was pushed to the back of my mind, my punishment overtaking everything.

'What marks did Ember and I get?'

'Ember got ninety-one per cent, and you got ninety-eight.'

Shock ripples through my body as I realise I beat Ember. I grin tiredly, finding Roux's features shifting into amusement.

'How pissed off is she?' I ask.

'Pissed enough to burn her entire bed. So don't ask her why she has new bedding,' Roux warns with a sly smile.

18

I sleep for the rest of the day and wake up early the next morning. I decide to sneak out before Roux can catch me. The last thing I want is a lecture on why I should quit the trials and how we will find another way to save Roux and her children. Frustration wells up inside me. If Ember ended up being our only hope, we'd be in deep trouble.

Today I want to be alone, with no Ravens, no family members and definitely no chances of walking into any of the masters. I decide to spend time at the stables, and I take the day to clean the stalls, polish the tack and groom the horses, along with plaiting their tails, all ready for riding.

'Okay, Joby. Let's take it easy, shall we?' I say, adjusting the saddle on the black-and-white stallion.

I lead him out to the training area, and we enter the large oval. It has several lanes of dirt to race the horses on around the outskirts, while the centre holds a sand school for learning the slower, more precise elements of equestrianism, such as jumping.

Joby stands patiently as I lift myself into the saddle and adjust my stirrups before securing my feet. The school is somewhat busy today. A few female Ravens are already riding around the track, no doubt testing their skills in case they need them for the next trial.

I kick Joby on, encouraging him to trot, and we find the rhythm immediately. Riding is one of my favourite hobbies, not that I would tell anyone. If word got out I actually *enjoyed* it, I'd probably be given another job, and I wouldn't want that.

I gently pull the reins to the right, and Joby obeys my silent command. I keep him trotting in a large circle, making sure to keep to one side of the school.

As I squeeze gently on Joby's sides, the horse eases into an effortless canter. His hooves pound against the sand as we stay within the circle I keep him in. 'Good boy,' I say in praise, making Joby's ears flicker. 'Nice job.'

A wind blows over us, and I feel a shiver run up my spine. I become rigid in the saddle, making Joby stumble and gradually slow to a walk. Peering around, I watch the Ravens training from afar. No one, as far as I know, has the ability to manipulate air in the House of Raven, and we certainly don't get a breeze through this part of the cave.

The feeling of being watched returns, a similar sensation to the one I felt yesterday leaving Dimitri's house. Once again my hand displays a silver scar. Whoever this presence is must only be curious.

'Who is there? I know you are following me. Show yourself,' I demand.

Joby comes to a halt as I pull the reins, hoping to hear where the phantom may be. Another gust of wind twirls the sand on my right side. From nowhere, a hand reaches out and strokes Joby's neck. His slight nicker makes me ease up on the reins, but only slightly.

'Are you invisible?' I ask, surveying the floating hand. Making a note of the slim fingers and manicured nails, I predict they belong to a female, and from the colouring of her skin, a deep tan, I guess she is Hanrae.

A voice so quiet speaks in my ear, making me jump. The woman's hand is still in front of me. 'No, I am not invisible.'

'Are you dameer?' My mind stutters, trying to figure out how the voice can be right next to my ear on top of a tall stallion, yet the hand is still roaming through the mane on my horse's neck.

'Of course I am,' the female voice replies.

'What magic do you have, exactly?' I don't dare move in case I frighten the voice away. I want to know the reason for her visit.

'That's a good question. One I can't answer right now.'

The hand disappears.

'Wh—' I begin before the voice rings in my ears once more.

'Enough questions. I'm here to warn you, so listen carefully,' the voice whispers, seeming to know the Ravens riding nearby could potentially overhear. 'The Elder Raven has plans for your next trial, and it's not going to be easy. You won't be alone, but make sure to wear long-sleeved clothing and to cover your skin with this.'

A small tub lands in my lap. I grab it before it falls.

'What is this?' Carefully I open it up and find a white jelly substance inside.

'Humans call it skinseal. It will be a protective barrier for you if you wish to use it,' the voice says, switching to my other ear, 'which I *highly* suggest you do.'

'This stuff is used to stop the skin from getting burnt in fires,' I mutter before looking up to see two Ravens staring in my direction. Clearing my throat, I pretend to check the saddle so the onlookers don't wonder why I'm standing around. 'What is the next trial? Why are you giving me this?'

By Joby's feet, the sand reveals two footprints, fairly small in size, but nothing else shows itself. This is magic unlike any I've seen before.

'Because I've been watching you. They say you are a curse on the House of Raven, but I see something else.'

'And what is that?'

Noticing more Ravens staring, I start to fidget. My clothes ripple slightly, making the hair on my arms stand on end.

'I have to go,' the dameer claims abruptly.

'Wait! What is your name?' I whisper.

'My name is Leo, but tell no one about my visit.'

Air twirls the sand by Joby's feet, and I immediately feel the lack of presence and know I am alone once more.

The pot of skinseal feels heavy in my hands as I peruse Rubien city, my mind swimming with questions. I'm meant to be meeting Dimitri for another training session, but I'm an hour early, so I decide to stop into one of my favourite spots: the Tea Shop.

The door opens to a pretty chiming bell, alerting the staff to my arrival. Eyes turn my way, but no one looks alarmed. I've visited enough times that I'm not seen as a threat any more, and it's one of the few places where I feel safe from judgement.

Waiting in line to order, I take in the feminine decor. The shop has low ceilings to give a cosy feel and flowery yellow wallpaper, and the tables have antique bronze legs and matching chairs with pink velvet cushions.

The owner's daughter greets me with a smile as I approach the counter, where cakes are displayed in towers for customers to pick and choose from. The smell of cakes and pastries fills me with deep joy.

'Scarlet! We haven't seen you in a while. How have you been?' Matilda says, wiping her flour-covered hands on her apron.

'Just the usual – working and working even more,' I answer with a shrug.

'I feel you there.' She nods with pursed lips. 'Do you want the special?'

'Yes, please.'

She rummages behind the counter, getting a tray ready with a steaming pot of tea and a matching teacup. Along-side them she puts several cakes on a plate. She hands the tray over, and I head outside to my usual spot, where I can watch the world go by.

The outside is as nicely decorated as the inside. Lace tablecloths, cushioned seats of pinks and yellows, as well as flowery umbrellas looming above the tables for shade, even though the shop doesn't get any rays of sunshine in this part of the cave.

As I'm arranging my teapot and cakes, a flicker of some-thing catches the corner of my eye. A cloaked figure in the street makes my heart jump with recognition. Leaning against a wall, leg propped up and arms crossed over his chest, is the Teacher, and I can tell by the tingles over my body that he's been observing my every move.

Holy Hanrah, I think as he walks my way.

Fumbling for my teacup, I try to act normal, pouring myself a hot beverage and sipping it delicately. The hot water burns my tongue.

Shit. Shit. Shit.

'Good morning,' the Teacher says, looming over me like a sentry. His gaze takes in my excessive number of cakes.

Without thinking, I'm studying his frame, watching his gloved hands as they flex and hating the fabric that covers his face.

'Why are you masked like a vigilante in the middle of the city? Don't you get tired of hiding yourself away?' I ask with a huff, trying to calm the sudden warmth in my chest.

'It's nice to see you too, Raven,' he replies, taking a seat.

I raise a brow. 'I don't remember asking you to join me.'

His eyes light up with amusement, and he lifts up a small container for inspection – my container, which I didn't notice he'd taken.

'Hey! That's mine!' I protest, grabbing the skinseal and putting it in my lap for safekeeping.

'Why do you have that?' he asks curiously.

'Are you following me?' I blatantly ignore his question like he did mine.

'No. Well, yes, but for good reason,' the Teacher remarks, waving a gloved hand. 'I was following you when you left the Badger's Sett one morning. I meant to catch up with you to talk.' He leans forward, hands up and eyes wide as he tells his story. 'But when I was approaching you, I noticed some other people following you too. You didn't seem to know they were tracking your whereabouts, but they've been doing it for days now.'

My mouth twists with suspicion. My first thought is he's been observing me without my knowledge. What could he have seen? Then I force myself to focus on the real problem. Strangers I don't know have been monitoring me. Why?

'*Days?* Are you sure?'

The Teacher nods. 'Yes. A pair of men – dameer, I think. I thought I'd warn you.'

My stomach grumbles, and the Teacher chuckles, his worries evaporating instantly. 'Hungry?'

'No. These delicious cakes are here just for show,' I quip, motioning to the delectable variety before us.

'Delicious indeed,' the Teacher drawls with a wink, making a small flicker of something light up within my chest. 'You need to be careful. I assume whatever they're following you for is something to do with the trials.'

I gape at him. 'How do you know about that?'

Ocean blue eyes study me. 'Dimitri told me when I asked why you've been absent from Storm's place.'

Another flicker of heat licks up my chest and into my throat.

He's been asking about me?

Before I can say much more, his hand clamps onto my chair. He drags it closer to him and puts his hand on the small of my back as he shuffles in, so close our faces are nearly touching. His scent overwhelms me sitting this close. I breathe in the ocean smell, and I find myself smiling.

He smells so good.

'I'll keep an eye on you for a while longer, until I know you're safe, but be on high alert for anything strange. I don't want to have to come swooping in to save the day because you're off guard.'

Frowning, I bristle at this and push his hand away from me. 'Because I can't take care of myself?'

He looks between his hand and my back as if he doesn't know what to do. Placing his hand on the back of my chair instead, he shrugs. 'I know you can, but I'd like to be the knight in shining armour sometime.'

Those sapphire eyes crinkle in what I assume is an arrogant grin, and I scrutinise him.

'Are you flirting with me?' I murmur, noticing people

looking our way, but for the first time, it's not because of me.

'Have you only just noticed?' he murmurs back, his intense gaze making my eyes widen.

My cheeks flame up as he gets to his feet.

'Scarlet, as always, it's been a pleasure,' the Teacher says, eyes intent. 'I'll be around.'

And just like that, he departs, leaving me feeling frustrated and wanting more. Again.

But as I finally take a bite of cake, I slowly realise he used my name. A name I certainly never told him, but a name he's gone out of his way to learn.

I smile to myself.

19

Stiff from hours of doing zilch, I sit alongside Ember in a cold room beneath the arena. It's only us in here, and I can't hear anything besides the relaxed rhythm of my sister's breathing.

This morning, we were woken up by the bell chiming, announcing the second trial's commencement. It was a flurry of chaos, and the remaining competitors were put into pairs. They decided who went together by alphabetical order, so that left me with Ember.

'Are you nervous?' I ask, more to fill the silence.

'No,' Ember states, crossing her arms.

My lips purse. We are heartbeats away from another deadly trial, and she can't even bother to make conversation with me. 'Good talk,' I mutter with annoyance.

The door opens, and Ember is on her feet, ready.

'Seraphine sisters?' a male Raven asks, watching me come to a stand. 'Right this way.'

We follow him, travelling through tunnels as long and windy as those in Songbird Castle. My body is tired from waiting, though, having become rigid from hours of doing nothing except worrying over every potential threat that could involve fire.

The Elder Raven has plans for your next trial, and it's not going to be easy, Leo said. Shaking off the feeling of impending doom, I check under my shirtsleeves. The skin-seal I was given is still thick and gloopy across my arms and body.

Our footsteps echo along the dark tunnel as we approach a heavy metal gate. In the middle of the entrance is a thin sliver of glass. The male Raven instructs Ember to stand on its left and me on its right. 'Go ahead. The Elder Raven is waiting for you,' he says, pushing us both forward. The gate closes as we step through.

Finding only red sand, I feel a small sense of relief that the lava is gone, but the glass wall between my sister and me piques my interest. I look along it. The whole arena is split in half by the barrier.

'A wall,' I hear Ember murmur to herself. She touches the clear glass before knocking on it. 'It's pretty solid, most likely unbreakable.' Her eyes lift to mine, aiming the words at me.

'Why would they pair us together to separate us now?' I ask, receiving a shrug in response.

My scar begins to bleed, and I attempt to hide it, squeezing my hand into a fist. *Shit.*

'Danger is coming, I assume.' Ember nods towards my palm, noticing my reaction.

'So it seems,' I reply, trying to calm myself, but my heart is beginning to pound.

Nothing seems threatening. Nothing seems out of the ordinary. It's just an arena full of red sand. Turning to the audience, I notice the royal family and the Elder Raven sitting together, guards surrounding them. They all watch us with anticipation except for the heir, Prince Julian, whose smile is as sly as a fox's.

A glint across their faces catches my attention as I walk around the edge of the pit, and I realise what the shine is.

'More glass,' I point out.

'Why is the audience caged in?' Ember asks.

Right on cue, we hear an ear-splitting roar from above. My head snaps up to find a gigantic dragon perched on a floating platform near the ceiling of the cave.

Blood red in colour, its enormous tail swishes with intimidating speed, emphasising its size in comparison to us. I can't help but gulp at the sight of it, suddenly wide awake. My body tingles with panic as my mouth goes dry and my hands begin to shake.

This is what Leo warned me about. *A fucking dragon.*

Along the centre of the creature's spine runs a straight line of sharp spikes, from its head all the way down to the end of its tail. Its wingspan makes me quiver in fear as I note this isn't even a fully grown dragon but a mere *baby*.

'I don't think the audience is caged in,' I remark as I edge slowly away from the monster. '*We* are.'

Ember has the audacity to look excited, while I feel near to pissing myself.

A voice we all recognise booms from the audience.

'Welcome, Seraphine sisters!' the Elder Raven announces excitedly. 'Today you must retrieve the bell from around the dragon's neck. Once you recover the bell, you will then be allowed out of the arena, but as you can see, there is an issue. A wall has been erected between you. To complete this task, you must *both* exit the arena, whether dead or alive. Good luck!'

Dead or alive?

I try my best not to curse, wiping away the sheen of sweat already developing across my forehead. Questions fill my head. My panic grows more intense the longer I stare at the winged animal. I should have slathered myself in way more skinseal – or rather, *bathed* in it.

My heart is like thunder within my chest as I look for any weakness, like Ruby told me to. There is none. What could possibly bring down a dragon of *this* size?

'Holy Hanrah! Any ideas?' I keep my sights on the creature in case it moves, and I find the bell wrapped around its neck, a gold ribbon keeping it tied in place.

'I'll distract it; you figure out how to lower the glass wall,' Ember orders. Then she runs off before I can have a say in her plan.

Turning for the stone wall that borders the fighting pit, I start searching for something that looks mechanical. Behind me, the dragon seems unfazed by Ember, her arrows of fire shooting towards it but unable to find their mark.

'I think you need to try something a bit bigger,' I shout at her, earning a glare of warning.

'Shut up and do your job!'

A column of fire grows near my sister, flames flickering and the sound of crackling becoming louder as her magic begins to stretch and weave through the air like a mini tornado. It reaches so high the dragon's tail is consumed by fire.

'Yes!' Ember shouts in triumph.

The creature screams in protest, opening its wings in annoyance. Any moment, it's going to fly for her, and I have yet to find a lever or button.

I search through the sand, up the walls, pressing on stone, thinking perhaps the button is invisible. I wouldn't put it past the Elder Raven to make it as hard as possible to find.

I'm on my knees, digging, when a rumble vibrates

through me. The audience echoes my surprise above me. I don't bother to turn around, as I can hear Ember shouting curses at the dragon, probably enjoying the opportunity to kick its arse.

It's only when I hear my sister scream, my name echoing through the arena, that I turn and realise what's happened.

Before me, staring at me with beady black eyes, is the dragon, looming high and mighty before me.

I've never seen a dragon, let alone been in the vicinity of one, but right now I can't move, can't speak, can't *breathe*.

The dragon is menacing and intimidatingly big in size, and lucky me, it's landed on my side of the glass.

'Scarlet!' Ember yells. 'Run!'

20

F *uck!* is the first thought that goes through my head. The second is *I'm going to die.*

My legs wobble as I get to both feet, shaky hands out in front of me. 'Ember,' I say, hoping she can hear me. My legs are unable to move; my body is planted to the spot. 'Ember, what do I *do*?'

I'm near to crying at this point. An orange glow beneath the dragon's neck grows brighter the longer I stand still. My mind is blank, empty of answers, the thing before me too big for me to create a battle plan. This is nothing like a fight at the Badger's Sett.

'Run, you fool!' she yells, banging the glass. She sends roaring flames over the wall in hopes of taking the dragon's attention. Unfortunately, it doesn't work.

In seconds, the giant's mouth ignites, shooting fire straight at me. On instinct I bolt, surrounded by searing heat as it licks at my clothes and skin. Thankfully, I run just out of reach so that I can't feel anything. The skinseal is doing its job, but the moment it melts off, I'm in deep trouble.

As I run around the perimeter of the arena, flames

follow me everywhere I go. The audience shouts with excitement as the blazing element glosses over the glass before them like a pretty painting.

'What's the plan, Scarlet?' I shout to myself, pumping my arms in an attempt to outrun impending death. 'Think of a plan!'

I start to zigzag, trying my best to dodge the blazes shot my way. I'm aiming for the creature's tail. If I can somehow clamber up the dragon's body, I can retrieve the bell, then jump off and run for safety. Simple enough.

'Look out!' Ember shouts.

I've nearly reached my target when I nearly run into an inferno of red and orange. This close, my lungs begin to burn from breathing in the blistering heat.

'Holy fucking Hanrah!' I hiss, tumbling backwards into the sand before urging my body back up. Stinging sensations cover my weakening legs, the gel Leo gave me beginning to melt away from the close proximity to the dragon's fire. I can smell my hair is slightly burnt too, but I keep running, finally reaching the creature's tail.

Without hesitation, I jump upon it, grappling a large spike that protrudes from the dragon's back. The monster tries to toss me off, its face coming frighteningly near me in an attempt to bite me with its sharp teeth.

'Ember!' I scream, hiding behind a spike. The dragon is getting angry now, its throat beginning to glow – a sign fire is coming for me again, and this time, I won't have much more fireproof gel to save me.

A squeal of metal and glass and cheers of delight resonate through the arena. A wave of relief washes over me as the wall begins to lower, my sister having found the switch. Ember's glowing hands and determined face show me she's ready for the fight of a lifetime.

'Get the bell!' Ember orders me, her flames shooting at our opponent.

The beast roars in answer as a flaming ball hits its eye. It swings around to my sister, its attention no longer on me.

As if I am climbing a ladder, I heave myself up the spikes, my bleeding scar making the scales slippery.

Passing the halfway mark on the dragon's back, I hear Ember shouting for me to hurry up. I grit my teeth, ignoring her taunts, pushing down the fear that follows me as I'm tossed around, and haul myself higher. Looking up the beast's back, I find the gold ribbon that wraps around its neck, the metallic colour contrasting with the animal's scales.

At last!

I chant to myself to keep going, and I finally approach the creature's thick neck. Nearing the ribbon, I hold my breath. The ribbon feels like silk in my hand as my fingers wrap around it, and for a moment, I smile, enjoying its texture. It's so lovely and—

The dragon jerks roughly, and I lose my footing. I swing from the ribbon, the weight of my body making me drop around the underside of the creature's neck. My grip tightens, my fear now making it harder to breathe.

'Stop messing around!' I hear from below.

I attempt to find Ember, but all I can see is blasts of fire, waves of red and heat like no other blazing from below.

'A little more,' I tell myself as I inch closer to the bell. My scarred hand is bleeding even more now, dampening my palm, and blood slowly trickles down my arm.

The bell is small, the size of a human baby at most. Its surface is smooth and reflective, my frantic face shining back with a golden hue. I reach for the precious item and hold on tightly as I bite my way through the soft silk.

The bell falls soundlessly to the floor, thudding as it

lands in the sand. Still holding on to each side of the frayed ribbon, I shake with the effort of defying gravity, calculating the best time to jump.

Three, two, one ... I let go.

My body becomes weightless, wind wrapping itself around me as I plummet like a wingless bird. I hear nothing as I fall, and my mind is barren of thoughts. My bones jar inside my body as I hit the sandy surface. My instant reaction is to curl inwards and roll.

In seconds, I'm up and limping away, my fall not as graceful as I was hoping. As swiftly as I can, I scramble for the bell and tuck it under my arm as I dodge a massive dragon foot, claws coming down so close to me I can feel the vibrations through my limbs.

Screaming at Ember, I point to the gate that is now open, the bell heavy in my grasp, and I finally get her attention. Slowly she moves away from the creature, her fire protecting us both as we move towards safety.

Grinning with triumph I reach the gateway, slowing down to meet the male Raven who waits for us. His smile widening before he looks behind me, and then his expression turns into one of horror.

Glancing around, I find Ember sprinting for her life towards us, shouting for us to clear out. Blue and red flames trail closely behind her, the inferno larger than anything I've ever seen before, something stronger and much deadlier than Ember or my other family members could ever create.

'*What is that*?' I scream, never witnessing such a colour combination of flames before.

'Hellfire! Save yourselves!' the male Raven roars, pushing me away to get a head start as he escapes into the depths of the tunnels.

My legs move without hesitation, the fact I'm not immune to fire jolting me into action.

Ember reaches me and drags me along with such force I can barely keep up. My sister's strong arms warp around me as she practically drags me away, holding up my weight as I limp as fast as I can. Before we reach the corner, Ember's voice thrums through me, saying words I'll never in my life forget.

'Hold your breath, Scar, and prepare for the worst pain of your life.'

The last thing I feel is blistering agony as I am enveloped in searing hot flames.

21

The first thing I glimpse is white walls. Instantly I know I'm in the healing clinic, which is strange, as I've never been here except to visit family members.

I wiggle my fingers, and they move with ease. Then I test my toes, and they, too, feel normal. Lifting my arms, though, I grimace with discomfort. The memory of fire, so much fire, overwhelms me, and I sit up in bed, wringing my hands.

I look down and gulp at the sight of my poor body.

My fingers look red, blistered and sore. Higher up is even worse, my arms covered in burn marks all the way up to my shoulders. Peeking inside the oversized nightgown I wear, I find my chest has minor injuries to it, my guess being that the little amount of skinseal that remained at the end of the trial helped.

Arching my back, I feel the skin is tight and uncomfortable. I discover a looking glass across the room, and I traipse towards it. My right leg twinges slightly as I put weight on it, but as I slowly begin to walk, the tenderness eases.

I take a deep breath before uncovering my back. The sight makes me gag. My burnt arms in comparison look minor. The skin is red, purple, patchy and wrinkled – nothing like I remember it being. It looks like I've been torched, any skin scorched away.

This is why I despise fire – the element that destroys without remorse, the element that relishes in pain and torment.

A knock echoes through the room, and my eyes drag themselves hesitantly to the door as I lower my gown. A woman with midnight-blue hair and tanned skin walks in with a large smile, holding up a clipboard in greeting.

'Welcome back, Miss Seraphine. I'm Annie, and I'll be your nurse,' she says as she approaches the bed and pats it, motioning for me to sit down.

'You're dameer,' I blurt, finding the woman's dark blue eyes brightening with amusement. That explains why she introduced herself as a nurse and not a healer.

'Indeed I am.' Annie smiles kindly. She approaches me, forgetting the bed. Her hand reaches for my forehead, her touch cool as a faint purple glow comes from her palm. Magic wraps around my skull, and I find myself relaxing slightly. Nodding with satisfaction, she writes some notes down, the scratching of her pen the only sound in the room.

'Are you allowed within our side of the cave?' I ask, curiosity getting the better of me. I silently urge the nurse to explain herself. 'It's dangerous for humans here.'

'My dear, unless *you're* thinking of hurting me, then I can assure you I'm safe.' Annie laughs, giving me a look to say I'm ridiculous for thinking such a thing.

'*I* don't want to hurt you,' I clarify before giving the woman a raised brow. 'Why are you tending to me, and not the Raven healers?'

'The royal family has offered my services to your family.

You were in very bad condition, and they didn't have enough healers to tend to you, so I volunteered to help.'

It doesn't take a genius to know that Annie is lying. Having grown up in the House of Raven, I know that we have enough healers to care for every member of our House if need be – it's just none of them want to work on healing *me*.

'Are we lacking in healers, then?' I ask, wondering what else she'd lie about.

Annie leans in closer as if wanting to tell me a secret. 'If you want the truth, I think the scary old woman, your leader ...'

Our eyes meet, and I nod in encouragement.

'She said she didn't have enough healers to tend to you, but I saw many Ravens wandering aimlessly with nothing to do.'

'Is that so?'

'Yes. It made me very curious, so I looked at your file. You have an interesting history when it comes to the Ravens. You're what they call a half-blood.' She lifts her fingers to form quotation marks. 'Half Raven and half human.' She points to my hair. 'That is why you look different from the rest. The bright red colouring that Ravens are known for is diluted by your father's genes. Bright red mixed with brown. Very interesting.'

My ears prick with interest. *My father has brown hair?*

'Do you have any files on my father?'

Annie shrugs. 'No. He is a mystery, it seems.'

Pouting, I cross my arms in disappointment, grimacing at the feeling of my skin rubbing together. I release my arms again and let them hang beside me.

Annie seems to notice and gives me a sympathetic smile. 'However, I do know he's not in the city.'

'Is he dead?'

'No—'

Our attention whips to Ruby, standing in the doorway, an expression of grief covering her features. She smells of magic, her emotions running high, and she studies me.

'Scarlet.' Bright red eyes grow wider as they pinpoint my exposed skin.

I curl in on myself, feeling self-consciousness hit me like a ton of bricks.

'I'll leave you be. I'll come back later to check on you,' Annie says, removing herself from the room.

I glare at her, internally shouting, *I'm not done with you. Come back!* But Annie only smiles as she closes the door behind her.

Ruby and I stand in silence for a moment, and I debate whether to bring up my father with her, but before I can make the choice, she rushes me. Her arms wrap around me in a warm embrace, her naturally hot body making me flinch.

'I'm so sorry,' she utters, releasing me instantly before backing away. In seconds, I can sense her magic lessening, her fire power cooling for my sake. 'You've been through so much. I'm so sorry.'

'I chose this,' I remind her, but she shakes her head.

Slowly she reaches out a hand. I entwine my fingers with hers. She caresses the burns along my fingers, looking full of sorrow. Guilt winds through me knowing her expression is my doing.

'You didn't choose to battle a dragon, Scarlet. All you chose was to help your sister.'

'How is Ember?' I ask, wanting to move the conversation away from me and my injuries.

'In one piece. She was extremely fatigued but otherwise fine.' Ruby nods, giving me a look. The gaze shows me how much she wishes I could have been born with fire magic, like Ember was, how much she wishes I weren't mutilated and forever covered in a reminder of the Hex Trials.

'They told me you wouldn't make it. They told me you'd die instantly,' she whispers, lip quivering. 'I ran for you the moment I saw you and Ember consumed by fire.'

I imagine Ruby sprinting for the entrance of the tunnels, pushing anyone and everyone out of her way, not caring who watched, who thought her weak for showing obvious emotion.

'Annie told me Ember's fire is what saved you.'

My eyes jerk to her face to see if she is lying, but no signs point to her deceiving me.

Ember saved me?

'How?' I ask, not believing her.

'She cocooned you in her own fire. That's what all the burns on you are from. The dragon's fire battled against it. Ember was out cold for days. Otherwise, you would have been dead instantly.'

The information trickles through my brain, the words *Ember saved you* sinking in slowly. She helped me hobble along when she could have run off without me. She could have saved herself from the fire, but she decided to stay and fight. For me. For us.

'I'll have to thank her,' I say numbly.

Ruby shakes her head, looking to the ceiling to stop the tears from falling. The gesture reminds me of Roux.

As terrified as I was battling a dragon, I don't regret it. As much as my own skin horrifies me, I wouldn't change the past. My family has always been my priority, and to save them, I'd do it again without hesitation.

'They can't get rid of me that easily,' I murmur, holding Ruby's hand tighter. 'They'll have to do better than a *puny* dragon to get me to quit these trials.' My smile is forced, but I play the part, hoping to relieve Ruby of her worry for me.

My mother knows what I'm trying to do. She smiles wearily. 'Are you still feeling sore?'

I turn over my hand, pointing along the inside of my forearm. 'It doesn't hurt. It's just a little tight around my elbows and back, but I'm sure the healer will fix it in no time.'

Ruby doesn't answer, and for the first time, I really look at her. She appears drained, her naturally milky skin paler than normal. I wonder if she's ill, something rare among Ravens.

'Are you sick, Mother?' I whisper.

The use of the word *Mother* surprises her. Never in the House of Raven do the terms *Mother* and *Father* get used to address a parent. We don't breed for love and affection; we breed for duty and keeping the Raven bloodline strong. But in this moment, I feel like the term is needed, to show Ruby she is more than a keeper to me – she is a female I love and look up to.

'No, Scarlet, I'm not sick.' She shakes her head and wraps her arms around me once more, the heat now gone, a coldness sweeping through me. I'm not sure if I prefer it or not. 'I just lose my mind wondering what will happen to you every time you leave the house, every time a trial is announced. I'm worried sick for your well-being, but at the same time, I understand why you are competing. I'm so proud of you and what you have achieved so far. You've done so well.'

'But?' I probe, because I know there is one coming.

'But I feel like a terrible mother for letting you compete, for letting you be involved in something so dangerous, even when I know you'd go ahead and take part anyway. Your loyalty outweighs your fear, and that scares me immensely.'

I start to protest, but she stops me, pushing me to arm's

length, her hand on a sore patch of my shoulder. I hide my wince.

'I'm not discouraging this. Your devotion to Roux is admirable. I just wish you didn't have to go through all *this* to prove yourself.'

'I'm not.'

She gives me a motherly look, like she knows deep down how I'm feeling even if I haven't figured it out yet.

A big part of me wants to save my sister, but I guess there is a part of me that wishes to show everyone my status as a half-blood does not define me as weak, that I'm far from unworthy, like everyone in this House thinks me to be.

'My thoughts exactly,' Ruby murmurs, giving me a tired smile as I meet her gaze. 'You are so precious to me. Do not ever forget that.'

'I won't,' I reply, feeling a warmth inside my chest I haven't felt in a long time. A warmth I don't flinch from but welcome with open arms.

22

A few days pass, and I'm released from the healing clinic. Ember and Blaze wait for me at the exit. They wear their black fighting leathers, their belts filled with small knives and throwing stars.

'Are you guys on your way to or from training?' I ask in greeting, walking down the steps of the entrance. We stroll along the street together, taking a route I know well back home.

'On our way to. We've been instructed to make sure you get to your destination okay,' Blaze answers.

I turn to Ember, and she practically ignores me, eyes averted but body language showing she's relaxed. She's obviously in a quiet mood today, perhaps still fatigued and recovering from the trial.

'And my next destination is ...?' I ask, glancing up at Blaze.

'Ruby wants you at the tavern. I think she wants to see you before you head home,' he says, eyes flicking to my arm nearest him. 'You didn't get your scars removed.'

It sounds like a question, and I purse my lips in response.

The Elder Raven supposedly hates scars. I remember the twins coming home once from training years ago, saying how they'd been banned from entering the arena until their scars had been dealt with. Growing up, I realised that was because the Elder Raven sees them as displays of weakness, and to others, it looks like our kind can be wounded and, furthermore, killed.

'I was told my scars are too deep to be completely removed.'

'I thought Ember's flame protected you? Her fire should be healable,' Blaze says, his crimson brows furrowing.

I shrug, trying not to let my emotions show. 'Well it appears the hellfire got through her defences, and dragon fire is not as easy to cure as normal fire.' The backs of my hands and both arms still look sore and disfigured. It still takes me a moment to remember they will never go back to how they were. That this is my new normal.

'Do they disturb you? I can find something to cover them up if you prefer,' I say, getting the sense my brother doesn't like looking at my scars.

'Yes, cover them up. Blaze is too nice to tell you they're hideous and better left unseen,' Ember states, finally acknowledging me.

'Ember,' Blaze murmurs, voice low in warning. 'That's enough.'

The strength it takes not to shout at her in front of the street is immense. Of all people, Ember should know I don't wear these scars to make a statement.

'You know, it's all because of *you* that I'm even here right now, Ember. I have you to thank for these scars and not being deep underground. So thank you. These scars mean a lot to me, and I think I'll wear them with pride from now on.'

Ember's hand grabs me so painfully my skin stings around her nails, my arm hurting instantly.

'Ow, you're hurting me,' I protest, trying my best to remove her cruel grip.

'You will cover up from now on because otherwise you will bring the Seraphine household embarrassment,' Ember snaps, teeth gritted as her face leans close into mine. 'We will be seen as weak if you flaunt them around, and the last thing we need right now is our family to be under the spotlight more than it already is.'

At this proximity, I can feel uneasiness seeping into my body. My eyes watch her movements so intently I expect her to hit me. It's only when she finally lets me go, her message made very clear, that I release a breath. Blaze gives me a sympathetic look but doesn't say anything as Ember stalks off without us.

I thought Ember had saved me because she cared. I was planning to thank her in private for protecting me when no one else could. Now, though, I'm torn. Why did she do it if this is how she perceives me? An embarrassment. A weak link in our family.

Silently I follow her, no longer in the mood to chat when Blaze attempts conversation. It doesn't take long for him to give up, knowing Ember has removed any cheeriness I felt leaving the healing clinic.

Ember enters the tavern before us. Blaze's hand lands on my shoulder, slowing me before I open the entrance door.

'Ember has been stressed lately with the trials. She's just letting out her anger on you. It's nothing personal.'

'Nothing personal?' I scoff.

Blaze pulls me aside as a couple of Ravens enter the premises. Inside, Ember stands by the counter, where Ruby is cleaning some glasses. They look to be having a stern conversation, but with the amount of noise inside from the customers, I can't hear what they're saying.

'Your scars are a reminder that she could have failed the challenge, that's all.'

'A reminder?' I counter, crossing my arms in frustration. 'She doesn't seem to realise they're also a reminder to *me*. A reminder I could be *dead* right now.'

Blaze shrugs. 'I know, I know. Like I said, don't take it personally. You're just an easy target to let her fears come out on. She doesn't think you'll fight back, and that's what she needs right now.'

'Right. As long as *she's* all right. I'll allow her to talk to me like shit whenever she fancies it, because she's *stressed*,' I mutter back sarcastically. 'Thanks for the company. It's been lovely.'

After dismissing Blaze, I stride inside and ignore Ember like she did me. She leaves for training, dragging Blaze behind her.

The tavern is busy, so I watch Ruby work, the only bartender available, like I used to when I came here as a child. I'm given scowls and unimpressed looks by patrons, but I don't move from my seat.

It's only when a figure beside me rocks up, taking the seat next to mine, that I peer up from my thoughts, and I see a woman with dark blue eyes and long midnight hair.

I frown. 'Dameer aren't allowed in here,' I state, not sure why she is in the House of Raven, and even more confused as to why she'd choose to come to this tavern, of all places.

'I know, but royalty is.' Her hand reaches out, waiting for me to shake it, and that's when it dawns on me. The manicured hand that stroked my horse's neck, the voice that spoke in my ear.

'You gave me the skinseal.' I gape, staring at her hand like it's poisonous.

'Why, yes, I did.' She smiles, and her teeth are pearly white and wickedly straight. 'I'm Princess Leonore of Hanrah, and I want to make you an offer.'

Queen Adela has five children, and her youngest sits alongside me like it's a normal occurrence for her to come into the House of Raven and join me as if we are long-lost friends.

'An offer?' I echo, still not fully understanding what is happening. 'What could I possibly have that you don't already possess?'

The girl's smile is sly and mysterious. It reminds me of her mother, Queen Adela. The sight of it makes me squirm in my chair, uneasy that she has her attention solely on me.

'Let's just say I have a plan, and it requires you to accomplish it. You are exactly what I've been looking for,' she answers.

'Me? Why me?' I peer around the joint and find curious faces watching us, intrigued by the princess. She sticks out, but she acts like she doesn't notice the stares, most likely used to the attention.

'You are the half-blood Raven, no?' she asks, earning a hesitant nod in confirmation, because I can't really lie about that. 'Then you are the only one who can help me, and in return, I will help you.'

Uneasiness winds through my chest. I can tell already it's going to be a bad idea getting mixed up with royalty. I don't want any more stress in my life. I already have enough.

'I don't need help, but thanks for the offer. I'm going to be late for work.' I push my chair out and begin to stand, but she's quick as she drags me back down.

'Hear me out. We both know the stables aren't in dire need of your assistance right now.'

'How did you know—'

'Just assume I know everything.' She lifts a hand to Ruby, asking for two pints of beer.

Her choice of drink surprises me, but it's Ruby's expression that concerns me. Bright red eyes observe the princess with caution before settling on me.

Watch yourself with this one, my mother silently tells me, setting our beverages on the counter.

The princess pays double the amount needed before Ruby heads off to another customer.

Princess Leonore drinks half her beer before turning to me, her dark gaze watching me carefully, like I'm a puzzle that needs solving. There is no denying she is beautiful, her eyes deep blue and mesmerising. I can imagine her with a line of suitors, but with the way she carries herself, I get the sense she's independent and probably as mysterious as rumours suggest.

'We are two sides of the same coin, Scarlet. I am rich, powerful and loved by everyone because of *what* I am. You, however, are poor by Raven standards, magicless – except for that scar that determines how much danger you're in – and hated by everyone because of *what* you are.'

My scowl is prominent as my spinning mind tries to

find stability. I've had enough people making me feel terrible about myself today. I get back up, refusing to listen any more.

Once more she places her hand around my wrist, not caring about my burns, and shoves me back down with more force than I expected. The moment I'm seated, she gently strokes my wrist before letting go, as if silently apologising for roughly handling me.

'I assure you I'm not here to offend you. There is a point to all of this,' she clarifies with a sweet smile.

I instantly dislike her and whatever plan she has in place for me. 'Then get on with it.'

She sighs, leans back in her chair like she's had a rough day. The sight of it almost makes me laugh – a member of the royal family looking defeated. What could possibly bring *her* down?

'You are a half-blood because you have a Raven mother.' She motions to Ruby, and I find my hands turning into fists. 'Easy. I've not touched her, and I've known you are both related this whole time.'

She waits for me to say something, but I stay silent. I do not have time for her horse shit, and I sense she understands she's running out of time. Her words come out fast but rehearsed, like she's planned what she's going to say to me.

'Your father is a human, and your mother is Raven, which makes you different, makes you *special*. You've broken tradition, and you continue to break it every day by simply living. That is a sign you are the key to everything. This House needs a change, and it's going to start with you.'

At this point, I'm so tired I pretend to go along with her ramblings. 'Meaning?'

'You have to win the Hex Trials. It's the only way.'

'I'm already competing,' I state, looking at her like she's

slow-witted. 'You gave me the skinseal for the dragon I had to face ... remember?' I motion to my arms in case she's forgotten.

The glare I receive is intimidating, and it makes me feel a slither of guilt for being impolite. But she doesn't come across as someone who would be offended so easily, so I simply glare back.

'You aren't competing to become the next Raven of the Hex; you are competing to win your sister medicine. There is a big difference,' she says.

'Well, I'm not interested. I don't want to be in the Hex. And I certainly don't want the pressure of becoming an Elder after that. I just want to live my life without trouble.'

'Well, listen to what I can offer you first before you make a final decision.'

I reluctantly agree, and she continues.

'First, your sister needs Araside, which is a rare and expensive medicine. Only the Elder Raven has a store of it, and only enough for two people at most. Unfortunately, we don't have time to get more before your sister goes into labour, so that's the first reason you need to win the Hex Trials.'

Crossing my arms, I study the girl. *Round one to her*, I think glumly.

She smiles at me like she can see my mental tally.

'Go on,' I say.

'Second,' she continues, peering around to the bar where Ruby is momentarily absent. The princess leans forward, lowering her voice. 'I know you use the money you win from fighting at the Badger's Sett to help your mother put food on the table without her knowing. She's been thinking she's paid more than she actually is for years. Sneaky girl you are.'

I jerk upright. 'How do you know—'

Her tanned hands rise in defence. 'I know everything, *remember*.'

'Have you been following me?' I hiss, clutching the arms of my chair so hard I feel the metal digging into my palms.

'Yes, of course. I've been following your family too. One member being your oldest brother, Ash Seraphine.'

My eyes meet hers. She looks confident, and the more she speaks, the more reason I have to be afraid. Somehow she has infiltrated my life without me knowing, and she is grasping any vulnerability I have within one hand and squeezing to see how I will react.

'What have you done to him?' I ask, my fangs growing in length as my emotions run away with me.

The princess simply eyes my mouth but doesn't seem concerned. 'Nothing. But I know he is a breeder and that he's another asset I can bargain with to get you to accept my offer,' she responds before drinking the rest of her beer. She eyes my untouched drink and scoots it over to her side. 'I know he's a breeder. Ghastly job, isn't it? Your brother, unlike Roux, lives in that cramped residence without any freedom to visit family or friends outside the breeding clinic. He's depressed and used every day without a care for his mental well-being.'

As I attempt to remember when I last saw Ash, envy crashes through me. I've not seen him in so long, and here Princess Leonore has, keeping an eye on him for some reason.

'Why are you telling me this?' I protest, feeling the noose tightening around my neck, waiting for the final blow.

'I can give your family money to live freely without the stress of overworking. I can lend my royal healers to your sister when she goes into labour – which is more help than she'll receive with the Elder Raven's assistance. I can liberate your brother from the breeding programme. He can come home and choose what he wants to do with his life. I can take care of your family for as long as they all live. You have my word.'

'All of this for me to try and win the trials? That's it?'

The princess leans in closely, voice low once more in hopes those around us don't bother to listen in. 'You will receive all of that if you become my champion.'

'Your champion?' I scrunch my nose up in confusion.

'The royal family is allowed to choose champions – fighters that are expected to win the trials. It allows me to help you. If you win, you'll be under my guidance, and we will both benefit from it. However, we cannot reveal this agreement between us until I say so. You'll have a target on your head the moment it's announced, and I can't have that happen yet.'

'This is a lot to take in,' I mutter, putting pressure on my temples, a sudden headache coming on.

'You are the best person to win these trials, Scarlet. You are kind-hearted, loyal to the ones you love, and you know what it's like to be treated unfairly for something you have no control over. You will be the perfect advocate for the little people. You'll be the best role model for children all over the lands to look up to. People like your sister Ember want the role for glory, and they have been leading the House of Raven for too long already. We need a change, and I want *you* to be that change.'

Nibbling my lip, I debate her case. A princess of Hanrah has come to this side of the cave and is asking for my help in return for all the things I can only wish to give my family. Could it be a trick? A farce to kill me off? Would the princess work with the Elder Raven to get rid of me?

'If you agree, you'll never have to worry about your family again. You can live your life without the burden of wondering if they'll be taken care of,' Princess Leonore presses, her face finally showing open emotion, her expression hopeful.

Ruby talks to an older male, her smile forced as she speaks to him. I imagine her without a care in the world, not having to overwork for the basics in life. She's done so much for me and my siblings. I could do this for her.

'I'll do it,' I announce, reaching my hand towards her. 'I'll be the next Raven of the Hex, if it comes to that.'

The princess grins, taking my face between her hands instead. She pulls me closer and presses a light kiss on my forehead. It tingles for a moment, and I can smell magic wrapping around us, binding us together. I look up, and her face is open and lovely.

'I promise you won't regret this,' she says.

24

The Badger's Sett is extremely busy, as is usual for nights like this. I glance down from the Green Room as I put on my hand wraps, covering my scar. Dimitri comes up behind me, already wearing his glamour – the image of a father with his daughter.

'You ready?' he asks, voice huskier than normal.

'As ready as I'll ever be.'

With a wave of his hand, I smell the tang of magic. He lifts a looking glass to me to show his work has been successful. My dark red hair has turned blonde, and my usually red eyes are now bright blue.

Seeing my smile, Dimitri mirrors me and helps me secure my hood while I put on my mask. As all fighters are required to be, I am completely covered except for my eyes.

'Do you know who I'll be fighting tonight?' I ask Dimitri as we make our way downstairs.

He shakes his head, and as we come into view of the crowd, they erupt into cheers and bellowing.

Playing my role, I lift my hand in greeting, and I earn a roar in answer. The Phoenix, as I planned from the beginning, never speaks. She only talks through action, and so far it's worked out well for me.

The crowd makes a path for me. Dimitri follows closely behind until we reach the small wall that separates the audience from the fight. I leap over and turn to my friend. We clasp hands, and he pats my head for good luck – a tradition that's developed during the years I've competed.

'Go get them, Phoenix,' he whispers to me, knowing I'll be able to hear.

As I walk around the ring, hands shoot out for me to slap, spectators screaming in delight when I touch them. Drinks splatter over my boots and spill over my hands, but I don't mind – my followers have been loyal to me over the years, and they have helped me more than they will ever know.

'Okay, folks. We have our first contender, the Phoenix!' Storm commentates from his box in the corner, magic projecting his voice so the whole building can hear him. 'And facing her, our new fighter and rising star – the Teacher!'

My heart thunders at the mention of his name. My hands turn into fists as annoyance grows within me. How I didn't see this coming is beyond me, fighting the Teacher was bound to happen eventually.

Shit.

I come to the centre of the fighting ring and stand very still as I watch him clap backs with burly men, wink at giggling women and easily jump the wall before stopping to face me. His blue eyes study me, roaming up and down as if I'm an obstacle he doesn't know how to overcome.

You are the Phoenix. Do not let him unnerve you.

'Let's toss a coin to see whether the fight is with fists or weapons!' Storm announces, faces all peering in his direction as a coin flies into the air and lands back in his hand. 'It's weapons night!' he declares, and the crowd goes wild.

'My favourite,' the Teacher murmurs, thinking I can't hear.

Two men from the audience reach the fighting circle, holding a large wooden tray between them stacked with weapons. The Teacher and I approach to choose what we'd like to use. My opponent goes for daggers, and so I choose the same.

'Ready yourself, fighters!' Storm shouts, urging his patrons to buy their drinks quickly before our match begins.

I watch the Teacher intently, observing the way he spins his knives expertly around his fingers. He's clearly well versed in weaponry, as well as combat, judging by the first time I witnessed him, but compared to me, how will he fare?

I've never been obnoxious enough to think I can beat everyone who comes my way. My preference is to learn of my opponent's techniques and hope to sway them into making mistakes, and thus win with keen observation of the human body and strategy. If Ember or Blaze ever witnessed me, they'd probably laugh, their techniques much more ferocious and untamed than mine.

'Begin!' Storm announces.

Encouragement is thrown around in screams and shouts for both fighters. Around me, the men and women bellow their opinions, instructions and desire for blood. The Teacher approaches, but I've yet to move, thinking myself a statue. He walks around me at a safe distance, taking in every angle of me, and I let him. When he circles me a second time, I sense a thrust, and I dip into splits, missing a dagger to the back by a second, the blade a breath away from the top of my hood.

'Flexible,' the Teacher whispers to himself as if making a list of my skills.

For some reason, this makes me smile as I spin and come back to my feet, my body bending in an unnatural way.

Once more he prowls, looking for a chink in my armour, wondering where to hit next. His next lot of attacks are quick and precise, but his hope I'll falter under pressure is mistaken, as I parry each of his daggers with equal force and ease.

'Strong,' he mutters.

The sound of metal upon metal urges me on, our blades slamming together in all positions. I can see on the Teacher's face that he is clearly becoming frustrated. He wants to win, but I have yet to do anything but defend myself, my method of learning his technique earning me more points the longer he plays along with my game.

'Patient,' he adds, jumping away, seeming to need space to rethink his plan of action.

Observing the growing distance between us, I calculate his next move. He seems eager for victory, as most fighters here are, but he wants to *earn* it. I've made a name for myself here at the Badger's Sett – a fan favourite, some may say – and to beat me would put a gold star beside his name.

With all my previous opponents, I've never had the desire to chat while in a battle, but I find my mouth opening, wanting to do just that. I realise too late it's a moment of weakness, one made by Scarlet – not the Phoenix.

Before I can utter what's on my mind, a dagger comes flying for me. It lands in my upper arm, and I hiss in pain, the blade not only hitting a tender part of my limb but also making my still-healing burns sting like never before.

You fool, you let your guard down, I chide myself.

My eyes water, and I'm suddenly vulnerable, having been preoccupied with wanting to talk with him. In seconds, I'm flat on my back, distracted enough from the agony in my arm to notice the Teacher's swift movements. His body towers above me, his eyes staring down with delight as he aims his next dagger, but he forgets I still have both of mine.

Make him think twice about using a weapon against you.

Gritting my teeth against the pain, I use my uninjured arm to slash the inside of both his legs – sensitive areas for any being. He crumples heavily on top of me, and I quickly roll him over so I am now on top. I stab my dagger into one of his shirtsleeves, pinning him down. I repeat this on the other sleeve before he can counter-attack.

Lying on the floor, he's temporarily restrained, and I leave him there, stalking around the perimeter of his body as I watch him wiggle to try to set himself free.

The knife in my arm throbs, but I don't dare remove it. I pretend it doesn't affect me, thinking of anything but the feeling that trickles down to my fingers, the numbness beginning to take over.

'Finish him!' I hear above all other voices. It's Dimitri telling me it's all right to end the fight.

I step up to the Teacher, whose face is no longer glittering with determination but instead shows frustration. I take his dagger out of my arm and throw it in between his legs to land inches away from his manhood. The crowd goes crazy, but I only have eyes for my opponent.

His sapphire eyes narrow in distrust, and I smile behind my mask, hearing Storm announce my win to the audience around us. They thump their fists along the wall, drinks flying through the air in glee, and Dimitri laughs with satisfaction at my win.

I peer over the Teacher's head, bending down so our faces are upside down to one another.

Ever so quietly I whisper, 'Don't forget to add *exceptional* to your little list.'

PART TWO

The Guardian

25

Songbird Castle is much bigger than I initially thought. With Queen Adela and Prince Julien in the front, leading us Ravens through their Rubien home, and the royal guards following us in the rear, we pass ballrooms, kitchens, areas set up with art supplies and rooms full of paintings before we finally reach our destination.

In the back of the stronghold is the undercroft, an open area whose ceiling is held up by arched pillars made of stone. Beside the pillars are various archery targets in the shape of animals. Along the ceiling hang ropes with bars to climb across, and the floor has strange arrows pointing in different directions.

Hanging on a random pillar sits the chalkboard that tallies how well we are doing in the trials. I scan the names and find my name higher on the list than last time but still close to the bottom. Relief swells in my chest. I'm thankful that at least I have a chance.

Searching the board for other names, I see Winella is still competing and falls in the top twenty. Merlot, I find, is higher, taking ninth place, and my sister, who stares at the leader board with disapproval, is in second.

'Ravens! Today is a particularly special day. We have never incorporated this type of meeting in the Hex Trials before, but I am truly excited for such an interesting time ahead of us.' Queen Adela smiles slyly, instantly reminding me of her youngest daughter. The sovereign glances at Prince Julien, who looks particularly excited for the day's events, his dark blue eyes studying us with amusement and eagerness.

Movement from across the undercroft catches my attention, a line of people heading our way with the Elder Raven in the lead. I glance questioningly at Merlot, who stands beside me with an equally confused expression – all of the people are dameer.

'That's an interesting sight to see,' Merlot mumbles.

'We have introduced a new asset to the Hex: those we call guardians.' Our sovereign continues, waving a hand towards the ever-nearing line. 'The guardians are keepers of rules and regulations. They will keep our Ravens as disciplined outside the House of Raven as they would be here in Rubien.'

The group seems wary of the Elder Raven as she urges the humans to move faster, the mixture of scents making me feel on edge. I'm used to the sweet scents of human blood, of course, but I'm not sure how all these other Ravens present will react. After all, we are part vampire.

'For each Raven, there will be a guardian. These are hand-picked men and women who have studied and trained their whole lives purely for this momentous occasion.' Queen Adela watches the newcomers with keen interest.

'Line up, Ravens!' Prince Julien shouts suddenly, clapping his hands.

We are hesitant to obey, but the queen's glare is enough to make us move, and quickly.

'Today our guardians will choose carefully whom they want to pair themselves with. Those not chosen will go home and will no longer take part in the Hex Trials.'

My head swings to Merlot. 'Are they joking?' I whisper in a panic. No doubt this is a plan the Elder Raven has conjured up to try to boot me out of the game. The dameer will choose everyone but me, most likely not wanting to be stuck with the only half-blood.

A royal guard comes along our group, pushing us into an orderly fashion, Ravens in one line and humans in another, and he hands out scraps of material.

'You are being given a blindfold,' Prince Julien instructs, walking in front of us like a true leader commanding his people. 'You will put it on and let destiny decide your fate.'

I'm handed a blindfold, and I reluctantly put it on. Feeling exposed, I can hear uneasy shuffling, some of the other Ravens no doubt feeling the vulnerability I do.

Footsteps surround me as I sense what is happening. Humans of various smells circle us. Merlot grabs my hand and squeezes. I squeeze back quickly before letting go.

Nerves swirl in my stomach, my worry growing greater the longer I stand without someone claiming me.

When a scent I'm familiar with grows stronger, I turn towards it. Fresh air and salt, like the ocean. Heavy footsteps stop behind me, and I feel a shiver creep up my spine. I'm being observed.

'Hello,' the voice says, low and at ease.

I don't move or speak, not sure if the word was aimed at me.

'Hello, Raven. What's your name?' the voice says, breath tickling the side of my neck. I shudder under its coldness.

'Hello,' I echo. 'I'm Scarlet.'

'What is your favourite food, Scarlet?' It's a man, and he is so recognisable, but I can't pinpoint where he's from exactly or where I know his voice from.

'Mint chocolates,' I state, wondering if anyone else is listening to his bizarre line of questioning.

'What is your favourite colour?'

I can't help but frown at that one. 'Um, yellow?'

'Are you sure about that? You don't seem too convinced by that answer.'

I nod, deciding that playing along with this stranger is better than being stranded and sent back home. If I don't succeed in being friendly and approachable, Princess Leonore may take back her offer of providing for my family.

'Yellow is bright and warm. What's *your* favourite colour?' I ask back, feeling him walk around to my front – examining my face, I assume.

'I quite like the colour red. I thought it would be your favourite too, as you come from the House of Raven.'

I lean in slightly as if wanting to tell him a secret. 'Red is actually my least favourite colour, for that exact reason.'

He hums in answer. 'Interesting.'

He walks away, and I lock my jaw in frustration. I thought I'd done a good job of being conversational. *Don't humans like that?*

The sound of a throat being cleared echoes through the area. The clip-clop of heels sounds as the queen orders us to remove our blindfolds.

'Behind you is a guardian that has chosen to pair with you for the Hex Trials,' she says, her sapphire dress gleaming even with the dimmer lighting. 'If you find no one there, please make your way over to the Elder Raven, and *do not* make a scene.'

The royal family observes us with scrutiny, expecting us

to cause trouble, but when our Elder silently motions for us to turn, it's only grunts of disapproval that I hear.

Slowly I turn on my heel, keeping my head down. The first thing I note is someone's shoes, and I sigh in relief.

I've been chosen.

Peering up, I see that my guardian is tall and broad-shouldered. He wears an all-black outfit that accentuates this toned body, and he has a welcoming smile. But what grabs my attention isn't his messy silver-blonde hair or outstretched hand but his eyes.

Ocean blue – not the same dark blue shade the royal family and all Hanrae people share but Tellian blue, light and alluring.

I know who he is instantly. We've met before, and he's chosen *me* to be his partner. My attempt to keep my expression neutral is difficult, my face straining not to give myself away.

'Nice to meet you,' the Teacher says. His unmasked face is more brilliant than I could ever have imagined. My hands wrap around his numbly as he studies me closely. 'I hope you don't mind being stuck with me.'

My smile is genuine, and I feel my chest tighten with excitement. Not only have I been chosen by the Teacher himself, a mysterious man I've been longing to know the true identity of, but now I have the opportunity to learn about him and see behind his facade without his knowing that I know who he is.

A little piece of me screams to expose the truth up front, to tell him what a bastard he is for throwing a dagger at me the other day. But the other half, the more prominent part of me, wishes to see how this goes. It won't hurt to keep my secrets a little longer, to play along for a while before I confess what I know.

'I'm sure we're going to have a lot of fun together,

guardian.' I grin, making the tops of his ears flush a slight pink shade. The sight of it delights me, this unmasked side becoming more intriguing the longer I stare at him. 'Do you have a name?'

Our hands melt together as he squeezes lightly, something I can only describe as soothing warmth seeming to course through our touch. I find myself not wanting to let go.

'My name is Jack Wilde.'

JACK WILDE

26

J*ack Wilde.*

Finally, a name to a face.

'Amazing,' I find myself muttering, the puzzle pieces within my mind all clicking together.

A scuffle ensues to my right as a stubborn Raven is escorted out by our Elder. Out of the thirty-five Ravens, seven have failed to entice a guardian to pick them. I wonder about what they've lost, not being in the trials any more.

'Ravens,' Prince Julien proclaims, grabbing everyone's attention. 'Your guardians have worked very hard to get this far. They will be helping you on the rest of your journey. Make sure you learn each other's strengths and weaknesses, and *remember* ...' He pauses for effect, putting a finger up. 'If one of you is kicked out of the competition, you are *both* out,' he states, and a rumble of murmurs washes over our group. 'Throughout the area are stations with certain items. Use them while getting to know one another. The more in tune with each other you are, the better.' The prince waves a hand at the nearest station, a pair of silver swords sitting up against a pillar.

Jack and I end up at the station furthest away. Out of the corner of my eye, I see Merlot, and she is paired with a young girl with long blue hair and matching eyes. I look for Ember, who is across the room. She's with a lanky guy whose black hair looks like the midnight sky against his pale skin.

'So we have bows and arrows,' Jack says, holding up one of each. 'Have you used these before?'

'Of course. Let's see who can get a bullseye first,' I suggest, earning a glimmer of a smile from him.

'I don't know if I could take you on.'

I shrug. 'I guess we won't know unless we try.'

I reach for a bow and strum the string. It's fine, but nothing like the one I use at Dimitri's – the vampire is serious about his weapon collection.

Jack readies himself before facing me. I can't help the mischievous smile that blooms across my face on seeing him like this, so different from how he acted fighting the Phoenix at the Badger's Sett.

'You ready?' I ask, and he nods. We scan the pillars for targets. I point to the closest one. 'Let's go for that one first.'

He nocks an arrow and aims. My eyes wander over Jack's face, the curve of his lips, the wisps of his silver-blonde hair. I stare without shame, pretending I'm studying his stance rather than drinking the sight of him in. He releases the arrow, and it hits the centre of the target.

'Nicely done.' I clap, impressed. 'So, Jack, how long have you been training for?'

He looks pleased with himself. 'I've been training for several years now. Started when I was seventeen, which is the starting age for guardianship.'

I aim my own arrow at the target and take the shot, and it easily hits its mark. He doesn't seem surprised by the ease I show, but his expression is amused.

We point to a target slightly further away, and this time I go first.

'And what exactly are you supposed to do as a guardian?' I ask, hitting the bullseye once more.

Blue eyes stare at me, at first blankly and then with swirls of confusion. I blink, wondering if I've offended him somehow, but he continues with his go, the bow making a twanging sound when the arrow is released. Again it hits the red circle in the middle.

'Being a guardian means to serve, to protect and to honour,' he states, like this sentence has been ingrained in his mind.

Biting my bottom lip, I ponder this a moment, but the longer I question the statement, the more I don't understand. 'Serve, protect and honour the sovereigns? Why are you involved in the trials, then?' I ask, watching him study me.

He shakes his head, merriment tainting his features. 'No, we don't serve the queen.'

We pick out the next mark – it's quite a distance, and I wonder if he feels nervous yet or if his beating heart is a little faster because of me.

'So what are you guarding, exactly?'

'The next Raven of the Hex, of course,' Jack answers cryptically, probably enjoying my curiosity. It seems that with the Teacher, I am always full of questions, and now as his unveiled self, he is the master of keeping answers from me too. It frustrates me, but I try not to let it show.

'I don't follow. Why do Ravens need guarding now?' I ask, forgetting target practice momentarily.

'Because of what happened before the Red Raven,' Jack replies, referring to the title my aunt Brande has gained over the years for her role as Raven of the Hex.

I've never met my aunt before, Ruby's sister having

never visited the House of Raven since I was born, but I've heard many stories about her. However, none explain how she came to be the winner of the Hex Trials.

'The Red Raven had to replace the previous Raven of the Hex – her sister, I think it was – after she got involved with a human. Apparently, your kind are forbidden to have relationships.' He shrugs as if this fact is truly unfortunate.

My heart stammers to a halt. 'What?'

Jack's face is smooth and relaxed. He doesn't seem to pick up on my growing emotions, and it's probably for the best. His attention is mainly on the next target. He has his go even though I'm supposed to go first this time, but I'm too distracted to care.

'Well, from what I know, the Raven of the Hex had a baby with a human, and it was all a scandal. The pregnant Raven was taken away, and the man disappeared – supposedly killed off by the Elder Raven, but no one is really sure what exactly happened, except for the Red Raven and her guardian, who happens to be my mother.'

'Your mother,' I repeat numbly as his words sink in. A thunk echoes through my head as another one of his arrows hits the bullseye.

I'm the only half-blood Raven to exist. My hand slithers up to my chest, the pounding of my heart so prominent I think it's going to burst out of my chest.

My mother was in the Hex? Brande wasn't the original winner of the last trials?

Jack nods and grins. 'Another one!' he announces, turning to me before his smile quickly disappears. 'Are you all right?'

I leave abruptly and go in search of Ember.

Ravens and guardians stare at me as I travel, watching me with curiosity. I don't care that the Elder Raven is around – I *need* answers.

Finally I find my sister and kneel before her. She is trying to light a fire without her magic. Her guardian watches me with suspicion.

'Was Ruby in the Hex?' I force out through gritted teeth, my mouth near her ear.

She swats me away, but I don't budge. I stay beside her until she is glaring at me, warning me. 'Go away.'

'*Was Ruby in the Hex*?' I demand, my voice low but firm. I sense the moment my sister realises that I won't be leaving her side until I get the answer I want.

Ember doesn't answer for a moment, but her expression changes from annoyance to reluctant surrender. 'Yes. Then Brande took over. Now go away.'

She pushes me, and I stumble away. Jack is beside me, asking too many questions as he leads me back to our station. The only voice I do listen to, however, is that of a woman. Her serene voice whispers in my ear, but she's invisible to everyone.

A trickle of air wraps around the back of my neck like a soft caress, and I find myself wanting to cry.

'What is wrong, my champion?' the princess asks, the concern heavy in her words.

I shake my head, my vision blurring, but I won't let the tears fall. I don't let myself be vulnerable in the presence of competitors, who would savour the moment I'm not on guard.

'Did you not know of your mother's past?' she asks, earning another shake of my head. The invisible princess sighs, having obviously been listening to me and Ember converse. Air wraps around my hands, which grip one another. The element eases them apart, making me realise how tightly I've been holding on. Little crescent moons are left on the backs of my pale hands. 'She was given a choice,

Scarlet. To keep or terminate you. She made her choice. *You were her choice.*'

Guilt fills me, and I find Jack stroking my back carefully, his eyes latched on to the burns along my hands.

'Are you okay, Scarlet?' he asks, and this time I hear him, my mind coming back to reality, my heart calming as I muddle through the information I've learned.

'Sorry. I had a minor panic attack,' I lie, hoping he will understand.

He nods slowly.

'You did really well.' I point to the targets he's hit bullseyes on. On the one furthest away, I see he's missed the centre mark. 'Although a little off over there.'

His smile is soft and gentle before his eyes lie upon the arrows I used. 'Like you could do any better,' he challenges.

'Oh, you've asked for it now.'

I ready my arrow and aim, but instead of hitting the bullseye, my arrow lands straight through his, splitting it in half. The bottom half falls to the floor with a clatter, and I can't help but beam watching his reaction.

'Show-off,' he mutters, blinking with surprise. 'But I'll let you have it. Next time, though, I won't be so easy on you.' He winks. His consideration for my feelings is a quality I've rarely found in people here in Rubien, but with the way he gazes at me, I know he will be a marvellous guardian.

27

The next day, I'm following both my sisters and Ruby to the healing clinic.

Since our time at the castle, Ember has been avoiding me, no doubt wanting to stay out of whatever episode I'll have when it comes to confronting our mother. But I've been strong and have held in my ever-growing list of questions until the right moment, a moment when I'm alone with Ruby and I can unleash my hurt for being kept in the dark about her past.

I help Roux up the steps of the clinic entrance, her belly much bigger now she is in her second trimester. Her hand lies upon it with protectiveness as we wait in the waiting room. We are instructed to take a seat, and one by one we are called to be seen. Our annual medical check is due, and the gender reveal of Roux's babies.

Raven's stare openly at me, most likely wondering what I'm doing in the clinic but this is one place I'm allowed to be – *forced* to be, in fact. It was made very clear at a young age that I was forbidden to fall pregnant, or else I'd be punished by the Elder Raven herself and most likely killed for my transgression.

One reason on a long list to why the House of Raven is so fucked up.

Ember is called away first, and she looks eager to escape our company. As I sit between Roux and Ruby, my leg jumps with impatience. I hope my sister will be called next.

When we have waited more than half an hour, I can't stand it any more. I get up and go to the water bowl and acquire us all a drink. Once sat back down, I hand them over, and my sister and mother thank me while they begin to sip from their cups. It's another five minutes before I give up caring that Roux is present for what I have to say to my mother.

'I learned something yesterday that I thought was really interesting,' I murmur, aiming the words at Ruby.

She turns and looks down at me with a lifted brow, drinking a mouthful of water.

'I was told that you were a member of the Hex before Brande had to take your place.'

Water spurts out of her mouth, spraying the backs of the Ravens before us. They turn and growl with displeasure. Ruby apologises profusely before glaring at me.

'Who told you that?' she demands.

I don't dare mention the Teacher – or rather, Jack. My family knows what happens in training when under the queen's care, but I am not going to put the blame on him.

'Ember confirmed it,' I say. I feel Roux's gaze on my back, burning into me. 'Is it true? You got pregnant and were thrown out because of me? You never told me my father didn't live in Rubien.'

'Neither was I going to indulge you with that information,' Ruby counters, making me scowl.

'Why not? Don't you think I'm entitled to know *something* about my father, the man who helped bring me into this world?' I ask sarcastically, annoyance and frustration flowing through me. 'Did you know about Ruby being in the Hex?' I turn to Roux, whose guilty face makes me even more bitter. 'So everyone knew except me?' I hiss, receiving glares from those who are waiting quietly in the room.

My mother's mouth opens and closes several times before she says, 'You weren't supposed to know, because it no longer matters.' Ruby avoids eye contact, and it irks me. For my whole life, my family has known I was the main cause for my mother's downfall, from being a fighter to becoming a worker.

'Right. Silly me. I'll stop asking about you and your life, or about my father, because you clearly don't give a shit.'

Ruby winces but doesn't answer me, instead crossing her arms. Wave upon wave of emotions rush through me, and I don't know whether I want to punch a wall or sob on my sister's shoulder. There is no way I'm letting this all slide under the rug. I have to find out who my father is and why he, of all people, caused so much trouble within the House of Raven.

Roux's hand finds my knee, and her warmth flows through me. She seems to sense my churning thoughts. Our gazes meet, and she looks apologetic. I simply nod in answer. They kept it from me for a reason. I get it, but all of them making a pact to never tell me seems wrong somehow.

'How are the burns healing?' Roux asks before her face scrunches up slightly.

My hand flies to her stomach to feel the twins kicking. Love fills me up, replacing all other emotions as I imagine what they'll look like when they finally arrive. My smile is faint, but Roux notices it, and her smile is enough for me to forget I'm angry at her.

'Fine, I guess. A bit tight in places but nothing I can't handle.'

'Well, we got a delivery the other day. Some salves and medicines were in the package. You may want to try some of them. They could ease your trouble areas.'

My brow creases in confusion. 'A delivery?'

We don't get deliveries, let alone packages sent to our door, unless the tailors have sent back Ember's or Blaze's amended training gear.

'Yeah. Every Raven competitor receives a parcel with every trial. We got a whole bunch of stuff, didn't we, Ruby?' Roux says, making our mother nod in agreement. 'We got extra food rations, money allowance for uniforms and whatever else we need, new cutlery and even some medicinal teas for me to help with the cramps and heartburn.'

Medicinal teas?

'Really?'

'Yes. Apparently, we're to get them every month you and Ember are in the trials. The note mentioned something about keeping promises.' She scrunches up her nose. 'I thought maybe that would make more sense to you, but it was a nice letter.'

It's then I almost cry, but for a reason other than anger. Princess Leonore was true to her word. She's sent a box of goods to our home, things we need, things that will help us. I mentally add thanking her to my list of things to do.

An envelope arrives at our house soon after we return from

our medicals. The moment Ember announces there is a letter addressed to the family, I come rushing to her side.

Once Ruby permits it, Ember opens the envelope enthusiastically. 'It's an invite from the queen. She requires us all in one hour.'

'For what, exactly?' Blaze asks as Ember hands the invitation over to him.

'It doesn't say.' Ember shrugs.

'Well, let everyone put on their finest gear.' Ruby claps, sending the household into a flurry of excitement.

I follow Roux up the stairs before walking with my sisters into the room we all share. My small bed sits in the middle, while my sisters' beds are pushed against the walls.

Peering under my single bed, I rummage around in a box for any clothes that would be suitable for meeting the royal family, but most of my clothing has been worn at the stables, and it's obvious, the smell of horse lingering on my belongings.

Ember, who searches under her own bed, looks over at me when I lay out a pair of slightly stained trousers and a faded black tunic.

'You can't be serious. That isn't what you are wearing to meet the Queen of Hanrah, is it?' Ember asks, picking up my worn out shirt with two fingers as if it's contaminated.

'Are you going to offer me something of yours, then?' I counter, giving her a pointed look.

Ember sighs heavily, searching among her own garments. She pulls out a long-sleeved black shirt and tosses it at my face.

'Here. Don't say I'm not helpful sometimes,' my sister declares, changing into her all-crimson uniform.

Roux taps my shoulder and hands me a pair of trousers, leather and slightly too long but cleaner than any pair I own. I take them gratefully, thanking her.

Besides looking like a child wearing adult clothes, my outfit doesn't look horrible, but standing in the hallway, watching as my family parades down the stairs in all their impressive uniforms, I feel self-conscious.

'Let's go! The royal family is waiting!' Blaze shouts with excitement.

28

The official throne room in Songbird Castle is extravagant and decorated so luxuriously that I can't help but gape. Never have I seen real gold, or tapestries as detailed as the ones that hang on the stone walls. A sapphire carpet lies upon a set of steps leading up to three thrones, each gold in colour and bordered with beautifully carved engravings. On the largest throne, I can see several names wound through what looks to be a design of flowers and naturesque patterns.

Guards stand all around the border of the room, waiting along with my family. They have an assortment of weapons hanging from their belts – one carries an axe, another a sword, and one even has a length of silver chain.

A shuffle of movement makes my family stand up straighter, my curiosity growing greater the longer we wait. With Roux and Ember standing either side of me, while Ruby and Blaze cover my back, I feel small. Circling me like a protective barrier is one of the most powerful fire-elemental families. It's almost laughable.

Queen Adela walks in first, her sapphire-and-emerald dress trailing behind, showing off her figure. Her make-up also matches her attire, giving the illusion of dark, mysterious eyes.

Behind the queen, her son enters, and Prince Julien has a regal air about him today. He wears a dark blue waistcoat on top of a crisp white shirt, with his hair combed neatly out of his face. He smiles at us before sitting down on one of the thrones. The other stays empty, but now I realise why. The princess.

The two royals sit looking over my family with piqued interest as they settle into their seats. The queen clears her throat and gets straight to the point.

'Welcome, Ruby Seraphine and family. We have invited you here today because we have some important matters to attend to, but first, I must congratulate your daughters on their success so far.' The queen's look of displeasure at my outfit doesn't go unnoticed, my all-black outfit contrasting with my family's all-red uniforms. 'Also, congratulations on the wonderful news of your daughter Roux's pregnancy. What gender are you expecting?'

Ruby bows. 'Thank you, Your Majesty. We are delighted to be having twins, one of each,' she replies, well versed in speaking with royals – now I know why.

'Marvellous! The best of both worlds!' The sovereign's expression of happiness seems genuine. 'And, Scarlet,' Queen Adela adds, turning her attention to me. My hands become sweaty instantly. 'Are you faring well after the dragon challenge? That was quite the remarkable show you and your sister put on.'

'I'm well, Your Majesty. Your healer was much appreciated,' I reply, bowing awkwardly.

For a moment, Queen Adela looks confused by my statement, and I ponder over what part of my answer isn't clear, until I realise that perhaps the queen's *daughter* is the one I should thank for Annie.

Damn that girl. She does *know everything.*

'Yes, well, now you're all here,' Queen Adela continues, taking hold of Prince Julien's hand and squeezing it fondly, 'I will pass you over to my son, who will reveal the reason for your invitation here today.' She nods to her heir, who stands, straightening out his waistcoat, and pulls something out of his pocket.

'I want to start by saying how impressed I was watching your last trial and that I appreciate how hard you have worked during our training sessions together here at the castle.' He starts slowly descending the steps, his voice clear and commanding. 'It's tradition that the members of the royal family give out tokens to contenders in the Hex Trials whom they favour to win.'

I steal a sideways glance at Ember, whose mouth tilts upwards in answer, as if she also knows who he's talking about.

'What I mean by this is I and my mother –' he waves towards Queen Adela – 'are to give tokens out to a Raven we want to win, whom we deem *worthy* enough of a place in the Hex. This token is not to be taken lightly and can give you an advantage within the challenges.'

The prince walks further down the steps, coming to stand in front of my family, his midnight hair and dark blue eyes a contrast to our red features. I can feel a slight resistance as he closes the distance between us. Looking down, I see a familiar silvery line upon the floor. As I peer up again, I find the queen's gaze on me. *Her shield magic*, I realise. She is protecting her son without him realising it.

I'm nudged in the side by Blaze, whose expression tells me to pay attention. My frown doesn't go unnoticed as I try to show him the shield line. His eyes lower to where I'm trying to subtly point to, but he only looks away disinterested.

Can no one else see the queen's shields?

'I was taken by this particular person's bravery throughout the challenges, the strength and the power that was shown by her.' Prince Julien looks Ember dead in the eyes, his face expressionless as he hands over what was in his pocket. A necklace made of pure gold. 'You have impressed me beyond belief, Ember Seraphine. I wish for you to take this necklace and wear it for everyone to see. This is a claim that you are *my* champion. I wish for you to succeed in all the remaining trials and represent the House of Raven with pride and honour. Do you accept my token?'

The prince's hands hover in front of my sister, the piece of jewellery glinting in the light. Ember admires the rubies adorning it.

'Yes, Your Highness.' Ember beams. She turns her back on the prince and catches my gaze, giving me a smirk as the golden chain slides around her neck. Ember touches it tenderly, her smile growing wider than I've ever seen it before.

'Beautiful,' Prince Julian murmurs.

Faintly I can hear his heartbeat quicken. His interest in Ember is perhaps something more than professional, by the speed his pulse is racing at.

Slowly the prince moves away, unable to take his eyes off my sister. A smitten look comes over his face as he sits back on his throne, resting an ankle over his knee.

'We wish you all the best in the trials to come.' Queen Adela smiles, politely dismissing us. She gives her son's hand a quick pat as they are escorted out by several guards.

The moment they are out of the room, I hear breathing like my family members have been holding their breath the whole time. Everyone turns to Ember, whose hands still touch her new jewels in admiration.

'It's beautiful, Em. It really suits you,' I say in compliment, coming up beside her to look at her neck with approval. 'Makes you look like royalty.'

'It does, doesn't it?' Ember murmurs, looking ecstatic.

Guards shuffle us out of the throne room, and I watch as my mother fawns over the necklace. Blaze follows the females, pretending to add to their conversation, but I see a glint of envy in his features. Once more Ember has exceeded everyone's expectations and left him in the dust.

Their bubble of excitement is so loud that when a whisper sounds in my ear, they are none the wiser. 'Trust my brother to make an important moment look romantic. Did you see the way he looked at your sister?' Princess Leonore whispers, making me smirk in amusement.

'She'd eat him alive,' I answer, keeping to the back of our group. My family travels down a hallway with faded blue-and-green rugs that fit perfectly over the stone floor of the castle.

'Maybe when I present you as my champion, I'll have you wear a flower crown and give out chocolates to children in the street in a horse and carriage,' she muses, the laughter in her voice evident.

'I'd rather not.'

'Of course not. You'd rather blend into the background.'

'Nothing wrong with that,' I reply.

'I didn't say that, but that's no fun.'

I imagine the princess pouting, and I find myself trying to hide a grin.

'Thank you, by the way,' I say. 'My family got your little gift, and Roux is already drinking the tea. She tells me it tastes better than anything else she's tried before.'

'It's nothing.'

I shake my head. 'To you, it may be nothing, but to me, it means everything.'

'You are more than welcome, Scarlet.' We enter a

drawing room, the portal we arrived through earlier still crackling with life. 'Now, hurry along. Next time we meet, we'll have to think of a better way to announce you as my champion. We clearly have competition, and I don't want to turn down the opportunity to make my brother look like a fool.'

'And here I thought the royal family was too high and mighty for such devilment,' I claim, earning a mischievous laugh.

'Never. Being a princess only means I can get away with a great deal more.'

'That makes me feel so much better.'

'You should. You have the most powerful ally in your corner.'

'The most humble too,' I add.

'You'll appreciate it one day.'

A sliver of air caresses my temple, 'Take care, my champion.'

And with that, I feel her presence leave me as I step through the portal to the House of Raven.

29

R ubien is busy as I make my way to the Tea Shop, people filling the streets, holding bags of fresh food, and children playing games in between groups of wandering people.

Dimitri waits outside for me, hands in his pockets as he watches Matilda, the owner's daughter, completely engrossed in what the human girl is doing.

'Maybe one day you'll have the courage to ask her out,' I say, tapping him on the shoulder.

He turns and, as expected, gives me a pouty look. 'I'm happy with how things are now.'

Dimitri has reservations about a girl Matilda's age being interested in a being hundreds of years old. I think that no matter the age gap, he would treat her the way she deserves, and that's all that matters. But without Dimitri hinting at his affections for her, I know the girl will continue to have no clue how my friend really feels about her.

'You keep lying to yourself if it helps you stay awake at night,' I state, going inside to pick up our cakes.

He follows begrudgingly.

'Are you here to pick up your order?' Matilda asks in greeting as I approach the counter.

'Yes. We need a sugar fix to reward ourselves later. We're on our way to donate some blood, and this one is still not over his fear of needles.' I jerk a thumb behind me to where Dimitri stands quietly.

'Have you always been squeamish about them?' Matilda asks him, collecting our box of goodies and looking at him expectantly.

'Yes, unfortunately,' Dimitri replies, with a tight smile.

My unimpressed look when the girl turns her back on us doesn't go unnoticed. I wave my hands frantically, silently telling him *Really? Two words? That's all you've got?*

But his *mind your own business* glare, is enough for me to sigh and force a smile once Matilda faces us again.

'Well, I hope all goes well,' she offers, handing over our container of goodies before helping another customer.

I watch Dimitri's face, and it flickers with disappointment – maybe even a bit of regret. We leave the premises, earning a wave from Matilda before we hit the streets once more.

'If you want to pursue her in deep and meaningful conversation, Dimitri, simple answers aren't going to help,' I mutter, opening the cake box and looking at the beautifully decorated slices inside. My mouth waters looking at them.

'Thanks for the advice,' he deadpans. 'But if I need your help, I will ask.'

I scowl. 'Someone's in a mood.'

'Can you blame me?' he asks, motioning towards our destination in the distance.

'I'm only trying to help.' I peer up at the vampire, guilt beginning to bloom inside my chest. 'I want you to chase anything that will make you happy and if Matilda can offer that to you ...'

'I know,' he relents, peering down at me with a soft expression. 'I appreciate your concern.'

I scoff, 'No you don't, you're simply too much of a gentleman to tell me to fuck off.'

He tilts his head, a smile creeping along his handsome pale face. 'I would never say that to you.'

'But you want to?' I surmise, making him chuckle.

'No, never.'

'Now I *want* you to say it. I've never heard you curse before.'

'You don't need to curse at people when you have fangs the size of mine.'

It's my turn to laugh when he flashes me a big grin. 'I suppose you're right.'

Rubien's hospital is quite small in comparison to the healing clinic within the House of Raven. However, the doctors and nurses that work there are much nicer to converse with, having gotten used to me and Dimitri visiting every month.

We head for the back entrance and sign in, then follow the path we know off by heart to the donor wing.

'Back again so soon?' a nurse called Meela calls out as we enter the ward. 'Didn't get put off by the last visit?'

Dimitri grimaces at the memory. The last time we came to donate blood, we were given a trainee nurse. She dealt with me first and was doing really well until she attempted to find Dimitri's veins and messed up, too distracted by his looks to concentrate on what she was doing, and ended up getting flustered. Dimitri was so traumatised we ended up leaving without him giving a drop of blood, and we spent the rest of the day in the bookshop in hopes of calming him down.

I beam as if our last visit wasn't a disaster. 'No, not at all. I'm sure this time will be more pleasant.'

We're escorted to the room with a bed, and without instructions, we take our places automatically. Every month, Dimitri and I book ourselves in. The blood that flows through our bodies is full of healing properties that help the hospital with special cases. Of course, being partially a vampire, my blood isn't as strong as Dimitri's, but I visit more for moral support of my friend than to help the stocks of our high-demand blood.

'You brought cakes with you this time. Good idea!' Meela smiles, always warm and kind. She knows of Dimitri's fear of needles, so she usually gets him to lie down first. The first time he donated blood, he fainted and cracked his head open on the edge of a table.

Sitting beside him on the bed, I hold his hand like usual. In the beginning, he would fret that I was mothering him, but after his fall, he allowed it as long as no one mentioned it outside the room – Meela included.

The nurse prepares the vials, more than would be normal for a human if they were donating blood, but over the years, she's perfected the amount she can take from a vampire without making him feel light-headed or sick.

'Distract me,' Dimitri murmurs, and I oblige.

'So you know I have a guardian now,' I begin, earning a nod from him. His bright red eyes are pinned on me so he won't watch what Meela is doing. I stare back, leaning forward as if telling him a secret. 'I never told you who it was, but you've met him before.'

He frowns, brows creasing together in confusion. 'I have? Where?'

'Guess.'

He ponders for a moment before tilting his head. 'The Badger's Sett?'

I nod excitedly. 'Uh-huh.'

'Is he a friend of ours? A regular customer?'

'Nope.'

'A fighter?' He gapes, earning a smile in confirmation from me. 'Please tell me it's not the Pirate.'

'It's not the Pirate,' I confirm, imagining being paired up with the annoying, burly beast. I don't know if I could handle him on a daily basis.

'The Destroyer?' Dimitri guesses.

Meela pricks him with the needle, and he winces. I squeeze his hand, and he squeezes even harder back, his nails digging into my skin. I've become accustomed to hiding the pain, but with my still-healing burns, it hurts more than I remember from last time.

'Breathe,' I order, watching him carefully. He breathes in through his nose and out through his mouth a few times.

'You're doing so well,' Meela says in praise, patting his shoulder before removing the first full vial of blood.

'Not the Destroyer. Think of a fighter who is newer in Storm's little collection of soldiers.' I squeeze his hand in a random pattern to keep his mind off the needle poking out of his arm. He in turn repeats the pattern back in an attempt to focus solely on me.

'No.' He grins in a way I know is forced, anxiety still etched on his face. 'You got paired up with the *Teacher*?' The smirk that spreads across my face makes him chuckle. 'That's hilarious, and here you were wondering what he looks like underneath that mask, and he walks straight into your life without it on. Classic.'

'You can't tell anyone, though. He doesn't know I have unravelled his identity.'

Dimitri blinks. 'You haven't confessed to knowing him already? And he hasn't told you about it either?'

'Not yet. I want to wait it out to see how he acts and if he'll mention his alter ego.' I shrug with a smug look.

Dimitri's smile turns more genuine as he seems to forget about Meela temporarily. 'You sly girl. Will you tell him about *your* other identity?' he asks, leaning his head back on the pillow and looking down his nose at me.

'I mean, I don't think so, not until it's completely necessary.'

Dimitri looks thoughtful before nodding in agreement. 'You hardly know him, so it's probably for the best. Until we know he's trustworthy, we should keep it discreet.'

'We?' I scoff.

'Well, I'm part of Team Scarlet, so if he's being added to the group, he's also *my* problem.' He winks, making me beam.

'We should get matching uniforms,' I muse, stroking my chin in thought. 'Perhaps something in purple. I look good in purple.'

'But purple clashes with red.' He motions to our eyes. 'We should do black.'

Meela removes the needle finally. He sighs with relief knowing his monthly good deed is over.

'But you always wear black,' I protest, motioning to his sable attire.

'And don't I look dashing?' he counters, making Meela and me chuckle as I take his place on the bed.

I've never fainted before, but I never complain about having a moment to put my feet up.

'You're all right, I suppose,' I say, my mind suddenly conjuring up the image of Jack in a dark uniform, his body the portrayal of strength and power. I bite my lip unconsciously before the needle pokes into my skin. The stinging sensation expels all lovely thoughts of my guardian in seconds. I lean back and try to think of anything but him.

30

Day one of training together, and I meet Jack at the tunnel that separates the Ravens and humans, the place where fresh air and heat mix.

His hair is messy, and the smell of sweat lingers on him. I wrinkle my nose.

'You didn't even bother to bathe for me. I'm offended,' I say as he approaches.

Jack smiles warmly, his ocean scent wrapping around me as he closes the distance between us. 'I just finished some training,' he answers with a shrug. I imagine him fully covered up in his costume as the Teacher, fighting in the Badger's Sett. I smirk, wondering if I can somehow bring the topic up. 'Thought there wasn't much point if we were training some more. I deemed a fresh shirt would be enough.'

We walk side by side as I lead him through the House of Raven, the lava rivers making his silver-blonde hair shine faintly orange.

'Well, about that ...' I trail off, meeting his blue gaze.

'Uh-oh. That doesn't sound good.'

Challengers in the Hex Trials have been given special

permission to bring their guardians into the Raven side of the cave, but I don't trust anyone. In our House, Jack is my responsibility, so I'll keep him safe in the few places I know we won't find trouble.

'I promise we *will* train, but I have to do some things first,' I say, leading him over a stone bridge, the lava below bubbling intimidatingly. He pauses to take it all in, the scenery here so different from Rubien. Already I can see a faint layer of perspiration along his neck from the muffling heat, something the human city doesn't have.

'Some things as in …' He quirks a brow as if insinuating something, and I chuckle.

'I have a bit of work I have to finish off. I've fallen behind lately, with the trials, but you can potter around in the meantime.'

'You're letting me have free rein here?' he asks, eyes bright with delight.

Shaking my head, I scoff, 'Holy Hanrah, no! You're not allowed anywhere within our House without me beside you. This place is not Rubien. The Ravens will take advantage if they see the opportunity, and the moment you turn your back, you'll be a target.'

When we arrive at the barn, Jack watches as I unlock the doors. This is the number one place I feel comfortable bringing him to, and the only place I feel we can train in safely.

'Stables,' Jack says with surprise. 'This is not what I expected of you.'

'And what did you expect?' I open the barn doors wide, leaving them spread apart for the horses to enjoy the outside world while I work.

'A dungeon of weapons?'

My laughter echoes through the barn, and horses nicker

in answer. 'Hardly. The only weapons I have around here are broomsticks and stirrups.'

Jack walks to the first horse on his left. His hand hovers in mid-air to let the creature take a sniff before he strokes her nose affectionately. A little part of me swoons at the fact he likes animals.

'I hear you have a giant arena here,' Jack says, his hands roaming over the mare's neck.

I grab him, spin his body and point to the large building across from the stables, lava around its perimeter. The structure was one of the first to be built when the House of Raven was created.

'The arena is full of fighters. I don't think it's a good idea going in there. I've only seen the inside a handful of times, and it's intimidating.' I head for the tack room, where cleaning supplies live. 'I have chores to do. Do you want a bucket to sit on while I work?' I motion to put one outside the barn doors. That way, I can keep an eye on him.

'I'll help you,' Jack insists.

My look is questioning. 'Really?' I ask, receiving a nod in answer.

It doesn't take long for us to get into our rhythms. While I empty the stalls of horses and replace the dirty straw, Jack sits on an upside-down bucket, polishing riding boots and cleaning bridles. I try not to stop and stare as he works, but every so often, I find myself mid-movement looking in his direction, engrossed in his human quirks.

'Why are you different from the other Ravens?' Jack asks out of the blue, making me jump slightly. The bucket by my feet threatens to topple over. I grab it before any horse shit goes flying.

'Really? *That* is your first question?'

'Your leader specifically said to know our advantages

and disadvantages. I'm trying to figure out what to cate-gorise your difference as,' he answers curtly.

His thought process makes me lift a brow in surprise. 'Yes, I'm different,' I murmur, refilling a bucket of food. 'I'm what they call a half-blood. Half raven and half human.'

'I figured as much.' Jack nods before dragging a hand through his hair, a large black strip coating his locks. His gaze roams over me, taking in my darker hair, the rake I hold and the outfit I wear. 'I assume you didn't know your mother was in the Hex. I'm sorry if I overstepped. I didn't mean to upset you before.'

My heart stutters, but I continue to place a fresh load of straw in the stall I stand within, spreading it evenly throughout. 'It wasn't your fault. No one told me, and I went into shock, but I'm fine now.'

Jack stands from his bucket and approaches me, his face scrunched up in thought. 'Are you, though?' He pauses, rubbing his hands together, feeling the black stains on them. 'It takes time to absorb news that big.'

With him leaning against the stall gate, I can't help taking him in. My eyes drop towards his chest, his shirt tight across his body as he crosses his arms. I look away and continue to work, pretending I'm immune to the view. He is my guardian now, I shouldn't be feeling *any* kind of way towards him.

'Yes, I'm fine,' I insist.

Dismissed, he walks away, heading out to get a fresh load of straw for me. Once he returns, Jack starts covering the floor with it while I carry the stale load out.

'Finally,' I say, studying the finished stall.

Exiting, I walk to the horse who patiently waits outside. The mare nuzzles me as I bring her into her newly cleaned pen, becoming a pain when I want to close the door on her.

From behind, Jack reaches around me to stroke the

mare's nose, distracting the creature while I close the door. His chest is so close to my back I feel my cheeks flush with heat.

'She's a good girl,' Jack murmurs, oblivious to the butterflies in my stomach. 'What's her name?'

'Torment,' I offer.

'Bit of a morbid name, isn't it? She seems too sweet for such a name.'

'Unfortunately, I don't get to pick their names,' I reply, walking around him. My mind feels instantly clearer with the distance between us.

I aim for the next horse, Misery – a perfectly ghastly name – and take him outside.

'Okay. What are your weaknesses?' I ask, needing to distract myself.

He makes his way back to his bucket and picks up a boot. 'Attractive women?' He winks, letting me know he's joking, and I can't help smiling.

'Ha ha, very funny. Are all you humans so full of horse-shit?' I ask innocently, holding up my rake of poo for emphasis.

'Ouch!'

Dropping the manure into a large bucket, I wait for Jack's real answer. So much time passes that I end up looking around and finding him staring at me. I clear my throat in an attempt to hurry him up.

'I don't know what weaknesses I have. I don't think people really know until something tests them, but I can tell you I'm not strong with all weapons,' he admits, putting up a finger. 'Unless you're talking about archery – I'm rather fantastic at that.'

I nod as he keeps counting.

'I can't run as fast as some of the other guys either,' he continues, holding up a second finger. 'And I guess I'm a sucker when it comes to kids. They get me every time. I just can't say no.' He shrugs as if this answer is sufficient.

'I was thinking more like ...' I wave my hand in the air, trying to find the right word. 'Do you have a weaker left knee or a part of your body you have to defend more? Or do you have a tragic flaw that could be your undoing?'

'My body is in excellent shape because of training,' Jack answers matter-of-factly, polishing the boot. 'And if sarcasm and kindness could be classed as tragic flaws, then I'll choose them as my undoing,' he declares with a grin.

After wiping his hands with a rag, Jack moves on to cleaning the bridles that hang up in the tack room. They hang neatly in a line across the wall, the only evidence of my organisational habits.

'I don't think it works like that, but good to know. So what training do you do? And where do you even go for something like that?' I'm baiting him, wondering if he will mention the Badger's Sett. As the Teacher, he knows that I visit the establishment, but as Jack, he shouldn't.

'I go to a boxing place that lets me train. Some friends and I have been going for a while, so we get together regularly to practise.'

Discreetly I look him up and down. He has the body of a boxer, as he's mentioned, his muscled arms and extremely toned legs on show. I ponder whether he dresses as the Teacher when he is with his friends.

'The only place I know of is the Badger's Sett. It's not near there by any chance?' I ask, filling a tub with horse feed.

Indecision coats his features, and I know instantly he's deciding whether to admit he goes there or not. 'Yes, that's one of the places I go.' He smiles, making me hide a grin.

'I visit there sometimes to train with Dimitri or to watch the fights. They're great entertainment,' I say, observing his body language as he wipes his face with the crook of his arm.

Somehow Jack smears a line of black polish across his forehead and temple. I shake my head with amusement. I find a rag, approach him and kneel before him. He freezes in place as I wipe at his face, then his hair. Our eyes meet, my heart racing with the realisation of how close we are right now. Seeing the black come away on the rag, Jack looks amused but doesn't say anything. He only stares at me.

'We should train there,' I blurt, leaning away before temptation makes me do something foolish. 'It'll be safer, for one, and I know the owner, Storm. We could watch a fight sometime too. I really want to watch the Teacher. He's a new fighter everyone's raving about.' I'm still kneeling, but I'm in the perfect position to study his face as it shifts.

My guardian's heart rate accelerates but his voice is steady. 'Yeah, he's pretty good.'

'You've seen him in action? What's he like?' I ask, leaning forward as if eager to hear what Jack has to say. He swallows thickly before waving a hand.

'Oh, you know …'

I eye him closer.

'He's fast,' Jack eventually says.

'That's it?'

'And skilled when it comes to weaponry.'

'Anything else?' I probe. If I can figure out what skills the Teacher has, it'll help me learn more about Jack.

'Um, he's very intelligent.'

'Intelligent, huh? I heard he got trounced by the Phoenix.' I grin.

'He's new.' Jack shrugs. 'He's got to lose sometime, or he won't learn.'

I smirk, thinking back to when the Teacher and I first met. 'He told me that he calls himself the Teacher to teach people a lesson. I think the Phoenix was the one giving out lessons that night.' I stand up with a laugh, and I wander back to the stall, grabbing Misery on the way. I pull the stallion back inside before taking the next horse out of his stall to clean it. I notice Jack's frown out of the corner of my eye.

'You've met the Teacher?' he asks.

Change of subject, I note. *Interesting.*

'Once or twice.' When I turn for my rake, Jack is right there, blue eyes so close my breath hitches.

'What did you think of him?'

My mouth tugs up of its own accord, making Jack grin playfully.

'Oh, is that a blush across your cheeks?'

I don't dare react, refraining from reaching for my now burning face. I narrow my eyes at him and think of the parallels of this happening with the Teacher. *Bastard.*

'Get back to work,' I utter, getting frustrated.

'I'm sure you're not the only girl who is fawning over him. I've heard he has a long list of admirers.'

My hands sit on my hips as I tilt my head. 'I am not *fawning* over him.'

'Looks like you are. Your pupils are dilating, which usually means someone's in love.'

My body stiffens. *Love?*

I wouldn't label my interest in him as *love*, more like fascination, perhaps infatuation that will eventually pass now I know the face beneath the mask.

I scoff, 'Yeah, right. I'm in love with the *Teacher*. That's hilarious.'

Jack's smug look annoys me, and it spurs me back to work, ignoring his jibes. I was supposed to be messing with *him*, not the other way around.

Two more stalls are done before he speaks up, and

thankfully, it's unrelated to his alter ego. 'What do you want to do with your life, Scarlet?'

I pause. What a heavy question.

'Win the Hex Trials,' I murmur, because that's the first thing that pops into my head that makes sense.

'That's it? You don't want to help people or go travelling, perhaps? The Hex Trials are all you live for right now?'

Sighing, I peer over the stall door and discard my rake. 'Winning will help a lot of things in my life right now. So that is my only focus. Nothing else matters.' I nibble my bottom lip in thought, and he lets me have the silence for a moment, as if sensing I have more to say. 'What do *you* want to do with your life?' I ask, hoping to get the topic off myself.

'To be your guardian, of course,' he answers without hesitation.

My eyes narrow as I observe him. He cleans his hands, which are stained with dark splotches, his nail beds full of gunk. He could have walked away the moment I announced I needed to finish work, but here he is, keeping me company, eager to finish the job.

'Why do you want to be a guardian so badly? Don't you know the risks?' I can't help but ask. I wonder if Jack would still be as eager to fight by my side if he had been present at my last trial.

'Isn't the risk what makes it rewarding?' he counters, looking more serious, his easy demeanour gone. 'If it were meant to be easy, everyone would be a guardian.'

I don't answer, thinking over his words. For me, the trials aren't a choice. I don't get a say in my future. But for Jack, they are the opposite – they are an opportunity, and one he's grasping tightly with both hands.

He takes my silence as permission to continue, blowing a strand of stray hair out of his face. 'Have you ever felt that you never quite belonged? That something about you made everyone treat you a certain way?'

'Every day,' I admit.

'My mother joined the Hex when I was small. Everything she told me sounded like something I wanted – something I *needed*. I knew from an early age I wanted to be a guardian and help people from all across the lands.'

'If you want to help people, why not become a healer, or if you don't have healing magic, a nurse?'

Ravens who fight for a living usually die young. Jack can fight, I've seen that first-hand, but even I have brushed hands with death since the beginning of these trials. What makes him any less likely to face such a fate?

He shakes his head. 'For a long time, it was just me and my dad,' Jack explains, replacing a bridle on its hook on the wall. Taking a moment before he reaches for another, my guardian stretches out the kinks in his body, muscles rippling with the movement.

I squint at him with annoyance, wondering if he's doing it on purpose.

'But when my father died, I felt like I wasn't living to my fullest potential. He always told me I could conquer any obstacle, that my sense of justice was my biggest strength. He never doubted I could be the next guardian to the Raven of the Hex, and I promised him I would work my hardest to make the dream come true.'

'You want to keep a promise to your father,' I state, earning a nod. I understand the sentiment but wonder if Jack's father knew of the risks and dangers of such a career.

'My mother was the first-ever guardian, and she's away a lot. I've seen her a handful of times in the last few years, but she's been my idol for as long as I can remember ...' He trails off, seeming deep in thought.

I watch as the tips of his ears begin to turn pink. The

quick change of his scent makes me blink. The smell of his embarrassment is nothing I've encountered before.

'Sorry. I didn't mean to load my problems on you,' Jack says hastily, fiddling with the black-stained rag he holds.

A glimmer of affection for the dameer boy swells in my chest. To be so open and vulnerable, to have such dedication and devotion to his family, it's highly attractive.

'I'm not used to such ...' I try to find the right word to ease his awkwardness.

'Confessions?' he finishes for me with a wary look.

I step out of the stall, reach for his forearm and give it a warm squeeze. I realise he is waiting for my judgement, or for me to belittle his dream.

'I was going to say "openness". Your honesty is refreshing. You'll learn quickly that here in the House of Raven, people don't always say what they mean.'

'Well, I can promise I'll always be hon—' He stops, and I quirk a brow.

He was going to say honest, I realise.

He can't finish that sentence, because he's already lied to me.

I study his face and tilt my head. 'You don't need to make any more promises to anyone. Let's just try and fulfil the one to your father first and win these trials,' I offer, earning a relieved nod from him.

'Do you think we can do it? Win, I mean.' Jack's heart beats a little faster, and I find myself wanting to touch his chest to feel it for myself.

Studying him, I find his strength combined with his unguarded nature charming. How could someone be so many things at once?

I smile warmly, hoping my words sound truthful. 'With a mindset like yours, we can do anything.'

31

I 'm waiting in the grounds of Songbird Castle with Merlot and her guardian, Mercy. Mercy is a pretty Hanrae girl whose ability to talk to animals makes me envious.

'You don't have to wait, guys. You can start warming up,' I assure them both, the pair nice enough to stay with me while I wait for Jack to rock up.

'You sure?' Merlot asks.

'We don't mind,' Mercy adds.

'Yeah. He'll be here any minute. I'm sure of it.'

They finally relent, and I watch the duo choose a circle that's been reserved for training sessions. The other Ravens in attendance, my sister included, train with their guardians, and I hate to admit it, but the humans look pretty good.

'What are you doing slacking off so early on?' I hear from behind me.

My frown is on full display when I turn. Jack stands with a hand on his hip, motioning to me where I'm sitting down.

'Waiting for an unpunctual guardian,' I quip, letting him know how irritated I am with my tone.

His mouth twists as he kneels down beside me, his hands out as if to reassure me. 'I'm sorry. I got caught up doing something and lost track of time. I'll make it up to you.'

I quirk a brow still scowling. 'Will you?'

'Yes,' he promises. 'Shall we?' He waves towards a training circle near Merlot, who gives me a thumbs-up. 'Friend of yours?' Jack asks, and I nod briefly, still annoyed with him.

'Okay. How much do you already know?' I query as we step inside the ring.

'A fair bit,' he admits with a shrug.

Of course, I know this is not true, having fought him myself. He knows much more than he is letting on. I push his shoulder roughly, and he staggers back slightly.

'I know you're angry with me, but—'

'When you fight, you need to focus. The moment you are distracted is the moment it could all be over,' I interrupt, kicking his feet into a wider stance. 'Your body needs stability *and* flexibility. If I push you, it shouldn't affect you.' I push his shoulder again, and he doesn't budge. 'Good. Now, if I hit harder, you will move and recover in one fluid motion. Think like a cat, elegant and always landing on your feet.'

Shoving him harder this time, I make sure to be slightly quicker. I'm aware he's going to be fine. His reflexes, as expected, are on high alert now he knows I'm not in the mood for small talk. I go on the offence, and his hand snakes out, but as I'm distracting him with my hands, I curl my foot around his ankle and pull hard.

He begins to topple over, but I grab the front of his shirt, and I watch with amusement as he flails his arms before grabbing my wrist – the one anchor preventing him from falling onto his back.

'If you're tardy again, I won't be so easy on you,' I purr, noting his mischievous look.

'And if you're moody, I'll have to try harder to earn that pretty smile back.'

He wrenches my wrist down, and I swing downwards, unprepared. When I'm near to falling on my face, his hand comes from behind and wraps around my neck. He forces me upwards and against his chest.

'Hmm, it seems you're letting your feelings get the better of you today, Raven.'

Unable to see his face, I roll my eyes, my back feeling the warmth of his chest. Without thinking, I reach backwards and let my hand trail down his leg. A gust of his breath tickles the back of my neck, and I smirk at his body's response.

'Don't distract me, woman,' he mutters, but he doesn't protest.

Before I can reach any part of him that would bring pleasure, I elbow him – hard. He groans, and I spin on him, forcing my feelings down and remembering we are here to warm up, not fight out our feelings. Doing that will cause slip-ups, and I don't want any of those.

We spar, his own training coming into play, his body reacting well to my speed and strength, which he now seems to realise surpasses his. I jab him in different areas, his arms up in defence as he blocks my attacks. The more I strike out, the faster he springs back, ready for more. His body is somehow graceful as he dodges and ducks, diving away and blocking my hands and feet.

'Good,' I say occasionally, not wanting to feed his ego too much.

When I feel he is starting to pant heavily, I slow it down until we eventually come to a stop.

Other Ravens have water breaks, and I offer to get us both a drink. Coming back, I feel Jack's gaze on me.

'What are you staring at?' I ask.

Jack grins as he reaches over to me and gently tugs on a strand of my hair, accepting the water graciously. He swallows the whole cup, and I offer him my own drink, not really needing it myself.

'I didn't know how good you are at fighting.' He shrugs.

'That wasn't fighting; that was warming up,' I quip, making his smile appear once more.

'Now I know how mouthy you are when irritated, I'll take my time coming to training more often.'

I swat his arm, and his laugh echoes across the grounds. A few people turn towards the sound. It's only when a hand slithers over Jack's shoulder that he stops.

The hand belongs to Winella, the girl who, along with her friend Carmine, started the fight that ended up with me getting punished by the Elder Raven. My frown doesn't go unnoticed by my guardian.

'Good morning,' Winella purrs, admiring Jack's physique. She seems impressed and maybe a little jealous. 'I couldn't help but admire your fighting skills. You are very well trained for a human.' She smiles warmly, and Jack mirrors her hesitantly. They exchange a handshake, and I refrain from dragging him away. 'You're Jack, aren't you? It's a pleasure to meet you. I'm Winella, and that over there is my guardian, Everett.' She motions briefly to a buff older man with tattooed arms who is currently conversing with another guardian by the water fountain. He reminds me instantly of the Pirate, their physiques very similar.

'What do you want, Winella?' I ask, making it obvious I want her to leave.

The female glances between me and Jack with bright red eyes that shimmer with trouble. I make sure not to move, knowing that if I shift closer to Jack, the subtle message of protectiveness would only challenge her to advance.

Winella circles us. 'Oh, I came to check up on you both. I heard about the Elder Raven's punishment. It must have really *hurt*.' She displays her fangs as she slowly grins.

Jack faces me with a questioning look. I don't bother explaining to him what she means.

'We've got to finish warming up. Perhaps we can converse some other time,' I suggest curtly.

'Don't disregard me as—'

A bell chimes as several royal guards approach, requesting us to come inside the great hall. Without hesitation, I grab Jack and drag him away from Winella, her face showing frustration that she didn't get to carry out whatever wicked plan she had in mind.

Inside, the hanging ladders, climbing walls and all the training equipment are still there, but the floor area is cleared of everything except a few rows of tables. We are greeted by the Elder Raven, who stands among the desks. The royals are sitting upon their thrones on the dais, speaking quietly as we enter from warm-up.

'Come in, come in. Grab a seat,' our Elder shouts, waving us to certain tables to hurry the group along. 'We have been through much already but have a long road ahead of us before we find our worthy Raven.'

The sound of shuffling continues as we find seats. Merlot and Mercy sit next to us, and Ember is sat at the front somewhere.

'Today we are testing our teams on their ability to make decisions together.' The Elder Raven looks across the room to some guards before signalling. They create a flurry of movement around the tables as racks of test tubes are handed out to each pair.

I peer closer, and at first glance, they all seem identical, crimson in colour and fairly liquid in consistency. Jack and I share a questioning look.

'Today we want to assess you on your abilities with toxins. In this little test, you have been given a number of substances, and your mission is to find which one is harmless. However ...' The Elder Raven pauses, revelling in the silence.

Here we go, I think.

'The vial you deem harmless must be tested on your Raven. So choose wisely – your lives are at stake.' Our Elder smiles, showing her fangs with silent joy.

The rack before us makes me gulp. I've never been great at identifying poisons. Dimitri has taught me what signs to look for if I ever thought my food had been laced, but the tubes all look the same, and my doubt starts to creep in.

'You may start. Extra points will go to those who finish quicker, and points will be deducted from those who end up being the slowest,' the Elder Raven states, pointing to the chalkboard. Our guardians' names have now been added to the list – those who weren't chosen by a human have been crossed off the list completely.

Guards roam around the tables, making sure teams aren't conferring, while the prince stands up and begins to make his way around the teams, watching for any cheating, no doubt.

Jack lightly grabs the rack that holds five tubes full of red liquid. He chooses the vial closest to him and swirls it before he puts the vial near his nose and inhales gently. 'Thick consistency, and is that lavender?'

He lets me take a sniff. 'Yeah, that's lavender,' I confirm.

I watch him as he carries on swirling the concoction, his

mind busy identifying the substance. 'This is the poison called Noose 003, known to be a non-lethal poison, but it blinds the victim for life,' he states matter-of-factly before putting it back in the rack.

He picks the second tube up, repeating his process. 'Again thick consistency. Is this one the exact same shade as the one before?'

Picking them up together, letting the bright lights seep through behind them, I check them – my eyes are better than Jack's. 'The first is slightly lighter, but not by much.'

'And with no scent at all.' His mouth pulls downwards.

He isn't sure of that one because it smells of magic, I think.

'Next one,' I instruct, making sure he doesn't dwell on the second.

He does as he's told, swirling and smelling the third.

'This one is citrusy, but I'm not sure what type.' He hands it over, a silent command to take a whiff.

'Lime, orange and a hint of raspberries,' I declare, making him nod thankfully.

'That means we have one that causes blindness,' he says, pointing to the first tube.

I nod, knowing that one is correct.

'Something I'm not quite sure of,' he admits, pointing to the second vial. 'And this one is Noose 533, made to close the throat up, causing the victim to suffocate in minutes.'

I cock a brow, impressed by his knowledge and glad he's so educated, because I don't have much faith that I'd make it through today without him.

'You have a significant amount of knowledge on poisons,' I say, noticing his leg jiggling up and down – probably with nerves.

'You sound surprised.'

'Well, yes. Why would you need it? Surely it's not *that* bad in Rubien city.' My wink makes him smile, even though it's slightly forced. His nerves are growing more intense the longer we sit here, and I can't figure out a way to help him other than trying to ease the tension.

'I dabble because my mum said it would be useful.' He smells the fourth substance before handing it over to me with a shrug.

'Jasmine, turmeric and raisins,' I say, grimacing. Its scent is extremely potent.

'Raisins aren't a normal ingredient in poisons,' Jack declares, making me nod in agreement.

'No, but that could be just to throw us off.' I lean in to smell the substance again, Jack tilting it slightly towards me. 'And this vial is diluted with water.'

'Diluted to trick us somehow?' he asks.

'It could just mean it's concealing something. Either way, I'm pretty sure it's poisonous, so let's move on.'

Jack doesn't question my theory, nodding in agreement.

The last vial is the lightest shade of red, although still similar in appearance to the others. So far I know that all the substances have been poisonous except concoction number two.

'This is a strange one,' Jack remarks. He sniffs the final vial, then hands it over. 'Does it smell like smoke somehow?'

'Yes, it does.'

He seems to notice my lack of participation. 'Do you know what it is?'

'No. I'm terrible at poisons.'

Jack's face drops, and I realise I've put an immense amount of pressure on him to keep me alive. What started out as a normal day training has turned into a morning trying to keep me from keeling over and losing us the trials.

'You're kidding, right?' he asks.

'I wish I were. The last time I was tested on poisons, I

was sick for a full week.' I grimace, thinking back to when I consumed belladonna and had to recover from a fever and hallucinations. I beat Dimitri up when I felt better, and to my relief, we never tried his way of testing toxins again.

'What if I kill you?' Jack frowns, voice low but slightly frantic.

'Well, we've narrowed it down, haven't we?' I say, keeping my voice calm and smiling like we're going to be fine. 'Number two and number five. That's all we have to figure out now.'

A loud thump sounds beside us. A dead Raven has rolled off her chair onto the floor. I look her over and wince.

'That's not good.' Jack grimaces, looking away quickly. His eyes close as if to remove the image from his mind as he refocuses on the task before us.

'It seems they were wrong in their assumptions,' I agree, peering down to find my scar bubbling with crimson blood. Quickly I hide it away so Jack can't see it. We have enough on our plate right now.

Another body behind us gurgles with obvious pain, the scraping of nails against the table echoing through my head. All around, several bodies drop dead from different causes, and Jack's heart rate shoots through the roof, my own mirroring his.

'Tick-tock!' the Elder Raven shouts, making me jump.

'Pick one, Jack,' I urge, grabbing for the two remaining substances we've yet to identify and lifting them between us, my blood dripping into my sleeve. 'Which one do I drink?'

'I think it's this one.' Jack motions to the fifth vial, jaw tensing.

'Time is running out. Which one are you drinking?' a nearby guard asks, motioning for me to drink something.

Some Ravens have drunk their tubes without harm and

now sit patiently for the trial to end. Merlot is one of them, and she nods encouragingly. *You got this.*

'I'm drinking this one,' I say, lifting up number five. Slowly I bring it to my lips, but Jack swipes it away before smelling it again. He takes number two and sniffs that as well.

'It's number two,' he blurts, shoving that one into my hand instead.

'Are you sure?' I study the new vial before turning to him.

'Um, yeah.' But he doesn't sound convinced.

I lift the tube between us, hoping I sound confident in his decision. 'Here's to living another day.'

Jack winces but nods.

I swallow the liquid and wait.

At first I think I can feel a heat in my chest, and I think back to the Elder Raven. Finding her in the crowd, I see she's not paying attention to me or anyone near me, so it mustn't be her magic.

'How do you feel?' Jack asks, hand briefly touching my knee as if that will fix whatever goes downhill from here.

I wait a few more moments and nod hesitantly, my scar slowly closing back up. 'I think I'm fine. It gave me a warm feeling here,' I reply, rubbing my chest.

'Wine.' Jack sighs, head bowing as a long relieved breath escapes him.

'Well done. That's twenty points next to your names,' a guard announces.

Taking in the hall, I note how many Ravens lie motionless, how many guardians are distressed or angry for losing a supposedly simple task.

Searching the tables, I finally find my sister talking quietly to her guardian, both unharmed. I exhale my unease.

The royals watch on, unfazed by the bodies piling up in their home, but what terrifies me most is the look I find upon the Elder Raven's face.

Now staring straight at me from across the room, she looks angry – no, full of rage. Her hateful eyes pin me down, letting me know she's disappointed I'm still breathing, that she gave us all poisons hoping to get rid of *me*.

'What's wrong?' Jack asks, hand across the back of my chair.

Averting my gaze from the Elder Raven, I focus on him, smiling softly. 'Nothing. I'm just glad this test is over.'

He nods in agreement before helping a guard clean up our rack of poisons.

If my prediction is correct, the Elder Raven will double her efforts to get what she wants most of all. A dead half-blood.

32

The great hall is emptied of everyone, the group of Ravens trickling out into the castle grounds once more as the bodies are collected.

'I'm glad to see you in one piece,' Ember says by way of greeting, eyeing up Jack.

I lift a brow, wondering why she's making an effort to talk to me today when usually she ignores me.

'You too.' I reach my hand out to the human male beside my sister. 'Hi there. I'm Scarlet, Ember's little sister,' I say before motioning beside me. 'And this is my guardian, Jack.'

Ember's guardian, once given a nod of approval from my sister, hesitantly takes my hand. His is clammy, and I refrain from wiping it on my trouser leg once he lets go. 'Taylor,' he replies with a smile that seems strained.

'How did you both go, then?'

'I drank a vial of red wine.' Ember shrugs easily, unlike her guardian, whose hands wring together. 'Not that *this one* knew much about poisons.' She gives Taylor a disapproving look.

Opening his mouth, Taylor turns to answer, but I notice

a sore-looking patch behind his ear. Ember's initials are scorched there, for everyone to see, looking horribly painful.

'Holy Hanrah! What is *that*?' I cry, leaning closer to take a better look, but Taylor jumps back in alarm at the sudden close proximity. Wincing at his reaction, I step away immediately, bumping into Jack. His hands steady me. 'Don't tell me you *branded* him, Ember.' My glare doesn't intimidate my sister. She merely shrugs.

'What's wrong with that? I don't want others thinking he is here for sharing.' Ember's face shows no remorse but rather confusion at my reaction.

Shaking my head in disgust, I wonder how she can do such a thing. Then I realise this is Ember I'm talking to. 'He's not your property.'

'He is. If someone touches him, they will have *me* to deal with. It's for his own protection – something I suggest you consider. If you need me to do it, I'll lend a helping hand,' she declares, scrutinising Jack.

My guardian glares back, unyielding as my sister steps closer.

'What power do you possess, human?' Ember asks.

'None of your business,' Jack retorts, crossing his arms defensively.

Ember laughs, but it doesn't sound like she's amused. Rather, she sounds vexed that he would defy her. 'Arrogance will get you nowhere.'

'Neither will being a snake,' Jack snaps.

Fire roars to life, and my sister becomes a human torch, her eyes blazing with fury.

My first instinct is to run, to drop to the ground and cover my head. 'Holy Hanrah!' I squeal, images of being consumed by fire again racking my body with fear. Arms wrap around me, and they pull me away, lifting me off the ground to widen the distance between me and my sister.

Looking back in horror, I watch as a gallon of water douses Ember, a heavy ball of it that comes out of nowhere, soaking her through so she looks like a drowned cat.

Feeling the arms around me shaking, I peer up at my guardian, who still holds me, his body vibrating with silent laughter. Jack looks unsurprised, eyes glowing bright blue and the smell of ocean potent on his now cold skin.

His magic, I realise. He's a water elemental.

Pursing my lips to stop myself gaping, I take in my sister, who coughs and splutters. Taylor looks surprised but also slightly amused. The sight of my sister being held accountable for her words brings me so much joy. I etch it into my memory so I'll never forget it.

'You never seem to understand, Scarlet,' Ember snarls. 'You are weak-hearted. You don't know what it's like to do the hard stuff. To fight to remain on top.' Her eyes flash, never leaving Jack's face.

I move subtly in front of him, his fingers wrapping around my elbow in answer.

It's almost laughable to have Ember, of all people, say I can't understand hardship. For as long as I can remember, I've been fighting extra hard for money to help Ruby put food on the table. I've been trying to survive everyday to stop myself from being punished or killed by another Raven simply because of *what* I am. As well as currently risking my life to save Roux and her babies, and yet all Ember can see is my guardian. An obstacle, in her eyes, not the very person who could *help* our family.

'I understand well enough, Ember. You're letting these trials and tests go to your head. This isn't a move to gain power; it's a trial to teach us *unity*. How can you be a team if your guardian is afraid of you?' I ask, motioning to Taylor, who becomes tense from the sudden attention. 'Perhaps think about how you are both going to cope in the outside world if he is constantly living in fear of what you'll do to him if he messes up.'

I leave Ember to think her words through as I pull Jack away in search of Merlot. We walk in silence, my anger and revulsion churning in my stomach.

'Hey.' Jack stops me, placing his hand on my shoulder. 'I wouldn't have let her hurt you.'

'It's not *me* I was worried about.'

He looks down at me with a thoughtful look. 'And here I was hoping to protect you.'

Rolling my eyes, I dismiss the insinuation of his comment. 'What was that magic?' I blurt, refraining from looking into his ocean-blue eyes. He shrugs self-consciously.

'Water?' he replies, like it's not a big deal.

'I gathered that,' I mutter, stomping away, making my way around the group of Ravens.

'Did I embarrass you?'

I spin, and he nearly bumps into me, so close our hands go out to steady one another.

'Embarrass me? What? No.' I shake my head, a laugh escaping my lips as I remember the look on Ember's face. 'You were *incredible*, Jack, but also incredibly foolish. Ember won't forget what you said to her.'

'And I won't forget what she said to me,' he answers defiantly.

Searching his face, I try to find even a sliver of fear, but I see none. 'You really aren't concerned? She's one of the strongest Ravens here, and you're most likely on the top of her list of targets now.'

He scoffs, 'Strongest?'

'Haven't you seen the leader board? Ember is in the top

three. She could burn you alive.' My frustration is growing with his lack of understanding, or rather, his lack of seriousness at the situation. 'She will *hurt* you, Jack. She won't care if you're with me; she will take down anyone who gets in her way.'

'Did *you* get in her way?' he asks, voice low.

I follow where his eyes land. He takes my hand and lifts the sleeve of my shirt up, exposing the burnt skin underneath. I pull away, but he won't let me, placing a cool hand around my mutilated wrist.

'No. She'd never do this to me,' I say, but the moment the words leave my mouth, I'm not sure I believe the statement.

From the look on Jack's face, I think he realises it too. He's silent as he releases me. It's suddenly tense, and I hate it.

'Let's find Merlot. I think we all deserve a feast,' I say, earning a nod from him.

33

Merlot and I stop in front of a large building called the Silver Snake Tavern. Neither of us has been here before — on the outside, it's slightly older-looking, its windows dark and dingy, but the place is full of noise on the inside.

'It has character,' Merlot says, unconvinced.

'The people won't judge you both for being here,' Jack insists.

'And the food is great,' Mercy pipes up, dragging her Raven up to the entrance.

Following behind the trio, I step through the door of the tavern, the sound of drinking, laughter and drunken conversations echoing throughout the joint. I can barely hear myself, and I love it.

Mercy leads us to a free booth. 'What shall I get us all? The special is pretty damn good.'

'That's my favourite. Let's get two. Maybe some jugs to share as well,' Jack answers, seeming to know what he's talking about.

'I'll need a helping hand to carry it all,' Mercy says, giving Merlot a subtle glance.

Jack seems to notice and doesn't offer. Neither do I.

'Lead the way,' Merlot says, waving her hand towards the bar.

Smiling, I watch the pair wait in line, a group of burly customers making conversation with them as they queue. Looking around, I find no one giving us funny looks, and it's refreshingly nice.

'This is so strange.' I take a seat, my guardian sitting opposite me. He flings an arm across the back of the bench, looking relaxed with a half smile.

'What is?' he asks.

'Not being noticed.'

'You mentioned being a half-blood,' he says, leaning forward across the table, his face closing in on me, 'but you never mentioned *why* that's a bad thing in your House.'

Pursing my lips, I wonder what to say as I fiddle with my bracelet. Jack's someone I've come to trust, maybe not in *all* aspects of the word, but in having one more person to confide in as I attempt to conquer these trials, I'm starting to understand he is my ally, and he would benefit from knowing.

'Everyone believes the human side has tainted my Raven side – although I'm sure the Elder Raven despised me the moment I was born.' I think back to the Elder's gaze, the horror and hatred on her face that I survived another test.

'Does she hurt you?' Jack murmurs, looking at my hands once more.

Feeling self-conscious, I go to shove them under the table so he can't study them any more.

Fast as a whip, his hand stops me, palm over my right hand. 'No, don't hide away. I'm not asking because I want to make you feel uncomfortable, I want to know what to expect if she ever does harm you.'

His fingers circle my hand. I stare at them. 'My burns weren't given to me by either Ember or the Elder Raven, but they share the same sort of power.'

'Fire,' he states.

'Yes, but the Elder Raven is different. We call her magic Unforgettable Fire.'

'Unforgettable?'

'She's a fire elemental, like everyone in my family, only her flames are invisible. Ravens say that when burnt by her magic, you'll never forget it – it even haunts you in your dreams.'

'And have *you* ever experienced it?' he asks, eyes hardening as we speak.

'Yes. I had a fight with Winella, that girl who approached you earlier. She and her friend targeted me, so I defended myself. As punishment for wounding two full-blood Ravens, I was disciplined.'

'That's what she was talking about?' My guardian asks.

I nod glumly.

Leaning back, Jack lets out a long breath of air, a hand running through his messy silver-blonde hair in surprise. 'That's fucked up.'

'It is, but our Elder makes the rules. She can do what she wants.' I shrug because, honestly, how can the system change with a female like the Elder Raven as its leader? That is why Princess Leonore wants me to win: to change our House, to hopefully make it better.

Jack reaches across the table, hand facing up. I look at him with confusion.

'Am I supposed to hand you something?' I ask, looking between his face and palm.

'No. You hold my hand, and we have a moment.' He laughs, wiggling his fingers at me to hurry up.

Secretly his words please me, but I try my best to act otherwise. 'You're kidding.'

'No.'

Feigning reluctance, I do as I'm told, my eyes briefly checking for our friends, who are now at the front of the queue, leaning against the bar and talking animatedly.

'Have you always had this scar?' Jack's thumb rubs over the jagged silver line across my right palm, stroking it up and down and causing my body to tingle. Magic wraps around my hand, and I stare in wonder.

'What are you doing?' I murmur, looking on in awe.

'Some water elementals have the ability to heal through their magic. It's something my father taught me.'

Our hands glow a bright blue, but when it fades, the scar is still there. His frown makes me smile, the concern etched into his features strangely attractive.

'It's a scar I've had since childhood,' I claim, his eyes meeting mine in questioning.

His lips turn into a frown. 'But I swear I noticed blood on it before.'

'It opens up every now and then,' I answer cryptically.

'You know my abilities. Don't you think it's fair I know yours?' Jack's brow lifts as he gives me a meaningful expression. 'You're clearly not a fire elemental like the rest of your family, or you would have used your power by now.'

Rolling my eyes, I point to my scar. 'Fine. I don't know how or why it does this, but it bleeds when I should expect trouble.'

'So when you're safe, it closes back up? It stops bleeding?'

'Yes. For example, it has opened up with every trial, and then at times like this –' I wave towards the people and our surroundings, feeling him watch my movements – 'when

I'm deemed secure, it closes back up. It's like a warning bell but in blood.'

'I bet that's been helpful.'

'Yes, it certainly was when I—' I stop myself, on the verge of telling him about when we met at the Badger's Sett the first time and how I knew he wouldn't hurt me.

To my relief, Merlot and Mercy approach the table with a large tray each. Upon them sit bowls of roasted potatoes, colourful vegetables and slabs of meat that look fresh and juicy. They place the trays down on the table and slide one our way.

'Is this the special?' I ask, studying the massive tray of food. 'It looks delicious.'

'Just wait until you try the beer.' Mercy grins, going back with Merlot to get our drinks.

In minutes, we're digging into our feasts. Jack and I share one tray while the females share the other. The afternoon turns into evening, and we keep the drinks flowing long after our meal.

By the time we leave, Mercy and Jack are drunk, their voices loud and obnoxious as they debate whose Raven is better. Merlot and I, however, are unaffected, as alcohol has no ramifications for us.

'I vote we leave them here so they can make their own way home,' Merlot says with a smirk.

'Tempting,' I reply with a chuckle, looking back to see Jack trip over his own foot.

We walk in silence for a moment, Merlot looking tired and slightly paler than usual. In the absence of her smile, I wonder if she's actually as happy as she lets on.

'How are you holding up? How are you coping with all these tests and trials?' I ask, subtly watching her features.

She shrugs, keeping her eyes forward. 'I'm alive, so fine, I guess. You?'

'The same ...' I trail off and bite my lip. 'How's your mother been?'

Merlot's whole demeanour drops at the mention of her, her mouth twisting in distaste. The whole reason we became friends is we have a mutual goal – to save the ones we love.

'She's not great. The sickness is spreading quicker than anticipated,' Merlot murmurs, avoiding my eyes.

My heart sinks for my friend, knowing by the way she speaks of her mother that Merlot cares deeply for her. 'Aren't the healers doing anything about it?'

Merlot meets my gaze briefly before searching the streets around us. 'I think the Elder Raven has ordered anyone related to the Hex Trials to not be healed. As if keeping our family members sick will spur us competitors to fight harder against one another.'

My scowl is prominent as I say, 'I can imagine the Elder making such a horrendous command but surely the queen wouldn't allow that.'

My friend shrugs. 'I overheard one of the healers saying as much. They are keen to empty the healing beds but they can't go against strict orders.'

The questions pile up. How did Merlot's mother become sick in the first place? How long does she have till it's too late to save her? *Can* we save her?

'And you're still covering your mother's work at the market?' I ask instead.

She nods glumly, looking back at Mercy briefly. Our guardians are still arguing about something inconsequential. 'Yes. My days are so long trying to fit everything in. I feel like I'm going to start drowning soon, and I won't be able to swim back up to take a breath.'

My hand snakes across her shoulder, pulling her into my side as we stroll. Her hand lifts, finding mine.

'If there is anything I can do to help, let me know, and I'll be there,' I offer, earning a tight smile from her.

'Thank you, Scarlet. These trials are so important. If I mess up, I'll lose so much, and I don't know how or if I'll be able to handle it.'

Tugging her to a stop, the guardians a distance away still, I bring her face to face with me. 'You are doing great, and you're not alone. With Mercy by your side, you guys are crushing it. You have nothing to fear when it comes to the trials. You're powerful, and Mercy is obviously fond of you. She has your back. You just have to stay focused and remember what you're fighting for, and like we promised, I'm working towards helping your mother like you're helping my sister. Together we can't fail.'

Nodding slowly, Merlot smiles appreciatively, closing the distance between us. Warmth spreads through me as we hug, and I think of how thankful I am that we met. Never has she thought me a misfit because of my differences. Rather, she sees me as an ally she can come to trust.

'I better get Mercy home. She looks like she's about to collapse at any moment, and I have a feeling once she's down, I won't be able to coax her back up,' Merlot says as we stare at our guardians, the pair of them helping to keep each other up, their steps wobbly.

Merlot approaches Mercy and takes her arm gently. Waving goodbye, they leave me and Jack in the dark street, the lanterns no longer illuminating the cave around us.

'And then there were two,' Jack murmurs, coming to my side.

'Where do you live? I'll walk you home.'

He lifts a brow, a smug smile crossing his face. 'You want to come back to my place?'

'I'm walking you home, not coming for a sleepover,' I state, but his eyes are half-closed with intoxication, and I know whatever I say, he probably won't remember it in the morning.

'Oh, how lucky I am, to be taking a Raven home,' Jack slurs as he leads the way. 'Lucky me.'

Jack lives in a home with three other males. Stepping into his place, we're quiet until my guardian walks into an empty flowerpot discarded on the floor. He jumps around, clutching his foot and cursing in whispers that are loud enough to wake everyone up.

'Shush!' I put a finger up to my mouth, and his eyes linger on it.

'You have a lovely mouth,' he confesses, to which I lift a brow.

'And you're drunk. Why is that pot there?'

Jack scowls at it, seeming to wonder the same thing.

'Never mind. Where's your bedroom?' I ask.

The grin upon his face is bright with excitement. 'Why? Are you going to take advantage of me?'

Taking the initiative, I go in search of his room, opening doors silently and finding sleeping figures in their beds. Finally I find the one room that's empty and point towards it. 'Is this one yours?'

'Why, yes it is!'

My hand covers his mouth to shut him up, but he wiggles his brows in drunken delirium.

'I quite like it when you manhandle me,' he murmurs through my fingers, his tongue running over my skin.

I jerk my hand away and swat him, pushing him inside and closing the door behind us.

Taking in his room, I find it's rather tidy and organised. The bed is made. All surfaces are clear of clutter, and the scent in the room smells like vanilla. Strangely enough, this is the exact room I'd imagine the Teacher owning.

'Do you wear nightclothes?' I ask, searching his

wardrobe for something that looks comfy enough to sleep in. When I find some grey trousers that are soft to the touch on the inside and a plain shirt, I toss them at Jack, who fails to catch them, the items falling to the floor.

'Uh, sorry.' He goes to bend down, but he wobbles and collapses on the bed instead, sighing heavily as he curls onto his side. 'I'm so tired.'

'Okay, well, I can't dress you like this. At least let me change your shirt.'

My hands reach for his arms, and I lift him into a sitting position. He brings his arms up, and I smile fondly down at him, seeing his eyes are closed.

'All right, I'm taking the top half off,' I warn, to which he smiles mischievously.

'Please do, Raven.'

After tossing his old shirt on the floor, I unfold his fresh top, but I don't avert my eyes from his chest. It's as muscled as I expected it to be, the skin unmarred, and his toned chest expands with every inhalation he takes.

'Like what you see?' he murmurs, eyes now open, catching my gaze.

I smirk, doing a terrible job at hiding my embarrassment that he's caught me looking.

'It's satisfactory.' I shrug, tugging his new shirt on.

He lies back and lifts his legs in the air.

'What are you doing?'

'I can't stay in these clothes. I've been around dead people, and my bed is clean,' he answers tiredly.

'Fine, but no funny business,' I caution before I tug his trousers off. I keep my focus on getting his fresh pair on. Getting his feet through the holes is harder than I expected.

Once he's changed, I pull a corner of his bed cover over and try to push him inside. He slithers in without prompting, his head sinking into his pillows. Jack's breathing changes, easing into a steady rhythm, and I can't help but stare at him for a while.

'See you later, guardian,' I whisper, reaching out to stroke a piece of his hair away from his face. His mouth tugs upwards slightly. 'Sweet dreams.'

34

The next day, I stand waiting for Jack by the tunnel. He looks weary and zapped of energy, but my smile is enough for him to scorn me.

'Don't say a word,' he warns, and I chuckle.

'You look refreshed today, guardian.'

My smile isn't reciprocated. Instead, I'm given a groan. 'Don't talk so loud.'

'Poor baby. Perhaps we should give training a miss today.'

'No. I want to see the arena. You promised I would see it sometime.' He looks down at me with a pleading look. 'Please. I can't train in the stables again, not today. I think I may vomit if I smell horse manure.'

'But the arena is not safe,' I insist. 'You're not exactly in peak condition. If something goes wrong ...'

'I am. Look, I can protect you.' He stands up straighter even though it looks like the gesture makes him feel queasy. 'If not, I won't hesitate to play dirty.' He points a finger at me, and a squirt of water shoots out, wetting my face.

'Argh,' I mutter, wiping the droplets away. 'Fine, but keep your guard up. I'm not babysitting you.'

The entrance is unlike anything found in Rubien. The twin archways are tall and intimidating, made of cold grey stone that looks as unbreakable as the House it represents. Finding red sand in the distance, I steal a brief glance at Jack. His face lights up with amazement, the whole scene enough to make him forget his hangover temporarily.

'Wow, this is incredible.' He gapes, turning full circle to take in the complete arena. 'Those seats are high. I guess Ravens aren't afraid of heights.'

Gazing up, I take in the tiered stone seats. Every time I've been in the arena, I've been in danger, under observation and high on adrenaline. This time, I can really take in the beauty of the structure, even if it's become a symbol of foreboding for me.

'What's first, Raven?' Jack asks as we aim for the centre of the sandpit.

Several teams of Ravens and guardians are already training. Being a bit later, we find every section that's been reserved for fighting purposes is full.

'Endurance training. Let's run as many laps as we can until you feel like passing out,' I reply, earning a moan of protest.

'Today, of all days,' Jack mutters, studying the perimeter of the pit in silent loathing.

In this instance, I'm glad I can't get drunk. I'd hate to be doing this while feeling unwell.

'You asked to train in here today, and this is what it's got to offer.' I put my hands on my hips, challenging him to object, to ask to come back another day. By the look on his face, though, he knows I won't yield.

'If I'm sick, where are the closest facilities?' he asks, making me grin and point to the nearest bathroom.

'You champ.' I punch his arm gently and walk to the

edge of the pit, watching as other guardians do the same laps. 'You ready?' I ask, making him purse his lips.

'As I'll ever be.'

We're slow to start, his feet sounding exhausted with every step, but I don't urge him to go faster. If we can sweat out his hangover, perhaps we can have a longer training session, maybe even grab a fighting square once a pair is done with it.

'You're doing great. Just keep breathing,' I say, finding his eyes hard and determined.

He pants in a steady rhythm, sweat lining his temples, but he doesn't complain. He keeps going.

We pass training classes full of Ravens still honing their skills, their bodies lithe and strong as they go through movements together.

I was never allowed to join any lessons as a child, but I heard stories from my siblings and wondered what it was like to be in a classroom setting. Unlike my family, I've never trained for anything other than cleaning horse hooves.

No one takes notice of us as we run lap after lap. Jack's breathing is horribly loud until we pass Master Lennox's defence class for the fourth time. His voice is loud and authoritative as he shouts at us.

'You two, come here,' he orders, making us slow down.

I notice Blaze is among the students, his face neutral, as expected, but his eyes show concern. He bows his head in greeting, the movement subtle enough not to be seen by his peers.

'Who is that?' Jack whispers, chest rising and falling quickly.

'That's Master Lennox. Do not speak unless spoken to,' I advise quietly, even though the male can probably hear our conversation.

'What is a master? Is that a teacher?'

'Yes. Now shush,' I utter, my heart pounding.

Master Lennox's bright red eyes study us as we approach, his gaze roaming up and down with obvious distaste but also a sliver of curiosity. This worries me.

'I see,' Master Lennox murmurs. 'Scarlet Seraphine, isn't it? You are Blaze's younger sister, correct?'

Sticking my hands to my sides, I find Blaze's stare. He gives me a meaningful look.

Tread carefully, he seems to say.

I nod. 'Yes, Master.'

'And this is your *human*?' Master Lennox asks, circling Jack with such slowness that my guardian looks extremely uncomfortable.

'Yes, Master,' I repeat.

Males aren't considered high-ranking in the House of Raven, but I've learned with Master Jepp that any of the masters could send me to the Elder Raven for punishment. In their world, I was the lowest of the low. I was to respect them or suffer the consequences.

'Why are you competing in the Hex Trials?' Master Lennox asks, aiming the question at Jack.

My guardian straightens, realising everyone is now watching him. 'I've always wanted to be a guardian for as long as I can remember. My mother was the first guardian, and I hope to follow in her footsteps.' He forces a smile, trying to gauge a reaction. Sweat drips down his back, and his forehead shines from our run.

'So your mother is Marie Wilde? How wonderful,' Master Lennox muses.

I quirk a brow.

'Do you know that without one of our Ravens, your mother would be without such a job?' he asks, and *that* is when I realise my mistake in bringing Jack to the arena to train. 'Marie was given the opportunity because one of our Ravens deemed sleeping around with a lowly human to be more important than following her duties.' His fiery red eyes turn to me.

I can't help but shrink back slightly.

'How fitting you are paired with the vermin offspring.' Master Lennox chuckles, looking at his class with amusement.

They all snigger except Blaze, who merely stands and watches. It hurts to know he won't defend me, but at the end of the day, surviving is all a Raven can do here. If he pipes up, he'll be punished for simply arguing with a master.

My ritual begins. *Think of something else*, I chant inside my head. *Imagine your mouth is stitched closed with thread.* I grit my teeth, wanting so badly to curse at the male, to give him a piece of my mind, but I don't. I can't afford to be hurt with an upcoming trial. I have to be smart, and right now, that means keeping my mouth shut and taking the insults.

'I think that's a harsh judgement.' Jack scowls, his face scrunching up in distaste. 'Scarlet had nothing to do with her mother's decisions.'

'Jack, don't.'

Master Lennox seems taken aback by a human speaking up against him. His demeanour changes instantly. 'That half-blood's mother is a *slut*.' His pale finger jabs towards me, and I move away instinctively. 'Her actions should have been dealt with accordingly. Yet here we are, having to accommodate such a creature.'

'You clearly know the whole story, then, if you can make such accusations,' Jack returns, crossing his arms defensively.

My hand finds his shoulder as I try to make him listen to me, to be quiet before he makes it worse.

'You,' Master Lennox shouts, directing his wrath at me. 'Come here. *Now*.'

When I meet Jack's eyes, my guardian looks furious as I obey the master so willingly.

Standing beside the towering male, I wait for what's to come. Hopefully, I'll receive a slap, and we can go back home, but instead, Master Lennox finds a cane in his belt.

'Ten lashes,' he declares.

'No, not him!' I yell, running to Jack with my arms out so no one can get to him.

'No,' Master Lennox states cheerily, his anger having been temporarily replaced with amusement. 'Ten lashes for bringing your guardian here and distracting my class,' he clarifies, making me grimace. 'Twenty now for speaking without permission.'

'That's ridiculous!' Jack shouts, his fist shaking towards the male.

Pushing him back so he won't get us into more trouble, I hiss at him. '*Shut up*!'

'Thirty,' Master Lennox decides, his face brightening with delight. 'Do you want to make it forty?' he asks innocently, clasping his hands together with quiet delight.

Thankfully, Jack stays silent, but his eyes harden, glowing bright blue, and I predict that today is not going to end well.

'Seize them!' Master Lennox orders.

Ravens restrain Jack and me with obsidian-coloured chains.

35

Three small pillars I've never seen before stand proudly at the far end of the arena. Master Lennox drags me towards them, and I note the splattering of blood over the grey rock from previous wrongdoers.

'Obsidian chains are a wonder,' Master Lennox remarks, yanking the black shackles around my wrists, pulling me towards my ruination. 'I know *you* don't have any magical powers – you're a weakling – but your guardian ...' He trails off as we both stare at Jack, who is attempting to fight three other males. 'I can smell the power in him, and he can't do a thing about it.'

My fanged sneer doesn't go unnoticed. Master Lennox knows he's won this fight – obsidian metal being one of a very few materials in the world that repel and douse magic. Jack, when wearing these chains is as good as an ordinary human. No longer can he use magic to defend himself – or me.

'Do what you want with me. Just don't harm him,' I plead.

'Oh, how noble. Make sure you don't sleep with him as

well, or you'll follow in the footsteps of your miserable mother.' Master Lennox smiles wickedly.

My anger rises several notches, and before I can think over my actions, I spit in his face for disrespecting Ruby, earning myself a slap.

'Play nice now. We are going to make a lesson out of you.' Grabbing the back of my neck, Master Lennox jerks me towards a pillar and thrusts my head into the hard stone.

'Holy Hanrah,' I whimper, my skull blooming with pain.

Taking advantage of my disorientation, the master connects me to a metal loop that sticks out from the pillar, a loop so high my arms are above my head. My hand, I realise, should be bleeding by now, but because of my special restraints, my scar stays silver and unopened.

'Get off me!' Jack yells, causing havoc with his sentries. They're stronger than my guardian, but his will to provoke and cause trouble makes it hard for them to contain him.

One of the male Ravens grabs something from his belt and quickly wraps it around Jack's neck. A wire, I realise. The cable begins to light up with electricity, making Jack's body spasm. I can't help but yell out to him as I watch him fall painfully to his knees.

'Now,' Master Lennox shouts, gaining the attention of those nearby, who are curiously observing what is unfolding. 'This is why we must not talk back to our masters. If any other class would like to join and be reminded of such discipline, then please, do join us.' He waves for those close by to come watch, as if inviting them to a party.

Spinning around in my chains, I search for any kind of help. In the distance, I detect my sister's face. Ember's frown shows her disapproval, with Taylor standing timidly beside her, but she watches on, unfazed that I'm on a platter for Master Lennox.

'Thirty lashes,' the master announces, making me squeeze my eyes shut.

'Please, don't do this!' my guardian shouts, his face pleading as he looks up. 'Take me instead! Take me!'

He tries to stand back up, but his neck restraint lights up once more, shocking him enough to cause his body to jolt and fall to the floor again. The males that loom over him grab his shirt and pull him back to his knees, laughing loudly.

My gaze automatically goes to Blaze, silently pleading with him to do something. I've been whipped before but not with so many lashes. He gives me a look of hopelessness, letting me know I'm on my own.

'Count for me, guardian,' Master Lennox orders as he brings the cane down against my front, the tip of the whip catching the side of my face. The pain is sudden, abrupt and vicious. My body swings from the force of the blow, the skin around my wrists stinging as the shackles dig into me.

The master glares at Jack, admonishing him to count, but he stays silent. 'Do you want me to add to her punishment?'

'One,' Jack utters finally, his face sagging with defeat. He meets my eyes, and I try to give him a reassuring look, but the master whips me again, causing me to yelp in pain. My guardian's face creases into dismay, and I decide I can't face him, knowing if he sees my agony, it will only make him feel worse.

Master Lennox revels in the whipping, becoming breathless as his adrenaline heightens. My flimsy tunic tears with every powerful strike. Time seems to slow down, and I find myself whimpering quietly, hating the arena and everyone in it.

'Fifteen,' Jack croaks as he tries to stand, the electricity shocking him more often than not now. 'Please. Stop this,' he begs, shaking his silver-blonde head in defeat.

'Count, or I'll add more' is all the response Jack gets as Master Lennox brings down blow after blow.

It takes a total of ten minutes for Master Lennox to conduct thirty lashes. By the time the punishment is over, my blood covers the sand, the pillar I'm cuffed to, and Master Lennox's beaming face. I can barely open my eyes. My whole body is throbbing, and my cheeks are stinging from where the tip of the cane has caught my face several times.

'That's enough for now. Back we go,' the master declares. He unties me and releases my mutilated wrists from their restraints.

The moment he removes the metal, I crumple to the floor in a heap, my body screaming. Tears stream down my face, my suffering too much to keep in.

'Take this as a lesson, half-blood,' Master Lennox says, leaning over me, his shiny black boots beside my face. 'If I see you back here to train, I'll make sure your punishment isn't as trivial as today's.'

Wishing to respond with something witty, I peek up through my blurry vision. My mouth opens, but nothing comes out, only a sniffle. The master smiles down at me before walking away, passing my brother who hasn't moved since my first lash.

'Traitor,' I whisper, thinking he won't hear, but from the hurt that flashes through his eyes, I know I've hit my mark. The betrayal that he would stand and watch me suffer is enough to make my mind up – I don't care anymore.

'Release the guardian. I've had enough of these two,' Master Lennox orders from a distance.

Jack is finally released, and he wrenches the chains and

wire off himself. He stumbles to my side, and his shaking hands hover over me with indecision.

'What have I done?' he whimpers, touching my side.

The moment his finger grazes my skin, I jerk in response, my body covered in slashes and oozing wounds.

'Find Dimitri,' I instruct him before letting the darkness consume me.

36

Waking up, I find myself lying on my front on a squidgy sofa, and two males are looking down at me with tension in their eyes. Jack sits patiently on the floor next to me, clutching my hand, while Dimitri is perched on his armchair across from us, holding a glass of crimson liquid.

'Dimitri?' I wince, but the pain is less than I expected. The males must have been working hard while I was passed out.

'I'm here,' he answers, coming closer, putting the drink down. Jack moves out of the way, and Dimitri takes his spot. 'How are you feeling? You look rough.'

My glare makes him smile timidly.

'I jest. You look lovely as always.'

'Liar.' I smirk but take his hand when he offers it, his fingers squeezing mine in hopes of comforting me.

He brings over the glass that I know is his blood.

Wrinkling my nose, I stare at it. 'Must I?'

'Jack healed you as best he could, but you still look quite awful. I went all the way to the hospital to get this extracted for you. It's fresh and will get rid of the remaining damage.'

'You got your blood taken without me?' I ask as he purses his lips.

'I had to.'

'I'm so proud of you,' I murmur, attempting to roll onto my side.

Dimitri grasps me tenderly, helping as I manoeuvre myself into a sitting position. A wave of nausea hits me, and my eyes shut until the feeling subsides, my nails digging into Dimitri's steady arms.

'Are you all right?' Jack winces, leaning closer.

'Give me a second.' My skin feels tight and tender. My face is sore and most likely bruised, but ultimately, I feel numb to any other pain. 'I bet Meela was surprised to see you,' I remark, trying to bring back the conversation.

Dimitri obliges. 'She kept talking like you usually do for me – telling me secrets of the other nurses. I can't look at them the same now.'

He brings the glass to my face, and I take a gulp, trying to forget the fact it's my best friend's blood that I'm consuming.

'This never gets any less weird,' I mutter in between sips.

'I know.' Dimitri tips the glass, urging me to finish the last drops at the bottom. 'A little bit more. That's it. Well done.' He takes it away, and I wipe my mouth with a shudder.

'What's weirder is that it doesn't taste that bad,' I admit with a grimace.

'As long as you don't have too much,' Dimitri reasons.

Vampire blood can be extremely addictive, and the drinker can become dependent – one of the many reasons Dimitri is selective with his blood donations. History has shown that people will do anything for it, like an addict needing their fix.

'I don't plan on doing that,' I reply.

Jack sits quietly in Dimitri's armchair, staring at the floor.

'Dimitri, do you mind giving us a minute?' I ask.

The vampire lifts his brow, following my gaze. He nods without hesitation. 'Of course.'

Jack is silent as he regards me, the sound of Dimitri busying himself in another room lingering between us.

'Scarlet, I'm so sorry,' my guardian whispers, his sky-blue eyes showing sorrow, guilt and grief like I've never seen before.

'It's not your fault.'

'He literally whipped you because of *me*,' Jack says bitterly. He drags shaky hands through his hair, the light strands making me scowl as I notice blood coats them. 'I should have shut up. I should have listened to you and not stepped foot in the arena at all.'

'You couldn't possibly have known,' I try to reason, but he won't have a bar of it.

'Scarlet, you could have *died*. If I hadn't managed to find Dimitri, you would still be bleeding out. Raven or not, those wounds would have killed you, and it would have been *my* fault!' His voice falters, and I motion for him to come closer. He obeys without question, kneeling in front of me.

'Look at me.'

Jack hesitates, and my chest tightens at the sight of him. I imagine him carrying me through Rubien in search of the one person I asked for, not stopping until he found him. My hand reaches out, sliding down his arm until I am holding his hand. Raising it slowly, I place his palm against my chest where my heart is. My guardian's eyes harden before rising to meet mine.

'I'm alive,' I say quietly. 'I'm breathing. I'm still here, fighting.'

He lowers his head, shaking it defiantly, but he does not pull away. Instead the hand on my chest moves up, cradling my face like I am something delicate – something precious. 'I could have lost you today,' he whispers, his other hand coming to frame my face. 'I made a mistake, and you suffered for it. You deserve better.'

'Jack.' I sigh, gently holding onto his wrists. The need for his touch is great, the coolness of his fingers on my skin making me feel suddenly warm. 'I saw you fight for me with every ounce of your being. Any Raven who has a guardian like that is lucky. *I* am lucky.'

Studying him closer, I inspect his clothes and his skin, which is still coated in splotches of my own blood, with faint stains of crimson smeared through his hair. But what makes my heart thunder is the harsh line around his neck. Without thinking, I reach for him, touching his wound. His fingers fall away from me, my guardian's eyes falling to the floor.

'One day I'll repay the favour for what they did to us,' I murmur.

'It doesn't hurt,' he promises, but I don't care. I would gladly have my revenge on Master Lennox, do gruesome things to him without remorse for electrocuting Jack. 'It's nothing compared to what you endured.'

'I didn't realise this was a competition,' I jest, trying to ease the tension.

He doesn't laugh, doesn't smile, only stares at me.

'I'm sorry I put you through that,' I say. 'I hate that you saw me like that.'

'I wanted to kill everyone there. I wanted to drown them all for hurting you, for mutilating you, when I couldn't do anything but watch and hope it ended quickly.'

'You don't have to go through with these trials,' I offer, my voice hoarse.

'I won't leave you to suffer in that place alone,' he answers without hesitation, his voice low and harsh.

'You don't owe me anything.'

'No, I don't,' he agrees, bringing my hand to his chest. My fingers feel his heartbeat beneath his shirt. It beats so fast it's as if he's been running, when for the last half hour, he's been here, watching over me. 'But I'm here because I want to be. I want to be by your side every step of the way. I chose you for a reason.' His eyes shift over me, the movement intimate and protective. 'You're my Raven, and we fight together.'

Tilting my head, I study him. He isn't lying, and his confidence is endearing. Taking a leap of faith, I snake my hands around his shoulders and pull him close. I breathe in his ocean scent as we embrace, letting the feelings of the day merge into each other's body.

'I don't want to lose you, Scarlet,' he whispers into my hair, his arms tightening ever so slightly.

My wince is hidden, but I don't dare complain. The safety I feel in his arms is nothing like anything I've experienced before. 'You won't. You're stuck with me whether you like it or not.'

Reluctantly I pull back, and the longing in his eyes is intense. My thumb lifts to his chin, tracing his jaw tenderly. 'I'm sorry I got blood on your clothes,' I whisper, wanting more than anything to kiss him, to let him know how much I worry about losing him too, but the words of Master Lennox ring through my head, flaring with a red flag.

Make sure you don't sleep with him as well, or you'll follow in the footsteps of your miserable mother.

If I allowed something to happen between us, I would ruin everything. Not just for me and helping my sister but for helping Jack live a dream he and his father have always wanted for him.

Slowly I release him as I come to my feet, wobbling slightly. His hands are there before me, holding me up so I won't fall.

'My clothes can be replaced,' he answers, implying that I am quite the opposite. 'But I'll send you a bill for them when you're feeling better.' He winks, finally letting himself smile – even if it's strained.

'I'll make sure you address it to Dimitri, then.' I smirk, hearing the vampire yell from the other room.

'I heard that!'

37

Bandages wrap tightly around my body for days later, my injuries slowly healing with the help of Dimitri's blood and Jack's magic. My guardian isn't free to train, not that he wants me to exert myself yet, but he claims to be doing something he can't get out of. I surmise he's at the Badger's Sett as his alter ego, so I don't push for details.

I return home from the stables with a plan. Having been busy with the trials, I've neglected my scheme of finding out more about Ruby and my father, so today I intend to find some more concrete answers.

'You're home!' Roux cries, coming to her feet the moment I step foot inside. She lifts my shirt without permission to check my bandages underneath. 'Good, good,' she murmurs to herself.

Since I came from Dimitri's looking like a wounded soldier, she and Ruby have been hovering around me like protective mother hens.

'Roux,' I protest, pushing her hands away. 'I've just been working. Stop your worrying.'

'If you keep straining your body, the wounds will open

back up,' Roux warns, crossing her arms defensively as best she can with her big belly. She doesn't know I have Dimitri's blood slowly healing me, so I give her an appreciative look.

'I know. I'm taking it easy. Promise.'

'What else are you doing today, then?' she asks, taking a seat at the dining table while I make us a drink of hot tea.

'I'm thinking of doing some reading, actually.'

'You are?' She turns in her chair to face me, most likely wondering if I'm lying.

'Do you want to join me?' I ask, a plan forming in my head.

'Sure. I could do with a walk. I didn't think you had access to our library, though.'

'Who said anything about the Ravens' library?'

Roux is incredibly on edge, and I don't blame her. For the first time in her life, she's visiting the human city of Rubien. She marvels at its wonders, at the people who stare our way and at the different shops that line the streets.

'How is it so different?' she asks, touching the petals of a flower that's potted on a windowsill we pass. 'There is so much colour and so much fresh air here.'

Her questions are constant, and by the time we arrive at the library, I breathe a sigh of relief. With my pregnant sister and her aching feet, our walk has taken double the time, but I don't complain. She's trying to watch over me in my current state, and I'm glad at least one of my sisters is doing that.

The library is an old building, larger than anything around, and it looks a little run-down. The maintenance on the outside, I know, is worse than on the inside, but Roux scowls up at it.

'You'd think they would take better care of it.'

Walking around the back of the premises, I locate a window I need and search for any passers-by. Deciding the coast is clear, I pull the window up. It's hard at first, and it takes time to wiggle it free, but gradually I can feel it creak and loosen under the pressure.

'What are you doing?' Roux hisses, looking around for anyone who may see us. 'Why don't you go through the front entrance like everyone else?'

Gritting my teeth from the effort, I finally push the window up enough for my body to slip through. I swing a leg over and slide on my stomach. 'Because I'm banned from here too.' I grin, making her red eyes widen in disbelief.

'You're kidding me! You're telling me we came all the way here to break in?'

I jump through the window and land quietly on the wooden floor, which is covered in faded red rugs. I sneak across to the nearest door, find no one present and quietly open the entry for Roux, waving her over from the window I broke in through.

'Hurry up,' I whisper loudly, keeping an eye behind me for any unexpected humans.

'I can't believe this. We are breaking so many rules right now,' Roux huffs, clutching her stomach in indignation.

'You wanted to come along,' I remind her, earning a frown. 'Besides, this part of the library is always empty. We can read here in peace.'

'What exactly do you want to read?' Roux probes, looking around with new interest.

I'm not sure what the House of Raven's library looks like, but I assume it looks much more updated than this one. Here it smells of dusty books, burning wood from the various fireplaces and tea leaves.

'I'm looking for any information about what happened with Ruby and my father,' I admit, earning another horrified look from her.

'This is a disaster.' She shakes her head as she follows me down aisles of novels and other publications. 'You dragged me all the way here to break the law *and* go behind Ruby's back to figure out her past? Is there anything else I need to know about this little excursion?'

Frustration coats her features, and I try to feel guilty, but I can't. I have a right to know what happened with my parents, what happened with my birth that affected the Elder Raven so much she has a vendetta against me.

'Ruby wasn't going to tell me anything, so I thought I'd take the initiative and find some answers myself,' I claim, fingering the spines as I pass them on the way to the history section.

'And you know why, right? Ruby can't tell you, because she physically can't.'

Turning slowly, I face my sister. 'What do you mean?'

'From what I've gathered, Ruby has been hexed to never mention your father, in hopes people eventually forget. The less people find out, the more likely the Elder Raven will keep control of the situation that happened all those years ago.'

Remembering every time I've mentioned my father, I recall my mother opening her mouth and closing it several times. Did she want to tell me more but couldn't? Guilt swells in my stomach. I told Ruby she didn't care when maybe she really did. Perhaps my not knowing the full story isn't because Ruby wants to keep me in the dark; it's because she has no other choice.

'Well, perhaps we can find a way to release her from this hex she's under.' My feet quicken, the need to find answers strengthening. 'And find out more about this mystery man that created so many problems.'

38

It takes fifty minutes to find a sliver of information about what occurred in the House of Raven. Roux sits in an armchair, tending the fire with her magic when it grows too low for her. She is flicking through the pages of an old newspaper when suddenly she lifts a fist in excitement.

'I've got something!' she exclaims, making me run from an aisle to her side. 'Look, here is an article dated twenty years ago.'

The report is quite lengthy, the writing small, but there is a picture of our mother. Ruby looks young, strong and every bit the fighter I know she is. Her features are relaxed, and she is surrounded by a group of people, all in impressive uniforms.

'"Ruby Seraphine and her fellow Hex members,"' I read out loud, taking in the males and females she once worked with.

Roux places a finger on the first line and drags it across the page as she reads aloud the article. '"The House of Raven continues to guard its secrets in the hopes of furthering its reputation as indestructible and everlasting.

At the conclusion of the sixth Hex Trials, a winner was chosen, the Vermilion Fang victorious in gaining the title of Raven of the Hex."'

My sister and I share a look.

'Vermilion Fang?' I scoff.

'"Becoming the world's most distinguished Raven, the Vermilion Fang exceeded expectations and was loved by all who met her. She created a new brand for the House of Raven, displaying the compassion and justice few people knew the House could portray. However, all changed when the Vermilion Fang was discovered to be with child."'

Pursing my lips, I sit on the armrest of Roux's chair, looking down at the pictures on the page, and my sister reads on, her voice clear.

'"The child is said to be a half-blood – half human and half Raven. Some rumours state the Vermilion Fang was banished from the House of Raven. Others state she was killed along with the human lover she had acquired. But my sources have proven that those rumours are not true but only a ploy to steer the people away from the scandal – that is, Ravens *can* fall in love."'

Roux pauses, eyeing me up. 'This makes me feel strange, Scar – to hear Ruby's story from another person. It's like we are invading her privacy.'

'Do you want to go home?'

As she studies me, I silently wait, hoping she'll decline to leave. Seeming to sense my eagerness to learn more, she averts her eyes back to the article, clearing her throat before she continues reading.

'"The Vermilion Fang has not been sighted for eleven days, making us theorise she has been taken back to the House of Raven to be dealt with by Garnet Cerise – the Elder Raven. Within days, the Fang has been replaced by one who we now know to be our beloved Raven's younger sister, Brande Seraphine – now dubbed the Red Raven."'

My nose crinkles at the Elder's full name.

'Holy Hanrah, this is insane,' Roux utters, having got to the bottom of the column. 'Now we know people were talking about it, we can find out more about what happened in the papers when you were actually born.'

Rummaging through some weathered stacks within some discarded boxes Roux was searching through before, I look for the issues dated later, for any front-cover pictures of my mother. One pops up from a few months after I was born, and I start to flick through it.

'I think I may have—'

Footsteps sound, accompanied by the smell of humans coming closer. I grab the paper and shove it into my pocket, then run for Roux, who has heard them too. Gently I rush her out the door and lock it back up, then sprint to the window and jump out before anyone sees me. With a quiet thunk, I close the window to where I found it and lead Roux back into the streets of Rubien.

'Were you seen?' Roux asks, out of breath from the small burst of exertion.

'No, I don't think so.'

'Did you find anything else?' she asks.

The paper burns in my pocket, but I know if I tell her I stole a printed publication from a local library, she'll scorn me, perhaps even make me take it back.

'No, nothing,' I answer, leading her to the Tea Shop to buy her a cake.

39

It seems fate has cursed me. Every time I go to read the article, I'm suddenly in the company of someone. It's only when I'm waiting for Dimitri in the Badger's Sett that I have a private moment to sit down and survey the write-up.

I sit within the Green Room, dressed ready for my fight with someone called the Mentalist. My mask lies beside me, ready for when Dimitri comes to glamour me and help with securing my hood.

Leaning over my knees, I unfold the paper and read, taking in every word.

NEWS HAS SPREAD THAT THE VERMILION FANG HAS BIRTHED A HEALTHY BABY GIRL. WITH A HEAD OF DARK RED HAIR AND FANGS LIKE HER RAVEN BRETHREN, SHE IS ONE OF A KIND. THE FATHER OF SAID CHILD IS YET TO BE FOUND, AND THE ELDER RAVEN CLAIMS TO HAVE KILLED HIM FOR HIS INDISCRETIONS. BUT WE KNOW BETTER.

. . .

Footsteps echo outside my private room, but I keep reading, eager to know the rest. Dimitri will be here soon, and I can show him what I've found.

SPECULATION CLAIMS THE YOUNG HALF-BLOOD'S FATHER IS NONE OTHER THAN AARON RUSH, SON OF THE ROYAL GUARD KILLIAN RUSH. REPORTS STATE THE YOUNG RUSH WENT INTO HIDING AND HAS YET TO BE FOUND. WHEN QUESTIONED, THE LEADER OF THE HOUSE OF RAVEN DECLARED THE HUMAN HAS BEEN DEALT WITH ACCORDINGLY. MY SOURCES, HOWEVER, PROFESS THIS IS NOT TRUE — RUSH WAS TOO QUICK FOR HER CLUTCHES AND ESCAPED.

My head throbs. I blink in disbelief at what I've read. He escaped the Elder Raven. My father, Aaron Rush, is alive. The paper feels heavy in my hands, and the weight of what I've learned sits on my shoulders suddenly.

The door to my room swings open, and I quickly get to my feet, waving the paper in the air before I realise I'm standing face to face with the Teacher. His blue eyes land on me, blatantly looking me up and down. I go to approach him like I would any time I need his advice, but then I remember I'm not masked or glamoured to hide my true identity.

'Scarlet?'

I'm speechless and unsure whether behind his mask he's mad or just in shock. Self-consciousness seeps through me as I look at my own mask, discarded on the seat before me. 'I was hoping to tell you sooner ...'

'Were you?' he states, calmer than I expected. What gives him away though is his heart, pounding like a drum, revealing his true emotions. The Teacher may be a disguise but right now I'm looking at Jack, my guardian, and I've clearly hurt him.

'Yes, of course. I wanted to make sure I could trust you first. Surely you can understand that.'

'And do you?' His eyes are hard like stone, and I'm still unsure how this conversation is going to play out. My mind is still spinning from learning about my father. 'Trust me, that is.'

I close the distance between us and shut the door so no other fighters can enter. I lean up against it, needing the solidness of it behind me.

'Yes, I do.'

He shakes his head, voice low. 'If that's the case, why have you been lying to me all this time?'

It's peculiar how a person's voice can portray how they are feeling. At first he was able to cloak his emotions, whereas now he seems genuinely wounded that I couldn't entrust him with this secret.

'The same reason you've been lying to me, Jack. I was waiting for the right time.'

Startled, he jerks back, his sapphire stare pinned on me. Swallowing down my feelings, I take his hand. He doesn't move away but rather stands stiffly.

'We both needed the time to get to know one another, to trust and to bond with our lies as a safety net. Perhaps now we can be ourselves completely. We can start over with no secrets between us.'

Peering up into his hood, I silently will him to see sense in this. I want him to be all right with me, to still be my friend – my guardian, who I've come to care for. Blue eyes roam over my face, telling me little about how he is taking the news.

'I understand if you no longer wish to be partnered with me,' I say, pouting my lips in a way I hope will make him yield. 'But so you know, the day you became my guardian, I knew I was fortunate and that I had a chance of winning the Hex Trials with you by my side. But if you don't want me any more ...' I trail off. I know I'm laying it on thick, but I reach for the door handle as if to leave the room.

'Don't,' he relents, grasping my hand to stop me.

Turning slowly, I see the amusement in his eyes before he pulls his hood off and lowers his mask. He truly is a sight to see in his fighting gear.

'You're so dramatic.' He shakes his head but doesn't let me go.

My face morphs into innocence. 'I don't know what you're talking about.'

A laugh escapes when he rolls his eyes good naturedly. 'How did you know it was me? I was so careful.'

Giving him a tight smile, I shrug. 'Well, other than the fact you smell exactly the same? Your eyes are pretty memorable.' Pink faintly covers his ears, and I chuckle.

His mouth curls up, and I find myself staring at it. My feet move forward, closing the gap between us. A tightness in my chest unfurls as I continue to gaze at my guardian.

'I—'

The entry flies open behind me, and Jack grabs me out the way before I'm bashed by the metal door.

'Oh,' Dimitri says, seeing us both maskless, my body in Jack's clutches. 'So you both know now. That's great. Your fight is about to start, Phoenix. Are you ready?'

40

The stables are somewhat clean when I'm visited by my brother, who edges into the barn with caution.

'If you want a session with one of my horses, we're closed for the rest of the day,' I declare with a scowl, his betrayal still fresh in my mind.

'I'm not here for a horse,' he claims, eyeing up Jack, who sits on his usual bucket, cleaning a pair of riding boots. 'I'm here because I want to apologise and ask if you want to take a stroll with me. We haven't spent much time together lately, with you conquering the daily tests and tribulations of the Hex Trials.'

Taking my time to answer, I study him, hoping to make Blaze sweat a little. 'Fine, but I don't feel chatty today,' I state, stretching my back out, my spine cracking. I need a break, and this is a perfect opportunity to hear him grovel. 'And Jack has to come along. I'm not leaving him here by himself.'

We walk along a lava river, the dameer trailing behind us to let my brother and me speak privately.

'So how has training been?' Blaze asks, glancing back at

Jack, who peers over the edge of the river, lava making his hair shine a faint orange.

'Don't go too near,' I warn my guardian, and I see him take a noticeable step away. 'It's been tiring, but we've been working really hard. I feel more confident every day.'

My words are half true. The upcoming trial is playing on my mind, and my fear is growing. We've yet to hear of when it will be, but I don't show Blaze my unease, knowing Ember will most likely hear of it, otherwise.

'Look, Scar, there is a whole list of things I want to say sorry for, but I apologise for not standing up for you when you needed me most. I was a coward.'

Life has taught me one thing: survival is all that matters here in the House of Raven. The day I was whipped in the arena is something I'll never forget, but I would have hated myself if both my guardian *and* my brother had been hurt because of me. Besides, the wounds I received have fully healed now. It's all in the past and ignoring my brother has been more draining than I imagined.

I sigh, 'I understand, Blaze. At the time, I didn't like it, but I'm glad you didn't step in.'

My brother's shoulders sag with relief, his face peering down at me with new hope. He purses his lips, scratching his head in deep thought. 'Have you spoken to Ember recently?' he asks.

'No. Since you retrieved me from the healing clinic, she's been avoiding me like the plague. Except the one time she nearly burned me for getting angry with Jack.'

'Hmm. I heard about that.' He nods.

'Did you know about her branding her guardian? Poor guy, he's petrified of her.'

Blaze's mouth twists in answer, always loyal to his twin. He's unable to say a bad thing about her, even though I know he agrees with me.

'She's got her reasons—' he begins, but I elbow his side.

'Don't even think about it. I'm not having a bar of that rubbish you give me. She's a lunatic, and she may one day be the next Raven of the Hex!' I exclaim in mild horror. I've never brought myself to think about how the world would be with my sister running free through the lands, but it wouldn't be good.

'And you? You might win at this rate. You've lasted longer than I thought you would.'

My punch is forceful as it connects with his arm. He scrunches his nose up but otherwise gives me no indication that I've wounded him. It seems I'm in a violent mood today.

'I was—'

Instinct makes me peer around in search of Jack, checking he's all right. My heart stops suddenly. He is nowhere to be seen, with no evidence to show he was even here. Immediately thinking the worst, I sprint to the lava river to see if he's fallen in, but if he had, I would have heard a splash or tortured cries.

Whirling on Blaze, I point a finger at his chest, fury boiling inside me. '*Where is he?*'

He looks worried but shrugs. 'I don't know.'

'Where is he?' I repeat, grabbing the collar of his uniform, my fangs growing in a fit of rage. 'Ember put you up to this, didn't she?' I seethe, shaking him roughly.

'No, I swear. I don't know where he is!' he declares, gripping my wrists tightly and trying to pry my hands off him. His claims of innocence are silenced by a voice booming above us, echoing across the entire cave.

'Ravens,' the voice drawls, making me close my eyes in recognition. 'It seems the remaining Ravens for the trials have misplaced their guardians,' the Elder Raven says with amusement.

I meet my brother's gaze, loosening my hold on him slightly.

'You have ten minutes to meet in the arena. Here you will retrieve your lost possessions.'

Hissing with dismay, I reluctantly let go, my face twisting in sudden fear.

'But hurry. They don't have much time left,' the Elder Raven announces with a cold laugh.

'I'm going to kill her,' I fume, imagining my hands around the Elder Raven's neck.

Sprinting as fast as my legs can go, I don't bother to consider Blaze running after me as we head for the arena. As I speed under the twin entrances, I vaguely hear him shouting, 'Good luck!'

Stopping in my tracks, I take in the monstrosity before me. The arena is covered in glass domes, as high as two men and wide enough to lie down in. Inside these clear cages are the twenty guardians still competing, waiting for their Ravens to show up.

It seems I'm the first to arrive, and I spot Jack immediately, his silvery-blonde hair standing out. I sprint towards him, but he begins to wave at me, shouting for me to stop. As I approach his enclosure, I'm repelled by an invisible force that sends me flying, and I crash into the red sand.

'Are you all right?' Jack frets.

'Yeah,' I groan, rubbing my throbbing head. Getting to my feet, I notice by my feet a silver line that crosses the sand, preventing me from stepping any further. When I reach out to touch it, it's cold. When I push against it, it resists me.

'A shield.' I hum in thought. It looks strangely familiar, like the queen's own magic. Peering towards the other domes, I don't see any with the same line around them. 'Is everyone's task for releasing their guardian different, Jack?'

He purses his lips in thought, seemingly unharmed, but that doesn't dull the worry I harbour. 'Every dome has its own trap,' he confirms. 'I wasn't sure what ours was, but it seems you've found it.'

I stare up into the audience, wondering if the royal family is watching. Situated in the prime spot, the queen and her son sit in a glass box among the Ravens, watching me with keen interest. Eyeing Queen Adela, I see her faintly nod, urging me to solve her unique task.

As if on cue, a shimmer of colour washes over the clear dome Jack is stuck within. Across the glass, words begin to appear in mid-air.

AS QUEEN OF THE HOUSE, I HAVE ONE TASK.
WITH SHIELDS OF DEFENCE YOU NEED ONLY ASK.
WITH MAGIC RUSHING THROUGH YOUR HALF-BLOOD VEINS,
THE ANSWER WILL RELEASE WHAT THIS DOME CONTAINS.

I'm about to curse the stupid riddle when a sudden hissing sound distracts me.

As I scour the arena for where the sound may be coming from, Jack's yelp of concern grabs my attention as thick red smoke begins to cloud inside his prison, his feet slowly being consumed by gas.

'Uh-oh,' Jack utters, his back pressing up against the glass in an attempt to keep away from it. 'I think it may be poisonous,' he warns, trying to kick it away from him.

'Poisonous! Why do you say that?' I blurt, pushing myself up against the shield to see better.

'Well, as the obvious toxins expert out of the two of us, I would say it's never a good sign when your eyes start to burn and your throat suddenly starts to feel like sandpaper,' he answers, his voice hitching.

My hands clutch my head, demanding to find an answer to this problem. 'I need only ask ...' I mutter to myself, banging against the shield once more. 'Magic in my veins ...'

Cries of help echo around the arena as guardians yell out to their arriving Ravens. Merlot is one of them, frightened and pale as she searches the arena for Mercy. She spots me and comes to my side, then spins in a circle to find her partner. By the looks of it, she has come prepared with various weapons – a coil of rope, an axe and some throwing stars attached to her person.

'What's happening?' she asks, reading the clue my dome has written across it. 'We all get clues?'

'Not sure, but every dome has a trap.' I point to a few enclosures down, directing my friend to where Mercy is waving in our direction. 'She's over there. Be quick about it,' I order, pushing her away.

'Meet you at the finish line,' Merlot answers, rushing away.

Focusing back on my own guardian, I peer down at my hands, imagining the blood in my veins, magic the queen thinks I have swirling through them. Does she think I have magic, or is she taunting me?

'Ask the shield to step through,' Jack orders, the smoke, to my dismay, is up around his knees now, the crimson fog rippling peacefully as if promising a quiet demise.

'Please can you let me through?' I ask out loud, pushing against the barrier, but it still resists. 'Please may I gain access to my guardian?' I try, but with no success. 'It's no use,' I complain, pressing my head against it. 'Why won't you let me in?'

A shiver runs through my spine, making me stagger back in shock.

'The answer you seek is within your veins, the magic you possess to save those restrained,' a voice murmurs to me, the sound thick and heavy inside my head, like the sound of death itself.

'Of course!' I cry out.

Without thinking, I sprint for Merlot. She's carefully treading around the dome Mercy is kept within, poking and prodding the glass with caution.

I point to her weapons. 'Can I borrow your axe, please?'

She yanks it from her belt and hands it over without hesitation.

'I'll bring it back!' I promise, rushing back to my own dome.

Carefully I cut across my hand and let my blood bubble up, hoping it will be enough. After smearing it across the invisible shield, I wait for a moment, staring at the bloody handprint I've left behind.

'Please may I enter?' I whisper once more.

A crumpling sound echoes through my mind, and finally I'm able to pass the magic barrier.

41

The smoke is around his chest now, the fear in Jack's face evident. It makes my heart tighten in panic – there is no way I can fail.

'Nearly there,' I reassure my guardian, studying the glass around him. There are no keyholes, no gaps and no other written-out clues.

Without any other options, I decide to chip away at the enclosure, the metal of my axe sending fragments flying into my face. If I can't find a logical solution, then I will force it down with brute strength.

'Scarlet,' I hear Jack murmur, his voice faltering.

'Yes?' I huff.

Crack, crack, crack. I pound against the cage over and over again, my arms beginning to ache, but I grit my teeth in determination seeing the smoke has now risen to his shoulders. This *has* to work.

'If I don't make it—'

'Don't even *think* about saying what you're about to say!' I yell, heaving my body weight into every swing of my weapon. 'I'm getting you out of here if it's the last thing I do. Now keep your head above the smoke!'

He's quiet. Too quiet.

Crack, crack, crack.

'Please hear me out,' he begs, watching me chip away shard by shard. The cage is thicker than I expected. 'You are the best Raven I could have asked for. You accepted me. You welcomed me into your life without question, and you made this a better experience than I could ever have imagined.'

'If you think you're going to die, you have very little faith in me,' I spit, angry he would give up so easily, angry he doesn't have a sliver of hope.

He sighs, and I try to ignore him, focusing on the task at hand. My shoulders scream with the effort to break this damn glass.

'Of course I have faith in you.' He coughs so violently I stop, axe in mid-air, and glare at him, watching as little puffs of red smoke are sucked into his mouth.

Quickly! Keep swinging!

'If I don't make it out, I want you to know I would have loved to travel the world with you, to stand by your side and fight alongside you,' Jack continues, his hands upon the glass to help steady him as he stands on tiptoes.

'Stop it!' I shout, forcing back tears, blinking rapidly.

Crack, crack, crack.

It's only when he's quiet for longer than I expect him to be that my eyes flicker upwards, his face right there where I'm about to lay the axe down. Crimson smoke fills the dome, and all I can see is red.

'No!' I scream. I swing again and again, listening to his heartbeat slowly fade, dimming with every second.

Crack, crack, crack.

'Don't do this!' I beg, hoping he can still hear me, can still listen to me fighting for him as I know he would for me.

Crack, crack, crack.

The sound of collapsing glass sends hope through my chest. Another crack, and the axe falls through the thick glass. My hands grab for the weakened shards and pull the wall down enough to clamber through.

Smoke smothers me the second I enter the dome, the gas filtering out around me to escape its cage. I hold my breath and step through with stinging eyes, hands out to feel where I'm going.

'Jack.' I cough harshly and crawl on the floor, stretching my hands out for his body. The fog is so thick I can hardly swallow without the feeling of knives in my lungs.

My hands feel material, his trousers in reach as I slide over to him. 'I got you,' I assure him. Cradling him under his shoulders and knees, I lift him with all the strength I have left, drained from breaking the glass.

I stagger over to the hole in the glass and carefully manoeuvre him into the fresh air, my lungs gulping down the oxygen like they have been deprived for years.

As I carefully lay him down on the red sand, his face is relaxed like he's in a deep sleep. I press a hand to his chest – it doesn't move.

'You're not leaving me that easily,' I declare, pressing on his chest roughly to try to restart his heart. I breathe into his mouth after a time, holding his nose, and I silently demand that his body cooperate. 'You can't leave me like this!' I hiss, pressing harder and faster. I give him more air until I start to feel dizzy.

Finally I find a heartbeat, so faint my tears become a sob. I prop him up against my body, then cut my hand once more and dribble blood into his mouth, stroking his throat in the hope he will swallow.

Gradually the rhythm of his heart becomes stronger, my blood slowly working its magic.

'Stay with me, Jack. I'm not leaving you.'

I hold his hand and watch as his eyes flutter briefly, his face so pale it's like he's gone to hell and back. Stroking his cheek, I can't look away. The arena is no longer important. The screams of others being slaughtered are silent, and all I see is him.

'Scarlet,' he murmurs, peering up at me.

I wrap my arms around his head and pull him towards me, his hair brushing against my chin as I cocoon him against my chest and laugh with relief.

'You're okay,' I sigh, telling myself he's alive, that he's breathing again. 'You're really okay.'

Slowly he sits up. I wait beside him, watching for any warning signs. Carefully he turns, and warmth envelops me as he embraces me, his hands in my hair, his lips brushing my neck, and I feel my body shudder with relief, with grief for losing him for those few moments and with hope that he's still here with me. Fighting with me. Hugging me.

'You scared me,' I whisper as I stroke his back, needing the feel of him. 'I thought I lost you.'

'I'm all right,' he murmurs before inhaling deeply. His body stiffens, and I back off instantly, seeing his wince.

'Are you still hurting?' The axe is in my hand, ready to cut my wrist, when his fingers lie upon mine, stopping me from draining any more blood.

'No, Scarlet. You've lost enough. I'm fine, just a little tender.' His eyes pour into me, urging me to understand that he is telling me the truth. 'I'm fine.'

I help him to his feet, and we slowly make our way to the arena exit, where healers in red coats wait. Annie, who healed me after my second trial, stands in a white uniform, ready and waiting to take Jack out of my clutches, but I wave her off, needing the weight of my guardian now more than ever.

'Do you not want to let me go?' Jack asks, our arms wrapped around one another.

'No,' I admit, finding his wide smile when I look up.

42

It's early when I wake up. Ruby is already at the dining table with sheets of paper, her fingers covered in ink splotches as she writes letters.

'Good morning,' I murmur, setting myself down at the table, letting myself take a moment to wake up.

My mother goes into the kitchen and begins to make me a drink, heating it within her palms before handing it over.

The smell of tea leaves wafts around me, and I hum in pleasure as I take my first sip. 'Thank you.'

'How is your guardian?' Ruby asks, slowly organising her writing equipment to the side, her attention focusing on me.

'He's on the mend, a little delicate when he inhales deeply, but he'll survive.' I smile, thinking of him last night, when I kept him company with Annie in the healing clinic.

Letting the warmth of my drink spread through my fingers, I clasp my cup to my chest and study my mother. She looks uneasy, but I'm not sure why. Since the trial, I've made sure to come home, to show my family I'm safe, that I am well.

'Are you all right?' I ask, watching Ruby shuffle in her seat.

'Actually, there is something I wanted to speak to you about,' she admits, her hands finding their way to her lap as if she doesn't know what else to do with them. 'You and your guardian are quite close.'

Instantly I'm on edge, but I nod. 'Obviously.'

It takes Ruby a moment to articulate what she wants to say, her eyes flickering with thought. 'What I mean is, you care for him.'

'Yes,' I answer hesitantly, taking another sip of tea.

'We can care for people, Scarlet, but please, whatever you do, don't fall in love with him.' Her words aren't harsh or demanding. They don't make me feel small and inferior, like I thought they would. But they do sound concerned, worried for my well-being, like she knows what it's like to be in my position. 'It never ends well, especially if the Elder Raven hears of it.'

'You know this from personal experience?' I ask, wondering if the hex Roux mentioned will allow her to answer.

As expected, my mother's mouth opens, but nothing comes out. She clears her throat and tries again, this time carefully wording her response. 'I've been hurt before, and I don't wish the same to happen to you. I want you to live without that fear, without being hunted down for making the same decisions I once made.'

'I don't love him,' I claim and I know it's the truth.

Do I think Jack is a nice person? Yes.

Do I think Jack is attractive to look at? Again, yes.

But I know where the line is, I am reminded constantly by everyone around me what would happen if I were to step past it.

The sad smile upon my mother's face is heartbreaking, like she knows something I don't.

'My little bird,' she murmurs softly, stroking my face gently, her red eyes bright with affection. 'Love always finds its way to the surface. It shines brighter than anything else in the world, fixing every scar, every crack, every break you've ever endured. It is a wonderful feeling to face but something you must hide if you ever experience it. The Elder Raven has spies. She has people undercover to stop anything that occurred from happening again.' Her voice is low and rushed, like she's trying to reveal the words to me before the magic binding her realises what she's saying.

'Did *you* have to hide your feelings?' I ask, feeling extremely close to a truth I've been wanting to know for so long.

Do you love him? I silently ask.

'Since the day I met him,' Ruby confirms, surprising me.

'And my father, did he feel the same way?'

My mother's mouth tugs up at one side, saying nothing. But it's her expression that reveals the answer – the truth that's been carefully hidden away from others like a sin.

Very much so, she seems to say.

Emotion swells through me at finally knowing that my father wasn't a mistake. They *loved* each other. They had me out of adoration – not lust, like everyone suspected.

'Do you miss him?' I whisper. Silence envelops me as I watch her struggle for words.

'I'm sorry. I can't say much more.'

My hand slithers across the table to hold hers. Her skin is warm as she squeezes my fingers tenderly. 'I understand. Thank you.'

A loud knocking echoes through the room, making me jump to my feet and making Ruby set her hands alight.

'Delivery!' someone shouts from outside our home.

Sharing a look, we both smile at our overreactions.

I open the front door to find a Raven child with two crimson envelopes. 'For Ember and Scarlet Seraphine,' he announces, and he pushes them into my hands before running off.

'What have you got there?' Ruby asks, sitting herself back down.

Handing over Ember's envelope, I take a seat and look at the letter addressed to me. My name is written in cursive handwriting, the ink dark against the paper. Inside I find six red cards that match the wrapping, but drawn upon them in metallic gold ink are six animals, one on each card.

A lion, a beetle, a hare, a snake, a fox and an owl.

'Interesting.' I hum, looking at the back of each card for a clue, but I find none. Picking up the envelope once more, I find a small scrawl on the inside, small enough that I would have missed it if I hadn't gone looking for it.

CHOOSE ONE CARD AND BRING IT ALONG TO YOUR NEXT TRAINING SESSION.

My brow quirks.

'What animal will you choose?' Ruby asks, admiring the lion picture.

'I'm not sure. Are these cards supposed to mean something?'

My mother's face doesn't give away any indication she understands what the deck means.

'I assume you never had this when *you* competed for the Hex Trials.'

Bright red eyes meet mine as she shakes her head.

'Unfortunately, this makes as little sense to me as it does to you, but I suggest you go with your gut instinct.'

Pursing my lips, I decide to shuffle the cards and pick one at random. When I choose the snake, I crinkle my nose in distaste.

'No?' Ruby ponders, watching me with amusement.

'No, that doesn't feel right,' I decide, and put it back. Taking a second card, I pull out the fox. I sigh, feeling like this is a foolish way to select an animal.

'Just pick the one you want,' Ruby urges, taking the cards away and placing them all back on the table, facing me. 'Choose the one that *feels* right.'

My hand hovers over them all, and finally it stops over one I didn't think I'd choose, but somehow I know it's the right choice.

My mother smiles fondly, her eyes warming. 'Ah, the hare.'

PART THREE

*The Raven of the
Hex*

EMBER SERAPHINE

43

Never have I seen Jack ride a horse before, so I decide to train on horseback today.

'Horse riding? Really?' Jack asks, stroking the muzzle of a dappled grey.

'It's safer to cover all bases. The last trial could be *anything*,' I argue, watching him intently. He wears a dark top today that shows off his toned arms. My eyes follow the lines of his muscles, but I remember what Ruby told me. I have to keep my feelings hidden, for my sake and Jack's.

'Fine. I want Misery, then.' He knocks on the stall of the biggest stallion, who's known for his temper tantrums. His reputation for bucking off Ravens is notorious, and it's the reason I'm one of very few who get to ride him.

'He's difficult, even for the best of riders,' I warn as Jack unlocks the door and steps inside.

He begins to tack him up, ready for training. 'I'm sure he will be splendid,' he insists.

Jack leads Misery out of the barn and hops on without trouble. The sight of him upon the great stallion does strange things to me, and I have to remove myself before he sees the heat in my cheeks.

Impressively, Jack's right. His riding is admirable as he canters the stallion around the sand school, his back straight and heels down like a true equestrian, his horse listening to every prompt.

'I was hoping you'd be thrown off,' I admit from my own steed.

'Sorry to disappoint you,' he replies. He pokes his tongue out as he circles me.

We've set up some jumps, and the pair fly over them as if they've worked together for years. Never have I seen Misery look so, well, not miserable. They suit each other, the pair looking annoyingly magnificent together.

'All right, Torment. Let's go show them how it's really done,' I say, squeezing the mare's sides.

She starts in a steady trot before easing into a smooth canter. We soar over three parallel oxers – extremely high metal poles that need Torment to use full effort to clear. We excel at each jump, the mare extremely talented in that area. Her tail flicks with every obstacle.

'Impressive,' Jack says in compliment when we finish the set, coming to our side.

We shift into a fast-paced walk around the sand school to cool our horses down, my guardian clearly not in need of any more teaching.

'I don't just work with horses because I'm good at scooping up manure,' I chirp happily. 'When did you learn to ride?'

He runs a hand behind Misery's ears for a scratch. 'Mum taught me when she came back from guardianship one time. She said they learned it when they joined the Hex and thought I would enjoy it.' He smiles as if remembering the memory fondly. 'After the first lesson, she paid for me to continue even when she went back to work. I think it was partly out of guilt for leaving me again, but I continued riding for a few years before I decided to train in other areas.'

'It must have been hard not having her around,' I muse, keeping an eye on some males riding around the track outside the sand school. They shout and laugh loudly, being generally rowdy while racing their steeds, and I can't help but shake my head in frustration. No wonder I have to attend to so many of the poor horses for injuries – not that anyone listens to me about their care.

'I guess it's the same as you not having your father around,' Jack says.

Whipping my head towards my guardian, I frown. 'That's nothing like your situation.'

'Of course it is. I bet you miss him just as much as I miss my mum when she's away.'

'I can't miss someone I don't know,' I counter.

'Sure you can. You can miss the presence of a father figure. You can sense the void of not having a second parent around – even if you've never met him,' Jack offers, making me think his words through.

Do I miss my father? *Yes*, I think. I certainly miss having the opportunity to know him – to have someone else to look up to like I do Ruby.

'See, you're thinking it through. That means I'm right.' Jack grins. He walks Misery nearer so he can tug a piece of my hair before trotting away, aiming for the exit gate.

Unable to help myself, I smile and follow him out. Out of the corner of my eye, I see the males ride towards us. The group beats us to the exit and blocks the gate, making Jack stop. Misery stomps a foot in frustration.

'What a pleasant surprise to see you, half-blood, and with your human too.' One male smirks. His long red hair is slightly greasy and pulled back into a slick ponytail. I've worked with him before, and it's never been pleasant.

'Carnelian,' I say nonchalantly. 'I see you're *still* distressing Wraith. I thought we spoke about this.'

The mare looks on edge, her eyes wide and alert for her rider's command, and it makes me sick. Carnelian is a serial abuser when it comes to his steeds – he kicks and slaps and doesn't give a shit what condition he returns them in.

'She's fine. She's just calming down.' He waves me off, then nudges the mare up against Torment's side. Thankfully, the horses don't mind one another's presence, but he knows I ask to give them their space when possible – some of us actually respect their boundaries.

'Ease up, Car. I know you like to be near me, but you don't have to sit in my lap,' I quip, earning an annoyed expression from him when his friends snigger.

'You wish,' he scoffs, turning to his friends, who instantly quieten. He spins back to me, hatred shimmering within his eyes, and I know he's about to spew some hostile words. 'Surprised you have lasted this long, to be honest, Scarlet. I thought you'd be buried by now.' He grins, now edging closer to Jack's horse, knowing of Misery's temper. 'Alas, we all know your sister will be the one to win. You should step down now before she burns you more than you already are.' He sneers down at my hands – the only part of me I can't cover with clothing. 'Because let's face it, you're no match for her, are you?' The male laughs, his friends joining in.

'We'll see about that,' I reply, squeezing my legs in silent command for Torment to push forward, pushing through their group. Their horses are calm enough I know it won't cause problems, but when I look back, Jack is still standing in the same spot.

'We will,' Carnelian says, a glint of malice in his gaze. 'I'll enjoy watching you being torn apart. Ember has a knack for making a spectacle out of everything, and I'm sure when she tears you to pieces, we'll all save a little bit each to remember the abomination we used to know and love.' Carnelian smiles, his teeth sharp and wicked.

My mouth twists in distaste. I'm not a stranger to horrid words being thrown my way, but the mention of my sister does something to me, like sharp nails clawing into my chest.

A strand of water whips out from nowhere, grabs Carnelian around his neck and tightens, making him gurgle. He's lifted off his saddle, suspended in mid-air. Wraith instantly bolts, finding the opportunity good enough to escape her rider.

'Get off me!' Carnelian chokes, trying to grab the water, but his hands pass through the substance, unable to get a grip on it.

My stare lands on Jack, whose face is as hard as stone. His hands are tight around the reins, his eyes glowing bright blue. 'Jack,' I say urgently, wondering what he's doing. 'Jack, that's enough.'

'Apologise,' Jack states harshly, his expression finally creasing into fury. 'Apologise to Scarlet *right now*.'

The gurgling continues as I watch Carnelian wither and jerk. Indecision crosses his eyes, and I wonder if he would rather die at Jack's hand than express regret to me.

'I'm s-sorry!' he blurts finally.

'That's enough, Jack,' I repeat.

Reluctantly the water unravels from Carnelian's neck and evaporates. The Raven drops to the sand, gasping and groping at his neck for relief. He wheezes, trying to breathe in as much air as he can. The male glares at my guardian, pointing a finger at him, but before he can say a word, Jack walks Misery straight up to him, the stallion coping with the close proximity for his rider wonderfully.

'If you ever insult my Raven again, I will hang you from

the ceiling of this cave, and I will stuff your mouth with water and watch you drown.'

With that, he kicks Misery on and pushes through the group of surprised males, leaving them watching his back with mixed looks of disgust and approval. The outburst surprises me, but I try not to show my shock.

'Come on, Scarlet,' Jack urges, his voice soft as he rides away.

The ride is silent as we approach the barn, swinging the doors wide open. We tie the horses up to groom them, and neither of us talks before we've settled them into their newly cleaned stalls.

I'm hesitant to bring up Carnelian but my guardian is quiet. Too quiet.

'Jack ...'

He turns to me with a grim look on his face. 'I'm sorry. I didn't mean to talk on your behalf. I know you can look after yourself, but they just—' He stops, clenching his hands so hard his knuckles turn white.

'They're only words,' I assure him, wrapping my hands around his fists to ease his anger.

Slowly his hands relax, coiling around mine. He brings our hands up to his face and leans his chin on them.

He sighs in defeat. 'I don't want you ever thinking what they say is true, that you don't have a chance at winning the trials,' he murmurs, his voice low and on edge.

'I don't take their words to heart,' I promise.

'You're talented, incredibly intelligent, kind-hearted

and loyal – those are all qualities a Raven of the Hex *should* have. You have every chance Ember has of achieving your goals, and they'll be eating their words once we are crowned the winners. Just you wait.' My guardian's mouth tugs up in an attempt to smile.

'Thank you,' I say. 'That means a lot coming from you.'

Staring up into his face, I realise how close we are. I see my face mirrored in his clear blue eyes, and the clear desire in my reflection. He looms over me, seeming to be getting closer the longer we stay holding hands.

Love always finds its way to the surface. It is a wonderful feeling to face but something you must hide if you ever experience it.

My hands hesitantly release him, the sound of his heart thundering in his chest causing me to avert my gaze. I have to step away, have to distance myself from him. Love may not be what I'm feeling right now but I'm afraid if I allow myself to grow close to Jack, it will eventually grow into something wild and untamed.

'Jack, I can't do this.' My palms begin to sweat, my nerves growing under his intense gaze.

He considers this, heading dipping closer. 'Can't what?'

'Let you get too close.' My guardian's eyes flash to outside the barn, to the arena beyond, before landing back on me. 'I feel this pull towards you but I cannot let it become more than intrigue.'

Jack does not reply but nods, pressing his lips together.

'This is purely temptation,' I continue. It sounds more like a statement than a question – my belief being the more I say it, the more I'll trust the words are true. 'We are friends. We are Raven and guardian. But that is all we *can* be.'

He moves away slightly, expression hard to read. 'You're right. It's safer for you and I to remain platonic.'

Something twinges inside my chest but I don't let it stop from forcing on a smile. 'I'm glad you agree.'

'I do.'

'Good.' I nod tightly.

He nods back. 'Good.'

We stand staring at one another, the seconds passing between us. My eyes trail over his handsome features, dropping to his lips, mind wandering for a moment. I bet his mouth tastes as good as he smells ...

'Oh fuck it,' Jack relents seeming to read my mind, taking my face in his hands. 'Just this once.'

And then my guardian kisses me, and like the fool I am, I kiss him back.

44

The kiss is urgent, greedy and delicious on my lips. I'm consumed by his nearness, and his ocean scent washes over me, making me want *more*.

'Just this once,' I repeat, as the need for him grows with every second he is devouring me. 'Then we can put these feelings behind us.'

My hands grab him excitedly. His moans are a melody to my ears when I push him inside an empty stall, and his body slams against the stone wall as I pin him with my body.

Our tongues entwine, and our breathing becomes urgent as our hands wander hungrily, needing to feel every part of the other. I stroke Jack's chest – he's broad and strong as I slip my hand under his shirt, the muscles I reach tensing under my eager touch.

'Fuck,' he murmurs, breaking our lips apart as I trail my nails down his back next. The shudder that escapes his mouth makes me smile. 'Remind me not to enjoy this so much.'

Suddenly he lifts my body up, and my legs naturally fold around his waist, squeezing tightly as I take possession of his lips once more. A gasp leaves me when he spins and pins *me* up against the wall, his strong body pressed against mine.

The stone wall is cold against my back, the temperature making my back arch into him. I can feel him hardening beneath me, my eyes peering down to his tightening trousers.

'You are hating every moment of this,' I prompt with a smirk.

He follows my gaze and chuckles. 'We should stop.'

Please don't.

'We should,' I murmur halfheartedly, shivers erupting down my spine at the feel of his fingers slithering under my shirt and across my back, leaving cool kisses along my imperfect skin. My breath hitches when Jack's lips lower to my neck, biting and licking. 'Because this feels terrible,' I finish lamely.

My guardian laughs against my skin, the heat of his breath causing my cheeks to flush and my body to ache.

In this position, I feel small and protected, his body cocooning me like a safety blanket, and I can't help enjoying the feeling. My guardian's strong hands move over my stomach and roam higher against my chest. I hold my breath as he skims the underside of my breasts, my nipples visible through my shirt.

'The sight of you does nothing to me,' he whispers breathlessly.

What a pretty lie.

'And the sight of you does nothing to me,' I murmur back, groaning when he pinches my nipples.

'I can see that,' he murmurs sarcastically, palming my breast, kneading it gently to watch my reaction.

My moans become more frequent as I throw my head back, hands clinging to his shoulders, part of me unable to stop listening for anyone who may stumble across a Raven and her guardian getting caught in a forbidden moment.

Jack presses my mouth to his – mostly likely to silence my continuous groans. I taste him, taunt him and in response his hips begin to rock, making me breathe heavily as he rubs against the very parts of me that want him most.

'Please don't stop,' I murmur against his lips, done with pretending.

How does he taste as good as he smells?

Jack begins to kiss my jaw, peppering me with tiny bites that make my body jerk with pleasure. He lifts my shirt, unrestrained unlike the man I first met in the Badger's Sett.

'Remember to be quiet,' my guardian says before his mouth covers my breasts and sucks, making a wave of emotions course through my body in answer.

'Oh, Jack ...' I pull his hair in silent demand.

My whimpers become obnoxiously loud, and he laughs against my skin, covering my mouth with his free hand. I bite his fingers gently, and the fiery look I earn floods me with heat and passion.

It's only when I stiffen does Jack pause, looking up at me questioningly.

I listen closer, frustration and longing filling me. 'Someone is coming.'

Instantly I'm placed back on my feet, my shirt replaced to its former state and the locks of my hair that have escaped are smoothed away from my face by my guardian who places them behind my ear.

He grants me one last kiss before murmuring, 'We'll talk about this later.'

With that he leaves the stall – heading for the tack room to most likely calm himself.

A shaky breath breaks free, my hands unsteady with what just occurred.

I shouldn't have kissed him back. I should have stopped him before it got so heated.

Fuck. Fuck. Fuck.

A loud voice declares their arrival, making me glad Jack has left already. Clearing my face of any expression, I walk out in the main area of the stables and greet the Raven.

45

The castle grounds are filled with only fifteen Ravens and their guardians. Jack stands behind me like a sentry, his presence now more prominent to me than ever before. Every time I focus on him, I see his hungry gaze and remember the taste of his mouth on mine, and I thank the higher powers that the Elder Raven can't read minds, or else we'd be in deep trouble.

Our leader stands like a statue, staring at us as we wait in a line. The great hall has been cleared of all equipment, and it looks like the room it's supposed to be. The stained-glass windows look recently polished, their colours vibrant as they shine onto the floor, shapes and hues of blue, green and gold dancing across the space. It looks ready for a ball, minus the music and tables full of food and drink.

The creaking of a heavy old door echoes through the room, and I find myself standing up straighter. The queen and her son bring in a stranger, an old lady who waddles slowly with a walking stick.

The royals sit upon their thrones, the princess's empty as usual, looking down from the dais at us. The unfamiliar woman, however, makes herself comfortable upon a middle step, her clothing long and flowy as it pools around her. She smiles pleasantly at us, not a hint of fear in her features.

'Dameer?' Jack whispers.

I nod subtly, smelling the faint magic on her.

'Hello all,' the woman says, her voice high and full of merriment. 'I am Silva, and I am here to read your fortunes.'

Shuffling occurs, and the Elder Raven clears her throat. The movement stops immediately.

'You have been sent an envelope with six animals. You should have brought *one* card with you today,' the woman explains.

Peering down, I make sure I still hold my chosen card. When I showed Jack, he was surprised. When I showed Ember, she laughed.

'Every creature comes with a story of its being and personality. We will talk about that today. Please, sit down.' She motions to the floor, then brings out six cards from her skirts and holds up the first three cards as we all make ourselves comfortable.

'Let us begin with these. The owl, the lion and the hare.'

Looking across at Merlot, I see she has the owl with her. She looks at mine and smiles.

'The owl symbolises wisdom and knowledge.' Silva smiles wistfully, meeting my eyes briefly before moving on. 'The lion –' she holds the card up and moves it around for everyone to see – 'symbolises strength, courage and justice. They're great leaders.'

My stare finds Ember, who I know has chosen this card, and she smirks at the description, obviously finding similarities between herself and the animal she has chosen.

'And lastly, we have the hare, which symbolises diligence, ambition and swiftness in the face of oncoming change.' Silva takes a moment to let us absorb this information.

I peer around at Jack, and he looks as confused as I do. What is this all for?

'You are currently wondering what these animals have to do with the upcoming trial,' Silva guesses, studying our faces like it's her job to know each and every one of us. 'You have unwittingly chosen what animal you identify with most. If you have chosen the lion, please stand up.'

Ember and six others get to their feet, flaunting their cards.

'You are good contenders for the trials. You are natural-born leaders and are powerful. Please stand beside our sovereign.' Silva motions behind her to the royal family.

'Stand up if you chose the owl,' Silva commands.

Merlot and Mercy are among three pairs.

'You are independent thinkers, observant listeners and, in my opinion, lovely companions to have. Please tag along with your peers.'

Merlot joins the group with my sister, and my insides start to bubble with doubt. What do these animals mean for the royal family, and how will it affect the results?

Jack's fingers graze my knee, and my skin tingles at the contact. Looking up, I find his head tilted, silently asking if I'm all right. My hesitant nod makes him stroke a thumb across my leg before quickly pulling away.

'And lastly, who has the hare?' Silva asks.

It's quiet as I get to my feet. I'm the only person to have chosen this card. Everyone sits staring up at me with a mixed look of amusement and confusion.

'Only one person? My, my, how interesting.' Silva chuckles to herself.

I personally don't see what's funny, but I don't react.

'You, my dear, are careful with your choices, determined

when your mind is set, and you aspire to greatness. You are quick to adapt when the world around you changes. These are brilliant qualities for the next Raven of the Hex.'

The compliment warms me up, my smile growing. Jack and I are waved over to the royal family, who now have eleven Ravens and their guardians surrounding the throne.

'For those of you who chose the fox, the beetle or the snake, I regret to inform you that your future is not within the Hex. Your qualities are vast and numerous, but today you must understand we can only have *one* Raven of the Hex. Unfortunately, that person is not you.'

Silence fills the room, shock rippling through both groups as we all realise that the tiny decision of picking one animal has brought the verdict of success or failure.

'That's not fair,' someone protests, a Raven whose hair is so long it's pinned up in an array of knots upon her head. 'You can't determine our values from a fucking piece of paper.'

'Your sovereign has asked this of me. Are you saying her decisions are foolish?' Silva counters.

The Raven's mouth twists in distaste as she eyes Queen Adela, who watches in amusement, before she finds the Elder Raven staring. She quickly averts her gaze, and nothing else is said.

'Now that's over,' Silva says, slowly getting to her feet. A royal guard rushes forward to help her up. 'Shall we begin? I want the girl who has the hare card first.'

The chamber Silva occupies is small but cosy. A fire burns in the corner, its crackling sound filling the silence. My guardian and I sit at a small round table that is covered in an emerald tablecloth. Upon the material are depictions of magic, stars and crescent moons.

'So, you chose the hare,' Silva states from her place opposite me. She fans out a stack of purple cards so they lie face down on the table between us.

'Yes,' I answer, my leg fidgeting.

Jack's palm covers my thigh, urging me to stop.

'I need you both to choose two cards for me. These cards will indicate your future as Hex members. I will be able to see whether your pathways will join cohesively, and thus whether you will be a good choice for our sovereign to let you compete in the last trial.'

The purple cards are prettily decorated, with foxes and moonlight upon them, their foiling of silver and gold making the violet look deep and mysterious. My hand gravitates towards two cards, one on each side. Jack chooses two in the middle.

Silva takes them away before we can see what is on their other sides, her face neutral until she studies all four. Her dark blue eyes widen with alarm, and my heart races in answer.

'What's wrong?' Jack asks, leaning forward across the table.

'Nothing is wrong per se.' Silva's mouth twists unconvincingly. 'I must say, though, your lives will be full of adventure, full of exploit and deceit, but I can sense that together you will overcome many things. It could be both bad and good – nothing set in stone yet, though, of course.'

'How do you know? What are the pictures?' I wonder, peering around her cards, but she snaps them away and enfolds them in her skirts before I can get a glance.

'If I were to reveal your futures, you'd want to change your timelines.'

I share a look with Jack, his expression conveying my thoughts. We'd want to change our timelines? Why?

Silva continues, seeming oblivious to our worry. 'You must not know the path you are set on, because it is always changing. Right now it may say one thing, but tomorrow it can change and flow into something else entirely.'

'Then why do this at all? Why not do this *after* the final trial?' I ask, getting frustrated. Several Ravens have been sent home because they didn't choose the correct animal on Silva's list, and now she says they do not determine our fates?

'Because Queen Adela wishes to know more than what your destiny is. She wants to know more of who *you* are. And with your choosing of these cards, I have a fair idea of what type of characters you are, and what type of pairing you are as Raven and guardian.'

The look on her face is assessing, as if she knows *exactly* what type of pair Jack and I are. I refrain from looking his way and instead scowl.

'Well, I hope for our sake we are capable of being in the Hex,' I say.

'You are. Together you'll move mountains, but we shall see in regard to the last trial. It will not be easy, and it will test the very limits of you,' Silva says, aiming the words at me.

'Of me? Not Jack?'

'No. The guardians will not be present in the last trial. This challenge is for the Ravens only,' Silva confirms, making me gulp.

Jack meets my gaze, and I can see he wants to react but doesn't know how to in front of Silva. If we were alone, he'd probably tug on a strand of my hair, but in front of the older woman, he tries to smile reassuringly.

'You'll be fine, Scarlet,' he says. 'If anyone can win these trials, it's you.'

For Roux's sake, I hope so.

Jack's words spin inside my head long after we leave Silva's chamber of fortune telling.

46

The guardians are no longer asked to train with us at Songbird Castle, and this rattles me. Somehow I've become so accustomed to Jack being beside me that without him I feel unprotected, like my back will be stabbed at any moment.

Thankfully, I still have Merlot, so we warm up together, stretching out our limbs as groups of Ravens prepare for a day of testing. The great hall has been shuffled around so different weapons and equipment are laid out ready for whatever is in store for us today.

'Three days,' Merlot murmurs as she sits on the springy floor, bending her torso over one leg and touching her toes. 'It doesn't seem like enough time for the final trial. I feel unprepared, and we've been through this three times already. It never seems to get easier.'

Three days. My heart hammers at the statement. Three days until my fate is decided. Three days until we find out if Roux will be saved.

'I don't think anyone feels prepared. All we can do is improve our skills and hope the final trial will require our strengths rather than our weaknesses.' I shrug, hoping she doesn't second-guess my calmness, because in actual fact, I'm extremely anxious about what's to come.

Ember struts in and sits with some older females, the group reminding me of a pack of lionesses ready to pounce the moment they feel threatened. They whisper among themselves, eyeing the two of us every now and then.

'I just hope that the trial isn't something to do with creatures. The dragon scarred me for life – literally and figuratively,' I admit, earning a sympathetic look from Merlot. Her bright red eyes roam over my hands, the sleeves of my shirt covering the worst parts up.

'Ember saved you, didn't she?' she asks, briefly peering at my sister as she bends over her other leg. 'There seems no other logical way for you to have survived.'

'I don't really remember what happened, but I think Ember used her fire magic to shield us in a way.'

Merlot's brow rises, and I shrug, not really understanding either.

'The healer said if I had been hit full force by the dragon's fire, I would have died instantly. Something Ember did that day protected me but left me with these unhealable scars.'

'She doesn't seem the type to do that,' Merlot murmurs, not wanting our conversation to be heard by anyone else. 'No offence, of course. But I'm glad she did.'

My smile widens – I take no offence at all. Ember has never been affectionate, has never been the type of person to put someone else's needs above her own, so that day has stumped me. She seems to regret her decision to save me, and Blaze always defends her, as usual.

'It's a mystery, isn't it?' I ponder, hoping to continue my stretching off the floor. I lift myself to one knee before a pair of boots come into sight and a small knife is thrust up against my jaw. The metal stings my skin, and my scarred hand begins to bleed.

'How the fuck are you still here?' Winella seethes.

'A pleasure seeing you too,' I mutter, trying my best not to move.

'Is this some silly game? Why would the queen allow *you* to compete this far on? You're a fake and a fraud, and you can't even defend yourself without your bothersome guardian around to save you.'

'I think you've made enough of a ruckus, Winella. Don't make another scene, or I'll show you *again* how I can defend myself,' I warn.

The Elder Raven may have pinned the blame on me the day we fought, but I recall Winella's friend Carmine was unable to heal in time for the next trial and therefore had to forfeit. From the look on the female's face, she, too, recollects that episode.

'That was a fluke, and you know it,' Winella argues.

Standing up, I let the knife press into my throat, and I refrain from wincing. I close the distance between us and lower my voice, hoping she'll understand my threat loud and clear.

'What I think the problem is, Winella, is that you hate that people will stand by me, that others see something in me worth fighting for, whereas you ... you have *no one* – only a guardian who feels compelled to guard you out of duty, not because they actually care.'

This, of course, is not the right thing to say to someone who is holding a knife to my throat, but my tether of patience with this female has finally snapped. In seconds, she slices, but I lean back enough to avoid severe damage.

'I'm sure my guardian would act as loyal as yours if I slept with him too,' Winella spits. She twirls back from me, snatching a sword from another Raven.

Merlot in seconds throws me some daggers she has in her belt so I'm not weaponless.

'Ever heard of the word *kindness*, Winella? I am simply nice to him, and he answers in kind with loyalty.'

The sword is sharp as it arcs for my stomach. I jump back, and the other Ravens all turn to watch, gravitating towards us slowly. Merlot is there, ready to step in if need be, but this is between me and Winella.

'Ha! I don't need loyalty. That's for dogs. I much prefer showing those who don't matter what it's like to be on the wrong side of my anger,' Winella exclaims.

Her sword crashes against my daggers, the vibrations shooting up both my arms. My teeth grind together with the difficult move. I won't be able to beat her with my weapons.

'Loyalty lasts longer than fear. Eventually, people will get sick of your shit and will fight against you just to see you fall,' I scoff, pushing her away.

She smiles, hardly winded, while I feel myself tiring with my miniature weapons. Having run out of ideas, I briefly look around, and only one other person has a sword. Ember gives me a lifted brow as if to say, *Show me how capable you are. My sword won't help you today.*

Winella follows my gaze and grins. 'Oh, is that one person who *won't* help you? That's refreshing, and so lovely to see it's your very own blood.'

'She won't help, because she knows I'll trounce you without it. It's not worth her time,' I counter, hoping Ember won't speak up in spite of me. Thankfully, she keeps quiet, but she doesn't look impressed.

'All I see is shit running out of your mouth, half-blood.'

Winella stabs, and I dodge just in time, my knives useless against her.

She is quick, constant and precise with her strikes,

knowing I'll eventually misstep. It's when she's forcing me back that she effortlessly slices my leg, then my arm. I falter, my wounded calf suddenly weak, and I fall to the floor, one of my knives skidding away from me. A Raven steps on it but doesn't make a move to hand it back.

Winella readies her strike as I cower away, but Merlot advances, hands outstretched, and suddenly everything stops. 'Enough with this madness,' she commands, fingers fluttering as her power comes into play.

Never have I seen my friend use her magic against someone, but my eyes widen as I study Winella, who stands as if frozen in time, her arm up, ready to strike, her blood listening to its new master – Merlot.

'I'll release you, but only if you promise to stand down,' Merlot says. 'We will go our separate ways and leave the fighting for the trials. Understood?'

Winella's face creases – whether in rage or in pain, I'm not sure, but slowly she's allowed a nod.

As abruptly as it appeared, the blood magic evaporates from around us, and Winella's body relaxes once more as she massages her wrists and forearms back to life. She scowls at us before stalking away. The other Ravens watch in amazement and wariness of my friend's power.

Merlot stands guard a second before coming for me, kneeling before me with concern in her features. I notice the dark circles under her eyes – shadows that weren't there before. Was this the effect her blood magic had on her?

'Are you all right?' Merlot asks.

'Are *you*?'

Merlot nods tightly. She'd mentioned once she hated using her power against people. She points to the blood pooling beneath my leg, most likely wanting to change the subject.

'You'll need a healer for that.'

'I'm sure it's not life threatening,' I answer, noticing my bleeding hand, the scar still open. 'This should have closed up though ...' I trail off before the sound of skin and bone breaking echoes through my skull.

A quiet sound of agony and fear escapes Merlot's mouth, her eyes wide with terror as blood starts to trickle through her lips and onto my boots.

Drip, drip, drip.

'Merlot!' I shout, clasping my arms around her as she falls heavily into me. Winella's sword is embedded in her back.

The sound of the weapon being removed from my friend's body is something I'll never forget, the guttural noise that escapes Merlot's lips making me bare my fangs.

Winella looms above us once more, face full of fury, crimson eyes gleaming with desire to hurt – to kill. Unconsciously I cover Merlot as much as I can as the female takes her second chance to finally end me.

'I'll show you madness.' Winella laughs, plunging her bloody sword downwards.

Suddenly a silver glow sparks between us. I expect to feel the sharp blade, but no pain comes. Instead, a small layer of warmth coats me.

'*You will not touch my champion!*'

Shivers erupt through me at the sound, a loud and demanding voice that radiates with powerful energy and echoes through the great hall. The stained-glass windows rattle with the force. A small tornado of wind begins to circle us, and furniture around the room is lifted, flying in the air.

Finally the illumination dwindles, and I find myself peering up at a woman in a dark green dress, ice-cold wind rippling her gown like liquid emerald. Long midnight hair flows down her back as she stands before me, emitting a silver glow like an angel of death.

Shouts of horror resound around the room as I realise what's happening.

Princess Leonore now holds Winella's sword, turning it to dust as she approaches the female. She looms over my foe, who swiftly kneels before her. The princess's voice is predatory and menacing as we all listen.

'If anyone *dares* to touch my champion,' the princess declares, injecting terror into every Raven present, including me, 'I will curse you and your family for generations to come. You will feel my wrath every time you speak my champion's name, and you will feel fear every time you lay your eyes upon her.'

Winella's frame shakes, head down as she whimpers under the royal's gaze. Her bright red hair flaps around her face as the wind pushes into her. She offers her hands out in regret and supplication. 'My apologies, Your Highness. Please forgive me!'

As if Winella were a pesky fly, the princess turns her nose up at her to come before me, her usually dark blue eyes gleaming bright silver. The magic finally dims. The furniture in the chamber is discarded randomly around the room.

The Ravens don't speak, don't blink in her presence – the presence of the princess who is rumoured to have power beyond belief. Now they have seen a snippet of it, a shred of her strength.

'Leave us,' Princess Leonore commands, making everyone, including my sister, rush away, eager to put distance between them and us.

'Merlot,' I mutter, turning to my friend. Her body horribly frail in my hold. Blood continues to ooze from her mouth, the wound in her lower back too large for me to care for, for me to find a healer in time to save her. 'Please! Do something!' I urge the princess, who falls to her knees without hesitation.

Her hands shimmer with light as she touches Merlot's back, her power veining through the Raven, silver snaking through her skin like a living creature. Slowly the wound is covered by a thick layer of silver magic but the princess's grim expression sinks my heart. I clutch my friend tighter, watching her chest rise and fall, but only barely.

'My magic will stop her losing so much blood, but she will need a healer immediately. I'm afraid she won't be able to compete in the last trial,' the princess says, making me close my eyes in guilt.

'I'm so sorry, Merlot,' I chant into my friend's hair, stroking the bright red strands away from her face. 'I'm so very sorry.'

47

Hours later I'm escorted out of the healing quarters of Songbird Castle by Princess Leonore, my remorse for Merlot having been replaced with rage. I want to scream until I have no voice. I want to break something and smash it into thousands of tiny pieces.

The princess decides to stay with me while I travel through the city of Rubien. Civilians watch my companion with curiosity. They are not sure who the princess is, but they can sense she is important. She wears her long green gown, which complements her darker skin, and her hair is loose and silky behind her. In comparison, I look nothing short of dull, while she sparkles and absorbs everyone's notice, her smile gleaming as people stare, her bright eyes wondrous and open. A few people approach us asking questions, and Princess Leonore answers every one of them, replying with a sunshine personality and amusing wit.

I, however, am in a thunderous mood, wanting revenge on Winella. In the midst of Merlot's trauma, the bitch scampered away and is now nowhere to be seen.

'I need to let off some steam, or else I'll go in search of Winella and stab her straight in the forehead,' I confess, the memory of leaving Merlot in a room of highly regarded healers came to her aid fresh in my mind.

I only left when the princess reminded me there was nothing else I could do for her except let the royal healers do their jobs without hovering like a mother hen.

The princess wraps a hand around my forearm and tugs me close to her side. Magic surrounds us, pulling me gently into a more relaxed pace. I've been storming ahead of her, and I didn't realise it in my hurricane of emotions.

'I'm sure I could arrange for an accident to occur when she least expects it,' Princess Leonore utters, trying to humour me. 'Or perhaps I'll pull her out of the trials.'

'You can do that?'

She gives me a sly smile. 'As for Merlot and her mother, we will help them. I promise.'

I had revealed to Princess Leonore why Merlot not competing in the last trial was so detrimental to our plan – why it would weaken our chances of saving her mother and my sister.

'How? The Elder Raven specifically said we can only receive our prizes once we win the Hex Trials. Now that Merlot is out of the game, how will she obtain the treatment she needs?' I ask, watching the princess as she waves to a group of young kids.

'Unfortunately, the treatment Mrs Kinsman needs is under the Elder Raven's custody.'

Translation: I will have to find a way to win the trails to save her as I promised Merlot.

'For your friend, however,' the princess goes on, a hint of optimism in the tone. 'I have faith my healers will bring her back to her former glory. Or as close to it as possible.

They said Winella just barely missed her spine. She will take considerable time to recover but she *will* make a full recovery.'

Pausing, I turn to Princess Leonore. She mirrors me as I study her face. She's young, perhaps a year or two younger than me, but she has wisdom and intelligence beyond her years. She speaks as if she has experienced the world, as if she has grown up among the Hanrae people and knows them personally. For the first time, I feel a kinship with her, a sort of relationship where the lines feel blurred. Not a ruler and her subject, but two friends who understand each other's motives.

'Why did you *really* choose me as your champion?'

A midnight-blue brow lifts. 'I have a soft spot for the underdogs of our world,' she admits simply, the honesty evident in her words. We pass a shop window with small kittens curled up in piles of blankets. The moment the princess approaches, the creatures press themselves up against the glass, wanting her attention. 'I chose you because I saw something special in you, Scarlet. You have a never-ending fire of resilience and astounding strength. You have determination and something to believe in, and the first time I saw you, I knew I wanted you on my side.'

'The first time you saw me? When was that?' I ask, knowing she has done her homework when it comes to my family and me. She visited my eldest brother Ash at the clinic, watched the twins train in the arena and knew of Roux's pregnancy before she decided to show her face to me that day in the tavern.

'The day my mother made you fill in that writing test,' she confesses, making me think back to the first time I visited her Rubien residence. 'She asked you Ravens why you wanted to compete in the Hex Trials, and as we predicted, all the answers were variations on a similar theme: glory, money, or a formidable reputation like the Elder Raven's. It was dull to listen to, but then *you* came along, and you were like a breath of fresh air.'

I crease my brow, unable to remember what I said to make such an impression on the princess, but from her facial expression, I clearly did a good job.

'You didn't try to make yourself sound better. You didn't try to compliment my mother.' Princess Leonore smiles as if *that* alone was enough to influence her. 'You just said you need medicine for your sister, and that was it. Simple as that.'

Unable to stop myself, I make a face. 'Wow. If I had known I had to put in so little effort to dazzle you, I'd have tried a lot less from the beginning.'

'That's the point, though. You don't beg for recognition for your actions. You see a challenge and are determined to conquer it, only because you know the reward will be favourable for your sister but not necessarily yourself. That selflessness is admirable and beautiful and is something I can't overlook – even now.'

I bite my lip. It's lovely to hear someone acknowledge what I've done, what I'm doing for Roux, but my motivation isn't completely selfless – not really. 'I don't fight purely for selfless reasons,' I state, my voice quieter. 'I wish more than anything to spend more time with my sister, but to be with both her children too. It's just as selfish as someone who wants those other things – just *different*.'

'Wanting to keep your family alive is not the same, and you know it,' the princess says, looking around in confusion.

She stops, and I slow down, looking back at her questioningly.

'Where are we?' she asks. 'I thought you were taking me to the tunnel.'

Without realising it, I've brought the princess to the Badger's Sett, of all places. Finding relief in my surroundings, I pull her towards the entrance. 'Have you ever heard of the Phoenix?'

48

The building is busy preparing for the evening contests. The princess sits on a stall by the fighting ring while I keep an eye on her from the Green Room above. She's laughing with those around her, not caring when they spill drinks on her lavish outfit or knock her around. She looks like royalty but acts like a commoner, cheering with each and every match, drinking beer and booing when her chosen contender has lost.

A knock sounds at my door, informing me that I'm up. The Phoenix is ready for her duel and is a special guest tonight. I convinced Storm that I need the fight to let off some steam, and he agreed as long as he didn't have to pay me.

As usual, the crowd part for me as I approach the ring. I hear mostly encouragement from the people but also the odd jeer or heckle. Eyeing up my opponent, I clamber over the small wall between the fighting ring and the audience. I find I'm up against the Pirate.

His frame is massive, so the fact that each of his muscles is as big as my head is no surprise. He makes sure his wooden leg – the reason for his moniker – is secure before cracking his knuckles, watching me as I bow low to the princess. She dips her head in acknowledgement, knowing full well who I am, and hands me a handkerchief.

'My champion,' she says as I stuff the white cloth into my uniform, a token that she wants to see me win.

The Pirate snorts at the exchange and yells for me to hurry up.

'I can't wait to see him on his arse.' The princess smiles, her eyes lighting up with excitement.

The round starts with a coin toss, deciding the use of weapons. Today it's hand-to-hand combat. My mind whirls with ways to bring him down. His obvious strength and stature over me will be to his advantage. I'll have to be smart, or else he will overpower me in minutes.

The Pirate starts on the attack, swinging his meaty arms, but I dodge easily, sidestepping his attacks. I keep up this scheme, wondering if tiring him out will benefit me, if perhaps his infamous anger will be triggered and he will make a mistake.

Only one way to find out.

The strikes keep coming, the Pirate bombarding me with giant fists that are quicker than I first expected them to be. As fluid as water, I gracefully skirt around every lunge, every jab, and soon he is becoming fatigued, as I hoped he would.

'Phoenix!'

Shouting isn't uncommon in fighting. Everyone cheers on their hopeful, but this voice is familiar.

'Phoenix!'

At the side of the ring, Dimitri rushes through the crowd, waving at me to get my attention. My brows furrow when I realise he isn't wearing a glamour – the most telling sign something isn't quite right. When he meets my gaze briefly, he mouths the last words I want to hear: 'Something is wrong with Roux.'

My insides turn cold, my breathing suddenly hard to manage. *Roux?*

Pain courses through my face. The Pirate has landed a punch to my cheek in my moment of distraction. I hiss in pain, feeling blood fill the inside of my mouth but take no notice of him as I dash for Dimitri, climbing over the wall and pushing people out of my way.

'What happened? Tell me everything.' I spit out crimson, following my best friend as he escorts me outside. I'm ripping off my gear and handing it over to him, not caring who sees me.

The princess runs to join us. Dimitri looks startled but doesn't ask.

'I had a blurry vision of a pregnant woman,' Dimitri explains as we run for the tunnel. With his vampire speed, it wouldn't have taken long to find me – thankfully. 'She looked similar to you, but she was bleeding. She looked afraid, and I couldn't shake the feeling that I knew her. I thought if there is any chance it was Roux, you'd want to know.'

Sprinting through to the House of Raven, I shout my thanks to him as the princess and I leave him behind. The lava bubbles beside me as I take the shortest route home, and I crash the door open as I enter my household.

Four pairs of eyes glare at me, their fangs bared in warning. Ember and Blaze sit at the dining table with plates of food before them, while Ruby and Roux are in the kitchen, making something that smells delicious. The moment they realise it's me, they all visibly relax.

'Roux,' I breathe, my chest heaving. 'Are you okay?'

Roux looks surprised before slowly bowing. My confusion gives way to the realisation that Princess Leonore is now behind me, studying my family with concern.

'Your Highness,' Ruby says, bending at the hip. 'It's such a pleasure to see you. Would you like something to eat? To drink?'

My brother gets to his feet so fast he bangs the table and knocks over a glass of water in the process. 'Your Highness,' he echoes, showing his respect.

Ember looks pissed as she stares up at her twin. Reluctantly she mirrors him, but my sister's expression shows she'd rather be bowing to her prince.

Princess Leonore is quick to answer, her smile bright and warm. 'Oh, no. Thank you so much for offering, but I'm fine. I was making sure Scarlet returned home safely.'

'Are you sure? We have made enough food if you would like to come in,' Ruby insists, eyeing me up as if to say, *Get her to stay awhile.*

However, I'm too busy staring at Roux, studying her for any signs of distress or trouble. What I find, though, is no blood-covered person but rather a happy female, her skin glowing and face at ease in her last trimester.

'I ... yes, please, stay for a while. I'd love you to meet the rest of the Seraphines,' I say jerkily, earning an unimpressed look from the princess. 'It would be nice to spend more time in your presence,' I add, hinting that if something happened, she could be there to help Roux if needed.

Princess Leonore's eyes flicker with understanding before she slowly nods. 'Smooth,' she coughs before her smile widens. She gathers her skirts and steps through the door to my home. 'Thank you. I'd love to stay.'

A flurry of movement occurs as everyone gets her seated. Steaming hot plates of food are brought over to her, and drinks are served around the table. All the while, I keep an eye on my older sister, watching for any twitch or crease of my sister's features, but none come.

For the whole of Princess Leonore's stay, Roux is her usual self, laughing and joking with our mother and siblings, acting as if everything is normal as she rubs her swollen belly. But a small, niggly feeling in the back of my mind can't help but be on alert.

Dimitri's vision is sure to mean something.

49

Days pass too quickly, and it's the day of my final trial. Breakfast is a quiet affair. My family's minds are occupied with what's to come. My nerves gradually build, my body displaying telltale signs of growing anxiety – my leg jiggling under the table, my hands sweating excessively. I'm a mess.

When we arrive at the arena, Ruby stops us all before we enter. She takes each of her children in, looking unsettled.

'I want you all to know that no matter what happens today, I love you all so much, and I'm proud of each and every one of you.' She clasps hands with Roux and Ember, who stand nearest her. Ember doesn't look too worried about today, but Roux's eyes are solely on me. 'Today I wish for Scarlet and Ember to achieve their goals however they see fit, to walk out of this last challenge happy and content they have done their best, no matter the outcome, and for our family to unite once again.'

She brings Ember into an embrace, whispering into her ear. Ember nods in acknowledgement before giving our siblings a quick farewell, saying she'll see them all later. She heads off for the tunnels, where we are to meet the other nine final competitors, her crimson uniform shining intimidatingly under the lava lamps.

Ruby turns and gives me one last hug too, squeezing me so tight it makes me apprehensive.

'I'll be okay,' I tell her, hoping to reassure myself too.

'You'll be more than okay. You'll be brilliant.' The smile she gives me seems tense, like if she doesn't smile, she'll cry.

I try my hardest to look confident in front of her, to seem unfazed about the fact that I could be adding today to my list of nightmares.

'You are smart, talented and a worthy candidate to become our next representative. I have faith in you and will watch you every step of the way. I'm so proud of everything you've achieved, of who you've become,' she says, her eyes becoming misty. 'Now, let's go, everyone. Scarlet can't be late.'

Saying goodbye to my brother and sister is just as hard. Blaze pats my back. Our affection for one another never goes as far as actual hugging, but he gives me a cheerful smile nonetheless.

'You'll be great, Scar. See you on the other side.'

Embracing Roux last, I breathe her in before I go to release her, but she won't let go. Her hands wrap around my shoulders like a vice, and I can't move.

'Roux ...'

'Please, just a little longer,' she whispers.

I feel her body is rigid as I wrap my arms back around her, Roux's stomach poking into me a little more than is comfortable, but I don't complain. I tuck my head into the curve of her shoulder, wanting to voice my love for her, that no matter what happens to me, I don't regret a thing. But I also don't want to say the words out loud in case they jinx my luck.

'I want to thank you,' Roux says in my ear, her breath tickling my skin. 'You are so brave, so courageous, and you have done so much for me. These kids will love you so much. They will love their auntie Scarlet so much.'

Tears well in my eyes. The children have been my main goal this whole time – my sister too. I want so badly to meet my niece and nephew, to watch them grow up and to see Roux become the amazing mother I know she will be.

'Like I've said before, I'd do anything for you, Roux. I want you to have the life you deserve, and to me, that means you being around to see these children grow up. I'll fight to the end if I have to, because family means everything to me. *You* mean everything to me.'

Nails dig into my back as her body shudders against mine, her sobs coming out thick and fast. Releasing my sister, I hand her over to my mother, whose face is filled with a glimmer of pride. I stand up a little straighter and wave my last goodbyes before heading for the tunnels, remembering the reason I'm doing this. Remembering that *today* is the day that counts most.

I've been sitting in silence for three hours. In that time, my mind has been a tornado of thoughts, wondering how today will end, how my family will be affected, depending on the outcome. As this is the last challenge, I expect it to be the hardest – the previous challenges having been nothing short of dangerous and terrifying.

It's a relief when a male enters the room to find me lying on the metal bench, staring at the ceiling. He opens the door wide for me. 'You're up, half-blood.'

I stand up and wipe my sweaty palms on my trouser legs. Taking a shaky breath, I force my body into a state of neutrality. I have to be focused. I have to be smart. This is my last chance to win, to help my sister and Merlot's mother.

We walk out of the cold room, and I'm led down a stone hallway, approaching a gate that leads into the sandpit, a gate I now know so well. I'm handed a few weapons, including a heavy sword and two unhelpfully blunt daggers. My questioning look is answered with an uninterested shrug.

The entrance to the sandpit opens with a loud groan, and I step through without prompt.

Be fearless, I tell myself, willing my hands into fists.

At first glance, nothing obvious stands out. No dragons, no glass domes, no shields around the audience. It looks like the arena on any normal day – and that's scarier than anything I've been up against so far.

Standing taller, I feign confidence as I listen to my heartbeat, wondering if every Raven in the arena can hear it too. I wait for something to jump out, something to suddenly break out from beneath the red sand, but minutes later, still nothing has happened.

I search for my family in the crowd and find them near the front, watching with pale faces. They've been watching the trials unfold, and their expressions don't make me feel any more confident about what's in store for me.

A voice booms loud and clear, sending shivers through my arms and legs.

'Welcome, finalist,' the Elder Raven states sharply, her words cutting through me like a blade. 'Today you will fend off a vicious threat. If you defeat your opponent, you will be granted permission to leave the arena – it's a fight to the *death*.'

I gulp.

No pressure.

Walking further into the pit, I position myself centrally to all four tunnels, thinking the more distance I have between me and my attacker, the more time I'll have to prepare myself if they come charging.

My mind runs wild as I imagine all sorts of rivals. A fire-breathing chimera, a deadly basilisk, or perhaps it will be a giant troll – violent and brutal creatures that I told Merlot I wished this trial wouldn't include.

Just my luck, I think sourly.

My heart races when the audience starts to murmur, their eyes focusing behind me. Ready with my sword, I turn, and suddenly the weapon feels too heavy in my grasp. It drops to the sand as I nearly choke at what I find. Or rather, *who* I find.

My sister.

Ember walks with conviction, her fiery red eyes pinned on me, her smile sly and amused at my reaction. I feel instantly sick to my stomach.

She stops a few metres away and watches me like a predator would its prey. She doesn't seem fazed to see me, and my stomach flips with unease.

'You don't look too well.' Ember motions to my trembling body.

I can't answer. Unable to move my muscles, I'm paralysed with shock.

Is this really happening?

Yes, of course it is, a little voice in my head answers. *The Elder Raven wants you dead. This is the perfect way to get what she wants.*

'You don't seem keen to fight me.' Fire lights up along Ember's arms, roaming over her whole body, burning with delight at my disturbance. 'I always knew you wanted to test your skills against me, to see how you compared. Well, now is your chance, little sister. Do your worst,' she challenges, her arms outstretched.

I shake my head, unwilling to admit this is real.

I don't want to do this.

This isn't *right*.

'Are you scared of losing in front of all our peers?' Ember asks, walking closer, her movements dangerously smooth and lethal.

I'd forgotten about the audience, my thoughts only on who is in front of me. My family, I realise, have to watch me fight my sister to win these trials. No wonder they look so pale.

'This can't be happening,' I mutter, shaking my head.

'Believe it. Today is the day we decide who is *better*. Who do you think will win, Scarlet? Me, a born leader and warrior who is one of the top students within the House of Raven, or you, a sad, lonely stable worker who thought she could save the family single-handedly?'

My eyes narrow as I try my best to keep my sister's words at bay, to let them slide off me like oil, but I can't help but sense the truth in her words. She truly believes what she is saying.

Ember stands at arm's length now, her fiery red eyes looking down at me. My sister's powerful body is corded with lean muscle as she stands intimidatingly still, the perfect representation of a Raven as she glowers at me.

I can feel the warmth wrapping around me from her close proximity, but I don't move. I refuse to flinch away from my sister, refuse to let Ember see I'm afraid of what's to come.

'Being the youngest must be difficult sometimes,' she says, making my face crease in confusion. 'But being a *mongrel* must be even harder. To be born with no gifts, to be the result of a one-night stand. So disappointing.'

Of course, I know better. Ruby loved my father – and seemingly still does. I was a product of love, unlike my sister, who was made by the breeding programme, but I retain this little detail and tuck it away, keeping the small flame of hope alight within me. She's only trying to wound me for some reason.

'Having no magic doesn't mean I'm weak, Ember. Only *you* and the Elder Raven think that way,' I state, still reeling at the fact that she is even here.

'It's funny – I was expecting you to say that. Defending humans like that inadequate father of yours. What a worthless piece of shit.'

My mouth twitches. I want to say something, but I know this is her attempt to bait me. She wants me to land the first punch, or the first kick, but I won't. My goal is to save one sister, not kill the other in the process.

'I'm not falling for your tricks. Say what you want, but I'm absorbing nothing.' I shrug, looking around with disinterest, as if she's boring me. This seems to do the trick.

Ember chuckles, cracking her fiery knuckles. 'Oh, you little ...'

My hand begins to bleed, and my head snaps to the open scar upon my right palm. Never have I experienced it opening with my own family. Hesitantly I peer up at Ember, who observes with savage delight.

'You didn't think I would harm you?' she asks, finding me amusing.

It takes no time for Ember to answer my questioning look, her pale hand clutching my neck so fast my reaction to run away fails. Slowly she lifts me off the ground. I claw at her wrists, attempting to gulp down air, but I'm unsuc-cessful.

Ember smiles, her fangs glinting as she laughs at my reddening face. 'I could rip your throat out, but what fun would that be? These people want a *show*,' she declares, looking back at the audience. I notice a few faces frozen with anticipation – most with excitement. 'So I shall give them just that.'

I'm thrown forcefully into the air to land in the sand. I roll several times, then clutch my throat as I heave, my lungs filling with much-needed oxygen. Trying to stand, I feel my head spin with dizziness.

'What to do with you ...' Ember trails off, stalking towards me. She looks alive, her skin glowing with happi-ness. The sight guts me. How can she get so much pleasure from hurting me? 'You can't even form words you're so scared.'

'I'm not scared. I just refuse to fight with you,' I croak with as much bravado as I can muster, looking for any sign of my sister, because this monster can't be her.

She clamps her hands around my collar, roughly lifting me off the ground. 'You'll be wishing you had when I am done with you,' Ember claims.

A fist lifts and collides with my face. Pain courses through me, my eyes blurry as I stare up at the ceiling of the cave. Shouting echoes throughout the arena. It reminds me of when I fight at the Badger's Sett, but here I'm to be killed, not simply overpowered.

Ember's voice floats above. 'Fight back,' she urges, receiving no answer from me. 'Fight me!' she yells, cursing me, kicking me, again and again.

Hissing, I clutch my sore ribs, feeling one sticking out more than the others. I attempt to open my eyes, my left effectively blind, but my right watching as Ember seethes, her mouth curling with anger, crimson eyes ablaze with agitation.

'*Why won't you fight me?*' Ember screams before sauntering off in a huff, a trail of heat waves following behind.

I stagger to my feet, clutching my throbbing body, my lungs burning – no doubt from a punctured lung. Reaching for my tender eye, touching the skin around the socket, I can feel it swelling up already. My hands caress the knives in my belt, and I stare at them. A part of me wants to show her I'm capable of defending myself with them. But the other part, the more dominant part, knows I wouldn't dare touch them even if I wanted to. Ember is my *blood*, and nothing would make me want to maim her intentionally.

'I won't be told to fight you,' I say, wincing at the discomfort of talking, wondering what she's trying to prove through all this. 'I won't listen to someone who claims it's acceptable to kill my own sister. My aim is to save Roux, but I won't do that by killing you in the process. What good would that do? I'd break our family. I'd betray our brother. Blaze wouldn't want this. *I* don't want this. We may have our disagreements, Ember, but all siblings do. I'll always have your back, no matter how you treat me. You're my *sister.*'

We stand and watch one another for a long time, neither speaking nor moving. My body feels battered and bruised, my ribs sending waves of discomfort through me, but I don't dare shift. I only wait for her to absorb my words and agree this is madness.

'They said you would be like this. Perhaps you need a little *push*,' Ember decides with a sly smile.

From behind me a tunnel opens up, and my guardian is dragged out of the darkness, chained like an animal.

50

My mind can't comprehend what is happening as I behold Jack. He and Taylor both wear chains on their wrists that connect to chains around their ankles. Jack tumbles into the sand, unable to keep his balance as Taylor stands warily.

'No,' I murmur with horror.

'You won't fight me, but you will after I'm done with him,' Ember declares, running for Jack.

Without hesitation I follow, sprinting hard, ignoring the wave of pain radiating through me, disregarding the fact I can only see out of one eye.

Reaching Ember before she can grasp Jack, I throw myself at her. Both of us go sprawling on the floor. She rolls easily, finding her feet in seconds, while I grapple for balance, putting myself in between the guardians and my sister.

'What have they done to you?' I ask Jack, making sure to keep Ember in my line of sight. I note the marks along Jack's skin from his confinement, the colour of the chains – obsidian.

'You don't want to know,' he answers, making my chest tighten. 'But I'm all right.'

My sister's menacing laugh gains our attention. 'You will fight for him but not yourself? I never could understand you,' Ember says before charging, swinging a flaming fist my way.

After succeeding in blocking the attack, I give her a forceful jab to the stomach. The impact causes Ember to bend over with temporary loss of breath. Before she can recover, I knee her in the face, leaving her to wallow in self-pity.

Using her distraction, I grab Jack and drag him away, hoping to put distance between us.

'Run faster,' I urge, looking back regularly to see where my sister is.

We move as fast as my guardian can manage, but a wall of fire stops us, nearly causing us to run straight into it. We squint at the brightness of the flames, the sudden heat making me sweat profusely.

'I don't know how to get out of this,' I admit to Jack as we turn to find Ember stalking towards us. She looks angry, her bright red eyes lit with defiance and challenge.

'I can't use my magic either,' Jack warns, his voice high with panic as he rattles his magic diminishing restraints, confirming my suspicions.

'Well, shit,' I mutter, earning an apologetic look from him. Jack would be the perfect shield against Ember's power.

'You can't run from me. You either fight or find your guardian barbecued,' Ember threatens, nearing us with Taylor beside her. He looks wary, eyes wide at the amount of magic being used.

My sister suddenly throws her hands up and bends the wall of fire into a circle around the four of us – a cage of flames. She creeps closer, making the panic in me grow with every moment.

What should I do?

'Please, Ember. You want to be the next Raven of the Hex, right?' I ask, my mind spinning. As long as Jack is alive, I can manage any outcome. 'Just take it. I don't want it, anyway.'

Jack's hand finds my elbow. 'Scarlet, no,' he murmurs, urgency in his voice.

'This is insanity, Jack. What are we going to do? She has us cornered – literally!'

Unimpressed, Ember crosses her arms, waiting for me to continue.

'You win, Ember! Now take this all down,' I beg, motioning to the crackling fire.

'That's not how this is going to go,' Ember answers disapprovingly, a gleam in her eyes like this is a dream come true for her. 'You're going to *fight* for your life.'

Suddenly I'm on my knees, heat like I've never felt before searing my body, burning me alive.

Ember storms over and grabs my collar, dragging me away from Jack, who also withers in pain, the noises escaping his mouth reminding me of an injured animal.

'You'll regret ever defying me,' Ember mutters.

She headbutts me in the face, making me groan as stars fill my vision. She grabs my arm and wrenches it with such expertise and force that it dislocates with a horrid *crack*.

My screams echo through the arena.

'Scarlet!' my guardian gurgles, his own body pinned to the floor by Taylor, whose chains lie tightly across Jack's neck as he struggles.

'Stay away from him!' I cry, gritting my teeth as Ember pins me down.

My head fills with heat, and a terrible pressure begins to

build behind my eyes. My dislocated arm lies unhelpfully beside me as I kick at my sister, but she's at an advantage. She simply swats my attempts away, restraining my remaining arm beneath her body weight.

'Your cries are music to my ears,' she murmurs quietly, relishing in the destruction of my body.

Ember clamps my head in her hands, nails digging in as she bangs my skull against the floor, my thoughts jumbled and spikes of desperation surging through me.

Through the agony, I hear a crack of bone in the background and hope it's not Jack's.

'Why would you do this to me?' I whimper. It baffles me that my sister would want to cause me so much anguish.

Wondering how close to the darkness I am, I suddenly find myself staring at Jack. He appears behind my sister, his chains winding around her neck. His face is full of determination as he attempts to strangle her, to pull her off me, but he is unsuccessful.

Ember jerks to her feet, leaving my limp body behind. I watch with my remaining eye as a spasm of red-hot desolation ripples through my body.

'You weak human!' Ember laughs, finding Jack more amusing than threatening. She snaps his chains in half with her bare hands before striking at his face and tossing him to the ground near Taylor, who looks like he has a broken nose, blood rushing out of it.

Jack whimpers as I try to reach out for him, to grasp his hand.

'Pathetic,' Ember spits, raising her arms once more. A wall of fire shoots up between me and my guardian, separating us with blazes of crimson.

'Scarlet!'

Not caring about the pain, I crawl towards his muffled voice, listening as his words turn into screams of pain.

Warily I stay close to the blistering wall of heat, shouting for Jack but knowing I can't do anything to help him.

'Why would you do this to me, Ember?'

Her eyes widen with malice, with venom. She says nothing as she looms above me, pressing her boot against my dislocated arm so I can't move.

Slowly the smell of burning flesh fills my senses, and I gag. The scorching sensation grows and festers all over me, making my body spasm as Ember makes a trail of invisible fire roam over me, little by little.

'Stop! Please, stop!' I weep, the suffering is too much to handle.

Unable to take any more, I muster up the last dregs of my energy and grab my sister's leg, pulling her through the wall of fire beside me. The element catches my hand, and I recoil from the scorching heat.

Ember is temporarily out of sight, but the heat is still intense. I curse at my burnt hand, the smell making my stomach churn and eyes water as a new layer of discomfort lingers.

'Jack,' I mutter, still dizzy with the heat and agony running through my body, cradling my dislocated arm.

Before I can call out for him again, something grabs me and slams into me. My teeth ring with the impact. With a large grin, Ember rolls me over forcefully and slaps my face hard enough I can't see for a moment.

'Any last words?' Ember asks softly.

My sister's eyes burn as bright as the fire surrounding us, relishing the view as I lie defenceless. She presses down on my cracked ribs, holding down my head with her hands. I can't help but scream with the hotness rising under her touch like a wildfire.

Ember grins as she completes her last performance.

'I'll see you in hell,' she says before her sharp teeth clamp down on my throat and finally rip away the flesh.

The feeling of blood loss is overwhelming. My throat feels like a living inferno. It's a torture like no other, and I feel my veins pumping harder and faster but making no difference in keeping me alive.

I try to watch my sister in the last seconds of my life, finding Ember's appearance feral with satisfaction, but her features flicker in and out with a different face. Her face is there one second, and the next, there is another profile, with older and sharper features.

I don't understand, and my imagination runs wild, my mind quickly deteriorating as I blink through life and death.

As darkness falls around me, I hear the last words, a female voice that is sweet like poison. 'I told you I'd kill you in these trials, half-blood.'

51

Fire, flames, blazing heat. I wake up drenched in sweat, remembering the smell of burning flesh, and the warmth of my blood across my neck.

'Scarlet, breathe.' Four pastel-blue walls surround me, and Princess Leonore studies me with those dark blue eyes of hers.

I'm not being burnt alive any more. It's all over.

'*Breathe*. You're in the healing quarters at Songbird Castle,' the princess offers gently, stroking a piece of hair out of my face. She hands me a glass of water, and I drink it all.

'What happened?' I murmur, throat hoarse.

Princess Leonore sits on the bed, making herself comfortable. 'You've been healing for nearly two weeks. But I am happy to announce you passed the last trial, Scarlet. You're the next Raven of the Hex!'

A jolt rushes through me, millions of questions bubbling inside my head.

'What do you mean? How is that possible? I lost the fight. I shouldn't have—' Unable to wrap my head around the words, I clutch my chest. My heart beats rapidly beneath my skin.

I'm alive.

For a moment, I listen to my own breathing.

How am I still alive?

'You won because my mother values loyalty. Without that, how can six Houses who have never met before fight together through the Hex?'

'Queen Adela decided I won?' I ask, dumbfounded.

'Yes. She chose you as the champion of the Hex Trials. She thought you were very valiant, and I'd have to agree.' She reaches for my hand and squeezes it, her eyes trailing over my new burns, the stripes of discoloured skin lining my fingers. The sight doesn't scare me as much as when I woke up from the dragon trial, but it still makes my heart sink, my mood becoming sad that my skin is covered in more burns.

'But Ember killed me,' I state numbly as I process the information. 'Or should have,' I correct myself, noticing three bunches of flowers by my bedside. They are in full bloom and in all different shades of yellow, blue and purple. It's a rare sight to see, living underground.

'You didn't fight your sister. You fought an illusion,' the princess explains, watching as I clench my fist in the sheets. I peer at my once-dislocated arm. My flesh is still burnt but more noticeable now.

'If I fought an illusion, how am I injured? Aren't they figments of the imagination?' I ask, sweeping my fingers over my neck. The uneven skin is rough to the touch where it was ripped.

'Not an illusion in that sense, I guess,' the princess back-pedals with a shrug. 'The Elder Raven had a powerful witch to shape-shift her, to change her body into your sister's and pass her off as Ember.'

Silence fills the room, my head pulsing as I absorb everything.

'But she controlled fire like Ember. She didn't use her Unforgettable Fire ...' I trail off, remembering my body withering, the heat I felt in my lungs and skull, and I realise she *did* use her power on me. I was in so much agony I didn't notice at the time.

'The Elder Raven chose carefully. The witch was hard to track down but extremely clever with magic and spells. She was able to replicate Ember down to the tiniest details.'

'So if I was given Ember to fight, did Ember get given a replica of *me*?' I ponder, scrunching my face up with disgust. 'Did the Elder Raven fight her too?'

'No. Only you fought the Elder Raven,' Princess Leonore confirms, ignoring my first question, averting her eyes to the flowers. Her tanned hands twist together briefly before she looks at me again. 'Ember was pitted against Master Lennox.'

My lips widen into a smug smile. 'I hope she gave him hell,' I state, remembering the whipping he gave me and the faint scar he left across Jack's neck.

'She did.' The princess nods, nibbling her lip. The gesture instantly unnerves me. Princess Leonore has never come across as the nervous type, as unsure of herself.

'What's wrong?' I ask.

'Nothing. I was thinking how much I've come to enjoy your company, but now you are the Raven of the Hex, I'll have to let you go.'

Without thought, I force a smile at the compliment, but honestly, I'm not sure how to feel.

'A healer is coming for your last check-up soon,' Princess Leonore says. 'Make the most of your last moments here in Rubien. You won't know when you will be coming back. I'll be seeing you off on your new adventure in two days' time. Don't be late.' She stands up, brushing non-existent dust off herself, and approaches the exit.

'Wait!' I yelp, making the princess spin around. 'I assume Ember fought my replica. How did she do?'

'She won her fight,' the princess replies simply.

'She killed me?'

Princess Leonore nods sympathetically.

'She didn't know it was Master Lennox, did she?' I guess, hoping it's not true.

The princess nibbles her lip again, and I realise *this* is what she didn't want to tell me. 'Not until his illusion died with him. She realised it was a trick then.'

Numbness spreads through my body. My chest feels like it's been cracked open. My eyes begin to well up, and the princess approaches me once more, but I hold a hand up.

'No. I need time alone. Thanks for stopping by, though.'

She nods reluctantly and leaves me to my thoughts.

The next day I'm finally released from the healing quarters, my first question being if I can see how Merlot is faring.

'She's not awake yet,' Annie informs me. 'We've had to put her into a state of deep slumber to help with her recovery.'

I nod tightly, following the healer down a long hallway.

Peaceful is the word that springs to mind when I find her laying soundlessly in bed. My friend no longer has dark circles beneath her eyes, instead her smooth features reveal a new wash of colour in her cheeks. I notice her hair has recently been brushed too, her fiery crimson locks glossy across her pillow.

Merlot looks healthier than I've seen her in a long while. Leonore and those under her command have cared well for the Raven.

'It's good to see you on the mend, my friend,' I murmur, sliding my fingers through hers and squeezing gently as I perch beside her on the bed. Her flesh is warm to the touch, my marred skin a contrast to hers as I peer down at our entwined hands.

'I have so much to tell you.' A part of me hopes she'll hear me. A part of me wishes she'll wake up to the sound of my voice. But she doesn't. She remains unaware of my company.

'I wish I didn't have to leave you like this, to say goodbye without—' my voice cracks and I have to stop before the tears fall. 'I never told you how much I cherished your friendship, Merlot. How much comfort you brought me with your presence alone. I never thought I would find something so precious with a fellow Raven – but I'm glad it was with you.'

With no response, I reluctantly release her hand and place it back where I found it. I stand, taking a deep breath before exhaling all my thoughts and feelings into the quiet chamber.

Peering down at her once more, committing her face to memory, I whisper, 'Take care. I'll visit when I can.'

And with that, I leave the one person who defended me – who put her life in danger to protect mine – laying motionless.

If it's the last thing I do, I will make those who harmed Merlot Kinsman pay.

52

Time is passing too fast, and I'm numb to my emotions. The fact that I'm leaving home and going sooner than I expected has not sunk in yet.

I knock on the first door I always come to when I need comfort or advice. Dimitri answers in seconds, his face saying it all.

'I'm so proud of you, Scarlet,' he says, pulling me into a firm embrace. 'I knew you could do it.'

'Glad to get rid of me, I suspect,' I jest, squeezing him tightly.

He ushers me inside his home, then goes to the kitchen and comes back with two glasses filled with crimson liquid. 'Here,' Dimitri says, handing me one. 'Let's celebrate.'

Scowling at the drink, I wonder if it's blood, but then I notice its consistency. 'Dimitri, it's eight in the morning.'

'Perfect time for red wine,' he confirms with a chuckle. 'Just try it.'

Hesitantly I take a small sip and am delighted to find I actually like it. 'That's not bad,' I say with a smirk.

So for hours we sit and drink. My eyes roam over Dimitri as if for the last time while the vampire inspects my wounds. With a quiet mix of emotions, he watches as I flex my arm for him, his sad smile making me feel slightly guilty for keeping my scars on show. Instinctively I keep my chin down to cover my neck for his benefit. It will eventually heal but it's not what I want him to focus on right now.

'So how long till you go?' he asks, making me grimace.

'Far too soon,' I admit, shuffling in my seat. He watches me, waiting for a proper answer. 'Tomorrow,' I clarify, noting his face forming into shock.

'But—'

'I guess it will hurt less if I go sooner rather than later.'

'But that is *too* soon,' he protests, putting his glass down.

'Which is why I came to see you first,' I state, sitting on the edge of the sofa to be nearer him. 'Dimitri, there's not much time left and I need to get some things off my chest.'

His face displays sorrow, and rightly so.

I feel rushed as my nerves simmer inside my chest. 'I have so many reasons to thank you, but mainly for your friendship, which is the reason I've got to this point. If it weren't for your kindness and training, I would still be here, complaining about how I am wasting my days ...' I trail off, imagining a life without Unforgettable Fire, a life without being whipped for minor things. A bubble of excitement gleams within my chaotic web of emotions. 'You have given me a chance to really *live* and a chance to show the world my potential, even as a half-blood.'

His eyes widen, becoming watery, and I think he's about to cry.

'You have helped me much more than I can ever express, and I am so glad I met you all those years ago. You're my *family*, Dimitri, and I'm going to miss you so fucking much. You're my best friend and the best mentor I could ever have asked for. You've changed my life for the better and I can't thank you enough. I'm truly lucky to have met you when I did – even if you *were* in a state.'

His body moves so quickly I don't realise we are hugging until his arms are around me, his cool skin pressing against mine. My arms automatically wrap tightly around him as I think of a reality without him being a short walk away, without his advice and humour, without his support and help.

'You're one of a kind, Scar,' he murmurs into my hair, his breath warm. 'Go out there and show them all what you're made of.' He pushes me back to arm's length, wiping his face subtly.

I grin, and he mirrors me.

'You sook,' I jest, making us both laugh. 'How will you fare without me when getting your blood taken?'

'Don't even mention that. I don't want to think about it,' he says glumly. 'Oh! I have something for you before you leave.'

He leaves the room and comes back with several extremely large, jingling pouches.

'Money from fighting? But I didn't save this much.' I scowl, looking inside the pouches, and gape at the amount of silver and gold coins within.

'Well, it's rightfully yours,' Dimitri answers, making me even more confused.

'Where did you get all this from?' I ask, eyeing him suspiciously. 'You haven't been selling yourself, have you?' I wink, earning an eye roll.

'No, Scarlet. That's all the money I won.'

'Won? From what?'

'Betting on you,' he answers, waiting for a reaction.

My grin widens, something warm flooding my chest. All the money I've earned at the Badger's Sett has been put towards helping Ruby feed our family and, originally, escaping this life. Now Dimitri has doubled it, because he believed I'd win all my fighting matches.

'You're giving this all to me? Why?'

'Well, I have a feeling you may need it. After all, you did earn it.' He smiles timidly.

'Thanks, Dimitri,' I reply, gratefully looking at the coins and comprehending this is real. I'm really leaving.

He cocoons me in another long hug, making my heart tighten painfully.

'I have always bet on you, Scarlet, and I always will.'

After an excruciating goodbye with Dimitri and promising to keep in touch, I make a quick pit stop at Jack's apartment – after having a little difficulty remembering where he lives.

A boy with bright red hair opens the door. He looks surprised to see me.

'Hello,' I say with a lame wave. 'Is Jack in?'

'Yes. He's in his room, packing. Come on in.' He opens the door wide for me to step through.

Having been here once before, I head towards where I remember helping a drunk Jack get into bed. I knock gently on the door and enter.

Jack turns, and the moment he sees me, his face lights up. I'm in his arms in seconds as he closes the door behind me, squeezing me so tight I can't breathe.

'Scarlet!' He releases me temporarily, holding me at arm's length as he inspects me. The longer he studies me, the darker his eyes become, his gaze roaming over my

now-burnt hand and stitched-up neck. He hums disapprovingly.

'I know. They're not pretty,' I mutter with a self-
conscious shrug.

'You're beautiful, Scarlet – with or without scars.'

Slowly he leans down. His hands wrap around my hips,
pulling me closer. We've not had a moment to truly flesh
out what this is between us. Not a chance do I complain,
though, wondering what he'll do.

He tilts his head and plants a gentle kiss upon my
throat as if my scar is the most precious thing to him. My
eyes peek down at his own neck and his faint scar from
Master Lennox.

His head snaps up, and he stares into my eyes. His
hands roam up my sides, over my arms, and land either side
of my face, and I think he will kiss me properly. He seems to
debate the same thing but sighs.

'How are you feeling?' he asks, reluctantly releasing me.

Timidly I smile, slightly disappointed. 'I'm fine. The
skin around my hand is a bit sore, but the healers said it
will ease with use. How are *you*? Did you know we fought
the Elder Raven?'

He nods glumly, looking down at his shoes as if the
memory itself is too much to handle. 'I think I had an
inkling the moment she used her magic on me. I remember
you describing it as a feeling you'd never forget and would
have nightmares over.'

'I'm sorry I couldn't protect you from her, Jack.'

My words seem to unsettle him, his eyes closing like
he's in pain.

'Please, don't say that.' He shakes his head, rubbing my
arms up and down. 'She is cruel, and there is nothing you
could have done. We were at a disadvantage from the start.'

'We were?'

He nods and leads me to his bed, then sits on the edge. 'My chains were made of obsidian metal, so I couldn't use my magic, but Taylor's were normal iron. He was able to best me because he could camouflage himself with his surroundings.'

My eyes widen at the new information. 'Honestly, I don't know why I'm surprised. I bet it was the Elder Raven's doing.'

'I suspect so,' Jack agrees.

My hand covers his knee, squeezing it with affection. 'I guess it doesn't matter now. You and I are about to start a new chapter together.'

His delighted smile heats me up from within. The look I receive is a sight I'll never tire of. He embraces me, bringing my head to his chest. Slowly he leans back, and we topple onto our sides, clutching one another.

Kissing the top of my head, he says, 'I wouldn't want to do it with anyone besides you, my dear Raven.'

53

I travel back home, and when I take a step into the House of Raven, I realise with horror that one day I could be everyone's Elder. If I live long enough to retire, I will control the House and everyone in it.

Too soon, I tell myself. *Focus on right now.*

As expected, Ravens ignore me as I amble through the streets on my last stroll alongside the lava rivers and over the stone bridges for a long while. Visiting the stables for the last time, I stroke each and every horse, telling them how wonderful they all are and to be good for the worker who will take my place. I even feed them each an extra apple and a handful of sugar cubes to make sure they know I'll miss them.

This all takes up valuable time, and I realise, as I see my household in the distance, I'm stalling. Something inside me doesn't want to go home, to face my family.

Why am I so afraid?

After hesitating at the door, I grit my teeth and force myself inside.

The house is loud as I behold my entire family in the

dining area, but my heart soars at what I find. The table is full to the brim with people, and Ruby is spooning food onto every plate on the table. Blaze hands drinks to Ember and Ash—

Ash?

My eyes land on my oldest brother. He in turn stares at me. I've not seen him in years, and he's changed so much. After he was sent off to become a breeder, we were forbidden from visiting him.

'*Ash?* Is that really you?' I murmur, unable to believe my eyes.

He stands up, and he's a hulk of a male. Muscles bulge from under his shirt, his fangs on show as his smile grows, and he rushes me and spins me around in circles, lifting me off the floor.

'My little Scarlet, look how much you've grown!' he cries, his laugh echoing through my ears, making me want to cry with happiness. He finally sets me back down, so carefully I can't help beaming.

'You're home? I haven't missed you visiting, have I?' I ask in a rush, worried I've wasted valuable time.

'No. I'm here to stay.'

I blink at him – I don't understand.

He continues, his large warm hand on my shoulder, the subtle fire magic from him welcoming. 'Princess Leonore brought me back for good. I can decide what to do with my life now. I've decided to work like Ruby. I hear there is a place at the stables open ...' He trails off, seeming to wait for my reaction.

My head spins to our mother, who nods eagerly. 'Isn't that wonderful?'

'That's amazing,' I say before my heart sinks. 'I wish I could have worked alongside you.'

He seems to understand, patting my head like he would a child's. 'Don't worry about it, Scar. We can keep in touch, and you can visit whenever you want. You're the Raven of the Hex now. *You* make the rules.'

Reluctantly I glance towards Ember, whose back is to me. She peers around and meets my gaze. Heart stuttering, I avert my eyes quickly and notice Roux isn't present.

'Where is Roux?'

Everyone shares a look, and I find myself shuffling uncomfortably.

'Have I missed something? Is she all right?'

'There has been a big change while you've been healing,' Ruby says, motioning for me to head upstairs. 'Go to your bedroom, and you can see for yourself.'

'Come with me?' I ask Ash, taking his hand.

He nods eagerly, and we head upstairs together.

I aim for my room and find Roux leaning over my bed. Two babies with heads of bright red hair lie on their backs, gurgling and sucking on a rag as she wraps them up in blankets. The moment I set foot in the doorway, my sister stops what she's doing and takes me in.

'Scarlet,' she breathes.

Instantly I note her stomach has flattened significantly. Her skin is radiant, and she looks astonishingly happy.

'Meet your new niece and nephew.'

Stepping closer, I peer down at them. The eyelids of their bright red eyes flutter – they are unable to decide whether they want to sleep or not. My vision blurs, and I kneel down to touch them, caressing their heads of soft hair, gently stroking their velvety cheeks.

'You did it,' I croak, voice breaking.

My sister kneels beside me, watching her children wriggle with obvious pride.

'You did it, Roux. I'm so proud of you. But how is this possible? You weren't due for another few weeks.'

She sighs like she knows I won't like the answer. 'During your trial, I started to bleed severely. The healers suspect that because my body was under so much stress watching you, I made myself go into early labour.'

'If that's the case, how are you still here? What happened with the medicine? None of this adds up,' I blurt in confusion, realising Dimitri's vision came true – just not in the way I expected.

Ash sits on the bed before the children, stroking the nearest one's belly. On my bed he looks massive, his frame taking up most of the room.

'You won because you refused to fight back,' Ash answers. 'The trial could have ended earlier, but the Elder Raven was angry and wanted to make an example of you.'

'Angry? That seems too merciful for what Scarlet had to endure,' Roux says, mirroring my thoughts.

'*Anyway*, Princess Leonore was sitting with us during your fight. When Roux went into labour, she whisked her off to her family's castle and took the medicine you'd earned – because at that point, you'd already won. Roux had several of the best healers working on her, who made sure she was safe and well cared for. They were in the room across from yours, but you were still recovering.'

'I wish I had been there for you,' I say with a pout. 'It must have been scary all by yourself.'

Roux smiles but shakes her head. 'I wasn't alone. Princess Leonore was with me, and she was wonderful. She's a good ally to have. I'm not surprised she chose you as her champion. You're very alike in some ways.'

'Yeah, she's great,' I agree with a nod.

'She also helped your friend's mother, so I think that's all your prizes used up.' Roux makes a face, seeming to think I'll be mad about this, but my heart feels like it will burst with joy.

Everything is right in the world. My sister is alive and well. My niece and nephew are happy and healthy. My brother is finally home and able to live a normal life. And Merlot's mother has been taken care of.

'That's wonderful news, Roux.' My arm wraps around her shoulder, and I bring her in for a kiss, my lips landing on her temple. 'I'm still baffled that I won, to be honest.'

'Well, no one else did what you did. Everyone else killed their loved one, hoping to win the trials,' Ash says, making me frown.

'Goes to show what the Elder Raven has done to our House,' I say, earning glum nods from my siblings.

'You can change that one day,' Ash says, peering down at me. 'You could change our lives for the better, and hopefully, these two will grow up in a more pleasant House than we did.' He motions to the twins, who seem deep in sleep.

'No pressure,' Roux pipes up, making me smile timidly.

'Have you decided on names yet?' I ask, needing to change the subject.

My brother and sister share a secret smile, and I can't help but laugh.

'Should I be concerned?'

Ash picks up the baby nearest him, cradling him as if he's experienced babies before. 'This is your nephew, and Roux called him Vermilion.'

I glance at my sister with a smirk, remembering our visit to the library. 'You named him after Ruby's Hex name?' I laugh, looking into my nephew's face with a new wave of love for him. 'Vermilion Fang the Second. How fitting.'

Roux lifts my niece and hands her to me. I hesitate, but she doesn't relent. In seconds I'm sitting beside Ash with a baby in my arms. My niece makes a face in her sleep, dreaming of something I could never guess at.

'And my niece is called ...' I wonder out loud, trailing my finger along her tiny ear.

'Well, it was tough to choose, as there are so many lovely names, but ultimately, there was only one that fit her perfectly,' Roux says, taking her daughter's little hand. 'Her name is Scarlet Seraphine, after the aunt who saved us all.'

54

My heart is overflowing with love and adoration. After meeting my new family members, my siblings and I all go back downstairs to have our meal.

The others all become quiet as I descend the stairs. Scarlet is in my arms as I take a seat next to my brother. Blaze automatically goes to touch our niece, like she magnetises him. The sight makes my heart burst.

'The food smells amazing,' I tell Ruby, who beams in answer.

'We are celebrating,' she declares. She leans towards me and gives my head a kiss. 'Well done on your win. I hope you're feeling well.'

'For the most part,' I reply honestly.

She takes my burnt hand and inspects my fingers. 'Fire can be a dangerous element in the wrong hands,' she says, no doubt wishing she could take revenge on the Elder Raven. 'Watching you was terrifying. You wouldn't do anything, and a part of me was hoping for you to end her. Of course, I knew it wasn't really Ember, but to think you ...'

She seems to lose her words, her eyes looking up at the ceiling to stop the tears.

'It's in the past now. We should focus on the bright future ahead,' I murmur, not sure what else to say.

Across the table, Ember drops her knife. Everyone stops, but I feel rather than see my sister's gaze on me. Swallowing, I look up, meeting her stare.

My heart races, a sliver of fear rearing its head as I focus on her. No matter how much I try to calm my heart, it beats wildly as I remember the fire – Ember's strong hands on me as she rips me apart. It may not have been her who caused me so much pain, but knowing she fought the illusion of me makes me feel sick. Ember, unlike me, chose to end her sibling to gain what she wanted most in the world. Every time I look into those crimson eyes from now on, I will remember that she decided my life was less worthy than hers.

'Is there a problem?' I ask, making myself stare at her, forcing myself not to show my fear even as it crawls up my limbs and across my chest.

'No,' she states, her eyes lowering to my throat. 'I didn't expect you to come home with so many scars. What did they do to you?'

'They did less than what *you* would have done to me,' I snap, my voice colder than I've ever heard before. Awkward silence envelops us, and I feel guilty for ruining a nice family moment. 'I'm sorry. I didn't mean to—'

'You're entitled to your feelings, Scarlet,' Roux pipes up. 'Don't ever apologise for that.'

Ember's gaze twists to Roux, and the pair glare at one another. I sense something has happened during my recovery and it's not been pleasant.

'You know what? There is something else I'd like to say,' I announce, clutching baby Scarlet to my chest for support.

If I don't say it now, I never will. 'I'm glad you didn't win the trials, Ember.'

Blaze, beside me, stiffens, and I know instantly that it's a sore subject for his twin. But I don't care – she needs to hear what I have to say.

'Don't get me wrong. You have so many qualities to make a brilliant Raven of the Hex. But I can't help but feel hurt and betrayed that my own sister would want to *kill* me for some stupid competition.'

'The Hex is not stupid,' Ember counters.

'No, the *Hex* is not stupid,' I agree calmly. 'But the *trials* are.'

Ember doesn't look away. She pins me down with her glare, and for once I welcome it. My mind churns with all the things I'll achieve in my life now I've won, things that *she* will miss out on. My sister wanted to win so badly, and now she has lost so much.

'I'm saddened that you felt the need to eliminate anyone who got in your way, Ember. But I hope you realise I'm the next Raven of the Hex because you are a *traitor*.'

Ember's face darkens at the taunt, but she says nothing.

After that, conversation resumes like normal around her, but she doesn't say a word.

I'm packing a small bag, filling it with the remaining clothes I own, when I feel a presence behind me. Ruby holds a large box and puts it on my bed, then opens the lid and takes out a cloak. One side is made of glossy raven feathers, while the other side is made of silk of rich garnet red.

'Wow, that's gorgeous,' I gasp as Ruby lays the cloak on the bed.

She reaches inside the box again and takes out a thin band made of bronze with a small red stone set on top.

'These were the things I could save from my time in the Hex,' Ruby says, stroking the raven feathers affectionately. Her crimson eyes turn watery. 'I was stripped of everything when they found out I was pregnant with you, but I wouldn't change that for the world. You must know that.'

Patting the bed, I nod. 'I do.'

Ruby obeys and sits next to me. I take in the cramped room, wondering how it fits all us sisters in it. I imagine Ember and Roux replacing my bed with cots, getting rid of any evidence I ever existed. It makes me slightly sad to leave now that everyone is together.

'We were so happy when we found out. One of the best days of my life, in fact,' Ruby declares, still unable to mention my father.

Her hand slides inside her tunic, and takes out a small photo. The picture is old with curling edges, a dark stain on the back. Ruby looks dreamy as her eyes roam over the print, her brows furrowing as her lips quiver slightly.

'He was so excited he couldn't keep his hands off my belly.' She chuckles as if remembering the memory fondly. Her trembling hands offer me the photo.

'He is very handsome.' I marvel at the stranger's face, seeing my likeness to him. He is undeniably human. He has windswept hair that curls around his nape, and his wide eyes that display warmth and happiness. The photo shows him smiling as if he is staring straight at us, the mirror image of me.

'You're like him in so many ways, but you have his big eyes and easy smile,' Ruby says with a sad nod.

'How did it all happen?' I can't take my eyes off my father – his sharp jawline, his skin dotted with freckles from the sun and his strong, tanned arms.

Ruby's mouth opens then closes. She considers before saying, 'I joined the Hex when I was twenty-five and met him not long after. He worked in a tavern in Sapphire City, in Tealwaters. I made excuses to go there any chance I could.' Ruby smiles as I imagine the man in the picture with my mother. 'We were ...' My mother swallows, the words becoming difficult suddenly. She brings her hands together in a motion of togetherness to fill in the gaps of her tale she physically cannot say. 'I had you three years after.'

They were together for three years.

By the way my mother relays her story, eyes shimmering with memory, I can tell she really loves him. She loves a human despite everything the House of Raven has taught her.

Finding more similarities between the man in the picture and me, I run my thumb over his face. Unlike Ruby and my siblings, my hair is straight, and I note my father also doesn't have a curl on his head. My heart tightens with quiet joy at the likeness.

'Aaron Rush,' I murmur, startling my mother.

'How do you know his name?'

Guiltily I explain how I found the article in the library.

Ruby nods as if this makes sense. 'I thought it was a coincidence your sister named one of my grandchildren Vermilion.'

Grinning, I bump her shoulder. 'It's a classy name, I must say.'

'At the time, I thought it sounded intimidating, but now I'm not so sure,' she jests in kind before her face smooths into seriousness again. 'You have the chance to discover more of your past, Scarlet. If you wish it.'

Translation: You have the perfect opportunity to find your father.

My heart pumps louder in my ears. 'Do you think he'd want that?'

Ruby looks surprised. 'Of course! Why wouldn't he?'

I take in my scarred hand holding the photo of him and imagine him looking at me in horror or revulsion. 'Because I'm not a sweet little girl. I'm burnt and torn up and ...' I don't know how to finish the sentence.

'The scars will be alarming, of course, but everyone knows what our House is like. He'll expect you to look like a warrior, as I once did.'

'Like you still are,' I correct, earning a small smile.

Ruby's hand rubs my leg fondly.

'Thank you for everything, Ruby,' I whisper, my voice cracking slightly as I hand back the picture.

'No. I want you to take it,' Ruby insists, pushing it away. 'If you find him, he will know it's you, even though you look *just* like him.'

'I do, don't I?'

Ruby takes out her pocket watch and sighs deeply. 'It's getting late, and we don't want you to be tired tomorrow.' She points to the bracelet sitting alongside the cloak. 'They are both yours if you wish. Put the bracelet on, but make sure the Elder Raven never sees it.'

I do as I'm told, deciding to leave the cloak for my mother to keep.

'A family heirloom?' I ask, putting the band on next to my other bracelet. Their contrast is significant. My old, dull bangle, worn since birth to prevent me from abandoning the House of Raven, and the new, glossy bracelet that has not a scratch upon it. I run a thumb over the ruby stone.

'You could say that. Click the ruby down, but stand up first,' Ruby instructs, coming to her feet as well.

I push down on the jewel, and a whirring sound starts. I look cautiously at my mother as I suddenly smell potent magic, Ruby only smiles in answer.

'Give it a moment. It needs to read your body.'

Moments go by, and the bracelet begins to double in size, plates of metal shooting out section by section. In seconds, my whole right arm is covered in hardware, the material slowly covering my body until I'm fully protected in armour.

'Holy Hanrah!' I exclaim, moving my body to see how it feels. The metal feels light and is easy to move around in. My eyes widen as I notice the garnet-and-gold colouring. 'This is amazing.'

'It was my armour, and now I'm handing it down to you. With time, it will change style and colour depending on your preferences.'

'You're kidding,' I exclaim, admiring the details and colours that Ruby wore once upon a time.

'I'm so proud of you, Scarlet. You'll be a brilliant Raven of the Hex. I just know it.'

My arms wrap around my mother's shoulders, closing the distance between us. I try to remember every detail of this moment between us, holding on to this happy memory.

55

Being in the presence of the royal family seems somewhat normal now. Queen Adela, Prince Julien and Princess Leonore all sit on their thrones. The princess winks at me as I stand before the dais, Jack right beside me as we ready ourselves for travel.

Queen Adela is beautiful, with luxurious gold jewels wrapping around her throat and dangling from her ears. Her dark blue eyes sparkle as she looks down at me from her throne, her delicate fingers resting easily upon the armrests as she inclines her head.

'Young Raven and guardian. I congratulate you both on your win,' the queen says, looking at her children. Beside Prince Julien is the Elder Raven, her face stone cold and furious. I can't help but smirk at the sight.

'Thank you for your support, Your Majesty,' I reply, raising my hand to my heart. Peering at Princess Leonore, I add, 'We won't let you down.'

The queen smiles easily, her teeth extremely white. She stands, letting her emerald dress and gold cloak pool around her. 'I have been impressed with your loyalty and commitment to this cause.'

Out of the corner of my eye, I can see the Elder Raven's mouth turn down, the lines in her face deepening with distaste.

The royal guards all shift as Queen Adela and Princess Leonore descend the steps together to come face to face with us. With a wave of the queen's hand, a guard runs to pass her a silver goblet adorned with rubies, the jewel of the House of Raven's army.

'Scarlet, you are to do one more thing before we send both of you away,' Queen Adela says, holding the goblet out to me.

Taking it, I peer inside to find nothing is there.

'You don't *take* from it. You *give* to it,' Queen Adela explains, seeming to understand my confusion. She reaches for my hand, noticing the already present scar. 'You must bind yourself to our lands, to guard the six kingdoms along-side the other chosen Hex members.'

'A blood oath,' Jack states, making the queen nod.

From inside her cloak, Princess Leonore reveals a dagger. Its hilt is midnight black with gold stars orna-menting it, its metal blade shining like liquid gold. 'Do not be afraid, my champion,' she says.

'I'm not any more,' I whisper, earning a grand smile.

The princess takes my hand and presses the dagger into my palm, cutting a line parallel to my scar, and squeezes the blood into the goblet.

Queen Adela clears her throat before asking, 'Do you, Scarlet Seraphine, vow to serve all kingdoms above your own needs?'

'I do,' I answer without hesitation, voice clear and confident.

'Do you vow to protect the innocent above all else?'

'I do,' I repeat, watching as my blood drips into the

goblet. The liquid sizzles at the bottom. Smoke begins to rise from the cup, red clouds filling the air.

'Welcome, Raven of the Hex. I wish you many successful years of honour and duty, as your ancestors have had before you.'

The goblet is taken from me, and the queen steps back, arms out in approval.

'I wish you good luck, Scarlet Seraphine and Jack Wilde. I will give you a moment to say your goodbyes.'

Together we turn, and two groups stand waiting for us, my family on one side and Jack's friends on the other. We share a smile before going our separate ways.

As I approach my brood, Roux rushes me, claiming the first hug. She whispers how much she loves me and how she'll miss me being around but how proud she is of everything I've achieved.

Ash lifts me and spins me around, a new favourite greeting of mine since he's been back home. Last night I couldn't sleep, so together we drank Liquid Gold until the early morning, catching up on life and pondering what our new lives will entail, and a small part of me wishes I didn't have to leave him so soon.

Blaze and Ruby share their embraces, telling me they are happy for me and to take every opportunity life sends my way. I nod and tell them I will. Ember, though, stands and watches quietly, holding baby Vermilion like a security blanket. I make it clear I don't want to touch her, but I lean close anyway, looking down at my nephew.

'I may not forgive you today, but I hope one day we can move past this,' I say, looking only at Vermilion. I'm a coward, but I don't care – her eyes haunt me in my dreams. 'But I wish you all the best in your training. Perhaps now, with the children, you'll be more mindful, not just of yourself but of others too.'

I step away and finally meet her gaze. Her eyes don't show any emotion, but I hope one day my words will sink in, and perhaps when I see her next, she'll be a different person. Hopefully.

Lastly, I hold my dear Scarlet, her eyes not open but I don't mind. I put my finger into her hand, and she grabs on like she knows it's the last time in a long while that she'll be able to.

'You be good for Mummy now,' I say, earning a laugh from my family. 'You can't be giving us Scarlets a bad name while I'm gone. Although I've probably done a decent job of that already,' I admit with a chuckle. After kissing her forehead, I release her, giving Vermilion one last peck too before stepping away. Tears fill my eyes as I say my last goodbyes and words of affection.

Jack's hand grasps my shoulder. 'You ready?' he asks, and I nod, waving and walking backwards towards the princess once more.

Princess Leonore gives me a sad smile. 'I'm sorry you have to leave your family behind, but a new and exciting adventure awaits you.'

Princess Leonore gathers my bleeding hand and trails her delicate fingers over the bracelet I've worn since childhood. The bracelet that ties me to our House and prevents me from leaving. What feels like air wraps around the metal, and her magic glows a light silver colour. In seconds, the bangle turns to dust as if it never existed.

'Thank you, Your Highness. Not just for this but for everything. You've been so kind to me, my family and my friends too.' I bow my head, earning an amused smile.

'You are very welcome. I can now say my first champion is the new Raven of the Hex! My brother will never live this down.' She winks, making me laugh.

The princess waves her hand in the air, and the Elder Raven approaches, her face reminding me of Ember's.

'As much as I want you to stay, I must send you off. Your next destination is a land of ocean and bright sunshine,' the princess reveals, making Jack's eyes light up with delight.

The Elder Raven pulls out a penlike object before making a circular motion, and a floating oval appears. The border crackles like fire, and the centre bubbles like lava as it glows an orange-red colour.

My body jerks back unconsciously when I see the element, and I instantly feel on edge.

'You have nothing to be afraid of,' Princess Leonore murmurs, taking my hand and squeezing it. 'This portal will take you to the kingdom of Tealwaters. There you are to meet your mentors and other Hex members, who are eagerly waiting for your arrival.'

The portal soon changes from bubbling lava to a depiction of trees. A waft of something I've never smelled before surrounds me, and I sigh.

'Are you ready?' I ask Jack, who nods.

'Let's go, Raven.'

He leads us towards the portal, then steps over and into the forest setting. Turning back, he offers his hand to me, and I hold on as I step into the new kingdom.

I look back once more and wave to my family, who are in the distance, watching every moment. They all wave frantically, and I find my throat constricting.

My eyes travel to the princess next, who smiles softly back. *Good luck*, she mouths.

Lastly, my gaze lands on the Elder Raven as the portal slowly closes. She glares into the portal with hatred, the same loathing that I fought in the arena. Ever so subtly her mouth moves, I lean forward to hear what she says.

'Watch your back, half-blood. You're not safe yet.'

EPILOGUE

Shivers course through my body, the Elder Raven's warning making me feel on edge. She never did get her wish of killing me off in the trials, and she'll no doubt plan to dispose of me now I'm out in the big wide world – away from the princess's protection.

'Scarlet.'

My heart rate spikes, and I turn towards my guardian, who watches me with concern.

'Are you okay?'

I nod before taking in the new setting. My eyes scan everything from ground to sky, my heart thundering for a different reason now.

Greenery.

Woodland surrounds me. Various shades of green, orange and brown cover everything like a blanket. The bright blue sky and fluffy white clouds peek through the leaves, creating pockets of sunlight that I step into without hesitation.

My bones warm instantly. My face turns to the beaming sun, and I listen carefully to the rustling sound in the gentle breeze, salt and fresh air filling my lungs. It smells exactly like Jack.

'This must all be very new for you,' he murmurs, coming up beside me.

My body tingles with anticipation, his closeness making me smile. I face him, and he looks at me with amusement, his lips tugging up at the corners.

'This is nothing like being stuck inside a cave,' I remark, making him nod knowingly. 'The smells, the breeze ...' I find myself getting emotional, and I look up at the branches above to keep the tears at bay. I've come so far and left so much behind, but right now, in this exact moment, I feel wonderment. Nothing can ever compare to the awe that is washing over me.

'It's rather lovely,' Jack finishes for me, but his soft gaze makes me think he isn't talking about the kingdom we've found ourselves in.

My hand reaches for him, grasping his fingers as I let the sun shine down on me. Closing my eyes, I wish that this moment would never end, that our time together would never fade.

'I never want to forget this moment, this new feeling I'm experiencing,' I confess, feeling his grip tighten.

My guardian is quiet for a moment. I peer up to find him smiling, watching me closely. He nudges my side with a playful grin.

A part of me wants him to close the distance, to kiss me with no one but the trees to witness it. This would be the perfect place ...

My guardian's eyes dance with delight – as if sensing where my thoughts are leading. But he doesn't move closer, he simply holds my hand while I adjust to our new environment.

'We did it, Scarlet,' he murmurs. 'We won the Hex Trials.'

I grin. We fulfilled Jack's promise to his father and saved the people I care for most. 'It was a long road but—' My eyes flicker down towards the earth, feeling my feet tremble slightly. 'Did you feel that?'

He lifts a brow. 'Feel what?'

My gaze turns to the scenery around us, the tremors growing the longer we stand still. In the distance I see the trees begin to rustle, leaves falling from an invisible force. 'We need to go.'

'What—' I tighten my grip on his hand and yank him into a sprint. 'Where are we going?' Jack shouts, looking back every so often, growing panic coating his features now.

'I have no clue!' I admit, scampering down a small hill and racing up another.

'Don't you think—' But before my guardian can finish his sentence, a deafening explosion rips us apart. My body feels weightless for a moment before gravity claims me. Pain spikes through my back as I find myself lying among dirt and thick tree roots. My ears ring as I search through the chaos.

I'm suddenly surrounded by blazing red and orange as crackling fire ignites around me. It climbs the nearest trees and consumes every leaf it comes across. My heart hammers with fear.

Has the Elder Raven come for me already?

'Jack!' I scream, but I hear no reply. Terror creeps into my bones. The flames make it difficult to see, to breathe. No matter what direction I look in, I see no silvery head of hair and no bright blue of magic. Panic grips my body.

My guardian is nowhere in sight.

AUTHOR NOTE

Hi there!
I hope you enjoyed reading
THE CRIMSON SCAR.

Scarlet's story has been stuck inside my head for far too long and
finally it's here, in your hands, and I can't believe it!

Thank you so much for purchasing this book. Please consider
leaving a review or recommending it to a friend.

Thanks again,
Hannah x

DIMITRI THUNDERS

Turn the page for...

A CRIMSON SCAR NOVELLA

COVEN OF VAMPIRES

HANNAH PENFOLD

Based 150 years before The Crimson Scar

Dimitri Thunders has everything a young man could ever
want – a loving family, a devoted girlfriend and an exciting
future full of promise. But that all changes when he is
betrayed by the person he trusts the most.

Now Dimitri must make the difficult choice between
acceptance and revenge.

I

As I scan the numerous shelves, my arms are filled with books that need returning to their correct places. I amble past row upon row of novels, tomes and publications that have been in this library since the rebuilding of the city many generations ago.

Reaching up, I rearrange a line of history books before adding the three missing from this section. One catches my eye enough that I put my armful of books down on the edge of a low shelf and start flicking through its delicate pages. They are stained with age, and the depictions upon them are starting to fade, but my lips tug up into a smile.

'Found a treasure have we, Dimitri?'

I turn to my cousin and fellow librarian, Bennett. We share the same dark brown hair, tanned skin and blue eyes. For as long as I can remember, we've been joined at the hip – so much so that we work together here in the Rubien City Library, our love for all things books and knowledge something we have in common.

'I think so. Check this out.'

Together we peer down at the chapters before us, images of our city, which was once above the earth and in sunlight. 'Rubien before it was destroyed and moved underground.'

Bennett flicks through the pages, pausing on each picture to read the caption alongside it. 'To think that a city of innocents was annihilated by one hateful witch.' He shakes his head glumly. 'Now we all live in this cave. Who came up with such a strange idea?'

'Perhaps there was a particular reason the royal family moved their lives here,' I suggest.

A prince and princess of Hanrah – both only eighteen at the time – were the only survivors within the city's castle when the witch brought down her wrath on their people. No Rubien civilian is ignorant of the history behind our lands, of the drastic move all families endured from the sunny coastlines to the depths of this cavern, away from any other civilisation.

'A reason such as what, though?' Bennett mutters, running a hand through his hair. 'It still baffles me that they created this cave, that all within it was built by the hands of our ancestors.' He motions to our surroundings. 'It must have been a scary time for them all.'

I nod solemnly. *Scary indeed.*

'Anyway, I'm heading off now. I left the keys inside the desk drawer. Don't stay behind too late.' Bennett pats my head fondly as a farewell. He's done that ever since we were kids – he was once taller than me and happy to make me feel small, but now we are the same height. It still amuses me, though, so I never complain about it.

'Get home safe,' I say, watching him as he turns back briefly with a nod of acknowledgement. It wouldn't be the first time my cousin has been mugged. Like most people in our family, we are dameer – humans born with magic. And like most people in our family, Bennett's magical abilities are defensive rather than offensive. He can see through anything – a teenage boy's dream, or so Bennett claims.

'Always do. Make sure you check the streets before you leave,' he says before heading out the exit.

From a young age, I have been able to see the future. As I've gotten older, I've learned to control the random visions and prevent them from occurring. I can also conjure images on demand – to see *what* I want *when* I want. As with anything in the future, though, nothing is set in stone. What lies ahead adjusts and evolves depending on a person's decisions.

I close my eyes, and my mind moves forward in time to see if Bennett will come to any trouble. The streets of Rubien seem calm and full of people. The shops and market stalls are open and bustling, as is usual for this time of day. Thankfully, I see nothing out of the ordinary. His arrival home is all I need to open my eyes once more to the books before me.

It's only when I go to put a volume back that a sudden chill washes over me, and the library's quietness becomes a cold silence. A shiver runs over my arms as I peer around, sensing something – or rather, someone – watching me. I glance between the books stored on the nearby shelves, towards the reception desk.

I find a woman standing there, waves of dark brown hair tumbling over her shoulders, contrasting with her milky skin. She wears a dress in an attempt to appear innocent, but I know better than to underestimate her. As I scan her face, she smiles at me, noting my observant gaze. Her lips pull back to show long, sharp fangs, her bright red eyes sparkling with delight.

'Hello, Dimitri.'

2

Her steps are silent as she walks through the foyer – the way she moves reminds me of a predator approaching its prey.

'Victoria,' I say, kissing her cheek as she embraces me.

'My love,' she says, her hands roaming over my arms affectionately. 'Are you ready to head out?'

I peer down at the book still in my grasp, its companions unsorted on the shelf beside me.

One of Victoria's brows rises – she's unimpressed. 'Where are the keys? I'll lock up while you deal with them.'

After I reveal Bennett's hiding place for the keys, she's a blur as she locks up the building, checking every door and window in the time I take to put away six books. In moments she's back at my side, keys dangling from a pale finger as she watches me put the last book in its rightful place.

'All right, now I'm ready,' I tell her, receiving a smug look.

Victoria takes a step closer to me, making my heart race at her proximity. I am still not used to her – the unnatural speed, her desire for me. It's as if I'm dreaming, and I'll one day wake up and realise this was all a figment of my imagination.

'I'm ready for something too ...' She watches me from under her lashes.

'For what, exactly?' I ask. My voice is husky because, from the look she is giving me, I know *exactly* what she is ready for.

She doesn't answer but slowly pulls off my cloak and unbuttons my shirt, her lithe fingers cold against my skin as she unclothes me, and tosses my attire on the floor. My uneasy look towards the door makes her smile. 'It's all right. They are all locked, and all the "Closed" signs are up. No one will come in.'

'Good girl,' I murmur, making her cheeks flush with pleasure. My girl has always liked being praised.

Our lips crash together, our hands roaming over one another as she directs me blindly to a table. I sit on the edge, the perfect height to slide my hands up her body, my fingers tickling the skin under her dress.

'How was your day?' she asks, watching as my hand disappears under her frock. My fingers caress her breasts, making her lips tilt up in excitement.

'It's been eventful. The children came in today, and we had story time. We had a whole pile of book returns, and I had lunch at the Tea Shop,' I answer, knowing she doesn't really care but is trying to be polite.

Slowly I remove her clothing altogether and take a breast in my mouth, earning a groan. I move away slightly, looking up at her with an innocent expression. 'How was *your* day?' I mutter, grinning when her lips tilt down.

'Fine. You got me,' she concedes, crimson eyes upon me. 'I couldn't care less about what story you read today. Take me right here, on this very table.'

A zap of adrenaline shoots through me, and I scowl at

her. Her vampire persuasion makes my body move of its own accord as I manoeuvre her body, getting it ready to do exactly as she has commanded.

She grimaces at her power over me. 'Sorry. Let me rephrase that. Please will you take me right here, on this table?'

'Say no more,' I reply, lifting her up. Her strong legs wrap around me, cocooning me in their embrace, unyielding and unwilling to let me go. Our lips find each other in seconds, like magnets that can't stay apart. My tongue slides inside her mouth, and she welcomes me, causing me to harden when she sucks and teases.

'I want you,' she murmurs, biting my lip tenderly.

Without hesitation I slide one hand gently up her thigh and taunt her with my closeness, testing how much she can handle, coming dangerously close to her wetness. She whimpers, wanting more, and I oblige. I trace a thumb along the very place she wants me most. I move it slowly in circles, loving the sounds that are coming from her lips, our tongues still entwined, and her nails dig in painfully as I increase the pace. Soon she is arching her back, pressing herself against me.

'Dimitri,' she utters.

'Yes, my love?'

She grabs my occupied hand and brings it between us, stopping our kissing momentarily. She puts each of my fingers down until only two are up. My brow quirks at her boldness.

'Right now,' she commands, her persuasion taking hold of me once more.

'Right away, princess.'

Her eye roll makes me laugh as I dip my fingers inside her and build momentum. Her breathing becomes ragged, and my trousers tighten with my need for her.

'You are so beautiful,' I say as she comes close to climaxing. 'My beautiful girl.'

One moment I am making Victoria scream, and the next I am screaming along with her. Pain as hot as fire and quick as lightning strikes between my neck and shoulder, what feels like needles penetrating my skin.

Deeply embedded into my muscles are her deathly sharp fangs.

3

My lack of movement and paused breath makes her eyes open. Confusion seeps through her features before she realises her mistake.

'Victoria,' I murmur, voice barely audible. My body feels stiff. The adrenaline and desire are immediately extinguished as I stare down at her. This has happened time and time again, her desire getting the better of her, and I always suffer with the immense agony that comes along with it.

Slowly she removes her mouth, and I wince at the withdrawal, her needle-like teeth making me groan with discomfort – the pain is harrowing. As my blood beats through me, I watch Victoria fight for control of her bloodlust.

I move away because I need space, but her hands are upon me, and my eyes snap to her face. *She is a predator*, I remind myself. *Do not run, or she will chase you.*

In these moments, I am truly scared of her – fearful of the vampire that promises me I'm safe, when really we are both lying to ourselves. With Victoria, I am *never* truly safe.

'Dimitri,' she murmurs before I unsteadily move away.

It's my wobbly legs that make her move at superspeed

to my side. She sets me down on a nearby chair and clothes herself as she frets over me. 'Sit. Let the dizziness fade,' she instructs, used to looking after me following her episodes. 'I'm so sorry.'

'You told me you could handle it,' I say, looking up into her inhumanly stunning face. Her eyes are apologetic. 'If you couldn't, you should have told me. I wouldn't have been so ...' I wave a hand, the effort causing me to grimace. I can't finish my sentence, but she understands.

She kneels before me, edging herself in between my knees. 'It was so sudden. I didn't know what I was doing until you stopped. I thought I *was* handling it.' Tears brim around her eyes, and I find my hand hovering over her cheek, stroking lightly.

'That is no excuse, Victoria. When someone says no, it means *no*.'

She doesn't look at me but nods. We've had this conversation many times. I don't enjoy her biting me, and she knows that. But when I scold her for doing so, she makes me feel so guilty.

'I can't help it,' she whispers.

'You can.'

She meets my gaze then, my hardened eyes portraying how I feel. She claims to have no control when around me, but I know better. She wishes I wanted what she does. To become like her – a vampire.

'Did you know that younglings are most powerful in the first forty-eight hours? Even more powerful than mature vampires?' she says, hope lining her gorgeous features.

I sigh. I don't care about what I can and can't do as a vampire. I don't want the same fate as hers and never will.

'I promise it wouldn't hurt if you just relaxed. If you would let me—'

I shake my head, pushing her away from me.

She gets to her feet, a hurt expression on her face.

'I do not wish to be like you. I wish to be myself, in *this* body, with the life I already have.' It's been over a year now, and still she wants more from me – more of me than I'm willing to let her have. 'I don't want you to pressure me. My decision is mine and mine only.'

She takes me in from head to toe. Where I think an apologetic face will show is one of anger, of frustration. My heart races at the sight, her fangs gleaming menacingly.

'You have never accepted me for who I am. Never accepted my kind. You're just like the rest of them,' she seethes, tidying up her attire, making sure her hair is in place.

'Accepting you and accepting you turning me are two completely different things,' I say hotly, taking her actions as my cue to grab my shirt and cloak from the floor. 'Accepting *you* means having a life of love and adoration. Accepting your *lifestyle* means becoming something I'm not sure I'll ever be ready for.'

'"Something" being a monster?' she asks, quoting the term the civilians use for all vampires within Rubien city.

I know she's baiting me, wanting me to argue, but I don't have the strength to fight back. 'You are not a monster, Victoria. But you have to understand you are asking something life-altering of me. It means never seeing the sun or eating the foods I enjoy again. My family would live in fear of me.'

'We can protect your family. I won't let you hurt them.' She pauses from her pacing to look at me, to let me know she's genuine.

My mind wanders to my parents, their smiling faces as they hold my younger brother, Felix. He is only six, and if I turned into a vampire, like Victoria wishes, he'd be the first person I'd crave. A vampire desires the blood closest to their own – as my family, they share the very blood I'd want most in the world.

'That is not a risk I'm willing to take. And besides, I would never be able to live in Alba,' I reply, my mind wandering to the dream I've held since childhood.

'You have been applying to become a librarian in the Library of Wonders for *five* years, Dimitri.'

'So?' I challenge.

'If they haven't accepted you already, they may never do so.'

My heart drops at her words. For years I have been requesting work at the most prestigious library in the kingdom of Hanrah. The capital, Alba, holds the largest and most renowned collection of tomes in the northern lands. Any who are accepted to work there are usually over the age of forty – the royals want their books to be safeguarded by those with worldly experience and the ability to educate. At twenty-seven years old, I have yet to be accepted, but this year I have high hopes – or rather, I *had* high hopes.

'Shove a dagger through my heart, why don't you?' I whisper, the hurt clear in my voice.

Victoria spins. Her pale face instantly morphs into regret. 'Dimitri, I didn't mean it. I'm feeling terrible, and I'm lashing out at you. Please.' She grabs my arm as I go to leave. Distance. I need distance from her. 'Please, let's talk this out. I don't want us parting on bad terms. Let's forgive and forget.'

Watching her reminds me of all the other times we've forgiven each other – or rather, the times I have forgiven Victoria, for forcing something upon me that I'm not willing to give her. Most times I would nod, let her talk out her feelings, and contribute my own occasional comment, but this time I've had enough. This has happened too often, and I know deep down the situation will never change.

'Victoria.' She's instantly on alert, body stiffening as if sensing this isn't the usual fight-and-make-up situation. 'I can never give you what you truly want, and I will clearly never make you happy until you get that one thing.'

'No.' She shakes her head, hands on my arms, pulling me closer and with such force I can't fight it. 'No, don't say that.'

'You want me to become a vampire, like you,' I say more firmly, looking into her teary eyes. 'You want a partner who can be with you – understand you. I am *human*. I want to travel and see the world, feel the sun on my skin, experience new foods and cultures.'

'You don't love me any more.'

'I love you as much as I did the first day I met you.'

'Then why does this sound like a break-up?'

'I want you to understand. I do not want to be a vampire, and your pressuring of me will never help your cause. If anything, it deters me.'

'Because you don't want to spend your life with me,' she concludes.

'You know that's not true.'

She doesn't say anything.

I sigh, picking up her cloak and handing it over. 'This is for the best, Victoria.'

Reluctantly she nods and takes the cloak after a moment of consideration. She doesn't say a word as I escort her to the exit, open the door for her and watch her walk away from me.

4

It's early evening as I walk home. The stone streets of Rubien are unusually quiet for this part of my neighbourhood. Above me the stalactites hang precariously from the ceiling of the cave. My mind wanders to the sunny coastline somewhere above us, a city that used to be there, without stone walls.

Victoria will come to understand my decision. She will realise that once I've done my travelling, I'll be happy to settle down with her. We can find a home where she is safe and guarded from the sun – a place where I can be above the ground, away from the cold pockets of this cage-like cavern.

I continue to stroll towards the market, which is crowded. Shouts and the sound of smashing glass echoes through the air. I run towards the gathering of people, peering over their heads to watch the spectacle before them.

'Leave us alone!'

'Don't touch her!'

The yelling comes from a group of market stall owners. Their children and belongings are being roughly handled by two vampires who have decided to visit. Their bright red eyes keep the spectators at bay, and their fangs are sharp and intimidating as they hiss at onlookers.

One of them, with red lips and long dark hair, holds a young girl in her firm grip – at first glance I think it's Victoria, but I know she would never terrorise the people of Rubien.

The child withers under the female's hold, looking up with fright.

'I said I wanted some silks,' the vampire snaps, glaring at who I assume is the child's mother.

For years, the civilians of this city have been terrorised by these predators, their threats becoming more lethal as time has gone on.

The mother, whose hands are out as if to calm the vampire, has been crying – her concern for her child outweighs any loss to her business. 'Please, don't hurt her! Take what you want. Just don't hurt my girl.'

The vampire woman raises a brow as if pleased with the answer. She points a delicate finger towards a pile of silver material beside the silk she wants. 'Add in the velvet, or else I will snap her neck.'

'Don't you dare,' the mother seethes, her hands working quickly to gather the fabrics.

I'm unsure whether the woman is being persuaded or not, but she looks half terrified, half furious.

The mother's facial expression doesn't please the vampire. Her strong hands reach up to the child's throat in warning.

'Enough!' My legs move without my consent, my voice rising above the havoc. 'Leave the child alone, and leave these people be – you've scared them enough,' I say, winding through the throng of people until I'm standing next to the mother. My eyes are intent, warning glimmering in them. I've learned with Victoria that a human cannot afford to act weak in a vampire's presence. They only listen to strength and power – and as their inferior, I am naturally deemed puny in their eyes.

'Dimitri Thunders?' the vampire asks, to which I faintly nod.

I'm not sure how she knows my name, but I don't dare react. Glaring at her, I silently will the vampires to leave and never return.

Eventually, she nods, as if my request is a rather good idea. 'If you wish it, I shall go on my way.'

'I do wish it,' I state firmly, reaching for the young girl. The vampire lets go as I take the child's arm, and I hand her over to her mother, the woman's cry of relief making my heart race. 'Go back to where you came from.' I point to her companion, a female with short silver hair whose glare burns through me from across the street. Her arms are full of crockery, which I have no doubt she's about to steal. 'And take your friend with you once you've paid for your items.'

The pair share a glance before the silver-haired vampire lets go of the wares in her arms, and dishes crash onto the stone street. My jaw tenses in an attempt to keep myself from cursing at her. Everyone else seems to have the same idea – no one dares to insult her for ruining their products. Together we watch as the two finally walk away, looking back once before departing the market for good.

The mother alongside me grabs my arm. 'Thank you, young man. I can't thank you enough.'

'I'd say it's my pleasure, but I hope for all our sakes it doesn't happen again.'

The woman shakes her head, saddened eyes turning to where the vampires stalked off. 'I wish this were the last time, but they visit more often now, creating chaos and causing trouble wherever they go. It's the second time they've tried taking Anita.' She looks down at her daughter and kisses her head.

I've heard too many horror stories about missing children in our city – the vampires deem them worthy of killing and feasting on when they are hungry.

'If only there were a way of getting rid of them,' I murmur, knowing full well this wasn't my first and won't be my last time standing against one of their kind. The newspaper always has an article to share when it comes to vampires.

'They are a plague on our city. It's a good thing we have people like you who are willing to stand up for the little people.' She squeezes my arm in thanks before tending to her ruined market stall. The neighbouring stall owners are gathering pieces of smashed glass along the street – obviously the sound I heard before.

People from the crowd start to disperse then – the bubble of helplessness they were in has popped. They begin to help those who went up against the vampire women – other stalls along the way are also wrecked – and more than anything, I want to go home and check on my own family.

5

I can smell baking as I let myself into my family home. My mother, a small woman with dark, glossy hair, mixes a bowl of what I assume is flour, eggs and other ingredients for cake. She looks engrossed as I quietly approach her, tongue poking out as she stirs.

'Mother.'

She jumps in surprise, the bowl in her grasp tipping over. I grab for it, grinning as I save her creation from splattering over the floor. She frowns before meeting my eyes, but her smile eventually grows as she seems to forgive my scaring her.

'I nearly had a heart attack,' she says by way of greeting, nudging me away as she puts her bowl down. She has a line of cake mix along her cheek, and I wipe it away with a finger and smear it on her apron.

'And I nearly lost the opportunity to have cake.'

She smiles broadly now. 'How was work, darling?'

'Really good. We got some new volumes in today that we need to find homes on the shelves for – and they're all the way from *Siamoon*,' I say excitedly.

'That's wonderful. Did you have the chance to read

them all before putting them out to the public?' my mother asks, cleaning away the discarded cups and saucers that are dirty and no longer needed.

'No, but I plan on heading into the library early tomorrow morning before my shift starts.'

She smiles at me like this is unusual behaviour. It's not. I spend most of my time at the library, books being one of my favourite companions. When I was a child, my mother would spur me on to make new friends, friends that weren't in the pages of books.

'And did you have a good evening with Victoria?' She gives me a warm smile as her eyes study me – no doubt making sure I'm in one piece. 'Although you are home earlier than I expected.'

Like everyone in the city, my mother is wary of vampires. She hates the coven that roams the streets and brings trouble to our homes, the destruction it brings upon our buildings, businesses and people.

I grimace, because the last thing I want to talk about is Victoria. 'We broke up.'

She pauses only a moment before she wraps her arms around me, embracing me as if I were a child again. I find myself leaning into her touch, needing a small dose of comfort. Slowly her hand strokes my back, so tender and gentle – just like her.

'My darling,' she coos as she leans away, starting to stroke my arms. 'You'll be all right. Things will work out in the end.'

'I broke up with her, actually,' I admit, making her dark brows furrow slightly, her blue eyes suspicious.

'Has she been pressuring you again?'

My lack of answer turns her face to stone. She is a soft lady – everyone loves her, and she is well known for her kindness. But when it comes to her two boys, she becomes a mother bear – protective, strong as iron and unwavering in the cause of our safety and happiness. 'She is a lovely girl, but love is all about compromise. If she cannot accept your decision to stay human, perhaps she is not the one for you. A decision like that is nothing to be taken lightly.'

'I know,' I murmur.

'Have some food with me. That will make you feel better.'

Together we prepare the table with lots of small plates, forgetting her cake mix. Two assortments of meat, slices of cheese and freshly baked bread rolls that are warm and smothered with butter. My groan of pleasure fills the room.

'Tasty,' I mumble, covering my mouth, which is full of food.

My mother beams with joy.

A racket sounds outside, and moments later my younger brother, Felix, falls through the door. Shopping supplies fill his small, gangly arms, but the bag tips and falls to the floor. Leeks and a bundle of apples tumble free.

'Felix!' My mother scowls, bending to pick up a stray apple. 'What did I say about—'

'Sweetheart, we're home!' my father yells before realising we are all right there. 'Ah, lovely. Looks divine, pet. Are there any leftovers for your doting husband and –' he peers at Felix, who is still picking up his runaway food – 'your clumsy second-born son?'

My father unloads the bags he holds and nods approvingly at my plate, half-eaten now as I stuff some bread into my mouth. My mother quickly makes up two more places at the table, and my brother takes a seat opposite me.

'What happened to you both? It's been hours. I was starting to get worried,' my mother says, stroking Felix's hair affectionately.

He looks up at her with a strange expression, and my

father's grimace doesn't go unnoticed. Felix looks on edge, but his face softens slightly as he tucks into his food.

'The coven hit again. Stalls were turned over. We had fresh produce all over the streets ...' His eyes flick to his youngest son. I get the feeling they experienced the same two visitors I came across. 'I think it's best we stay away as much as we can,' my father finishes, giving my mother a meaningful look.

She nods in understanding. 'It will never change,' she murmurs miserably.

'They need to be handled by the royal family,' I pipe up.

'They probably don't get informed of such things,' my mother answers with a huff. 'The coven controls all the communication towers and postal offices, and now it dictates what comes in and out of the city.'

My frown shows how little I really know of the vampires. When did they take over such vital parts of our home? With Victoria, I guess I've become ignorant to what really happens in the outside world. The pair of us existed inside our perfect little bubble, not wanting to pay attention to the war between our peoples.

'But enough talk of them,' my mother says.

A knock at the door startles us. A letter slides under the door, and we all stare at the envelope. It's royal blue in colour, the stamp of the royal crest upon its front – the peacock and her beautiful feathers on full show.

Felix is the one to retrieve it, his blue eyes widening as he takes in the envelope, and he hands it over to our father.

Hope lines my father's features, the same eyes my brother and I have peering up at me. 'For you,' he says, handing it over.

My brother runs around the table, his smile growing as he jumps onto my lap. 'Open it! Open it!' My arm wraps around him as I manoeuvre him into a more comfortable position on my leg, his small body coiling around me as I begin to open the envelope.

My mother's face contorts into an anticipated smile, her hand reaching for her husband's.

'You've got this, son,' my father mumbles, giving me an encouraging nod.

My fingers fumble and my hand shakes as I take out the piece of paper I've seen so many times before. The letter is from the Library of Wonders. All those I've received over the last five years have contained a rejection of my plea to join the librarians of Alba.

My eyes scan the paper as I open it out fully, and my breath hitches.

I did it.

Looking up at my family, I say, 'I did it.'

My brother howls in excitement, and I jump to my feet with elation.

'I did it!' I laugh, my brother wrapping himself around me as I spin us around.

My parents are quickly on their feet, embracing my brother and me, our family in a huddle together, and I can't remember the last time I felt this filled with happiness.

I've been accepted. I've finally made the cut. My one dream of going to the capital is about to come true. I will be one of the famous royal librarians, like I've always wanted.

'We need to celebrate!' my mother announces. She looks at the discarded baking and eyes the door. 'I'll buy some cake – strawberries and cream, your favourite.'

6

I'm being fuelled with shot after shot of Liquid Gold, an alcoholic drink that tastes delicious to anyone over eighteen and disgusting to anyone underage. The beverage warms me up, staining my mouth gold, as its name promises.

My whole family now knows of my achievement, and so here I am, drinking in celebration with my older cousins, continuing the night from our family-friendly dinner.

The group is dispersed throughout the tavern, which is especially popular with dameer – a spark of magic shines in the corner of my eye every now and then. Most of my female cousins dance with a throng of people, while most of my male cousins are at the bar, talking among themselves – the rest are in the restrooms, chucking up their guts.

I, however, sit with Bennett in a booth, watching as the night unfolds, the alcohol swirling inside my head. I'm drunk enough to be humming to myself, singing along to the music, but not drunk enough that I will forget the night.

'I can't believe you finally got accepted,' Bennett says,

taking a swig of his drink. 'I knew you could do it. You're the most intelligent and capable person I know.'

His faith in me is not surprising. If I told him I wanted to fly one day, he'd be right next to me, encouraging me to make it happen.

'Thanks, Ben.' I peer around at my cousins, all having a great time, and my chest tightens at the sight. 'I'm going to miss you lot.'

'You deserve this out, Dimitri. You've worked your butt off for this opportunity. Don't get sad now – it's just the alcohol affecting you.'

'You're right, but I—'

My eyes begin to cloud over, and I know instantly I'm about to have a vision. Stuck in a trance, all I can do is wait for it to pass.

It's hot. My skin feels clammy and taut. I'm looking towards a large fire – so fierce it nearly burns my lungs being this close to it. Movement to my right warns me of company. Victoria doesn't seem to care about the fire but rather only has eyes for me. My heart swells seeing her, the beauty of her face, the desire in her eyes. She is talking to me, but I can't hear her. My heart races faster the longer we stand close, my teeth grinding in response to whatever she is telling me. Turning towards the fire once more, I can feel my hands closing into fists – something I do when I'm trying to keep my feelings under control.

Why am I angry? Or am I sad? What is Victoria saying?

My cousin shakes me, and I come back to reality. Bennett and his sister, Tillie, are staring at me.

'I think Dimitri is ready to go home now.' Tillie grins. Her dark hair is stuck to her sweaty face, and her shoes are off from all the dancing.

'I'm fine,' I insist, standing up to leave, but a wave of sickness washes over me. 'On second thought ...'

'Come on. I've got you,' Bennett says, grabbing my arm

and throwing it around his shoulders. 'Tillie, don't walk home alone. Make sure the others are with you.'

'I will.' Tillie nods in confirmation before turning to me. 'I hope you don't feel too terrible tomorrow morning. We all know how little you usually drink.'

'Thanks.'

My arm is wrapped around Bennett's shoulder as he leads me through hordes of drunks, heading for the exit. The moment we step outside, I feel slightly better. The faint ocean breeze from the cave entrance is flowing through the streets.

My cousin doesn't let me go as we walk across the busy road, the nightlife still roaring and awake around us. Some groups of young people practise their magic together, and swirls of colour rush through the air above our heads.

My mind wanders to my vision – will they be the cause of the large fire later on?

'What did you see?' Bennett asks, seeming to notice I'm lost in my thoughts. His steps are slow beside me, his body strong and steady as he keeps my arm around his shoulders.

I debate lying, but it's never been easy trying to bend the truth with him. 'A big fire. So big I thought I would melt if I stood too close.'

He quirks a brow, and I mirror him, equally confused.

'Yeah, I have no idea what it means either, but Victoria was there.'

'Maybe she started it,' he suggests, but I shake my head.

'No. I don't think so.'

We continue in silence for a while, and I realise Bennett looks completely sober.

'You haven't had many drinks. Do you want to go back? I can walk myself home,' I say, untangling myself from him, but he maintains his pace.

'I didn't drink much, because I wanted to make sure you had a good night and could get home safe without having to worry about walking alone.'

Seeing my goofy expression, he punches my arm. Before I can answer with something corny, a shiver runs up my spine. It seems Bennett feels the same sensation, as his blue eyes widen slightly.

Did you feel that? he seems to ask.

I nod.

A flap of material snags my attention. In the distance, a tall figure with long silver hair, dressed in a midnight-black cloak, leans against a wall, his leg propped up as he plays with a small knife. My gut tells me this stranger is dangerous. My pounding heart tells me the same when he faces us, fangs bared in warning.

7

Panic coils in my stomach and progresses through the rest of my body when I notice another vampire across the way, staring at us from a dark alley. The female's red eyes are observant as they roam over Bennett and me, scanning us from head to toe. A voice behind us jerks me out of my growing alarm as I clutch at Bennett, swinging him forcefully behind me.

'Which one of you is Dimitri Thunders?' the male asks, his red eyes curious.

This particular vampire wears a cloak of deep red with dark stains covering the front – I assume he's spilled something down it and conclude it's most likely blood.

My mouth doesn't move, my brain fogging with fear.

'Answer him!' the female shouts, her body suddenly up against mine. Her grasp on Bennett is strong as she rips him away from me. Her hands are around his neck too quickly for me to follow, her deft fingers ready to snap his spine if we don't obey. 'Silas asked a question,' she prompts, looking between the pair of us.

'Let go of him,' I demand, watching her hold my cousin as easily as if she were restraining a child and not a grown man. He tries but fails to ease her grip on him. 'It's me you want.'

Silas smiles menacingly. 'Excellent. We've been sent to fetch you, Mr Thunders – to make sure you get home in one piece.'

On any other occasion, I would keep quiet, but the alcohol in my system gives me courage. 'Thanks for the offer, but I'm doing just fine without you,' I say, motioning to my cousin, his face neutral but on guard.

The moment I reach for Bennett, the three vampires circle us, intimidating as they close in.

'We don't want any trouble,' I murmur, my eyes stuck on Bennett. I try to convey that the moment the woman loosens her grip, he is to run, but he doesn't look at me. Rather, he looks at the vampire closest to me.

'Come with us,' the one with long silver hair says, his teeth so sharp they could tear me apart without much effort.

'Only if you leave him alone,' I say, watching as the female's face slides into a sly smile. 'Unharmed,' I add, and her eyes harden with what looks to be dismay.

The three of them share a glance as if debating whether to punish me for speaking up against them. The female vampire pouts, stroking a thumb down Bennett's cheek, and his eyes widen with fear. The sight torments me.

'What do you say, Lazarus?' she says to the silver-haired vampire.

He debates the options silently for a moment before nodding once in answer.

I get the sense they are talking about something different.

'Very well.' She smirks.

My hair is yanked by the female, her long and sharp nails scraping along my scalp. For a wild moment, I'm ecstatic Bennett is finally free – until Lazarus takes hold of him instead.

My stomach blooms with pain as the woman punches me in the gut before kicking me in my knees. The hard stone street makes my legs bark in pain. She chuckles, watching me roll onto my back, my eyes wide as I study her. She is erratic, and I hate that – her unpredictability scares me.

'Thana,' Silas warns, as if telling her to finish her business and be quick about it.

She leans over me with a wide grin that makes my body stiffen. 'You never specified that *you* should be left unharmed.'

I refrain from answering, and she finds delight in my reaction.

'Go on. Say what you want to say, human.'

'Demon,' I whisper, knowing she can hear me.

She laughs, amusement gleaming in her red gaze. 'You smell too good to tempt me like that,' she says, licking her lips.

I move away, instinctively putting my hands up as a barrier between us. It's the wrong move. A predator and her prey. She senses me wanting to escape, and the beast inside her can't help but want to chase me.

She jumps for me, sharp teeth biting into my neck, and she sucks up big mouthfuls without my consent. A scream escapes my lips, my arms and legs thrashing, trying to get her off me, but the more she takes, the more I can feel my limbs weaken, my strength leaving me.

Bennett roars as he runs for me, having been thrown away by Lazarus. My cousin looks mad, his eyes glowing with fury as he tries to fight for freedom, to save me from the female's grasp, but he is stopped by Lazarus, who snaps his neck as if it were a twig.

My cries of horror and sorrow go unheard.

'Enough, Thana!' Silas barks, ripping the female away from me finally.

My shoulder aches and burns from her attack. The feeling of needles penetrating my skin makes me shudder – a feeling I wish never to feel again.

'Sorry,' she utters with no remorse, wiping her mouth with her sleeve.

My gaze stays glued to Bennett's body, his lifeless eyes staring up at the ceiling of the cave. My hand edges towards him to see if he is all right, but I know deep down he's gone.

'What have you done?' I whisper, my words hoarse.

Lazarus steps on my hand, preventing me from touching my cousin. My eyes turn upwards to see his amusement.

'He won't be pleased with either of you.' Silas frowns, looking at my wounded neck with an annoyed expression. He urges his male companion to remove his foot from my now-aching hand. 'He is damaged goods. You'd better pray he is in a good mood tonight.'

Silas – the only one who seems to have control of himself – roughly yanks me to my feet, but my legs feel unsteady and buckle beneath me. He takes it upon himself to throw me over his shoulder like a rag doll, his bones digging into my stomach painfully.

'Clean up this mess,' Silas orders his companions as he turns away.

My cousin is being left with the two of them.

'No! Put me down! Put me down! I can't leave him!' I kick my legs, but Silas's grip on them is like steel – immovable.

'Be quiet, human. The lord of vampires will not take kindly to your behaviour,' he answers, whisking me away at superspeed.

8

I'm close to vomiting by the time I'm dropped onto the floor, my breathing haggard and my eyes still trying to focus, the blur of the streets messing with my head.

We are in a large chamber that is strangely airy but reeks of blood. My nose wrinkles at the smell. I've been brought to a long, narrow room with an extensive table that can seat at least ten people. With a yank on my arm, Silas hauls me to my feet. My gaze falls upon a dangerous-looking vampire at the head of the table.

I stumble as I'm pushed roughly towards him. A strong hand shoves my head down upon the stone, pressing my cheek against the hard surface, while another holds my hands behind my back. The stranger, with his blood-red eyes, observes me with amusement. He has a goblet of crimson liquid, and I somehow know it's fresh.

'As requested, Lord Atticus,' Silas says in greeting, his fingers digging into my scalp and wrists.

Lord Atticus hums unfavourably. 'I didn't know this was Victoria's ... taste in men.' He sneers down at me but doesn't seem fazed by my reddening face. The hand pressing my face against the table is making my head start to throb. 'My daughter never asks for anything, however, so this is surprising.'

'Shall we chain him, my lord?' Lazarus asks, coming into my field of vision. Not too far behind him is Thana, watching me intently.

The lord of vampires studies me, as if considering whether he wants his prisoner to be caged or not. 'Yes. I think we should dine together. What do you say?' He peers up at his companions, and they share a smile.

My stomach drops. I know this can't be good.

'Victoria has spoken much about you,' Lord Atticus claims, making me frown.

'Victoria?' I repeat, wondering if my aching head is understanding him correctly. 'As in *my* Victoria?'

'He's not very bright, is he?' the lord says to his minions.

My nose wrinkles. Victoria never spoke of her family – she became touchy every time I mentioned my own. But when I first asked about relatives, she denied having any – yet here I am in the presence of Lord Atticus, the leader of the vampires, who claims to be her father.

'She never mentioned you,' I state, annoyance spreading through me.

'Strange. We have such a close bond,' the lord answers, making me think quite the opposite. 'Regardless, she wishes you to turn. So consider tonight an initiation present from us.'

Now I realise why they wanted me specifically.

Fear hits me hard in the chest. My vision blurs, and my head spins frantically. I think I'm going to pass out. 'No. Please, don't do this,' I beg, my head hurting more as I jerk against Silas's hold on me. My bound hands squirm against his iron grip.

'Oh?' The lord feigns curiosity.

'I'll do anything. Please don't turn me.'

The vampire's gaze doesn't waver as he stands. He clutches my arm and yanks me out of Silas's grasp. I hiss at the pain as my arm is nearly torn from its socket.

'Are you telling me you do not wish to be with Victoria forever?' Lord Atticus asks me, making me lean away instinctively.

'I want to be with Victoria, but not like this.'

'Your miserable human life will end shortly. That will not do. Victoria deserves forever.'

'I agree. She does deserve that,' I answer honestly, but I don't realise what I've implied until the words are out of my mouth. The vampires' smiles are devilish, and I flounder under Lord Atticus's hold.

'Then it is settled.' The lord releases me briefly.

Lazarus has me in his clutches in seconds, giving me no chance to bolt.

Chains from beneath the table are brought above, four of them, made of obsidian metal. The black-coloured restraints contain magical properties to stop a dameer, like myself, from using their powers – not that my abilities could defend me in a situation like this.

Slowly the vampires begin to clamp my ankles and wrists in the restraints, the vampires' eyes widening with anticipation. I flail and buck, hoping to deter them, but their hands are stronger than anything I've felt before. They are unmoving and unapologetic as they seal my fate – my body is sprawled upon the table like their own personal feast.

'You'll not regret the decision. You'll be powerful like us,' Thana says, as if that's what it really means to be a vampire – to have power over others.

'No, don't do it. I don't want this!' I cry, trying but failing against the chains that hold me.

Silas approaches my left, his fangs so long I blanch. Thana takes my right side, and she eyes my arm up like a prize, her desire for my blood no doubt tenfold now she's had a taste of me already. Lazarus steps back and lets the lord of vampires have my neck, while he watches and waits for his turn.

Lord Atticus doesn't mention the puncture marks already in my shoulder, but his glance towards Thana is enough to know she'll be dealt with accordingly. Instead, he moves to my other shoulder, a fresh side for him to work with.

'A little advice, Dimitri,' Lord Atticus murmurs, his voice soft and silken against my ear. 'Don't resist, or this will *really* hurt.' He laughs, making my heart stutter.

I am just a mouse caught in a very dangerous trap to these creatures.

'Please, it doesn't have to be this way,' I plead, feeling tears stream from my eyes. Panic consumes me – my future is fading away the closer the vampire inches towards my throat. I can't help but stare at his open mouth, the long, sharp fangs right *there* – taunting me.

'It's always the ones that don't want to be changed that end up enjoying it the most,' Lord Atticus declares as his fingers slide through my hair. He quickly yanks my head to the side, my neck a gift for him, and he clamps down without hesitation.

I scream. Teeth as sharp as needles pierce into my skin on all sides, Thana and Silas also taking their fair share of blood from me. My arms begin to feel heavy, lacking in strength. My neck feels sore, and a burning spreads through my shoulder, down my back and across my chest.

The trio suck up large mouthfuls of my blood, draining me slowly, and I start to feel my head spin. My mind reels with the agony rushing through my limbs, with the thought my blood is being drained from me – like a pig in a butcher's shop.

'How does he taste?' Lazarus asks with amusement as Lord Atticus lifts his head for a breath.

'Like Liquid Gold. But strangely, I don't mind it.' He smiles before dipping his head for more of what I have to offer.

My fighting body soon gives up, the life withdrawing from me as I lie upon the table, the lanterns above me blazing as my eyes begin to flutter. I feel weightless but with an incredible layer of pain throughout my shoulder and arms. My body hates every moment, wanting to expel the feeling of sharp fangs penetrating my skin and taking whatever they can get.

'The less you fight, the more pleasurable it will be for you,' Thana reminds me, but I'm not listening. I don't give a fuck if it will feel good. I don't *want* this.

'I'm begging you. Stop. Please,' I whimper, and the group laughs.

'You'll thank us soon enough.' Lazarus smiles.

9

I wake up in a room painted in gold and maroon. The bed I lie upon is soft and cushioned, and the room itself is cluttered with dark stone furniture. Finding a looking glass on the nearby dressing table, I grasp for it. The first thing I see is the change to my eyes. Crimson. Ruby red. The colour of blood.

'Holy Hanrah, no,' I whisper in horror. My hands reach up as I gape at my reflection, my mouth opening in disgust. Fangs – shiny and new – peep out from beneath my lips. I rear back as my tongue trails over them. Real – too fucking real. 'No, no, no, no.'

This is a horrible dream. A terrible nightmare that I will wake up from soon. Sounds from outside make me jump to my feet. Their voices are loud even through the walls, their words as clear as if they were standing next to me.

'See how the youngling is. He should be awake soon, and he will be very hungry, I suspect.'

I panic silently. I need to leave. I can't be associated with these demons. I need to go home.

Home.

What will my family say about me now? Will they think

I wanted this? No. They knew this wasn't what I yearned for. I had so many plans and now ... ruined. Destroyed.

Grief racks my chest, my sobs quiet as I think of my dream to work in the Library of Wonders – now lost, my efforts all for nothing. Thrown away because of these ... monsters. Yes, monsters. Victoria is a *monster*. Her father, the lord, is a *monster*.

I'll make them pay, I promise myself, hatred filling every part of me. My thoughts go to the hundreds of ways I could hurt them, how I can make them suffer as I have.

I clamber towards the curtain-covered window across the room. I heave the window open with such ease that I'm surprised for a moment before remembering my new vampire strength. I leap down from the second storey without a hint of pain and run.

As I travel through the city, I note how all the humans and dameer live on like nothing has happened, as if my life hasn't been tipped over and rearranged so violently. I envy them – hate them, even – that they have their own, normal lives to attend to while I ... I don't know what to do now.

Revenge.

The word clangs inside my brain, reverberating around my skull, spelling itself out over and over for me to see.

Revenge. Revenge. Revenge. Revenge.

I will take revenge on those who have wronged me. I will make them pay for what they have done to me, what they have done to countless others. I will make them pay for everything I have lost because of one person's decision – a decision that has ruined my life forever.

A memory pops into my head – Victoria as she feeds me more facts about vampirism after biting me, hoping to soothe me with stupid details about how being like her will make everything better.

'Did you know that younglings are most powerful in the first forty-eight hours? Even more powerful than mature vampires?'

I pause, hiding within an alley between a pet shop and a tailor's. Peering down at my pale hands, I can feel the strength course through me, my energy unlimited.

More powerful.

Forty-eight hours to complete my plan. Forty-eight hours to set things right in this city.

I head towards home, to where my family is, and with my new-found speed, it takes no time to approach my front door. Quietly I open the entrance. At this time of the morning, my mother is having a cup of tea while reading her book. She looks up, and the scent of her fear hits me as her face scrunches up, a scream about to erupt from her lips. As quick as an adder, I'm upon her, my hand gentle as I cover her mouth.

'Don't scream. I won't hurt you.'

She reacts strangely, her back straightening, her lips pressing together as if I've glued them shut. I reel back in shock. *Persuasion.* I just used persuasion on my own mother.

'It's all right, Ma. It's me,' I say, trying not to think too deeply about what I have just done.

Understanding forms in her expression. She studies my face, terror – not *of* me but *for* me – spreading over her features in waves.

'Dimitri,' she utters, her hands shaky as she reaches for my cheek. 'What's happened to you?'

'I don't have much time,' I rush, kneeling beside her, becoming smaller so as not to frighten her. 'I was turned against my will. I only have so much time before the blood-lust starts to creep in. But you'll be in danger the moment it hits. You need to get Pa and Felix out of this cave – along with the rest of the family. You need to get the next boat out of Rubien and go somewhere in the full blaze of the sun, where I can't follow you.'

My mother's mouth widens in panic, but I shake my head, not letting her interrupt me.

'You need to leave as soon as I'm out the door. You have to understand, I don't *want* to hurt you, but I don't know how much control I'll have. I'm not *me* any more, Ma. I'm something entirely different, and I'm *scared*.'

'Dimitri, we can figure something out,' she offers, but I take her hands in mine.

'Look at me. My eyes are crimson. I am without a soul now. It's been ripped away from me, and if you don't leave, *you* will get hurt. *Felix* will be hurt.' I know the mention of my brother will make her realise the gravity of the situation. 'He will not be able to run, nor will you or Pa be able to fight me off. I will *win*, and I will *hate* myself for it.'

Tears trickle down her face, and I squeeze her fingers as tenderly as I can.

'Promise me you'll leave. The last thing I want is to hurt any of you. I need your word,' I urge.

She reluctantly nods. 'I promise, my sweet boy. I promise I'll get us all out of the city.'

'You can write to me, but I must never know where you are.'

She purses her lips but doesn't disagree.

'I love you, Ma. Tell Pa and Felix I love them too, with every fibre of my being. Never *ever* forget that. I dreamed of a better future for us all, but you must live it without me now – for Felix's sake.'

'Dimitri, I—' She breaks down into sobs, and I hold her close.

'I'm going to miss you so much,' I whisper, making her cry even louder. 'I have to go.'

Her arms wrap around me then, and my instincts tell

me she is human. She is breakable and is potential *food*. I can tell she senses my change of demeanour.

'The change is coming,' she says with a sniffle.

I nod, getting to my feet quickly. I approach the door and swing it open, looking back one more time. 'Go get them right now. You don't have much time left, and when it does run out, I'll be the most hated vampire in the whole of Hanrah, and you'll all be targets too.'

My mother wrings her hands with nerves. 'What are you going to do?'

A flicker of hope fills my chest. I will do what it takes to keep my family safe. I will do what is needed to make my city safe once more. I will devote my new immortal life to saving those who can't defend themselves from creatures who have no morals and understand no distinction between right and wrong. I will take revenge for Bennett, my cousin and best friend, who was killed for being brave, killed while fighting for *me*.

My hands turn into fists, loathing coating every emotion inside me. 'I'm going to destroy the coven from the bottom up. Rubien will be free of vampires for evermore.'

VICTORIA MILLER

10

Victoria

S houts and screams erupt through the streets, and I'm alerted to a mass of running civilians. For once they don't care about my presence – they have found a greater danger in their midst.

Curious, I stalk towards the chaos, people shoving me, pushing me out of their way to get away from whatever has caused so much fear. The blood pumping through their fragile bodies makes me hungry, but not hungry enough to forget my curiosity.

It's a great surprise when I come across a large fire with one lonely figure standing before it, watching it burn and crackle as it grows more vigorous.

'How did you find enough kindling to light such a blaze?' I ask the stranger as I approach. He turns, and my throat tightens, my heart racing inside my chest. 'Dimitri?'

My hands reach out of their own accord, needing to touch him, needing to see if this is real. His blood-red eyes study me intently, his fanged mouth relaxed as he watches me process his new body. But what scares me is the blood splattered all over his clothes and skin. His face is covered in droplets of rust-coloured liquid.

'Are you hurt?' I ask, earning a shake of his head. He doesn't seem to want to talk about the blood on him, so I let the topic go for now. 'You look ...'

He peers into my eyes, his once ocean-blue gaze now ruby red, waiting for the rest of my sentence.

'Beautiful,' I can't help but whisper as I take him in. He looks leaner and much sharper than before – his human features were no doubt cut away by the brutality of his turning.

He steps closer to me, inhaling deeply as his fisted hands uncoil slightly. The fire before us somehow becomes hotter, and I can't help but ache for him.

Together. We can finally be together.

Nerves bubble up inside me as I wonder how he is feeling at this moment. When he was human, I could smell the emotions he experienced – could feel the heat rise in his cheeks when he felt embarrassed. But now his skin is colourless. His lips don't move, and his eyes are deep wells full of *nothing*.

'Are you all right?' I find him watching me carefully when I meet his gaze. 'Do you feel stronger?'

He nods, and I mirror him.

'It suits you – this body, I mean.'

He holds up a hand as if analysing it, trying to find a secret within his palm. 'I do feel stronger.' He turns towards the fire once more, and I find myself wanting his attention again.

'Why are you so quiet? Are you hungry? Do you need me to find someone for you to feed on?'

He stiffens but says nothing.

'If you don't tell me what's wrong, I can't help you.'

Silence envelops us a moment before he speaks, so quietly I find myself leaning in to hear better.

'Why did you lie to me?'

My brow rises at his accusation. 'I've always spoken the truth to you.'

'No, you haven't. You claimed to love me.'

My body jerks in shock. The moment I first laid eyes on him, I wanted him – wanted to protect him and keep him safe from my kind and their escapades in the city. Why would he think I *didn't* love him?

'My love for you has always been obvious. The turn has probably made you feel vulnerable, my love. Let us eat, and you'll feel much more like yourself.'

He reluctantly glances my way and lifts a hand to stroke my cheek, trailing his fingers through my hair. The touch brings me warmth, and I lean into his fingers.

I could experience this love for the rest of my immortal life.

The thought widens my smile.

'What are you thinking about?' he asks.

'How I'll never get bored of us, bored of this,' I say, motioning between us.

Slowly he lifts my chin, our faces so close together my eyes lower to his lips, wanting nothing more than to taste him. My hands roam up and down his body, feeling his new-found strength, and I feel my desire growing with his proximity.

'You're so much stronger,' I murmur.

'I am stronger,' he states, pinning me against his chest so our bodies are joined. His usual human warmth is gone, but in its place is a force I find myself magnetised by.

I raise my arms and wrap my hands around his neck, feeling the puncture wounds on both sides. I frown and peer up, finding his stone-cold face.

'I am dangerous,' he adds.

The words make my heart race. He and I will be formidable. We will have each other's back for eternity. Excitement lances through my limbs, making my fingers tingle as I run them over his cold skin, into his dark hair.

'I am a *monster*,' he whispers.

I stiffen. 'What—'

He grips my throat tightly, causing my words to come to a forced stop.

'You will let me talk. You will listen, and you will not move until I say so,' he commands, his words pushing against my will. His persuasion is stronger than my ability to block it. For once in my life, he has power over me. Before now, he could never hurt me. 'You betrayed me, Victoria. You asked your father to turn me against my wishes. I thought you *loved* me.'

'I do love you!' I choke out, but his grasp doesn't waver.

'No. You love yourself.'

My attempt to loosen his grip is futile. My body is no longer under my command. His hands are immovable, and for once, I feel small and weak in comparison – his power over me is unyielding.

'You took everything away from me – my life, my dreams, my cousin – all because you wanted me for *yourself*. That, Victoria, is not called love. It's called *selfishness*.'

His fingers press in dangerously tight, and my lungs begin to burn. I merely look up at him, meeting his hateful gaze.

'I made the choice you were too scared to make,' I whisper, knowing this to be true. I could see his curiosity from a mile away, but he was too frightened to take the risk.

'Yes, and now, in return, I'll choose *your* fate. I'll make a life-altering decision for *you*,' he says, his grip on me loosening.

I try to bolt, but his persuasion still holds me hostage.

He leans down to caress my cheek with his own. 'I'll deal with you the same way I dealt with your coven – with your father.'

My eyes dart towards the fire before us. I asked how he had got the fire blazing. It seems I've got my answer.

'Yes, Victoria,' he confirms, making my eyes close briefly. 'Your father and brethren are all dead. They were too weak to fight me, their powers no match for a youngling.'

'I don't believe you,' I murmur. 'My Dimitri would never hurt anyone.'

'*Your* Dimitri died the moment his cousin was murdered in cold blood. *Your* Dimitri died the moment he told his family to run away from him and never look back. *Your* Dimitri died the moment you decided he wasn't enough for you as a human.'

Our eyes clash, and I can finally see all his emotions on display. Every bit of hurt, grief, suffering and loss is in them. My heart shatters seeing him – all of him.

'I'm sorry.'

His hands are nimble as they smoothly wrap around my neck, a hand either side of my head in an affectionate hold. My own hands twitch, wanting to find his wrists and hold on to them like anchors.

'I am a monster,' he repeats quietly.

'Please don't do this. This isn't you,' I whimper.

Eyes full of cold, calm hatred stare back at me. He's right. My Dimitri is gone. Before me isn't the man I loved but a demon waiting to unleash itself.

'Goodbye, Victoria.'

Too quickly for me to register, he grabs my skull in between his hands more firmly and roughly twists with extraordinary vampire force, snapping my neck with a definitive crack.

EPILOGUE

150 Years Later

The bottle of Liquid Gold hangs precariously from my fingers, my eyes half-open as I stumble through the street. Passers-by keep their distance but don't baulk any more. They have become accustomed to me, the only vampire in the city now.

I am alone. *Always* alone.

My foot catches on something, and I go flying, too weak to save myself from face-planting on the street. I hear something smash, and I groan. The glass bottle is no longer full but now leaking over the ground I lie upon, dribbling slowly as I watch it with contempt.

'Fuck you,' I mutter.

'Are you talking to the drink?' someone asks.

My head turns, and I note two black leather boots. They are scuffed, and I'm certain I can see a sliver of toe through one of them. The hole is not quite big enough to be notice-able to a human, but to me, it's plainly obvious.

Further up I find a pair of small, gangly legs – both with patches on them, different-coloured materials stitched over the brown trousers they wear. The stranger's top seems like the only part of their attire that is somewhat decent, until the stain at the neck comes into view. My effort to see more is now making me roll onto my back.

Dark crimson eyes stare down at me with curiosity. My heart hammers, thinking I've missed a vampire in my life's mission to rid Rubien of them all, but I realise that is not what this child is – not quite, anyway. The young girl's hair is long and dark red, tied up with a piece of leather. Her arms are covered with cuts and bruises, and some of her fingers are bent at strange angles.

'Are you all right? Do you need help?' she asks, seeming to understand I'm not capable of answering her last question. 'You're a vampire, right? Is this what happens when you don't feed? You get weak and start crawling around the city? Do you need me to fetch you some blood?'

Blood.

My stomach clenches at the word. My mouth salivates over it. I want it so bad, but no. That's not the plan. The plan is to fade away and never open my eyes again. I've made it this far, and I can't stop now. I've failed too many times before – but not this time.

Sixty-seven days and counting.

'No. Leave me alone,' I mutter, my throat dry as sand.

She studies me, injured hands entwining, and winces at her movements. I see a large silver scar on her right palm. She notes my stare and holds it up.

'I would have left you alone, but it claims I'm safe.'

I have no idea what she's talking about, but my stare never wavers from her. The child's interest in me is somewhat beguiling. I've not spoken to another person in a *very* long time who hasn't looked at me with disgust, suspicion or fear.

'What are you doing here?' I ask.

'I escaped.'

'From whom?'

'The Ravens.'

'Ravens?' I utter, realising too slowly what she is. A Raven. Of course. Half vampire, half dameer. The magical race that lives within the deeper parts of the cave. 'How did you get to this side of the wall?' I ask.

'There's a hole.'

I tilt my head, knowing from experience there is no hole in the wall between the city of Rubien and the House of Raven. We've been separated for generations – unless they've built something recently.

'Lies. There is no hole,' I reply.

The girl's smirk is full of amusement. She seems like the quietly confident type. What surprises me more, though, is her fear is non-existent. I can't scent anything on her which confirms her vampire ancestry.

'There is now.' She shrugs. 'But I've heard the royal family wants to make a proper tunnel eventually. It's a pain for them to travel to us.'

'Is that so?'

She nods. 'Yes. I overheard one of the masters say so. He didn't sound too pleased about it.'

The view from where I lie nauseates me. I need to get up. So I roll to my side and attempt to get to my feet. In seconds she's clutching my arm to aid me as I stagger to a standing position. My hand is still holding the broken bottle of liquor. I pause and study her, wondering why she is assisting me and not fleeing.

'What? Do you not like touch?' she asks, her youthful face rippling with understanding.

The recognition in her features pains me. It's as if she knows exactly what it's like to hate people touching her. I ponder over what she has endured within her House – her arms are an obvious display of what she's experienced, marks coating her pale skin, alongside dark scabs and slowly healing wounds.

'What happened there?' I ask, pointing to a long gash across her forearm. It looks to have been stitched by a very inexperienced hand. I conclude she's done it herself – her handiwork is dismal.

'Master Jye sliced me open.' She hesitates before continuing. 'He asked me to perform a job, and I wasn't fast enough for his liking. It's all right, though. I'm used to it.' She smiles as if to calm *me*, to make *me* feel better.

My frown deepens. 'That's torture,' I state.

A scowl forms on her small face as I stand to my full form, looming over her. A predator and its prey. I can't help but feel awfully dangerous around her, like any moment I'll snap. I'll feed off her, and I'll be back to my normal state, and I'll be alone all over again. I don't dare move, knowing that with the thoughts in my head, I'm a threat to her. I need her to leave. To leave me be and go on her way. Or else she'll be the next dinner I planned on never having.

'Torture?' She scrunches her nose up. 'Master Jye calls it discipline.'

My snort is unexpected, surprising us both. 'No. Discipline does not involve hurting someone, especially when it's dealt out with weapons.'

She doesn't say anything but takes a step away from me, probably assuming I'm fine now I'm standing. 'Do you need some blood? I can see if the butcher has some spare.'

The offer is unexpected, but I shake my head. 'No. I have a plan that I can't get out of.'

'Which is?'

'To die of starvation.'

The girl cocks her head. 'How long have you been without blood?'

'Sixty-seven days.'

'No wonder you look so terrible. I heard vampires are supposed to have everlasting beauty.'

My unimpressed face makes her grin.

'Why starvation?' she asks.

'I killed all those who wronged me – wronged this city,' I admit, but she doesn't react. If anything, she probably understands more than anyone else – her House is notorious for being radical and unethical. 'And now I'm alone. But I'm too much of a coward to kill myself. I'm hoping if I weaken myself enough, someone will find me and finish the job.'

Dark crimson eyes widen only slightly. I've frightened her. Not with what I am but with my wish to end my life.

'Life is hard,' she mutters with a shrug. 'And some days are unbearable, but do you want to know what I tell myself when I feel like giving up?'

I refrain from sighing but shrug in response. 'What?'

'It's going to be hard, but *hard* does not mean *impossible*. You'll be alright. Things will work out in the end.'

The words clang through my skull, sending shivers down my arms. My eyes swivel towards her, studying her, taking her in. My mother said something similar once. She, too, was a person full of optimism. Memories of her flood my thoughts, something I've not allowed since her death.

'You've paled,' she says, voice filling with concern. 'I didn't think that was possible for someone who is already so fair.'

My eyes snap to the girl who pulls me out of my thoughts. She's so small, so fragile and so naive. She thinks that being tortured daily is a temporary situation, like each day is a step closer to seeing the sun, to finding a sliver of happiness.

My silence seems to spur her to fill in the gap. 'What is your name, vampire?'

'Dimitri Thunders,' I say after a moment, finding her dark crimson eyes looking up at me. They remind me of red wine – dark and mysterious, intelligent in more ways than one.

She wears a faint smile upon her face, her tiny fangs more adorable than intimidating. Somehow she seems to know she's had an effect on me. She sticks out her small hand, the one with the scar, a few of her recently broken fingers looking disturbingly mangled. The sight enrages me as I carefully grasp her small hand in mine, taking care not to squeeze too hard.

'Nice to meet you, Dimitri Thunders.' Her smile is genuine, and it creates a flicker of something inside my chest. I've not felt anything for so long. I have not felt the feeling of *hope* in so long.

How has this malnourished child slithered her way through my shields so easily?

Because you are desperate for companionship, and she is the first one to see you as a person and not the true monster you are, a voice says inside my head.

Ignoring my thoughts, I say, 'What is *your* name?'

She rolls her shoulders, looking around as if any moment someone will come for her. A small part of me wishes to protect her, to shield the girl from whoever is causing her harm.

'My name is Scarlet Seraphine.'

Want more of The Crimson Scar Series?
Scan Here For Book 2

ABOUT THE AUTHOR

Hannah is a huge lover of tea, a passionate writer and an avid reader who claims buying books and reading books are two completely different hobbies. She is also the author of The Crimson Scar series.

As a Bachelor of Criminology and Law, Hannah has spent years reading and writing fantasy stories with morally grey characters, villainous crimes and lots of blood.

Want to know more?

Visit: www.hannahpenfoldauthor.com

Socials: hannahpenfoldauthor